W9-CMR-085

J
FIC
NAYLOR   Naylor, Phyllis
         Reynolds

         Boys in control

DUE DATE

BOYS IN CONTROL

■ ■ ■ ■ ■ ■

BOYS
IN CONTROL

Phyllis Reynolds Naylor

DELACORTE PRESS

Published by
Delacorte Press
an imprint of
Random House Children's Books
a division of Random House, Inc.
New York

Visit us on the Web! www.randomhouse.com/kids
Educators and librarians, for a variety of teaching tools, visit us at
www.randomhouse.com/teachers

Library of Congress Cataloging-in-Publication Data
Naylor, Phyllis Reynolds.
Boys in control / Phyllis Reynolds Naylor.
p. cm.
Summary: Once again the Hatford brothers and the Malloy sisters find
themselves pitted against each other when embarrassing pictures of the boys turn
up in the girls' basement, and the boys try to figure out how to get them back.
ISBN 0-385-32740-4 (hardcover)—ISBN 0-385-90154-2 (GLB)
[1. Sisters—Fiction. 2. Brothers—Fiction. 3. Baseball—Fiction.
4. Garage sales—Fiction.] I. Title.
PZ7 .N24 Bop 2003
[Fic]—dc21
2002152828

The text of this book is set in 12-point Garamond.
Printed in the United States of America
September 2003
10 9 8 7 6 5 4 3 2 1
BVG

To two of my morning pool buddies,
John Doyle and Reid Cherner,
who taught me a little something about baseball

Contents

■　■　■　■　■　■

BOYS IN CONTROL

■　■　■　■　■　■

One

■

Stuck

Wally Hatford took two baseball cards from his dresser—Derek Jeter and Alex Rodriguez—and stuck them in a jacket pocket. Jake had given them to him a month before just because he had duplicates, but Wally was going to trade them at school for a magic trick—a box that took a quarter and turned it into a fifty-cent piece.

When he got downstairs and hung his jacket over a chair, he found his mother moving about the kitchen and talking to herself in a state of great agitation.

"I must have been clear out of my mind!" she said, lifting the teakettle off the stove and plunking it right back down again. "I don't know what in the world possessed me to say yes last year, when I had no idea what I'd be doing a year from then."

When Mrs. Hatford talked like this, Wally and his older brothers knew to lie low. Even their father knew

1

that as long as breakfast was on the table, it was better to sit down and butter a biscuit than to ask what she was talking about.

But Peter, who was in second grade, hadn't learned that yet. He licked the grape jelly off his fingers and asked, "What did you say yes to?"

Everyone else at the table gave him a silent shake of the head. When Mrs. Hatford started talking, it was sometimes hard to get her to stop, and the boys would be lucky to make it to school on time. But it was too late.

"The Women's Auxiliary of the Buckman Fire Department's Treats and Treasures yard sale," she said, and immediately sank down in her chair at the end of the table and rested her chin in her hands.

"Now, *that's* a mouthful," Mr. Hatford said, hiding a smile behind his mug as he finished the last of his coffee. "Did you promise to clean out our attic and look for things to give to the sale?"

"I promised to *run* the sale!" Mrs. Hatford moaned.

"At the firehouse?"

"Right here in our yard! Right out there on the driveway! Right up on our front porch!" Mrs. Hatford cried.

Now all the Hatfords were staring.

"Well, Ellen, that shouldn't be so hard," said her husband. "I'm sure the boys will help, and I'll do what I can."

"No, you won't, because the sale happens to be the last Saturday in May, and you know what *that* is!"

Wally tried to think, and then he remembered. That would be the day of the final game in the district elementary school baseball championships. And Jake, his brother, was on the Buckman Badgers.

"If the Badgers make it that far, you know we'll all want to be there rooting for Jake!" Mrs. Hatford said in distress. "I'm certainly going to be taking half days off from work each Saturday in May that he's playing."

Now it was a family emergency! Wally saw Jake's eyes open wide. Even Josh, Jake's twin, looked startled that his mother might have to be anywhere else on that fateful day. Jake had wanted to play for the Buckman Badgers ever since he was six years old. This was the year, and May was the month, and the twenty-ninth was the day of the championship game.

But it just so happened, Mrs. Hatford continued, that in the window of every store in town there was a poster about the Treats or Treasures yard sale, which would be held from noon till four on May twenty-ninth at the home of Tom and Ellen Hatford on College Avenue, rain or shine. So there was no getting out of it. On *that* particular day, she would need to take a *whole* day off from her job at the hardware store, but how could she be in two places at once?

There was silence around the kitchen table as sausage gravy congealed on plates and biscuits grew cold.

3

"Well, after all the practice I've put in pitching balls to Jake for the last five years, I've *got* to be at that game," said Mr. Hatford. "If I have to take four vacation days off for baseball, that's okay with me. We hadn't planned on going anywhere this summer."

"He's my twin brother! *I'm* going to be there!" said Josh.

"I've been watching Jake practice ever since I was born!" Peter declared. "I'm going to go sit in the very first row and I'll yell the loudest of all."

"Well, *I'm* Jake's *mother*!" Mrs. Hatford said. "How could I *not* be at the championship game when my very own son is one of the pitchers? At least, we *hope* the Badgers will be playing that game."

Jake scraped up some sausage gravy with his fork and put it in his mouth, looking very smug and important.

Wally knew what was coming. He knew it before the first word was spoken. He had felt that something was up the moment he'd stepped into the kitchen that morning, in fact. He wondered if he'd sensed it even before he got out of bed. And now the whole family had turned their heads and were looking down the table at him.

"No," said Wally.

"Now, Wally," said his father. "There are times when every member of a family has to stand up and be counted."

"You can count me, but I don't want to do it," said Wally.

4

"There are times you have to make sacrifices for the good of the family," said his mother. "And you have to admit that baseball isn't your favorite thing."

Wally didn't see that this made any difference. Maybe he *did* think baseball was sort of boring, and maybe he *did* like to lie back in the bleachers and study the clouds instead of watching the team practice. But did that mean he wanted to stand out on the driveway surrounded by old lamps and curtain rods and picnic hampers, arguing about prices and missing the game? The game that was going to decide the sixth-grade champion of the district?

"No!" he said again. "I don't know what any of that stuff is worth—all that stuff you'll be selling."

"Everything will have a price tag on it, Wally," his mother said.

"I can't make change!" Wally bleated. "I'm awful in math!"

"You can use my calculator," said his dad. "If you can press a button, you can make change."

"I'm only one person!" Wally wailed. "How can I look after all that stuff at once?"

"Mrs. Larson will be here to help you till the rest of us get back from the game," Mrs. Hatford said.

"Old Mrs. Larson is deaf!" Wally cried. "And she won't wear a hearing aid."

"Wait a minute, Wally. The game starts at nine in the morning and could well be over by noon," his mother told him. "The only people who will come by are folks who just want to look the merchandise over. It's against the rules to sell anything before the sale opens. The other women and I will be back by noon, and if we're not, we'll be there shortly after that."

"Besides," said Josh, "if the Badgers lose any game between now and the end of May, they won't even be playing in the championship game."

"Now, that is something we're not even going to think about," said Mr. Hatford. "We're all going to think positively in the weeks ahead. Jake is going to win for the Badgers, Wally is going to do his part by keeping watch over the yard sale till Mother gets back, and then we will all help out and, hopefully, will have something to celebrate that evening."

Wally tipped his head back and closed his eyes. Why did this always happen to him? Just because he was the middle child—Peter was in second grade and the twins were in sixth—did that mean he wasn't important? Peter was the youngest, Jake and Josh the oldest, but what did that make him? Chopped liver?

"It's not fair," he wailed.

"No, it's not," said his dad, getting up and putting on his postal worker's jacket. "That's life, Wally. You win some, you lose some, and it's not always fair. But you know yourself that you are probably less interested in baseball than anyone else in this family, and all we're asking is that you miss one game in order to help your mother out."

"The *championship* game," said Wally.

"Yes, but we'll be as proud of you taking care of things back here as we'll be of Jake out on the pitcher's mound," said his dad.

Wally didn't say yes, but it was useless to say no because he knew when he was licked. He went upstairs to brush his teeth before school.

As he ran the brush back and forth, minty foam on his tongue, he was thinking that there was at least one other person in Buckman who felt the same way he did about baseball: Caroline Malloy. But he would have to be nailed to the wall with a gun at his head to ask Caroline to come over and help at the Treats and Treasures yard sale while his family was gone. In fact, he would have to be brain-dead to ask Caroline Malloy to come over at all.

Because whenever the Hatford kids and the Malloy kids got together, there was trouble. When Caroline and her sisters put their heads together, there was mischief you wouldn't believe.

It didn't help, of course, that Eddie Malloy was the alternate pitcher for the Buckman Badgers and that some people thought she was even better than Jake. It didn't help either that Beth would be in the bleachers cheering loudest of all for Eddie. And it especially didn't help that Caroline would undoubtedly discover Wally's absence from the championship game and would probably come looking for him, just to see what he was up to.

"I feel sick," said Wally to the mirror. Still, having

Caroline there to help might be better than not having any other helper but Mrs. Larson.

"Wally!" called his mother. "You're going to be late. Your brothers have already left for school, and the Malloy girls crossed the bridge five minutes ago."

Wally sighed and went downstairs. He pulled on his jacket and picked up his backpack. Then he went outside into the cool sunny air of a May morning, past the swinging footbridge that led across the river to the house where the Malloys were staying, and on up the street toward the school.

It used to be that his friends, the Bensons, lived in that big house on Island Avenue, where the Buckman River flowed into town on one side of the island, ran under the road bridge to the business district, then circled back out again on the other side of Island Avenue. It used to be that he and his brothers and the Benson boys spent all their time together, thinking up new things to do.

But now the Bensons had moved to Georgia for a year, the Malloys were renting their house, Jake was on the baseball team, and Wally was stuck. There was no getting around it.

Head down, shoelaces flapping, Wally trudged on up the sidewalk, reaching Buckman Elementary just as the last bell rang.

■ ■ ■ ■ ■ ■ ■ ■ ■ ■ ■ ■ ■

Two

■

Dreaming

Caroline Malloy pushed up her sleeves, settled back in her chair, and lifted her long dark ponytail to cool the back of her neck. Wally was going to be late if he didn't hurry. Miss Applebaum was already standing up with her roll book, looking over the class.

It wasn't that Caroline was especially fond of Wally Hatford. He certainly wasn't very fond of her, but could she help it if she was precocious and had been moved up to fourth grade? Could she help it if she had strong ambitions to be an actress, and Wally was so laid-back he just seemed to slide from one day to the next?

What she missed was being able to trace her name on the back of Wally's shirt with the edge of her ruler. Tickling him behind the ear with her pencil, and then watching his shoulders twitch and seeing first his neck, then his cheeks, then his ears turn red. Where *was* he?

Riiiiiing! went the last bell. A few seconds later there was the sound of running feet in the hallway and then Wally Hatford skidded into the room, stumbled down the row, and crumpled into the seat in front of Caroline.

"Well, I heard you coming, Wally, so we'll say you made it," said the teacher. "You might want to hang your jacket out there in the hall."

Wally got up, went back out the door, then came in again, a little more slowly this time.

"Good *mor*ning, Wally!" said Caroline softly, leaning forward and blowing on the back of his neck.

Wally didn't answer. He just moved sideways so that she couldn't poke him with her ruler and pretended he was listening to Miss Applebaum talk about book reports and when they were due.

Caroline sighed and folded her arms across her chest. May was going to be the most boring month if she didn't think of some way to liven it up. All the attention was going to Eddie these days—Eddie and baseball. The middle Malloy daughter, Beth, didn't seem to care if anyone paid attention to her or not. As long as Beth had a good book, especially a scary one, she was happy.

But Caroline needed attention. She loved being the main attraction, and why not? She was an actress, wasn't she, and all actresses liked an audience.

". . . a choice," Miss Applebaum was saying. "You may read a book of at least a hundred pages and write a report, you may read two shorter books and compare them, or you may write a book of your own of at least ten typed pages."

Caroline's hand shot up into the air. "Could we write a play?" she asked.

Miss Applebaum looked thoughtful.

"A play is like a book. It's just mostly talking, telling what the characters are saying to each other," Caroline went on, as though her teacher did not know what a play was.

"Well, yes. I suppose it could be a play, Caroline, as long as it tells a complete story," said Miss Applebaum.

Caroline began to smile. "And will we get extra credit if we act it out for the class?"

"Yes, certainly!" said the teacher. And then she asked the class to stand for the Pledge to the flag.

"Wal-ly," Caroline whispered, moving a little closer to the boy in front of her.

"No!" Wally whispered back. "I won't be in your play."

"You don't even know what I'm going to write about," said Caroline.

"Neither do you," said Wally. "But you'll have to find someone else to do it, not me."

Caroline sighed again. It wasn't easy being a budding actress in a boring world. Still, a lot more happened here than had ever happened when she lived in Ohio. If only her family could stay here, and her dad didn't decide to move the family back again come fall.

". . . and to the Republic for which it stands," the class was saying, "one nation . . ."

I know! Caroline thought. *I'll write a mystery play, and then even Beth will read it. And if she likes it, maybe I could perform it for the whole school!*

The more Caroline thought, the more excited she became. How would you ever accomplish anything if you didn't dream? She was better at dreaming than almost anyone she knew.

There would have to be a main character, of course, with a wonderful part, and this main character would naturally be her. Maybe it would be such a good play that the newspaper would send a reporter out to review it when she performed it onstage. It might be such a great play that a talent scout would read the review and invite Caroline to audition for a part on Broadway. It might be such a brilliant play that—

"You may sit down now, Caroline," Miss Applebaum said, and there was laughter all around her. Caroline realized that the Pledge of Allegiance was long over and she was still standing. She sheepishly took her seat.

Never mind, she told herself. Someday she would be standing onstage on Broadway and everyone would be clapping. The ushers would come down the aisles carrying bouquets of roses, and she would bow to the audience—left, right, and center—and the name Caroline Lenore Malloy would be on everyone's lips as they left the theater.

When school was out for the day, most of the students went home. But those who were on the Buckman Badgers baseball team, and many of their brothers and sisters and friends, went right out to the ball field instead. The team would be practicing for the first big game of the season, coming up that Saturday. Many elementary schools had only a small field for baseball, and championship games had to be played at the local high school. But Buckman Elementary was one of the few that not only had an official ball diamond, it had bleachers as well, and on Sunday afternoons the field was open to men's amateur teams from the area.

There were sixteen sixth-grade teams competing for the championship, which meant there would be eight baseball games going on at once in different parts of the district the first Saturday in May. The eight winners would play each other the following week, the four winners would play the week after that, and on the last Saturday in May, the twenty-ninth, the two winners would play each other to see who would win the sixth-grade championship for the school district. Losing teams, however, still met at local schools to play each other, just for fun, with parents doing the coaching, so it wasn't as though you had one chance to play baseball and that was it.

But Caroline knew that Eddie had her heart set on the championship game. If the Badgers didn't make it to the finals, baseball season would be over as far as

Eddie was concerned. None of that Saturday-morning neighborhood baseball stuff for her.

Caroline had mixed feelings as she followed her two blond sisters out to the ball field behind the school. It seemed wrong to wish that Buckman would lose, and for Eddie's sake, Caroline hoped they wouldn't. But if the Badgers won the first game, and they played every Saturday in May, it would be hard to get anyone interested in her play till the games were over.

Beth, who was in fifth grade, crawled up on the bleachers beside Josh and Peter, but Caroline climbed up farther still and sat a couple of feet away from Wally Hatford, who was leaning his elbows on the riser behind him, studying a branch of the maple tree that hung out over the stands.

Wally moved a few more inches away from her, and Caroline decided right then and there that if ever she was to persuade Wally Hatford to be in a play with her, she would have to be nice to him, starting *now*.

"Hello, Wally," she said. "Nice day, isn't it?"

"We just saw each other two minutes ago," said Wally.

"So, can't I say it's a nice day anyhow?" asked Caroline.

"What do you want?" asked Wally, looking at her sideways.

"Do I have to *want* something? I just like sitting up here with you because I know you don't like baseball any more than I do," said Caroline.

"I never said I didn't like it," said Wally.

Down on the field, the coach was yelling at one of the players. "Hey, Mike! You playing baseball or chopping wood?" he called. "Don't start swinging your bat around until the pitch. You could let a ball go right past you if you're not ready."

Jake was on the pitcher's mound, and he threw a hard fastball. Sure enough, the boy in the batter's box wasn't ready. As he started his swing, the catcher had already caught the ball.

Eddie was playing shortstop in the practice game, and when the batter merely tapped the next ball, she leaped forward and caught it. Then the players changed sides and she and Jake were up to bat.

"I personally don't really care who wins the championship," Caroline said to Wally, "but Eddie and Jake will be unbearable if it's not the Buckman Badgers."

Wally shrugged. "I'm not going to be at the last game anyway, so it's no skin off my nose," he said.

"Why aren't you going to be at the game, Wally? *Every*body's going to that game if the Badgers make it that far."

"Everybody but me and Mrs. Larson," said Wally, and his voice sounded angry and disappointed.

"Where are you going with Mrs. Larson?" Caroline asked.

"I'm not going anywhere. I'm staying home. I have to be in charge of the Treats and Treasures yard sale of the Women's Auxiliary of the Buckman Fire Department the last Saturday of the month," Wally explained. "Somebody goofed and scheduled the sale the same day as the championship game, and it's already on posters all over town."

Caroline felt like laughing, but she checked herself in time and put on her most sympathetic face. "How did you get stuck with *that*?" she asked.

"Mom's making me, because everyone else in the family likes baseball more than I do. The sale's going to be in our front yard, right up on the driveway and the front porch. If the Badgers play that day, everybody will be going to that, and I have to stay home to watch over the sale stuff till the others get back."

"*I'll* help you!" said Caroline. "I don't think Eddie will miss me. I'll just come over that morning when everyone else is at the game. I'll make change or show people around or whatever you say."

Wally didn't seem to trust her, because he was still looking at her sideways. *When a person trusts you,* Caroline was thinking, *they look you right in the eye.*

"Well, okay," said Wally finally. "Maybe. If nobody else shows up to help."

And *maybe,* thought Caroline, beginning to smile, Wally had just said yes to taking a part in her play.

Three

■

Thinking Things Through

When practice was over, Wally and his brothers headed home. Wally and Peter looked somewhat alike, with round faces, brown hair, blue eyes, and thick, square hands like their father's. But the twins, Jake and Josh, had dark hair, and skin that tanned to a golden brown in summer. They were both string-bean skinny.

Usually their mother called them around three-fifteen from the hardware store where she worked to make sure they'd gotten home safely. But when they stayed for baseball practice, they called her instead.

Wally dialed the number, and as soon as his mother answered, he said, "We're all lying poisoned on the floor."

Mrs. Hatford seemed to know that meant everyone was okay because she said, "Peter didn't get his new shoes muddy, did he?"

"No, we kept him on the bleachers during practice. We didn't let him run around any."

"Good," said his mother. "You can have crackers and peanut butter, but the spaghetti is for supper, so don't touch that. The applesauce either."

"Okay," said Wally, "bye," and put the phone back down.

It used to be that as soon as the Hatfords got home from school, they would sit around the kitchen table with their afternoon snack and decide what kind of trick they were going to play next on the Malloy girls. It used to be that nothing was too awful for those girls, and the boys would do whatever they could to make them persuade their father to move them back to Ohio.

The Whomper, the Weirdo, and the Crazie, the boys called them. Eddie was the Whomper because she could hit a baseball so far—way out in center field sometimes; Beth was the Weirdo because she read such gross and scary books; and Caroline was the Crazie because she would do almost anything to be the center of attention.

But now, with Jake and Eddie on the same team, and with all the things they'd been through together, the boys had to admit that if they weren't quite friends with the Malloys, they weren't exactly enemies, either. The brothers had found themselves cheering every time Eddie made a really good play out on the field, and the Malloy girls cheered when Jake did something special.

"But if it wasn't for baseball . . . ," Jake said almost to himself, with a mouthful of crackers.

"If it wasn't for baseball, *what*?" asked Wally.

"Nothing," said Jake.

Wally seemed to know what Jake was thinking, however, because he said, "If you guys win the championship, you won't mind having Eddie around so much. You'll have your pictures in the paper and you can brag all over the place." While he spoke, Wally was fooling around with the magic trick he had traded for the two baseball cards at school. You put a quarter in one drawer, but when you pulled the drawer out a second time, the coin appeared to be gone. Then you closed it and pulled it out again and there was a fifty-cent piece in it. Except that it wasn't the same drawer. It only looked as though it was.

"And if we *don't* win?" said Jake. "What if we bomb on our very first game and then all we can play are neighborhood games for the rest of May?"

"Then . . . I don't know," said Wally, and leaned over to show Peter his trick.

"If the Bensons were here, and Steve was on our team . . . ," Jake said.

"Oh, Jake, good as he was, Steve was never as good at baseball as Eddie, and you know it," said Josh.

"Yeah, but at least if we lost out then, we'd have the guys to hang around with, do things with for the rest of the month."

"We can hang out with the girls!" Peter said helpfully.

"Eeee-yuck!" said Jake and Wally together.

"I don't need any more to do," Josh told them. "I

promised Mom I'd make signs for her Women's Auxiliary sale." He got up from the table then and went into the dining room, taking his colored markers from a drawer in the buffet. Then he reached around behind the buffet, where Mrs. Hatford stored sheets of white cardboard from the hardware store that she saved for Josh's art projects. He sat down at the table and began to make some signs.

Wally watched from the doorway. ONE TO FIVE DOLLARS Josh penciled carefully, and when the letters were straight, he went over them again with colored markers. Then he began to draw a decorative border.

Jake came and stood in the doorway too. "Hey," he said. "If we lose this weekend—if we're out of the tournament—will you guys go camping with me the rest of the weekends in May? I mean, I don't think I could *stand* losing *and* having to hang around with the Malloys."

"Sure," said Josh. "I'll go camping with you."

"Me too!" said Peter.

"Not me," said Wally. "*I* have to be here for the yard sale—" He stopped suddenly. "But if you lose, you won't be playing that day, and Mom will be here!"

"Smart boy," said Jake. "Don't go wishing we lose, though."

"Just look at it this way, Jake. No matter what happens, one of us wins," said Wally.

Jake opened his book bag and spread his homework out on the other side of the dining room table, across from Josh. Peter took a saucer of Oreo cookies into the living room to watch TV, and Wally checked the book-case to see if there were any books he hadn't read yet that he might like to read for his book report.

Hatchet he had already read. Same with *Maniac Magee.* There was another book by Jerry Spinelli he hadn't read yet, though—*Wringer.* Maybe he'd read that one.

Mr. Hatford got home from work first that day. He took off his postal jacket and hung it on a hanger. Then he went upstairs and put on a pair of sweatpants and a T-shirt. "Now, this is the kind of weather that makes me glad I'm a mail carrier," he said when he came back down. "Days like today I can drive with the window of my truck open. I can carry mail up the hill to a house, the breeze blowing at my back, and think I've got the best job in the world."

"Just the same, I don't think I want to be a mail car-rier," said Wally.

"Nothing wrong with that. You can be whatever you want," said his father. "What do you want to be?"

Wally shrugged. "I just like to study things."

"What kinds of things?"

"I don't know. Just things."

His dad poured himself a glass of cold tea from a pitcher, then put the pitcher back in the refrigerator. "Well, you could be a biologist and study cells under a microscope."

"Maybe," said Wally.

"You could be a zoologist and study animals."

"That'd be okay," said Wally.

"Or you could be a sociologist and study people."

"I'll stick with animals," said Wally. He settled down in one corner of the couch to start reading *Wringer*. It was about a town in Pennsylvania where there was a pigeon shoot every year to raise money, and boys about Wally's age worked at grabbing any pigeons that were shot but not dead yet, and wringing their necks, and this one boy didn't want to do it.

I wouldn't want to do it either, thought Wally. *What kind of a person would want to twist the head off a pigeon?* Maybe he *should* study people after all.

When Mrs. Hatford came home, she found all the members of her family busy. After checking on everyone in turn, she set about making supper, humming to herself.

"I feel so much better knowing you will be here to look after things at the sale, Wally," she said when he came in to see if the food was ready yet.

And I feel so much worse, thought Wally.

After supper he took his book bag up to his room to work on his math assignment. He was surprised to find two boxes, a lampshade, and a framed picture in one corner. He went to the top of the stairs.

"Hey!" he yelled. "What's that stuff doing in my room?"

His mother came to the foot of the stairs. "Oh, I hope you don't mind, Wally. We've told all the women not to bring their sale items to the house until the day before the sale, but some of them will be out of town then, and others just want them out of the way. Better to have them early than not at all, I guess."

"But what are they doing in *my* room?" Wally bellowed.

"Well, I looked in the twins' bedroom, and they've got so much stuff in there, and so does Peter, that—"

"What about the *basement*?" Wally wailed.

"Things might get musty down there, dear. Be a good sport, please, Wally. It's only till the end of the month, I promise."

Wally went back into his room and lay facedown on the bed. Just because he kept his room neat—just because he put things back in the right place—did he have to be punished? If he were a slob like Josh or Jake or Peter, would she have put the sale stuff somewhere else? Or did the middle child get the worst of everything? Wouldn't want to store stuff in the twins' bedroom because they're the oldest. Wouldn't want to put it in Peter's room. He's the youngest. So good old Wally—

The phone rang and he heard Jake answer at the foot of the stairs.

"Oh, hi, Eddie." Jake's voice was flat. ". . . No, I don't think so. I've got too much to do. . . . Yeah, bye."

Wally got up and went downstairs. "What did *she* want?" he asked, curious.

"Wanted to know if I would go over to the school and get in some extra practice. I told her no."

"How come?" asked Wally.

"Because Eddie doesn't *need* more practice. If I help her get even better, Coach'll let her pitch *all* the games. What kind of a fool does she take me for?"

"But you'd get better too!" said Wally.

The phone rang again. This time Wally picked it up.

"Is this the Hatford residence?" came a woman's voice.

"Yes," said Wally.

"I understand you are collecting things for the Women's Auxiliary sale on May twenty-ninth?"

"Yes," said Wally.

"I was wondering if I might come by early and look over what you've collected so far, and make a purchase."

"I don't think so, but I'll ask," said Wally.

He went to the kitchen and asked his mother. When he came back, he said, "No, we can't sell anything before the sale opens at noon on that day, but if you'll give me your name and phone number—"

The phone at the other end clicked as the woman hung up.

Four

■

Out!

"Jake Hatford is a jerk!"

Eddie Malloy stood in the upstairs hallway, phone in hand, before plunking it disgustedly down in its cradle.

"What now?" asked Beth from her bedroom.

"All I did was ask if he wanted to go back to the school later and get in some practice, and he said no."

Caroline followed Eddie into Beth's room.

"Maybe he had homework," Beth suggested, putting her finger between the pages of her book to hold the place.

"It was just an excuse, I could tell," said Eddie. "Doesn't he want to get any better before Saturday?"

"Maybe he just doesn't want to see *you* get any better," said Beth.

"That's ridiculous! We're on the same team!" Eddie fumed. "Doesn't he want us to *win?*"

"Not as bad as he wants to see you *not* win," said Beth.

"I will never understand boys as long as I live," said Eddie. "They were all born with half a brain."

"Peter's cute," said Caroline.

"Cute won't cut it," said Eddie.

"Josh is nice at times," said Beth.

"If you like the arty type," said Eddie.

Beth and Caroline exchanged glances.

"And what type do *you* like, Eddie? The sports type?" giggled Beth. "Maybe you thought Jake would jump at the chance to go over to the school with you alone, and he didn't. Maybe *that's* why you think he's a jerk."

"Give me a break," Eddie said. She turned on her heels, walked into her room, and shut the door.

Caroline sat down on the floor and leaned back against the wall. "What kind of book are you reading?" she asked.

"Mystery," said Beth.

"That's your favorite kind, isn't it? Scary stories?"

"Mystery and science fiction and romance—those are my three favorites," said Beth.

Caroline thought about that a moment. "If someone gave you a play that had mystery and romance and science fiction in it, all mixed up together, would you read it?"

"Whose play?"

"Mine," said Caroline.

"No," said Beth.

"Why not? Miss Applebaum said I could write a ten-page play instead of a book report, and if I can get it performed in front of the class, I'll get extra credit."

"Well, don't look at me. I'm not going to be in your play. I'm not getting up there on the stage at school and making a fool of myself."

"All I want you to do is read it when I'm done and tell me if it's any good," said Caroline.

"Sure," said Beth. "Now go away and let me finish my book."

It rained on Wednesday and Thursday, and the ground was still too wet for practice on Friday, so when the time came on Saturday, Eddie had been without practice and was feeling nervous.

Caroline had never seen her sister so jumpy. Usually Eddie was pretty much in control, but by the time the Malloys pulled into the parking lot of the high school in Elkins, where the game would be played, she was nibbling at her lower lip and looking tense.

"What's the matter, Eddie?" Caroline whispered.

"I don't know. I'm just jittery," Eddie confessed. She was sitting between her two sisters in the backseat, and kept taking deep breaths. "I feel rusty without practice."

"I don't know why you should be nervous," said Beth. "You're better than almost any boy on the team, and no one else got in extra practice either."

"But you know what will happen if we lose," said

Eddie. "Especially if we lose our first game. They'll blame it on me. They'll say it's because there's a girl on the team. And nobody will ever want to talk to me at school."

"Eddie, that's ridiculous," said her father. "You know what? You're a lot more nervous sitting here in the car thinking about how you'll play than you'll be when you're actually out there on the field." He turned off the engine. "Okay, girl. Go!" he said.

The Malloys piled out just as the Hatfords were getting out of their car. Peter was squeezed between his parents in front. Caroline studied the Hatford boys. Jake didn't look nervous at all. The Hatfords looked in control of the situation. Jake, in fact, looked as though he could handle anything. There was a swagger to his walk as he sauntered over to survey the other team, which was warming up out on the field.

Parents and friends took their places on the bleachers, Elkins parents on one end, Buckman parents on the other. There was an empty space, a no-man's-land, in between.

The Hatfords sat in front of the Malloys, and as soon as they were seated, Peter turned around and said, "Jake's gonna strike everybody out!" The others laughed.

"We'll see what happens, Peter. We'll see," said his dad.

The other team was at bat, and Eddie was the starting pitcher. But Caroline could tell just by her windup that she was off her stride. The ball didn't come as fast as it usually did, and the first batter hit it to center field. Fortunately for Buckman, it was caught. One out.

The next batter walked. The third batter hit a double, and the runner on first scored. By the time the first inning was over, Elkins had one run, Buckman, nothing.

The coach was talking to Eddie and Jake. And Caroline knew without hearing that Jake would pitch the second inning. While Eddie was waiting her turn at bat, she paced behind the catcher like a tiger. *Nibble, nibble, nibble* went her teeth on her lower lip.

"What do you suppose is wrong with her?" Mrs. Malloy asked her husband.

"Just the first time she's played on a real team," her husband answered. "No matter how much practice you get, there's always that first time." Mr. Malloy was a football coach at Buckman College. He was replacing Coach Benson for a year on a teacher-exchange program. Whether he would take his family back to Ohio when the year was over or stay in Buckman had not yet been decided.

Buckman struck out before Eddie got a chance to bat. When the Badgers took the field again, the coach put Eddie in left field and Jake on the pitcher's mound. Jake struck out two batters and got the third out on a weak infield fly.

When Buckman's players came to bat, Eddie was batting third. The first boy struck out. The second batter made it to first when the shortstop fumbled the ball. When Eddie got up, Mr. Malloy murmured to Caroline, "She's leaning too far forward." Eddie swung and missed.

"Strike one!" called the umpire.

Eddie didn't swing at the second pitch.

"Strike two!" the umpire said.

Eddie lifted the bat slightly off her shoulder. The Elkins pitcher wound up and threw the ball. Eddie swung.

Craaaaack! Eddie, surprised that she had actually hit the ball, let go of the bat as she started to run to first. The next thing anyone knew, the bat had traveled down the line of Buckman players waiting their turn and hit two of them across the knees.

The umpire stopped play.

"You're out of the game, Eddie," he yelled. "She's out of the game, Coach, for throwing her bat."

Down on the field, Eddie looked stricken. Dazed. "I . . . I didn't mean to," she kept saying.

Her coach shook his head. "You know the rules, Eddie. You never let go of the bat like that. You could have hit a player in the face. Go sit on the bench."

Beth covered her face with her hands, but Caroline couldn't take her eyes off her older sister. Seemingly in shock, Eddie went slowly back to the bench and sat down, her face blank.

The game continued without her. Jake had never played better. He was in control of his arm and his arm was in control of the ball. Buckman tied the score, then got a run in the eighth inning. No one scored in the ninth, so Buckman advanced to the next game the following Saturday. The team was greeted with cheers as they picked up their bats and balls to go home.

Eddie didn't say a word as she followed her family across the parking lot to the car. Coach Malloy reached out and put an arm around her shoulder, but Eddie didn't respond. It was only when they were inside the car that she said shakily, "I don't know what was the matter, Dad! I just blew it, that's all. I've never thrown a bat like that, ever!"

"And I don't think you will again, Eddie," said her father.

"I just felt like . . . like everyone was looking at me, expecting great things, and that no matter how well I played, it wouldn't be good enough," she said miserably.

Coach Malloy smiled a little. "Well, by next week, word will get around that you aren't very good after all, and nobody will expect much of anything. And *then* you can show them what you can do."

Eddie sat with her head down. "This is so humiliating!" she murmured. "Jake didn't seem nervous at all. He's going to hate me for letting the team down."

"Oh, I don't think so," said her dad. "The Badgers won, didn't they? Show up every day for practice, Eddie, and do your best."

The girls went upstairs as soon as they got home,

and Eddie seemed too tired even to talk. She certainly didn't want any lunch. When the phone rang, Caroline took it in the upstairs hall. It was Jake.

"Can I talk to Eddie?" he said.

"Eddie," Caroline called. "For you. It's Jake."

"I don't want to talk to him," said Eddie. "Tell him I'm sick or something."

"I guess she's too tired," said Caroline into the phone.

There was a pause at the end of the line. "Well, tell her I'm going over to the school this afternoon and get in some practice, and I wondered if she wanted to come along," said Jake.

"Just a minute," said Caroline. She walked to the door of Eddie's bedroom and told her what Jake had said.

Eddie was quiet for a moment. "Yes," she said finally. "Tell him I'd like that."

Five

■

Act One

When Jake set off for the school ball field that afternoon, he told his brothers to stay home.

"Eddie doesn't need to have people staring at her," he said. "She feels bad enough already."

Wally could only stare at Jake. It seemed to Wally that while Eddie had lost her self-confidence, Jake seemed to have found his. Now that Eddie had proved she wasn't so hot, wasn't superhuman, Jake could shine. And once he shone, he didn't have to dislike Eddie so much.

"We need her on the team," Jake said to his brothers. "If she doesn't play any better than she did this morning, we'll lose." He went outside and down the street toward the school.

Wally decided to spend the afternoon reading *Wringer* for his book report, but he was almost afraid to go in his bedroom anymore. It seemed as though every time he left, the bags and boxes along the wall had babies. All he had to do was leave the house for an hour or two and when he came back there would be another lampshade or Crock-Pot or toaster.

"Just hold on till the end of the month, Wally, and you'll have your room back the way it was," said his mother.

"What if some of this stuff doesn't sell?" he asked.

"Mrs. Larson's son has promised to haul away to the Goodwill store anything that's left," his mother said.

It was a beautiful spring day, so Wally decided he would rather read outside than in his room anyway. He went out on the back steps with a glass of lemonade and his book and tried to think how much lemon juice and water it took to make a pitcher of lemonade. And once he started thinking about water, he thought about how much rain they had had that spring. Once he started thinking about what a rainy spring it had been, he started to remember the year before, when it had hardly rained at all and farmers had worried about drought. The newspaper had asked people to take fewer baths and shorter showers. They were told not to water their lawns and to make sure their dishwashers were full before they turned them on.

Here's what Wally could not understand: If the water from your sink and your bathtub went into the sewer, and the sewers flowed into rivers, and the water you drank came from the river, through filtration plants, and then back on into your house, what difference did it make if you used too much bathwater or not? Didn't it just end up in the river again? He knew there must be a good reason, but no one had ever explained it to him.

He had taken another sip of lemonade when he saw Caroline coming up his driveway. He tried to pull his feet out of the way so that she wouldn't know he was out back, but it was too late. Around the house she came. She was holding a writing tablet and pencil.

"Hi, Wally," she said. "I guess Jake and Eddie are over at the school practicing, aren't they?"

"I guess so," said Wally.

"Eddie was pretty upset over the way she played this morning. Jake was nice to offer to practice with her."

"I guess so," said Wally again, studying the slice of lemon in his glass.

"I brought over the first act of my play, Wally. Can I read it to you for your frank and honest opinion?"

"I guess so," said Wally.

Caroline studied him. "You have to be one hundred percent honest or it won't help," she said. "When I get to be an actress on Broadway, critics will come to see me perform and the newspapers will publish their reviews. I have to get used to criticism, so say whatever you really feel about it. Okay?"

"Okay," said Wally.

Caroline cleared her throat, held the tablet out in front of her, and began: "A Night to Forget," she read. "Act one, scene one: A cottage on the beach. Ten o'clock at night. A couple is on their honeymoon."

JIM: Wasn't that a nice walk on the beach, honey?

NANCY: Yes, it was. And wasn't the moon beautiful?

JIM: Yes, it was.

NANCY: I wonder what those strange marks were on the sand, though.

JIM: Probably just a crab or some sort of seagull.

NANCY: I suppose so. *She yawns.*

JIM: Well, I guess we should go to bed.

NANCY: Yes, I'm very tired.

JIM: I'll turn out the lights.

NANCY: Wait a minute. What was that noise? It sounds like something trying to get in.

JIM: Probably just the wind. I think you're imagining things.

NANCY: I suppose so. Good night.

JIM: Good night.

They kiss.

Wally found Caroline looking at him. He also felt his neck beginning to get red.

"Okay so far?" asked Caroline.

"I guess so," said Wally.

"Act one, scene two," said Caroline. "Twelve o'clock at night. Jim and Nancy's bedroom. There is just enough moonlight coming in the window that the audience can see what's onstage."

NANCY: Jim! Jim! Wake up. I hear that noise again.

JIM: Huh?

NANCY: I hear it, and it's louder now! I really think someone's trying to get in.

JIM: But we're the only ones on the beach. There aren't any other houses for miles around. Who would it be?

NANCY: I don't know, but I think you should do something.

JIM: Okay. I hear it now too. I'll go downstairs and check.

There is a sloshing, thumping, scraping noise offstage.

NANCY: Oh, Jim! Be careful!

JIM: Don't fear, my love. I'll be okay.

Nancy sits up in bed with one hand to her throat. Jim grabs a golf club and goes out into the hall in his pajamas. The noise gets louder and louder, and then there is a terrible yell from Jim.

NANCY: Jim! Jim!

There is a gurgling sound from downstairs and then the house is quiet. Nancy leaps out of bed and backs up against the wall, her eyes wide. When Jim does not come back, she runs over and locks the bedroom door and then she gets back in bed. Soon she is sound asleep.

"What?" said Wally. "Her husband disappears and she just goes back to sleep?"

Caroline thoughtfully tapped her pencil against her cheek. "Okay," she said. "She'll lie there with her eyes wide open until morning." Caroline made a note on her tablet, then began reading aloud again:

Act one, scene three: Morning in the cottage. Nancy sits up in bed sobbing.

NANCY: Jim! Jim! Where are you? *There is no answer. She gets out of bed and looks out the window. The sky is dark and brooding.*

NANCY: I know! I'll call the beach patrol. They will come over and help us. *She lifts up the telephone.* Oh, no! The line is dead!

She puts on her robe and combs her hair. Then she takes another one of her husband's golf clubs and carefully opens the bedroom door.

NANCY: Jim? Jim?

She takes a step outside into the hall.

NANCY: Jim? Jim?

No answer. She screams. She puts her hands to her face. She screams again. She bends down and touches something on the floor. The floor and the stairs are covered with a thick green slime. Curtain falls. End of act one.

Caroline closed her writing tablet and looked at Wally. "Well," she said, "how did you like it?"

"It stinks," said Wally.

"What?" cried Caroline.

"You wanted me to be truthful," said Wally.

"But you have to say more than 'It stinks,' " said Caroline. "This play has everything! It has romance and science fiction and suspense and mystery!"

"It still stinks," said Wally. And then, thinking that perhaps he sounded a bit harsh, he said, "Of course, I've only heard the first act. I probably shouldn't say anything until I've heard it all."

"Right," said Caroline. "But what's the matter with it so far?"

Wally shrugged. "They don't sound like real people. Why didn't the wife call the beach patrol before? Why did she wait till morning?"

Caroline thought about that a moment. "Because I wanted her to discover that the line was dead at the end of act one, and that would be the next morning."

"Well, why wouldn't she go downstairs as soon as she heard her husband scream, then?"

"Because I'm saving that for act two," said Caroline.

"Well," said Wally. "Like I said, so far it stinks, but maybe the next act will be better."

Caroline sighed. "Maybe I'm a better actress than I am a playwright. But I wanted to write a play with a part especially for me."

"So does Nancy die a horrible death in the end? That would be a good part for you," said Wally.

"I can't give away the ending," said Caroline.

"Who's going to play the part of Jim?" asked Wally, and when Caroline just looked at him and smiled, he said, "No!"

"That's okay," said Caroline. "When I've finished it, it will be so good that every boy in school will want to play the part of Jim."

"Name one," said Wally.

Caroline thought some more. "Well, Peter, maybe."

Wally laughed out loud, and Caroline smiled a little too. "Just wait, Wally," she said. "Someday you will see my name in lights on Broadway and you'll be proud to say you knew me when I was just a little girl."

■ ■ ■ ■ ■ ■ ■ ■ ■ ■ ■ ■

Six

■

Scavenger Hunt

"Girls," Mrs. Malloy called up the stairs when the girls got home from school the following Wednesday. "When you finish your homework, will you take a half hour or so to check your rooms and see if you have any-thing—any *nice* thing—that we could donate to Ellen Hatford for the yard sale?"

"Like what?" asked Eddie.

"Oh, maybe a shirt you haven't worn much. Belts, jewelry, anything at all that might catch someone's eye. I've put a box in the hall up there for your things. But don't give away anything with holes in it. We'll put things like that in the rag bag, and I can use them around the house."

Eddie was the most generous when it came to give-aways. She stood at her closet door, sliding hangers from left to right. For each item she said either a soft yes or no. A yes meant it could be given away, and she would yank it off the hanger and throw it onto her bed. A no meant it was a keeper. To Caroline, it seemed as though Eddie had no second thoughts. No sentimental attachments. And when she had finished her closet, she started on her dresser drawers.

Beth was more of a problem, especially with books. Asking Beth to get rid of a book was about like asking Mrs. Malloy to get rid of a daughter. But Caroline was the absolute worst, and she knew it. Caroline, it seemed, could get rid of nothing, because every object, every item of clothing, every old sneaker, in fact, was something that she might, someday, in middle school or high school, be able to use as a prop in a play. It might be just the right necklace for the part, or the right music box, or even the perfect moth-eaten sweater for an orphaned child to wear onstage. When Mrs. Malloy came upstairs later to see how the girls were doing, she found a box full of Eddie's things, only a jacket from Beth, and nothing at all from Caroline.

Caroline sat on her bed, surrounded by things her mother thought she'd parted with years before, misty-eyed and clutching each one to her in turn.

"Good grief," said Mrs. Malloy. "I'm not asking you to sacrifice body parts, Caroline. If you haven't made use of something since first grade, let it go, for heaven's sake."

And so a little doll in a Swiss costume was donated to the sale, a *Bambi* video, a pair of patent leather shoes that were a size too small, and a wool cap.

"We're not supposed to take things over to the Hatfords' yet, so we'll keep them here until the night before the sale," Mrs. Malloy said. "But this will save us some work later if we move back to Ohio."

"*Will* we go back, Mother?" Beth asked.

"I wish I knew! One day your father thinks he'll stay on here for another year as football coach and the next he doesn't. It will depend partly on whether Coach Benson decides to move *his* family back from Georgia and take over their house. It's like dominoes. Everyone's waiting for the next piece to fall."

■

"Well, I feel great!" Eddie announced at supper. "I've done well at practice every day this week, and I don't think I'll be too nervous at Saturday's game. I was afraid the coach would take me off the team after last week, but he says no way. Just a question of the first-game jitters, he calls it."

"That's the spirit, Eddie!" said her father. "Where's the next game? Clarksburg, is it?"

"Yeah. Are you coming?"

"Wouldn't miss it for the world," Coach Malloy said.

■

At school, the kids in Caroline's class were beginning to read their book reports aloud. Every day in English two or three more students got up to tell why they had chosen a particular book.

Wally stood up and read his report about *Wringer*. Everyone listened intently, especially when they found out there really *was* such a town in Pennsylvania, and that there really *was* a pigeon shoot, and that boys really *were* hired to wring the necks of injured and dying pigeons.

"Very good, Wally," the teacher said. "Isn't it interesting how Mr. Spinelli took an incident from real life and turned it into a work of fiction?"

At recess, when people were putting their books away, Caroline said to Wally, "I think that sounds like a good book. It's sad, but I'll read it sometime."

"I didn't do a good job telling about it, though," said Wally. "There's a lot of stuff going on in the book that just doesn't come out in a report."

"Just like my play!" said Caroline. "I could see all kinds of things going on in my head while I was reading it that you couldn't see when you heard it. That's what actors and actresses do—they bring the words to life onstage."

Wally thought about that a minute. "Well, maybe," he said. "Maybe I'll like the second act better."

■

There was, of course, baseball practice again after school, and when the Malloy girls finally got home and were sharing a bag of chips, they noticed more bags and boxes in the hall.

"What's this?" Beth asked her mother.

"More things for the Women's Auxiliary sale," said Mrs. Malloy. "This is giving us a chance to clean house. When you girls finish your snack, would you go down in the basement and see if there's anything else that could go?"

"Most of that stuff belongs to the Bensons," said Eddie.

"I know. But we put some of our own things down there too."

So the girls sauntered over to the basement door and went down the steps. Eddie and Caroline rummaged through the old tires and garden hoses along one wall, while Beth stood back on the stairs, surveying the basement and holding the bag of chips.

Suddenly Beth said, "Hey!"

Eddie and Caroline turned around.

"What?" asked Caroline.

Beth stuffed another handful of chips in her mouth and pointed to the long metal heating ducts overhead.

"*What?*" said Eddie, and went back up the stairs to where Beth was standing, to see where she was pointing.

There, on top of a metal duct, almost out of sight, was a small notebook or something.

"What do you think it is?" asked Beth, still chewing.

"I don't know," Eddie said. "Furnace instructions maybe?" She went back down the steps, pulled the stepladder over, then climbed up and ran her hand over the top of the metal duct until she reached the notebook. She pulled it down and a shower of plaster dust and dirt came with it.

"Yuck!" she said, lowering her head and flicking the stuff from her hair.

It was a small photo album with no label on the cover. Still standing on the ladder, Eddie opened it up. Her eyes grew wide and a slow smile spread across her face. "Hey!" she said. "Pay dirt!"

"What is it?" asked Caroline, reaching for it. But Eddie only clutched it to her chest, came back down the ladder, and, grinning mysteriously, motioned her sisters to follow her up to her room.

"Find anything for the sale?" Mrs. Malloy called from the dining room.

"Only old tires, and those are the Bensons'," Eddie answered.

Up in her room, Eddie closed the door behind them and the three girls sprawled on her bed.

"You'll never guess!" Eddie said, still smiling, and opened the cover. There were color photographs of . . . who else? The Hatford and Benson boys, in the silliest pictures the girls had ever seen. They appeared to have been taken sometime in the past year, for the boys looked only a little younger than they were now.

Yet there was Peter Hatford dressed in a diaper, curled up on a blanket and sucking a bottle. There was Jake with strands of cooked spaghetti dangling from his nostrils, a cap with a propeller on his head. There was Wally in bunny pajamas two sizes too small, with sleeper feet and floppy ears. There was Josh in Batman

46

underpants and a Batman T-shirt with a cape around his shoulders.

The girls were too astonished to make a sound at first; then they burst into laughter at the humiliating pictures of the boys. The five Benson brothers had their photos in the album too: Steve Benson dressed as a ballerina; Bill bending over with a rip in the seat of his pants, blowing soap bubbles at the same time; Tony in white knee socks with a pacifier in his mouth and a Dr. Seuss hat on his head; Doug holding a teddy bear and sucking his thumb; and Danny wearing a T-shirt that said KICK ME HARD, holding a blueberry pie in which he had obviously just buried his face.

"What do you suppose made them take these pictures?" Eddie gasped in disbelief.

"I don't know," said Beth, "but this is too good to pass up." She went to the phone in the hallway and dialed the Hatfords' number.

Wally answered, and Beth held the phone out so that her sisters could hear.

"Hi, Wally, this is Beth," she said. "I just wanted to tell you that I think we've found something else for your Treats and Treasures yard sale."

"Good," said Wally. "Bring it over on the twenty-eighth, okay?"

"Oh, but I thought you should know about it first," Beth went on. "We found it in the basement on top of a heating duct."

"Yeah?" said Wally.

"It's a photo album, with pictures."

"Yeah?" Wally said again.

"And you look really great in those bunny pajamas," Caroline said over Beth's shoulder, giggling.

"What?" yelled Wally, and the girls heard him bellow, "Josh! They found those pictures!"

Josh's voice sounded from the kitchen. "Who did? What pictures?"

"The Malloys. The *pictures!*" he squawked.

There were cries of anguish in the background; then Josh took the phone. "Where were they?" he asked, his voice tense.

"On top of a heating duct in the basement," Beth explained. "We thought we'd offer them for the Women's Auxiliary yard sale. Unless, of course, you guys want to negotiate or make a trade of some sort."

"Trade for *what*?" asked Josh.

"I don't know, we'll think of something," Beth said, and hung up, still laughing.

Seven

■

Missing

Josh threw back his head and howled, Jake and Wally joining in.

Mrs. Hatford was just coming through the back door, and she paused as she dropped her car keys on the counter.

"Is this a braying contest or something?"

"That stupid Bill Benson!" Wally cried.

"Stupid Steve and Tony and all of them! They should have taken those pictures with them!" said Josh.

"What on earth are you talking about?" asked their mother.

Josh look at Jake and Jake looked at Wally and nobody wanted to say anything, but finally Peter, the only one who seemed calm, spoke up: "Pictures," he said.

"Pictures of whom?"

"Us," said Peter.

"So?" said his mother.

"Doing silly things," Peter answered uncertainly, looking at his brothers for guidance.

"Well, is that so awful? What kinds of things?" asked Mrs. Hatford as she went to the refrigerator to see what to make for dinner. She took out a package of pork chops and studied the lower shelf.

Josh did the telling. After all, Wally figured, he was making all those beautifully decorated signs for the yard sale. His mother could hardly get mad at him.

"Jake had spaghetti coming out of his nose," he said.

Mrs. Hatford straightened up and looked around. "He had *what*?"

"And I was wearing a diaper and sucking on a bottle!" Peter said, laughing.

Mrs. Hatford turned slowly to Wally.

"I was wearing my old bunny pajamas and Josh was in his Batman underpants and a cape."

Mrs. Hatford was trying not to laugh. "*Why* would you guys want your pictures taken like *that*?"

"The Bensons did it too!" said Peter. "One of 'em was in a ballerina costume and one put his face in a blueberry pie and—"

"*Why?*" Mrs. Hatford asked again.

The boys looked at each other.

"Just for fun," Josh said finally.

"So where are they?"

"The Malloys found them in the basement."

"Well, for goodness' sake, just ask the girls to give them back!" said Mrs. Hatford. "Now, let me see if we have any more applesauce in the cellar." And she went down the stairs.

The boys looked at each other. There were times, Wally thought, when their mother seemed to be the smartest woman in the world and times, like now, when she seemed to have no imagination whatsoever. Did she really think that the girls, who had thought of every trick in the book to play on them—girls, in fact, whom the boys had tormented from the very moment they moved to Buckman—were going to give back pictures of the boys in their underpants and bunny pajamas? Did she really believe that if Wally went over to the Malloys' house and said, "Could you please let us have those ridiculous pictures back, the ones with spaghetti coming out of Jake's nose?" the girls would say "Sure," and hand them over? Was she living on another planet?

They went up to the twins' bedroom to think it over.

"Why did we ever take those pictures in the first place?" Wally wondered aloud.

"You know why, Wally!" said Josh. "We were all in on it. We made a pact that we would always be loyal to each other, no matter what, and to make sure, we took the most embarrassing picture we could think of for each one of us. If one of us ever betrayed the rest, we were going to show his picture around school."

"Oh, yeah." Wally sighed. "It seemed like a good idea at the time."

"Until the dumb, stupid Bensons forgot to take the

pictures with them!" said Jake. "Just tell me this, Wally. Was Eddie on the phone? Was she doing any of the talking?"

"No. Only Beth," said Wally.

"Well, maybe Eddie didn't see the pictures, then," said Jake. "She might get them back for us, now that we're working together on the same team."

"And maybe pigs have wings," said Josh.

"Well, I'm not going to get upset before this next game!" Jake declared. "I'm not even going to think about it, if I can help it. Josh, you'll have to bargain with them."

"How?" Josh bleated. "The only Malloy who likes me a little is Beth, and it was Beth who was doing the talking!"

All eyes turned to Wally. "No!" said Wally. Then he shouted it. *"NO!"*

This time they must have taken him seriously, because suddenly the twins turned toward Peter.

"Peter," said Josh. "We really, really need you. We need you to go over to the Malloys' and ask for those pictures. Just get those pictures and bring them back. And don't come home until you do."

"Okay," said Peter. He went back downstairs and out the door.

Wally looked at his brothers. This was too easy. They stood at the window at the top of the stairs and watched the youngest Hatford go down the walk and cross the road. They watched him start across the swinging bridge. When he got to the center, where the supporting cables on each side hung low enough to grab as handrails, they watched him stop and peer over the edge.

"Why is he just standing there?" Jake asked. "What's he *doing*?"

"Spitting," said Wally.

"What?"

"That's what he's doing," said Wally. "He's spitting in the water to see how far it will float."

Jake and Josh stared at Wally.

"You can't see your own spit in the water. It gets mixed up with the river."

"I know," said Wally. "But that's what Peter's trying to find out."

His brothers were still looking at Wally strangely, though, and Wally wondered if he and Peter were the only boys in Upshur County who had ever passed a May afternoon by spitting in the Buckman River.

Eventually, however, Peter began walking forward again, stopping now and then to try to see the river between the slats in the bridge, and at long last he reached the other side and started up the Malloys' hilly lot.

"I sure didn't need this right now," said Jake. "I'm trying not to let *any*thing throw me off stride for Saturday's game. Clarksburg's going to be a tough team to beat."

"Well, I sure didn't need it either," said Josh. "What

if Beth brings those pictures to school and puts one up on the bulletin board or something?"

It went without saying that Wally didn't need this either. He didn't need it now or ever. He didn't need Caroline sticking the picture of him in his bunny pajamas on the end of a ruler and thrusting it over his shoulder at school. He didn't need her passing the pictures around the girls' table at lunch. He didn't need to walk by groups of giggling girls out on the playground and see them all point to him. No sir, he didn't need that at all.

"Do you think they'll give the album to him?" Josh asked as the minutes ticked by and Peter disappeared from view at the top of the hill.

"If they give the pictures to anyone, it will be Peter," said Jake. "They like Peter. They think he's just the sweetest thing that ever lived. Ha! They should check out his closet sometime. They should smell his breath after he's eaten cheese! But hey! If Peter gets the pictures back, he can smell like dog doo for all I care."

Mr. Hatford's car turned into the driveway, and the boys could hear his footsteps as he came into the house.

They heard the voices of their parents in the kitchen below, and the sound of the TV as Mr. Hatford turned on the evening news. There came the smell of frying pork chops, and the clatter of plates on the table.

Wally and his brothers stood at the upstairs window, noses pressed against the glass.

"Come . . . on!" Josh breathed.

"Where *is* he?" said Jake.

"Well, you can't expect him just to say, 'Give me the pictures,' and think they'll hand them right over," said Wally. "He's got to be sweet first."

"Man, I don't know how he does it. He's so sweet that the girls always feed him cookies when he goes over there," said Jake.

"They *bake* them especially for him," said Josh.

"Which makes him even sweeter," said Wally.

Five more minutes went by. Then ten.

"Boys!" came their mother's voice from below. "Wash up. Supper's on the table."

"Oh, man!" Wally whispered.

"Coming!" called Josh.

They went into the bathroom and washed their hands, doing everything in slow motion, hoping to stall for time.

Down the stairs they went, stopping at the front door to peer out again at the swinging bridge, looking for a lone figure coming down the hill from the Malloys' with a photo album under his arm.

Nothing.

They went into the kitchen, where mashed potatoes and green beans and pork chops sat on various platters, and a dish of applesauce stood in the center of the table.

Mrs. Hatford glanced around at her brood, then went to the kitchen doorway and called, "Peter?"

"Uh . . . he'll be back any minute, Mom," said Wally. "He's doing an errand."

"At suppertime?" his mother asked.

"He'll be along," Josh echoed.

The rolls in the oven were just beginning to brown around the edges, and Mrs. Hatford grabbed the pot holders to take them out. For the next few minutes she was busy with that. The boys helped themselves to the food at hand and amiably discussed the rolls and how good they were spread with their mother's cherry jam.

But right in the middle of supper, Mrs. Hatford said, "Where *is* Peter? Where did he go?"

"He should have been back by now," said Wally.

"Do you or do you not know where he went?" asked Mr. Hatford.

"He went to the Malloys' to get some pictures back," said Josh.

"Aha! So he's doing the dirty work for you," said Mrs. Hatford. "How long ago did he leave?"

"Twenty minutes, maybe," said Jake.

"Say thirty," said Josh.

"Well, for heaven's sake, he should have been back by now," said Mrs. Hatford, looking concerned.

And at that very moment the phone rang.

Eight

■

The Visitor

"Who do you suppose will come over to get it?" Beth asked mischievously.

"I don't know, but I'm going to let you two handle it," said Eddie. "Jake and I are getting along okay right now, and I don't want any trouble between us before the game on Saturday. He was awfully nice to practice with me last week, so if there's any negotiating to do, you guys will have to do it."

"Man oh man, do we ever hold all the cards!" said Beth. "We've never been in such a good bargaining position before, Caroline. What should we ask for in return? All their earthly possessions?"

"We'd better think about this a long time," said Caroline. "We don't want to blow it. Maybe we shouldn't decide until the championship game is over. We could tell the guys we'll give it back in June, and we'll make our conditions then."

57

"Good idea," said Eddie. "We're not saying we won't give it back. We're just saying we won't give it back right now."

"Let's take another look at it," said Beth. "I want to imprint these on my brain forever." She giggled.

The girls sat down on the bed again, and this time they savored every picture. They hooted and howled when they came to the photo of Wally Hatford in bunny pajamas two sizes too small, and Caroline even rolled off the bed in laughter.

There was a knock at the door downstairs, and Caroline continued rolling till she was on her feet again and was the first one to reach the door. There stood Peter, smiling his sweetest smile.

"Well, hello, Peter." Caroline grinned at him, then turned around and grinned at her sisters on the stairs. "Want to come in?" she asked him.

"Okay," said Peter, and stepped into the hallway.

"Who is it?" called Coach Malloy from the kitchen, where he was helping cut up vegetables for dinner.

"Just Peter Hatford, over for a little visit," Beth called back.

Peter came in and sat in a chair in a corner of the living room.

"How are you?" asked Eddie.

"Fine," said Peter.

"How is everybody at your house?" asked Beth.

"Fine," said Peter.

"How are things going at school?" asked Caroline.

"Fine," said Peter.

The girls exchanged knowing looks. "Well, did you come over to see us about something?" asked Beth finally.

Peter nodded.

"About what?" asked Caroline.

"Jake and Josh and Wally really, really, really want those pictures back," said Peter.

"What pictures?" asked Caroline innocently.

"You know. The ones of us acting silly with the Bensons," said Peter.

"Oh. *Those* pictures!" said Eddie. "Well, I don't think we've finished looking at them yet, Peter. Some of them are so silly we just want to look at them a long, long time."

Peter grinned. "Did you see the one of me in a diaper?"

"Yeah, that was silly, all right," said Beth. "But the one of Josh in his Batman underpants was my favorite."

"That's the one Josh really, really, really wants back the most," said Peter.

"Well," said Beth. "We're going to have to think about this, Peter. Of course we'll give them back eventually. They don't belong to us, after all. We just have to figure out what we want to do with them first."

Peter gave a long sigh. He leaned over and rested his

elbow on the lamp table beside the chair, then put his chin in his hand. "Well, I guess I can't go home, then," he said.

"Why not?" asked Eddie.

"Because Josh told me not to come home without the pictures."

The girls tried not to laugh. "Imagine that!" said Eddie.

"I guess you'll just have to live here for a while, then, won't you?" said Caroline. "Of course you'll stay for dinner?"

"What are you having to eat?" asked Peter.

"Chop suey, I think. But I know for sure Mom made a fudge pie."

"Yeah!" said Peter brightly, straightening up again. "I'll stay!"

"Are you girls ready for dinner?" Mrs. Malloy called.

"Yes, and Peter's staying for dinner too, Mom," called Beth.

"Oh? Really? Well, I'll put on another plate, then," said her mother.

When the family gathered in the dining room, Peter took a chair. He didn't seem too sure about the chop suey, taking only a little bit of rice and a small helping of vegetables but his eyes drifted regularly to the kitchen and the chocolate fudge pie sitting on the counter in plain view.

"So what's happening at your house these days, Peter?" asked Coach Malloy. "Everybody doing okay?"

"The answer to whatever you want to know, Dad, is 'fine,' " said Eddie. "I thought I'd save you the trouble of asking."

"I see," said her father. "Well, I imagine your whole family will be going to the game in Clarksburg on Saturday, Peter. Right?"

"Yes, we're all going," said Peter. He frowned. "I may have to ride with you, though."

"Oh? I'm not sure we have room. Our car only holds five," said Mrs. Malloy.

"Uh . . . Mom . . . Peter may be staying over tonight. He can use one of our sleeping bags, can't he?" said Caroline.

"What's this?" asked Coach Malloy. "You're not running away from home, are you, Peter?"

"Just for a little while," Peter told him.

"Doesn't your mother know you're here?" asked Mrs. Malloy.

"Just my brothers," Peter answered.

"Peter Hatford, you go to the phone right now and tell your mother where you are," said Mrs. Malloy. "Tell her it's fine with me if you stay for dinner, but she's got to know where you are. She must be worried."

"O-kay," said Peter reluctantly. He slid off his chair. "But Jake and Josh and Wally aren't going to like it."

Under his breath, Coach Malloy muttered, "Jake and Josh and Wally can go jump in the lake, as far as I'm concerned. We can't have kids appearing and disappearing whenever they get the notion."

61

"Excuse me," said Caroline. "I just want to make sure he really talks to his mom and not just his brothers."

"Good idea," said Mrs. Malloy.

Caroline went out into the hallway and stood beside Peter as he called home.

"Hi, Wally," said Peter. "Can I talk to Mom?"

Caroline bent down so she could listen.

"Peter, where *are* you?" came Wally's voice. "What's taking so long?"

"I'm eating dinner," said Peter.

There was an anguished wail at the other end of the line. *"Dinner?"*

"I have to talk to Mom!" Peter insisted. "Mrs. Malloy *said*!"

And the next thing Caroline knew, Mrs. Hatford's voice came on the line. "Peter? Is that you? Where *are* you?"

"I'm having dinner at the Malloys' and I'm going to sleep in a sleeping bag," said Peter.

"You most certainly are not!" cried his mother. "Peter, have you lost your mind? You can't just wander over to somebody's house and stay for dinner and sleep in a sleeping bag!"

"I have to," said Peter. "I can't come home."

"*Why* can't you come home?" Mrs. Hatford demanded.

"Because Jake and Josh and Wally said I couldn't come home without the pictures, and Eddie and Beth and Caroline want to look at them some more, so I'm going to live over here for a while."

"Peter Hatford, you pick up your feet and get yourself home this very minute!" Mrs. Hatford was practically screaming. "This house is a zoo, I tell you! A living, breathing zoo!"

"Okay," said Peter.

"Peter!" his mother continued. "You go back to the table and thank Mrs. Malloy for whatever you ate so far. Then you wipe your mouth on your napkin and carry your dishes to the sink, and you go out the door and come home. Do you understand me?"

"Okay," said Peter. He hung up the phone and walked back into the dining room, Caroline at his heels.

"Thanks for what I ate so far, but I have to go home. Mom said," Peter told them.

"Oh, I'm sorry," said Mrs. Malloy. "Can't you even finish your dinner?"

"Mom said to pick up my feet and come home," Peter told her. He wiped his mouth on his napkin, picked up his plate, and carried it to the kitchen.

"Now, what was *that* all about?" Coach Malloy asked.

"Don't ask, George, don't ask," said Mrs. Malloy.

Caroline went into the kitchen with her own empty plate and got there just in time to see Peter hurriedly stuff something into his pocket. He grinned at her sheepishly and went back through the dining room.

63

"Goodbye," he said.

"Well, it was nice to see you, Peter," said Mrs. Malloy. "We'll invite you to dinner another time."

"Yes, we'll see you at the game Saturday," said the coach. "Tell your dad hello for me."

Peter went out the front door and closed it as Beth took her plate to the kitchen.

"Hey!" she yelled.

"Now what?" asked Mrs. Malloy.

Beth came back into the dining room carrying the chocolate fudge pie. There was a large hole in the middle of it, as though someone, with an insistent thumb, had carved out a bite for himself.

■ ■ ■ ■ ■ ■ ■ ■ ■ ■ ■

Nine

■

Letter to Georgia

Dear Bill (and Danny and Steve and Tony and Doug):

Boy, did you guys ever goof up! You know those pictures we took a year ago? A really stupid picture of each of us, so that if one of us ever betrayed the others, we'd have an embarrassing picture of him to show around school? Well, guess who has them now? Right. Caroline and her sisters.

WHY did you leave them in your basement when you moved? WHY didn't you take them with you?

The Whomper, The Weirdo, and the Crazie have probably been having laughing fits over them. Beth found them on top of a heating duct and the girls won't give them back. Beth says they want to look at them a little longer.

I can't stand it. You know what I'm wearing in my picture? My old bunny pajamas—the ones with feet and floppy ears. They were way too small for me then, and now Peter wears them.

Just remember that you guys have pictures in that album too. Remember how you're dressed up like a ballerina, Steve? With a ribbon in your hair? One false move by us and those pictures will probably make the rounds at school. We tried sending Peter over to sweet-talk the girls into giving them back, but no luck.

The weird thing is, the only people who seem to be getting along right now are Jake and Eddie, probably because they're on the same baseball team. And somehow I have to stay home the day of the championship game because Mom's in charge of the yard sale of the Women's Auxiliary of the Buckman Fire Department, and someone has to guard the stuff that day till she gets back from the game. The sale, of course, happens to be on our driveway, in our front yard, up on our front porch the exact day of the game.

You guys sure did a number on us by moving away, letting the Malloys rent your house, and leaving those pictures in the basement. What do you have to say for yourselves?

Wally (and Jake and Josh and Peter)

P.S. I'd send this by e-mail but stuff for the yard sale is piled in my room blocking my computer. It'll have to go by snail mail, and no telling when you'll get it.

■ ■ ■ ■ ■ ■ ■ ■ ■ ■ ■ ■

Ten

■

Game Two

On the way to school the next morning, the only two people who were talking to each other were Jake and Eddie. They talked about the Clarksburg team—what they had heard about the pitcher and who was most likely to strike out.

Behind them on the sidewalk, Caroline and Wally glared at each other, and Josh glared at Beth, while Peter strolled along at the rear, humming a little song and running his hand along a row of azalea bushes.

Wally didn't think he could ever be friends with the Malloy girls again. If Caroline ever—*ever*—brought that picture of him in his bunny pajamas to school, with *whiskers* at the sides of his face, even, he would be laughed right out of fourth grade.

He didn't know if he was angrier at the girls for not giving the pictures back or at the Bensons for leaving them behind in the first place. How could they have forgotten *those*? You don't just take the most humiliating pictures of each other you can possibly imagine and then go off and leave them on top of a heating duct in your basement! You especially don't go off and leave them when a family of *girls* is going to rent your home for a year, especially girls like the Malloy sisters, who had caused Wally more trouble in the ten months they had been living there than the Bensons had caused Wally his whole life!

And yet . . . had *he* thought to remind the Bensons to take those pictures with them? Had he even remembered where the pictures were hidden? Had his brothers thought to remind them either?

When he was in his seat, leaning forward so that Caroline couldn't tickle him with her ruler, he tried to concentrate on the next week's assignments, which Miss Applebaum was explaining to the class. But when her back was turned and she began writing the new spelling words on the board, Wally heard a soft voice behind him saying, "Hippity-hop, little bunny, hippity-hop," and he felt his ears beginning to turn red. He didn't know which he disliked more at that moment—Caroline Lenore Malloy or his ears.

At recess, Eddie and Jake went over by the fence to practice pitching and catching. Wally stood glumly off to one side with Josh, but their minds were on other things. Finally Josh spoke:

"There's only one thing left to do: get embarrassing pictures of the girls. Then we'll say that if they don't give those pictures back, we'll put their pictures in that glass case by the auditorium, and by the time the principal sees them, everyone in the whole school will have seen them first."

"Yeah? How are we going to get embarrassing pictures of the girls? Hide in their bathroom? We *posed* for those pictures, remember?" said Wally.

"Yeah, that's the problem," said Josh. "I can't think of a way to do it either."

■

It was the day of the second baseball game, and cars full of excited players and their parents and friends were on their way to Clarksburg. It seemed to Wally that in every other car they passed was someone they knew. Horns honked. People waved to each other, and by the time they got to Clarksburg High School, the bleachers were beginning to fill up. Mr. Hatford, who had taken the day off work from the post office, and Mrs. Hatford, who had taken a day off from the hardware store, gave Jake a final pat on the back and a squeeze of the shoulder.

"Good luck, Jake. Just play your best," his mother said.

"Get out there and show 'em what you've got, son," said his father.

It seemed to Wally that Eddie was in better form than she'd been for the first game. She seemed excited but not too nervous. Buckman was to bat first, and Eddie was first in line. She swung the bat, the ball sailed right over the head of the center fielder, and Eddie made it home. Clarksburg was beginning to look nervous, and the Buckman fans, especially the Malloys, clapped and cheered.

But Clarksburg didn't have anything to be ashamed of, because they had just as good a batter on their team. Wally didn't study the clouds this time. He didn't hang over the edge of the bleachers looking for ants or think about whether the ball diamond might have been a battlefield in the Civil War and whether there were ghosts of soldiers around. He kept his eyes on the ball, and once, when Jake threw a really fast pitch, he caught Caroline Malloy looking down the bleachers at him and smiling, and he started to smile back before he remembered they were enemies. He turned his eyes toward the pitcher's mound again. All Caroline saw when she looked at him, he was sure, was Wally in his two-sizes-too-small bunny pajamas with floppy ears and feet.

Both teams played well, but the game wasn't especially exciting, Wally decided. After the one home run that Eddie made, there weren't any others. Not until the seventh inning did either team score again.

By the final inning, Buckman was ahead by a run. Clarksburg, however, was at bat, and tension was rising.

This time Eddie was pitching and Jake was at shortstop. There were players on first and second. A tall boy stepped up to bat, and the Clarksburg crowd began cheering. All he had to do was hit the ball between two of the outfielders, and his team might get not just one run, not just two, but three. Wally swallowed. So did Josh, beside him.

The boy gripped his bat, his eyes on Eddie. Eddie stood still for a moment, seeming to think it over. Glancing quickly at both runners, she faced the batter again, lifted one foot off the ground, and threw. Strike one. Maybe there was hope yet, Wally thought.

The umpire leaned forward. Eddie pitched again. The batter stood motionless.

"Ball one," the umpire said.

This time Eddie took a longer pause, figuring what to do. Then her arm went back, and before anyone expected it, the ball was on its way. The batter swung, the bat connected, and just as he must have planned it, the tall boy hit a line drive between third base and shortstop.

Jake was in control, however. One arm swooped down and he caught the ball with a soft *plop* in his glove.

"Out!" yelled the umpire. But Jake wasn't through yet.

Both base runners were going at top speed. They skidded around to head back. Jake tagged the boy from second on the shoulder.

"Out!" the umpire yelled again.

Jake wheeled around and fired the ball toward first base. The first baseman caught it and put one foot on the bag before the runner could get back.

"Out!" came the umpire's voice again over the cheers from Buckman fans. All three Clarksburg batters were out.

"A triple play!" Josh yelled.

Out on the field, Eddie was jumping up and down. The second baseman had leaped onto Jake's back, and the rest of the team was swarming around him, throwing their gloves in the air and cheering. The Clarksburg team wasn't cheering, of course, but they too had played well and the score was close.

"Jake, that was something else, let me tell you!" said the coach. "With Eddie's home run and your triple play, I don't think we've ever played better."

Jake beamed. All the Hatfords were out on the field now, slapping him on the back and talking excitedly. It felt pretty good to be a brother of one of the best sixth-grade ballplayers in the school district, Wally thought. Baseball wasn't so bad when he could sit up in the bleachers and watch his brother make a triple play. Maybe if there were triple plays more often, he wouldn't feel like watching the clouds, or the ants carrying crumbs, or a spider weaving a web. If baseball had a little more action, maybe there would be a little more to watch.

The car was full of excited chatter as the Hatfords drove home that evening. Peter thought the town should have a parade in Jake's honor, even though the triple play had happened so fast Peter hadn't even seen it and couldn't describe what it was if he tried.

"Well, at least your team will make it to the third game," said Mr. Hatford. "That much is sure."

"And I'll just bet they'll be one of those two teams playing the championship game," said Mrs. Hatford. "I'm certainly glad that Wally is going to watch over the sale tables on the twenty-ninth, because I wouldn't miss that final game for the world. Not if Jake is playing."

The Women's Auxiliary yard sale! Wally had almost forgotten about it. Now that baseball had suddenly gotten so exciting, he wanted more than ever to be at the championship game instead of sitting with a bunch of lampshades.

Still, that wasn't the worst thing that could ever happen to him. If that was all he had to worry about, it was only a little thing. Then he remembered: the pictures. The bunny pajamas. He had been feeling so good before, about being the brother of Jake Hatford, and now . . .

Wally began to think that for the rest of his life, perhaps, the Malloy girls would take those pictures with them wherever they went, and they would always, always be laughing behind his back.

■ ■ ■ ■ ■ ■ ■ ■ ■ ■ ■ ■ ■

Eleven

■

Act Two

"Well," said Eddie as her family went into the house after the game. "I guess I've got my zip back."

"You have indeed!" said her father. "You played like
your old self this afternoon. Between you and Jake, I'd
say the coach has himself a pretty good team this year."

Eddie, Jake; Eddie, Jake; Eddie, Jake; Eddie, Jake . . . ,
thought Caroline in the backseat. As glad as she was for
Eddie, as much as she wanted the Buckman Badgers to
win the championship, she was sick of hearing about it
all the time.

She was tired of Eddie being the center of attention
day after day, week after week. Yet, short of running
across the baseball field in her underwear, she couldn't
think of a single way to focus the attention on herself
for a change. Just long enough to remind everyone that
she was the girl who would someday—*some*day—have
her name in lights on Broadway, and people would say,

"Oh, yes! We knew her when she lived in Buckman, West Virginia."

The only answer was to get right to work finishing act two of her play, so as soon as they got inside, Caroline went up to her room and shut the door. She came down only long enough to have lunch and dinner, and by evening she was ready to knock on Beth's door.

"I finished act two, Beth," she said. "Do you want to hear it?"

Beth was in the middle of her math homework. When Beth did math, she put her notebook and papers on the floor, then stretched across her bed, her head and arms hanging down one side, and wrote on the paper from above. The way to do math, she declared, was to let the blood rush to her head. Only then could she figure it out.

"Okay," Beth said, wriggling her body back up on the bed. "I'm ready for a break." She propped her pillows against the headboard and leaned back, closing her eyes. "Shoot," she said.

Caroline perched on the edge of Beth's bed and held her tablet out in front of her.

Act two, scene one: Still morning in the cottage on the beach. Nancy sits at the table drinking a cup of coffee. The clock on the wall says ten o'clock.

NANCY: I think I must have dreamed it all. Jim has probably gone out for a walk. There isn't any slime here at all. And yet, the telephone still doesn't work. I know he'll be back any minute and then he'll explain the whole thing.

The lights fade out and come on again. The clock on the wall says two o'clock. Nancy is at the table having lunch.

NANCY: Well, if he's gone for a walk, it's a long one. Maybe I should go look for him.

The lights fade out and come on again. The clock on the wall says six o'clock. Nancy is at the table having dinner.

NANCY: Something's happened, I know it! As soon as I eat, I'll go look for him.

Act two, scene two: Daylight is beginning to fade and Nancy is walking along the beach. Suddenly she stops and a look of horror crosses her face.

"Like this, Beth," Caroline said, raising her eyebrows as high as they would go, opening her eyes wide, and shaping her mouth in the form of an O.

NANCY: Here are the same tracks that Jim and I saw in the sand yesterday. They are hardly human, and yet they don't belong to any animal I know. It's as though a creature from outer space was dragging something. Oh, no! Could it have been dragging Jim?

She faints.

Caroline put her tablet down. "Well, how do you like it?" she asked.

"That's it? That's the end of act two?" asked Beth.

Caroline nodded.

"Well, I don't see how a woman whose husband is missing can eat breakfast, lunch, and dinner," said Beth.

"She has to keep up her strength," said Caroline.

"Whatever," said Beth.

"You don't like it!" said Caroline.

"I didn't say I didn't like it. I just can't quite believe it."

"Everything will be made clear in the end," said Caroline. "Everything will come together in act three."

"Good," said Beth. "I can wait."

■

On Sunday afternoon, Caroline tucked the play under her arm and went over to the Hatfords'. She knocked on the door, and when Peter answered, she said, "I'd like to see Wally, please."

"Did you bring the pictures?" asked Peter.

"No," said Caroline. "This is business."

"Okay," said Peter. He opened the door wider and Caroline stepped inside.

Wally came downstairs in his stocking feet. He still had on his Sunday clothes, but his shirttail was hanging out in back.

"What do you want?" asked Wally.

"Come out on the porch, Wally. We're going to talk business," she said. And then, to Peter: "Go back inside, Peter. This is personal."

"Okay," said Peter, and shut the door after them.

"What is it?" asked Wally.

Caroline sat down on the steps. "I have a proposition to make. How much do you want those pictures back?"

"You're going to give them to us?" asked Wally, looking wary.

"I didn't say *give*," said Caroline. "I asked how badly you wanted them back."

"What do you think?" said Wally. "Badly. A lot."

"Okay, here's the deal," said Caroline. "I want something a lot too. You've heard the first act of my play. I want to read the rest to you, and you tell me how you like it. Then . . . *then* . . . you perform it with me in front of the class. If you do that, I'll give you the pictures back."

"No way! I can't!" said Wally. "I'm not an actor."

"Well, just read your part, that's all. You don't have to do anything."

"But I don't even like it!"

"You don't understand it yet, Wally. Once you hear act three, you'll understand it, and if you understand it, you'll probably like it. And even if you don't, well . . . you don't want that picture of you in your bunny pajamas to go around school, do you?"

"No!" said Wally.

"Okay, then. I just want you to sit right here and listen to act two, and then tell me what you think," said Caroline.

"If I listen to the play and read it with you in class—just *read* it—you'll give me the picture of me in my bunny pajamas?" Wally asked.

"Yes," said Caroline.

"And you'll give me the rest of the pictures too?"

"Yes," said Caroline. "But we can't tell *any*body. If Beth and Eddie find out I gave those pictures back, they'll kill me."

"Why? What do they want to do with them?" asked Wally.

Caroline looked deep into Wally's eyes. "Blackmail," she said.

"You mean they'd use them to make us do anything they want?"

"That's right."

"That's exactly what you're doing to me!" said Wally. "You're making me read a play in front of the class."

"Correct," said Caroline.

"That's blackmail!" said Wally.

"Bingo," said Caroline.

■

A half hour later, Caroline took her play home.

"Where have *you* been?" asked Beth.

"I just read act two to Wally Hatford and he listened," said Caroline.

"So?" said Beth. "What else could he do? Did he *like* it?"

"I don't know," said Caroline. "But guess what? He's

going to read Jim's part in front of our class so that I can get an A-plus. If he didn't like it, do you think he'd do *that*?"

"How did you get him to say yes?" asked Eddie from across the room. "Wally Hatford wouldn't do that unless he was hanging upside down over the Grand Canyon by his heels."

"Well, something like that," said Caroline, and went on up to her room to write act three.

■ ■ ■ ■ ■ ■ ■ ■ ■ ■ ■ ■

Twelve

■

Letter from Georgia

Wally (and Jake and Josh and Peter!):

You've got to be kidding! Did the girls really find those pictures? We are doomed, man! We are dead meat! We are roadkill!

I don't know how we could have forgotten to take them with us. Steve thought Tony had them and Tony thought Steve had them, and the rest of us didn't even know where they were.

You've got to get those pictures back, Wally! I don't care what you have to do to get them, just DO it! If anybody sees that picture of me blowing soap bubbles, with a rip in the seat of my pants, I'll never be able to show my face around Buckman again.

Just GET them, Wally! I'm begging you! Write and tell me you did!

Bill (and Danny and Steve and Tony and Doug)

■ ■ ■ ■ ■ ■ ■ ■ ■ ■ ■ ■ ■

Thirteen

■

More Visitors

When Wally's brothers went to baseball practice on the Monday before the third game, Wally walked home alone. He didn't feel like watching Jake practice. He was afraid that if he was around Jake and Josh for very long, he might let it slip—what he was going to do to get their pictures back. And the reason he didn't want it to slip was because he didn't entirely trust Caroline Malloy to keep her promise.

Not that she would deliberately lie to him, but she might not actually have the pictures. Eddie or Beth might have put them away for safekeeping, and no matter what Caroline told Wally about giving them back, she might not be able to do it. And he would have made a fool of himself in front of the class for nothing. No, if he was to suffer, he would suffer alone.

The second reason he didn't want his brothers to know was . . . well, maybe Wally would have to do a little blackmail of his own. The twins were always getting Wally to do things he didn't want to do. And if he had the pictures, he could say no and mean it. He could say that if they made him do whatever it was he didn't want to do, he would take their pictures to school. He could only do this once, of course, because they would pulverize him if he tried it twice and didn't give the pictures back, but maybe he should hang on to them for an emergency.

He opened the door with his key and went to the kitchen. Now that he was ten years old, he had his own key. His mother didn't call to see if the boys were all right because she thought they were all at the school watching Jake practice. So Wally prepared to enjoy having the house to himself.

First he got down the crackers and peanut butter. He got out the cheese. He found the corn chips and the pickles and the pitcher of cold tea, the applesauce and leftover macaroni. Then he sat down at the table.

It wasn't very often that Wally had the house to himself, and it was nice. It was great, in fact, without Peter's constant chatter and Jake's complaining and Josh's bragging about this or that.

Wally propped his feet up on the chair at the end of the table, smeared a cracker with peanut butter, placed a little square of cheese on top of the peanut butter and a piece of pickle on top of the cheese. He was just about to pop it all into his mouth when the doorbell rang.

Wally put down the cracker and walked to the front

door. When he opened it, he saw two women with purses tucked under their arms. One had on a pink jacket and the other wore her hair in a braid over one shoulder.

"Hello," said the woman in the pink jacket. "Are you one of the Hatford boys?"

"Yes," said Wally.

"We understand that this is where the things for the Women's Auxiliary yard sale are being stored," the woman said.

"Not till the last Saturday of the month," Wally said. "Sorry."

"Oh, but we've heard that some things were donated early," said the woman with the braid. She was wearing sandals and had bright red polish on her toenails.

"Well, some things, but most of the stuff is coming the Friday before the sale," Wally explained.

"We'd just like to come in and look at what you have so far," said the woman with the red toenails.

"Oh, I can't let you do that," said Wally.

"But we'll pay for anything we find now and take it off your hands," said the woman in the pink jacket.

"Well . . ." Wally hesitated. He wondered if she'd buy everything that was piled in his room. He didn't know these women, but then he didn't know a lot of women in Buckman. "I'll have to go call Mom," he said.

"Certainly," said the red toenails.

Wally shut the door, but not quite all the way because he didn't want to seem rude, and went to the phone in the kitchen.

The owner of the hardware store answered. "Your mom's with a customer, Wally," he said. "She'll be with you in just a minute."

Mrs. Hatford must have been selling a customer nails, because Wally could hear the sound of nails being poured into one of the metal scoops on the scales. The hardware store had a metal scoop where you put the object being weighed. Then Mrs. Hatford would take little round weights and put them on the other side of the scales, one by one, until both sides of the scale dangled evenly in the air. There was no digital anything in the hardware store, and that, said the owner, was just the way he liked it.

Finally Mrs. Hatford got on the line. "Wally?" she said.

"Mom, I came home from practice early because I was tired of watching Jake, and there are two women out on the porch who want to look at what we've collected for the yard sale so far."

"Who are they?" his mother asked.

"I don't know."

"Well, it doesn't much matter, because we can't let anyone buy anything until the sale opens on the twenty-ninth. That's the rule. We have to be fair. Otherwise people would be sneaking over all the time and buying the best things before anyone else got a chance. Tell them I'm sorry, but they'll have to wait till the last

Saturday in May. Goodness, I had no idea the sale would be so popular!"

Wally went back to the door and put his hand on the knob. "I'm sorry," he said as he opened it. Then he stopped. The porch was empty. At that moment he heard the floor creak in the hallway and when he turned around, he saw the two women poking around in the walk-in closet.

"Oh, forgive us, but we're just so eager to see what you have for sale," said the woman in the pink jacket.

"Mom says I can't let you buy anything before the twenty-ninth," said Wally. "Sorry."

The women looked disappointed. "Well, we won't even try to buy anything, then, but if you could just let us look the things over? Have a peek? Just show us where they are?"

Something told Wally that he didn't much like these women. He knew his mother's rule about strangers in the house. "No," he said, and opened the front door wide. "I guess you'll have to go now."

"Of course," said the woman with the red toenails. "We're just too eager. We do love a good yard sale. Thank you anyway, young man."

"You're welcome," said Wally, and shut the door.

He went to the kitchen again and ate his crackers. Then he called his mother and told her what had happened.

"You mean they walked right into our house while you were on the phone with me?" she gasped. "Why,

Wally, they could have been kidnappers! They could have whisked you away before you knew it!" There was a pause. "Did they take anything?"

Wally began to worry. "I don't know. I don't think so."

"Go look in the dining room and see if the green vase is still on the buffet," said Mrs. Hatford.

Wally went into the dining room and looked. "The vase is still there," he told his mother.

"Did they go upstairs?"

"No."

"Well, look in the living room and see if that little marble dish on the coffee table is still there."

Wally went into the living room.

"It's there," he told his mom.

"What about the little picture hanging beside the coatrack in the hall? Is that still there?"

"Just a minute," said Wally. He checked the wall by the coatrack. "Yes," he told his mother. "That's still there."

"Well, I imagine they were just curious, as they said. We get some frenzied shoppers at these sales, let me tell you! But in the future, don't let anyone in unless it's a member of the auxiliary, Wally, and you know who those women are."

"Okay," said Wally.

■

At school the next day, Miss Applebaum said, "Class, you have just one more week to turn in your book reports. I know that some of you may have been waiting for a certain book at the library that hasn't come in yet, and that baseball season is here and a lot of you have been watching the team practice. But there are eleven of you who have not turned in your reports, and you have only seven more days to finish the project." She turned to Caroline. "Caroline, are you still determined to write a ten-page play, or will you do a book report?"

"I'm working on the play, Miss Applebaum," Caroline said. "But I'll have it done in a week and I'll read it to the class."

"I'm sure we're all looking forward to that," the teacher said, and perhaps she didn't hear the low moans that went around the room. A precocious girl who *knows* she is precocious is not always the most popular girl in school. Especially if that girl is a year younger than everyone else, and especially if she is Caroline Lenore Malloy. From *Ohio,* as Caroline would say, meaning that much closer to New York City and Broadway.

After baseball practice that afternoon, the girls went on ahead and Wally walked behind with his brothers.

"Life would be great right now if only we had those pictures," Jake said. "That's the only thing in the world keeping me from being really happy now that I've made the Buckman Badgers."

"We *have* to get them back," said Josh.

"Maybe we should just go to the sheriff and tell him the Malloys have something that belongs to us," said

Wally. "Maybe Dad, as sheriff's deputy, could go over to the Malloys' in uniform and demand them back."

Josh and Jake stared at him.

"Are you nuts?" asked Jake. "Do you think for one minute he'd do that?"

"If it was important enough, he would," said Wally, beginning to waver.

"And what would you tell him was so important?" asked Jake. "A picture of you in your bunny pajamas? A picture of me with spaghetti hanging out of my nose? Get real."

The day didn't seem quite as sunny, somehow, as it had before.

Perhaps because they were out of sorts, everything seemed to irritate them. Peter had a spring cold, for one thing. His nose was dripping and he snuffled constantly.

When they got home and were getting out the cheese and crackers, Josh said, "Peter, you're disgusting! Wipe your nose, will you?"

Peter started to run his sleeve along under his nose, but Wally yelped, "Not snot on your sleeve! Get a Kleenex or something!"

Peter looked around the kitchen for a box of tissues and, not finding any, dug around in the pocket of his jeans and pulled out a rag. As he wiped his nose with that, he smeared chocolate across his face.

"Yuck!" Jake yelled. "What's that?"

Peter looked at the rag in his hand. "Chocolate," he said.

"Where did you get it?"

"When I was having dinner at the Malloys'," Peter said. And because his brothers were still staring, he added, "I went out in the kitchen and took some of their fudge pie, but then I saw Caroline coming, so I grabbed the dishcloth and wiped my mouth and stuffed it in my pocket so she wouldn't see."

Jake's face was wrinkled in disgust as he studied the rag in Peter's hand. "Now it's got chocolate *and* snot all over it!" he said. "What a weird dishcloth. It looks like it's got elastic, too!"

Josh leaned over. "It's got *words* all over it!" He looked even closer. "The words say *Let's play ball*!"

Wally took the rag from Peter's hands and shook it out. Then he held it up by two fingers. The four boys gasped in unison, for Wally was holding a pair of girls' underpants—old underpants with worn elastic and holes all over.

"*Let's play ball!?*" croaked Jake. "They could only be Eddie's!"

"You mean you've had Eddie's underpants in your pocket all this time?" Wally asked Peter.

Peter shrugged, not knowing if his brothers were angry or not. In a small voice, he said, "I thought it was a dishcloth. It was just lying up there on the counter."

Suddenly the kitchen erupted in wild shouts.

"We're *saved*!" yelled Jake.

"We'll get our pictures back!" cried Wally.

"We'll wash these up and parade them all around school unless the girls make a trade," said Jake.

"Man oh man oh man, have we got them over a barrel!" said Josh.

"Life is sweeeeeet!" said Jake, waving the underpants over his head like a lasso.

"Let's call over right now and tell them what we've got," said Wally. "I'll bet they bring back those pictures in a hurry."

"Wait a minute," Jake told him. "Not till after the championship game. I don't want to get Eddie mad before a game."

"And maybe we won't even tell them then," said Josh. "Let's just keep these *Let's play ball!* underpants secret until a really good time to tell them comes along. It's our ace in the hole. It's our lucky break. Have you got that, Peter? Not a word!"

■　■　■　■　■　■　■　■　■　■　■

Fourteen

■

Game Three

The next-to-the-last game was to be played in Weston, and almost everyone was going.

"Of course I want to see Eddie and the Badgers win," Coach Malloy said that morning, tucking a sweater over his arm, "but I've had to get a substitute to work with my next year's players these last three Saturdays. If the Badgers win, though, it will be worth it."

"And if we don't win?" asked Eddie. "Are we zero? Zip? Zed?"

"If you don't win but you played your best, you're still my spunky gal Eddie, and I'll love you just as much," said her dad.

Caroline had long suspected that Eddie was her father's favorite because she shared his love of sports. At the same time, she knew that if she or Beth ever really needed him, he'd be there for them. It was simply a question of where he'd rather be—at a baseball game watching Eddie pitch, in the living room watching Beth read a book, or at a theater watching Caroline perform. *Duh,* thought Caroline. No question at all.

"Well, I'm ready," said Eddie. "Jake and I play well together. It's good we're on the same team."

"Now, *that's* a switch," said her mother.

It wasn't a long ride to Weston, and Caroline didn't have much time to work on her play on the drive there. She had brought her tablet in case the game proved to be slow and boring, but she doubted, from the last two games, that that would be true.

At the high school ball field, the Malloys saw the Hatfords sitting up in the bleachers and went over to sit beside them. Caroline, however, sat as far away from Wally as she could get, because she didn't want Beth to even begin to suspect that she and Wally had made a bargain—that the gold mine of pictures of the Hatford boys was about to be turned over to the Hatfords themselves in exchange for Wally's taking part in her play.

"We've certainly lucked out on the weather for the games, haven't we?" Mrs. Malloy said to Mrs. Hatford as she sat down beside her. "Not a cloud in the sky! After all the rain in April, I'd say we deserve a little sunshine, wouldn't you?"

"We certainly do," said Mrs. Hatford. "The last thing I want on a Saturday in May is to have these four boys moping about the house because it's raining. Baseball gets us all out. Of course, Tom and I have had to take three days from our jobs to get to the games, but we enjoy it."

Out on the field, the players were warming up. The nine members of the Buckman Badgers were throwing the ball to each other in quick succession and then, at the coach's whistle, reversed the order of throw. They did limbering exercises and leg stretches. Finally, when all members of both teams were accounted for, the Buckman Badgers took their positions on the field, Eddie pitching this time, Jake on first base. The game began.

Eddie adjusted her cap with the big *B* on it. She *was* ready. She pitched just the way she pitched back home in practice games, and the first two Weston Wolverines struck out. But the third batter hit the ball to right field. The ball rolled out so far, in fact, that when the runner was halfway between third base and home plate, he stuck his thumbs in the top of his pants and slowed his run to a walk. He simply swaggered back to home plate.

"Well, *he's* feeling good!" murmured Tom Hatford, laughing.

The next batter struck out, so the Badgers came in to bat.

Three Badgers went to the plate before Jake. The first two struck out, the next doubled, and then Jake was up. He swung at the first pitch and missed. On his second swing he hit the ball to center field and started for first base, while the runner on second went to third and started for home. But as his family watched, Jake turned his ankle rounding first base. The center fielder came charging in to throw the ball to home plate. The runner on third was tagged out. Jake, who had sunk to the ground, had managed to stretch out one leg so that he was touching first base. He sat there rubbing his ankle, obviously in pain.

"Oh, no!" said Mrs. Hatford. "Not at the very start of the game!"

Jake got up, though, wincing, and rested his weight on his other foot.

"I think the coach should take him out," Mrs. Hatford said to her husband.

"Jake would have to be tortured before he'd admit anything was wrong," said Josh.

The coach walked over to Jake and stood talking to him for a moment. Jake smiled and flexed his ankle to prove he was fine.

Beth clapped. "He's okay!" she shouted.

Caroline began to wonder about sports. The slightest mistake, it seemed, could cost the game. A ball that was sent flying just two inches above a fielder's glove. A bat that moved only a fourth of an inch too far to the left.

In the theater an actress had several opportunities to correct a mistake. If she forgot her lines momentarily, she could simply pretend to be thinking. If a telephone rang off cue, she could pick it up and pretend to hold an imaginary conversation. If she tripped on her dress and fell, she could pretend it was part of the action and weave it into the plot. Who would know?

The game continued much as it had before, and when the Badgers batted again, Eddie hit the ball so far out that it was hard for a moment to see where it had gone. Around the diamond she went, touching each base, while the people in the bleachers yelled and screamed. The shamefaced Wolverines' fielder found the ball at last and threw it in.

The score seesawed between the Badgers and the Wolverines. The Badgers' right and center fielders collided during the third inning going after a fly ball, and in the fourth the Wolverines argued that Eddie had failed to touch second base while running from first to third. The umpire ruled in Eddie's favor. By the time the game reached the last inning, the score was tied 5 to 5.

The Badgers' first batter struck out. The next batter was out on an infield fly. Jake, batting next, tripled to right field, but Caroline could tell he was in pain. He was limping in spite of himself.

"Tom, that boy should be home with an ice pack on his ankle!" Mrs. Hatford said. "Do you think I should go down and speak to the coach?"

"I think you should sit right where you are and let Jake and the coach work it out," said her husband.

Eddie was up to bat, her last chance to win the game

for the Badgers. When the Wolverines saw Eddie take her place in the batter's box, they all moved back. The shortstop moved back. The center fielder, the right fielder, and the left fielder all moved back. The families and friends in the bleachers all leaned forward, knowing how hard Eddie could hit.

The ball came at her. Eddie tensed, but then held back.

"Ball one," said the umpire.

The next ball came flying toward Eddie, and she let it go by.

"Strike one," said the umpire.

"What's she waiting for?" Caroline heard someone mutter. "She's going to lose her chance if she doesn't take it."

Eddie gave a glance at Jake on third, touched the bill of her cap, and set her eyes again on the pitcher. The three boys in the outfield moved back farther still. The third and first basemen also took two steps back.

The pitcher, without winding up, quickly lifted one foot and threw.

The second the ball left the pitcher's hand, Jake was on his way toward home. As the ball came to the plate, Eddie turned and squared her body to the pitcher's mound. She slid her right hand up the bat and let the barrel just meet the pitch. It connected with only a little pop, not a pow, and rolled a few feet along the ground, down the first-base line.

Pandemonium broke out as the pitcher and the first

baseman scrambled to pick up the ball and tag Eddie, but she raced past them to first base. There was not enough time to make a play at the plate, and Jake, despite his aching ankle, made it home with the winning run. The Buckman Badgers were on their way to the championship game the following Saturday.

Three of the Badgers piled on Jake and almost knocked him down. Everyone crowded around him and Eddie.

"Smart play, Eddie!" said their coach. "Just as we planned. That was the perfect time for a bunt."

"I caught her signal," said Jake. "Everybody thought she'd whack it, but she took them all by surprise!"

"That's what baseball's about—surprises," the coach said. "Good game, guys! Congratulations, everybody!"

■

On the way home, Caroline listened to her sister chattering happily about the game. She was glad that finally Eddie's wish had come true, the dream Eddie'd had since they had moved to Buckman. If Beth had a dream, as far as Caroline could tell, it was simply to have enough good books to read for the rest of her natural life.

It was Caroline's dream that seemed farthest away. It would be years yet before she saw her name in lights on Broadway. It not only took talent to get to be a famous actress, she decided, it took patience. She could only get there one small step at a time, beginning with the play she had written for her class. And in a few more days, she and Wally would read it for Miss Applebaum and the fourth graders. They might even perform it on-stage for the whole school. And if they made it to the big stage in the auditorium, who was to deny that someday Caroline might even make it to a big stage on Broadway?

Fifteen

■

Act Three

When the Hatfords got home from the game and went up onto the front porch, Mrs. Hatford said, "Who left the window open?"

Wally looked where she was pointing. The window to the right of the front door was raised about six inches.

"I suppose any one of us could have opened it, Ellen," said her husband. "It's been a warm May."

"But we haven't opened any of the downstairs windows yet, only the ones in the bedrooms," she declared. "And if I did open it, I certainly would have closed it before we left."

"Well, it wasn't me," said Mr. Hatford.

Mrs. Hatford looked at each boy in turn.

"Not me," said Jake.

"Not me," said Josh.

Wally insisted he had not tried to open it, and Peter didn't even know how.

"Well, it looks to me as though someone might have tried to get in, then," said Mr. Hatford. "Lucky for us that old window only opens a few inches before it sticks."

"You think one of the girls knows we have Eddie's underpants?" Josh whispered jokingly to Wally. "Maybe one of them was over here looking for them."

Wally grinned and shook his head. "All three girls were at the game, remember?"

"Oh, right," said Josh.

"Who would want to rob *us*?" Mrs. Hatford said as they unlocked the door and went inside. "What do we have except a few items of sentimental value?"

"Maybe just kids fooling around," said Mr. Hatford, and after a quick check of the house, to determine that nothing had been taken, nothing was amiss, and no one had been inside, the Hatfords settled down to enjoy the rest of their Saturday with the memory of Jake's winning run.

Wally had already done his homework for the weekend and was looking forward to being able to do whatever he wanted with the rest of his Saturday and Sunday—namely, nothing. He just wanted to be free to do whatever came into his head. For one thing, he liked to go down to the end of the swinging bridge every spring, especially after a gentle rain, and lift up the large rock that rested just off the path.

He liked to see if the same kinds of bugs stayed there year after year. He always counted the different ones he found. It was a little like a bug hotel. Maybe bugs, too, liked to get away for the weekend.

He was squatting down next to the bare patch he'd uncovered and was trying to poke up the bugs that were scurrying around in all directions when he heard the hollow sound of footsteps on the swinging bridge. Looking up, he saw Caroline coming toward him with her tablet under her arm.

"Goodbye weekend," Wally murmured to himself. No one on earth could ruin a good weekend faster than Caroline Malloy. He didn't have to be in her old play, though. Sure, she was trying to blackmail him with those pictures. Well, he could blackmail her with Eddie's underpants. Should he do it?

"Finished!" she called. "My play is done, and all I have to do is type it up. Want to hear it, Wally?" And without waiting for an answer, she said, "Of course you do. Let's go up on your porch."

Wait, Jake had said. *Let's save the underpants for a time we really need to bargain.*

Well, if this wasn't the time, Wally didn't know what was. He prodded a bit more with his stick. "Can't you read it right here?"

"All right, Wally," she said, "provided you pay attention. Act three, scene one: Evening in the cottage by the beach. Nancy is fixing dinner."

"Doesn't she ever do anything but eat and faint?" asked Wally.

"She's just doing her ordinary everyday routine to calm her nerves," Caroline explained, and continued: "Nancy puts two plates and glasses on the table, then suddenly covers her face with her hands and cries when she realizes Jim is no more."

"How does she know he's no more?" asked Wally. "He disappears the day before and suddenly he's no more, and she goes on eating dinner?"

"Wally, if you keep interrupting you'll never find out," Caroline said indignantly. "Sometimes you have to wait till things reveal themselves. Please save your criticisms until I've finished."

"Okay, but at the end of the second act, she'd fainted, you know. And now she's making dinner. . . ."

"Well, sometimes you have to just guess what went on in between, Wally. A playwright doesn't have to show every little thing. Obviously she woke up or somebody came along and revived her. The audience has to figure some things out for itself."

"Okay," said Wally.

Nancy sits down on a chair and turns to look out the open window facing the sea. There is a faint sound of sloshing and sliding offstage. As Nancy stares mournfully out at the waves, her back to the doorway, the sloshing sound grows louder and louder. Nancy covers her face with her hands and sobs. The sloshing and sliding grows louder still.

A shadow appears in the doorway behind her and spreads across the floor, and the audience sees a kind of shapeless form coming in sideways, like a mass of primordial green slime, a sort of giant amoeba, and it slithers and slides closer, closer, closer, until Nancy hugs herself, as though she feels a sudden chill. She turns around and screams as the moonlight coming in the window shines on the giant amoeba, and the audience sees that it has the face of Jim. Curtain falls.

Wally put down his stick and sat back on his heels. "Is that the *end*?"

"No. Just scene one."

Scene two: Nancy has fainted again. The giant amoeba picks her up in his arms and puts her on the couch. Nancy wakes up and screams again.

NANCY: Jim! What's happened to you?

JIM: Nothing's happened, my darling. I've been an amoeba all along but you didn't know. I was sent from my kingdom down under the sea in disguise to choose a bride. Now you belong to me.

NANCY: No! No! A thousand times no! Never to breathe in sweet air again? Never to see the sun rise? Jim, how could you do this to me? I thought you loved me.

JIM: I have a greater love for the netherworld. Come with me and you shall be queen of the waves and caves of the deep. You shall rule over all the sea creatures of night and dark and ocean depths.

NANCY: No, no, no! I shall die if I leave my earthly home.

JIM: You shall die if you don't.

NANCY: Help! Help! Will no one come and save me?

The door opens and a fisherman comes in, an ice bucket in one hand, a fishing rod in the other.

FISHERMAN: What's the matter? Say, what's this? A giant amoeba?

NANCY: Help! He wants to take me down under the water and make me Queen of the Deep.

The fisherman lifts his ice bucket and hits the amoeba over the head, but he is only sucked into the amoeba and finds himself covered with green slime.

FISHERMAN: No! He's got me!

NANCY: There is no hope.

JIM: There is only night and dark and waves and caves, and you, my darling, Queen of the Deep.

The blob oozes back out of the room, dragging Nancy and the fisherman with him, and all that is left onstage is the fisherman's ice bucket and rod, Nancy's shoes, and Jim's tie.

The End

Wally didn't say a word. He was still thinking about the story.

"Well?" said Caroline, clutching her tablet, her eyes dancing with excitement and anticipation.

"If Jim was an amoeba all along, why did he yell when he left the bedroom that first time? And who was making the sloshing sound when he was with Nancy?"

Caroline didn't seem too sure. "Well, he'd sort of brought the netherworld with him. And the yell was just to trick his wife," said Caroline.

"It's a horrible, sickening play with a bad ending," said Wally.

"But you have to admit there's suspense! People like suspense!" said Caroline.

"Are you sure I get extra credit for being in this play?" asked Wally.

"Yes," said Caroline. "I checked."

"And if I read this play with you, I get to be the amoeba?" Wally asked.

"Yes," said Caroline.

"Then I like it," said Wally. Suddenly things began to look very bright indeed. Maybe Wally did want to be in the play after all. Where else could he cover himself with green slime and drag Caroline Malloy around?

"Really? That's wonderful! I knew you would!" said Caroline. "Who can we get to play the fisherman?"

"What about Peter?" Wally suggested, knowing the twins would never do it.

"Perfect. He'll do it, he's such a sweetie!" said Caroline. "All we need are a few props—a tie, some shoes, an ice bucket, a fishing rod, some golf clubs, dishes . . ."

"What do we do for the green slime?"

"We've got some left from Halloween," said Caroline. "I'll tell Miss Applebaum that we'll perform my play on Friday, okay?"

"Okay," said Wally. Oh, yeah! He was going to like playing an amoeba just fine.

He went into the house, where Peter was working a puzzle on the floor in the living room.

"Hey, Peter," Wally said. "You want to be in a play?"

"What play?"

"A play Caroline's written. We have to put it on in front of our class."

"What do I have to do?"

"Hit me over the head with an ice bucket and let me cover you with green slime."

"Cool!" said Peter.

Sixteen

■

Getting Ready

Thursday after dinner, Caroline went to the Hatfords' carrying some props for the play. She handed one of her father's old ties to Wally.

"You'll want to wear this, because it's the only thing left of Jim after he turns into the giant amoeba," she said.

She handed a fishing rod and a Styrofoam ice bucket to Peter. "When you swing at Wally, you only *pretend* to hit him," she said.

She held out an old pair of her mother's high-heeled shoes. "And these will be all that's left of me after the amoeba carries me off," she said.

They went through a brief rehearsal in the Hatfords' living room, and would have run through it again—all but the green slime, which they were saving for the real performance—if Mrs. Hatford hadn't called down from upstairs.

"Wally? The twins went shopping with your father, and I could use some help up here."

Wally went upstairs, Caroline behind him.

Mrs. Hatford was seated on a folding chair in the middle of Wally's bedroom, surrounded by bags and boxes and baskets.

"Everything that people bring tomorrow night for Saturday's sale will go downstairs," she explained. "The auxiliary women are coming over then to check it all in and put price tags on it. But meanwhile, there's all this stuff people donated in advance. I have to list everything we've stored in your room. Maybe Caroline could help too while she's up here."

"Sure," said Caroline. "What should I do?"

"As each of you picks up an item and tells me who it's from, I'll write it down on this clipboard. The women will price them tomorrow. After we've listed something, set it over there by the door."

Caroline sat down on the floor beside a bushel basket, and Wally chose a box crammed between his computer and a couple of paper bags.

"This basket is from Susan Kemp," said Caroline. "One sugar bowl . . . one cream pitcher . . . two candy dishes . . ."

"Wait a minute, don't go too fast," said Mrs. Hatford, writing on her clipboard. "Susan's grandfather started the Kemp Real Estate business, you know. She's been such a help to the auxiliary. . . ."

"One silver serving spoon," Caroline continued. "Four sets of salt and pepper shakers . . ."

When the basket of dishes had been cataloged, Mrs. Hatford turned to Wally. He dug down in the box beside him and took out an old photograph with a thick backing and frame. "A picture of somebody's grandparents, I guess," he said.

"Who donated it, Wally?"

Wally checked the box. "Jenny Bloomer."

Mrs. Hatford wrote it down. "Oh, yes. Jenny. She's descended, you know, from Amelia Bloomer, the famous suffragette of the eighteen hundreds."

"What's a suffragette?" asked Caroline. "Like a martyr? Somebody who suffers?"

"No, it's someone who stood up for a woman's right to vote and hold office and do the things women weren't allowed to do back then."

"Oh," said Wally. "One pen and pencil set . . . one leather dictionary . . ."

On it went. Everything in the bags and boxes and baskets in Wally's room had to be taken out and listed, until finally Wally's room looked positively naked and it was the hall beyond his door that was crowded.

"Can you imagine what our house is going to look like tomorrow night when all the women bring their things over?" asked Mrs. Hatford. "We'll hardly be able to walk through the rooms!" She looked at Wally. "Don't worry," she said. "As soon as the game is over Saturday, the women will all come back here to take over, and you can leave. We'll have everything in place before we go, and all you and Mrs. Larson will have to do is guard the tables and not let anyone buy anything before we get back."

"What if it rains?" asked Wally.

"It's not supposed to rain. If it does, we have large sheets of plastic you can use to cover the tables."

"What if there's a big crowd and I can't watch everybody at once?"

"There won't be. Most of Buckman will be at the game. The championship game's being played here, you know, right at your school."

"I'll be here to help too, Wally," said Caroline. "I'd be too nervous to watch Eddie play the last game. Just hearing them cheer will be enough excitement for me."

"Really? You'll be here? Hey, Mom. What about if we leave Caroline in charge and I go to the game?" Wally asked.

"We'll do no such thing," said his mother. "I need someone besides Mrs. Larson to keep an eye on the tables. People can look, but they can't buy, and three sets of eyes watching over the place are better than two."

"It'll be sort of fun, Wally," said Caroline. "We'll be like security guards at the mall."

When they had checked the last of the bags out of Wally's room, they found more boxes in his closet. There were even some under his bed.

"One toy tea set . . . ," began Caroline. "One child's dress, size four . . . one blue umbrella . . ."

"Who's the donor?" asked Mrs. Hatford.

"Catherine Collier," said Caroline.

"Catherine's great-great-grandfather opened the second bank here in Buckman," said Mrs. Hatford. "She herself helped found the Women's Auxiliary. We couldn't do half the things we do if it weren't for Catherine Collier." It seemed to Caroline as though every woman in Buckman had a history behind her.

Wally's room began to look so empty that Caroline began to wonder if they were carting half his own belongings downstairs with the rest. But Wally sure looked happy about having his room to himself again.

"Mom," he said. "Promise me you won't ever take on the job of running the Treats and Treasures yard sale again. Not at our house."

"If I ever do," said his mother, "it will not be for a long, long time, and you'll be off at college by then, I imagine."

■

"Okay," Caroline said at the front door. "I'll bring all the props to school tomorrow: golf clubs, ice bucket, fishing rod, green slime, tie, shoes, dishes, and special effects."

"I think a book report would be easier," said Wally.

"Of course it would be easier, Wally, but would it be better? No! Did you know that great actresses have plays written especially for them? When you're really famous, movies are made for you alone. People beg you to be in their plays or their movies. If I could write my own plays *and* star in them, I'd be a huge success."

"Don't forget the pictures," said Wally. "You know what you promised."

"Oh. Right!" said Caroline. "The pictures." Did she only imagine it, she wondered, or was Wally trying not to smile?

She started down the walk to the road and the swinging bridge beyond, and then she turned around suddenly to look at Wally again, up on the porch. He *was* smiling, but not at her. He was smiling to himself. He did not look like a boy who had to do something he hated. He looked like a boy who had a secret, and Caroline had a strange feeling that the secret had to do with her and her sisters.

■ ■ ■ ■ ■ ■ ■ ■ ■ ■ ■ ■

Seventeen

■

"A Night to Forget"

When it came time for Caroline to read her play to the class, she got permission to borrow Peter from his second-grade classroom and led him back to Miss Applebaum's room. Peter smiled shyly at the fourth graders, obviously feeling very important to be there.

Wally did not feel as embarrassed as he had thought he would. In fact, knowing how the play would end, he couldn't wait to get started. For too long the Malloy sisters had seemed to get the upper hand in their arguments with the Hatford brothers, but this time, unknown to the girls, it was the boys who were in control.

So when Caroline stood up and announced that she was going to read an original play, "A Night to Forget," Wally stood behind a file cabinet off to one side with Peter and did not come out until Caroline read, "Act one, scene one: A cottage on the beach in a faraway town. Ten o'clock at night. A couple on their honeymoon."

The kids burst into laughter.

"Ha, Wally!" one boy yelled.

"Your *honey*moon!" crooned another.

Wally ignored them.

"Class, let's be quiet now and listen," said Miss Applebaum, and the dialogue began. But as soon as Wally said, "Wasn't that a nice walk on the beach . . . honey?" the class giggled again.

Peter, however, had been assigned to make the sound effects, and as soon as the class heard the sloshing and sliding, which was the noise a balloon half filled with water made as Peter dragged it around the floor behind the file cabinet, the class gave the play its full attention.

"Act one, scene two," read Caroline. "Twelve o'clock at night, Jim and Nancy's bedroom." Then she and Wally had their conversation, and when Wally went offstage with a golf club to investigate the noise (Peter again, with his balloon), and a horrible scream came from behind the file cabinet, some of the girls even jumped.

By the time Wally reappeared as the amoeba, his clothes, his arms, his ears, his hair—everything but his face—were covered in green slime, and the class gave a loud *ohhhhh*. When it was her turn to scream, Caroline did it dramatically and fell to the floor in a faint so convincing that the principal, who was going by, stopped and looked in the door.

Peter tried to miss Wally and just make it look as though he had hit him with the ice bucket, but actually managed to bonk his head. Immediately, of course, he was swept up into the creature's slimy arms. And then the monster from the netherworld, dragging Peter in one hand and Caroline by her ponytail in the other, intoned, "There is only night and dark and waves and caves, and you, my darling, Queen of the Deep."

"Ouch!" said Caroline softly.

Wally looked and sounded so evil at that point, and seemed to be having such a good time dragging Caroline, bumping and thumping, across the floor, that everyone clapped and cheered him on, and when it was over, everyone wanted to feel the green slime for themselves. Wally grinned. He would never have believed he could enjoy performing as much as this.

Miss Applebaum clapped too. "Well," she said. "That was quite a story, Caroline. Thank you, Peter, for taking part. You may go back to your room now, though I think you'll want to wash up first. Wally, I do hope you brought a change of clothes."

He had indeed. When he and Caroline went out into the hall to head for the rest rooms, she said, "You didn't have to be so rough, Wally! But weren't we great? Did you hear how everyone clapped?"

"They really liked the green slime," said Wally, grinning a little.

"*I'd* like to think they liked the whole play! It had

116

everything—romance, suspense, mystery, terror, science fiction . . ."

"Whatever," said Wally, and went into the boys' rest room to clean up. He didn't even mention getting the pictures back now that he had kept his part of the bargain. He was having too much fun.

■

When Wally and his brothers got home from baseball practice that afternoon, they hardly recognized their house. There were women going in and out the front door. A woman sat at a card table just inside the door writing down each item as it arrived.

The living room looked like an antique store. There were lampshades and trunks and lawn chairs and books; there were coats and platters and galoshes and figurines. An accordion perched on the back of Mr. Hatford's favorite armchair; the couch was covered with dishes. The dining room table was stacked high with clothes to be sorted, and one end of the room was heaped with children's toys.

Mr. Hatford went out to buy Kentucky Fried Chicken for dinner, which he and the boys ate upstairs in Wally's near-empty bedroom, and afterward Peter went out into the hall and stared forlornly down at the women who were still coming and going.

"I liked us better before," he said.

Mr. Hatford laughed. "So did I, Peter, but after tomorrow, it will all be over. All the stuff is going to be moved outside, and we won't have to look at it any longer."

"Why do people buy so much if they just give it away?" asked Peter, coming back into the bedroom.

"A very good question, Peter. Very good. We'll have to ask your mother sometime. But right now we're all focused on tomorrow. Jake plays the championship game and your mom runs the sale. How are you feeling, Jake? Did you have a final practice after school today?"

"Yep. We're playing the toughest team, though—the Grafton Grangers."

"Well, *they're* playing the toughest team too, so don't let that discourage you."

"Hey, hey!" said Jake. "I'm ready."

■

When all the women had gone at last, Mrs. Hatford came upstairs and fell across her bed.

"Think you'll make it?" Mr. Hatford asked as he sat down beside her and rubbed her back, the boys gathering in the doorway.

"I've never been so tired in my whole life," she said. "Even my fingernails ache."

"Who's setting up tomorrow?" Wally asked.

"The men. All the husbands are going to come over at seven, set up the tables on the porch and lawn and driveway, and put out all the stuff. We've color-coded every item, so that the things that sell for between one and five dollars will go on one table, things going for five to ten dollars will be on another, and . . . so . . . on. . . ." Her voice dropped off as she sank into sleep. Mr. Hatford put one finger to his lips and sent the boys back to their rooms.

■

After Wally went to bed that night, he realized he had forgotten to demand those pictures back from Caroline now that the play was over. Well, when she came the next day to help with the sale, she'd just better have them with her, or perhaps *that* was when he'd tell her about Eddie's LET'S PLAY BALL! underpants that they were going to run up the flagpole if they didn't get their album back.

He turned on his side and smoothed out his pillow. With his ear off the pillow momentarily, however, he thought he heard a noise. Footsteps. He had thought that the rest of the family was in bed, but then the sound came again. It almost sounded as though it was coming from the front porch.

Wally sat up and listened. Then he got up and went to the door of his bedroom. All the other bedroom doors were closed, and there was no light shining from under any of them.

Wally felt his way along the dark hall and slowly descended the stairs, being careful to avoid the next to the last step because it squeaked. If there was a robber in the house, Wally didn't want to be heard.

At the bottom of the stairs, he looked all about him—the living room, the dining room . . . There was certainly no one there that he could see. Wally went over to the front door. For a minute he thought of turning on the light to see if anyone was out there. Then he saw a circle of light—the beam of a flashlight—moving across the grass in the front yard and disappearing at last in the trees.

Eighteen

■

Mystery

It seemed as though everyone in Upshur County was at the Buckman Elementary school baseball field on Saturday. Shortly after the Malloys were seated on the bleachers and the game with the Grafton Grangers began, Caroline whispered in her mother's ear, "I'm going over to the Hatfords' and help Wally with the sale."

"You're not going to watch the rest of the game?" Mrs. Malloy asked in surprise.

"I can't!" Caroline wailed softly. "I've got butterflies in my stomach. But I don't want Eddie to know I've left, so I'm just going to slide through the bleachers. You'll have to tell me about it afterwards."

Her mother understood. "All right," she said. "I don't want you fainting dramatically if Eddie misses a ball. I'm sure Wally can use you." She helped Caroline slip down to the ground below. Beth and Coach Malloy didn't even notice that she had gone.

It was very warm for a day in May, and instead of her usual jeans and T-shirt, Caroline had put on a sundress that morning. If she was going to be a security guard at the Hatfords', people were going to see her. And if people were going to be noticing her, she wanted to look her best. She hurried down the sidewalk toward the Hatfords' house but hardly recognized it when she got there.

It looked like a junkyard. An organized junkyard. Every square inch of ground, it seemed, had a table on it with a sign listing prices for those items. There were aprons and axes, teddy bears and ties. A hand-lettered sign at the bottom of the driveway said SALE BEGINS AT NOON.

Already, however, there were a few browsers wandering among the tables, fingering the embroidered bedspreads, checking the price on a cake pan, measuring the width of a plant stand, or trying on a raincoat. Mrs. Larson hovered over the cash box and tried to keep an eye on everyone at once.

"Hi," said Wally, and followed that up with, "Where are the pictures?"

"I couldn't bring them now, Wally, because I came from the game. I didn't think you'd want me taking them *there*," said Caroline.

"If you don't give them to me, Caroline . . . ," Wally said threateningly.

"I *will*! I *promise*!" Caroline said.

Mrs. Larson called them over and handed Wally a Polaroid camera. "I want you to take a picture of every table before we start the sale," she said, half shouting because she could hardly hear herself. "We want to put them in our auxiliary newsletter so the women can see what wonderful donations we had this year. The people of Buckman have never been more generous."

Caroline and Wally wandered up and down the rows of folding tables, checking to see that all was well and pausing while Wally took pictures of table after table. As the photos came out of the camera and began to develop, it appeared that Caroline had somehow managed to be in each one, looking directly into the camera and smiling.

The sugar bowl and creamer from Susan Kemp, the framed photograph from Jenny Bloomer, the copper lamp from Edna Ballinger, the ceramic figurines from the Wheelers . . . a place for everything, and everything in its place. All the while Mrs. Larson, whose voice carried all over the yard, chattered away with neighbors who had come by to check out the sale.

A woman in a blue jacket came up to a display and smiled at Caroline. She smiled at Wally. Then she began walking around the tables, not stopping to look at much of anything until she saw the framed photograph from Jenny Bloomer, showing two stern-looking elderly people in rocking chairs. She picked it up and examined the back.

Over she came to Wally and took a twenty-dollar bill from her purse. "I'll take this, please," she said. "The price says fifteen dollars."

"The sale doesn't start till noon," Wally said. "We're just letting people look."

"But I can't come back at noon," the woman said. She put the twenty-dollar bill on the table where the framed photograph had been.

"I can't sell it now. I can't give you change," Wally said, reaching for the photograph. "It's against the rules." He looked over at Mrs. Larson, hoping she would come and talk to the woman. But Mrs. Larson had her back to them and was chatting with someone else. When Wally turned toward the woman in the blue jacket again, she was walking down the driveway, the framed photo in her arms, the twenty-dollar bill left behind.

Caroline saw, and shrugged. "What can we do, Wally? She wanted it, she got it. She paid for it, after all, and the auxiliary gets to keep the change."

"I suppose so," said Wally. He picked up the twenty-dollar bill and walked beside Caroline to Mrs. Larson. They waited politely while Mrs. Larson said goodbye to the woman she'd been talking with and that woman turned to go.

Caroline nudged Wally. "Get a look at those bright red toenails," she giggled.

Wally turned and stared at the woman who had been talking with Mrs. Larson. Then he turned some more and saw her catch up farther down the sidewalk with the woman who had taken the framed photo.

Suddenly Wally grabbed Caroline's arm. "Caroline!" he gasped. "It's them!"

"Who?" asked Caroline.

"The women who tried to get in our house. The last time I saw them, the one with the photograph was wearing a pink jacket. And I'd recognize the red toenails on the other one anywhere."

"They must want that framed picture really bad," said Caroline.

"Yeah, but why? They must know something about it that Jenny Bloomer didn't know. Follow them!" Wally said.

"*What?*" said Caroline.

"You've got to follow them and see where they go! We might have to get that picture back."

"Are you serious?" Caroline asked. She had come over to be a security guard and now she was a detective?

"*Go!*" Wally said. "I can't leave here till Mom gets back."

"I'm going!" said Caroline. "What am I supposed to do if I catch up with them? Bring the picture back?"

Wally wasn't sure. His mother had said no one was to buy anything before the sale opened. "I guess so," he said. "At least find out where they live."

Caroline took off. This, she decided, was a lot more exciting than watching a baseball game. Even a championship game. Far off on the school ball field, she could hear the crowd cheer, then cheer again. Did that mean a hit for the Badgers? Or was it the fans for the Grafton Grangers who were doing the cheering?

No matter, she told herself. *Keep your eyes on that blue jacket, but don't let them know you're following them.* If she was ever given the part of a girl detective, she'd know what it felt like. They turned, Caroline turned. They went up an alley, Caroline went up an alley. At last they went around a corner and up the steps of Mrs. Ritter's Bed and Breakfast. As soon as they were inside, Caroline, too, bounded up the front steps.

Flattening herself against the wall just outside the screen door, she heard a woman's voice call from far inside the house, "Did you have a nice walk, ladies?"

"It was lovely, Mrs. Ritter," one of the women answered, and when Caroline peered around the corner, she saw them going up the big oak staircase to the second floor.

Her heart was thumping hard inside her chest. She softly opened the screen door and slipped inside. She heard an electric mixer back in the kitchen, and she smelled cinnamon as something baked in the oven.

Caroline crossed the oriental rug in the hallway and made her way upstairs, keeping her feet close to the wall, where the steps were less likely to creak.

Even before she reached the top, she could hear the women's excited voices from one of the guest rooms.

"We're in luck, Dorothy. If we'd waited for the sale

to begin, who knows who could have walked off with this!" said one.

"By the time Jenny finds out—"

"Why does she have to know? We're the ones who found the letter in Mother's things. What our cousin doesn't know won't hurt her. That's what she gets for giving away family pictures."

"Hurry up, Marva," the other woman said. "What did the letter say? Just that something of great value was hidden behind the backing?"

"Yes, and we're about to find out what it is," said the first woman. "See how it bulges out back here? You can feel that something's in there, but you probably wouldn't know just by looking. The letter said it was an heirloom the family would want to keep forever."

"Do you need a nail file or scissors or something?"

"No, I can slide the paper open with my finger and work it off the frame. Something's in here, all right."

Okay, Caroline told herself, peeping carefully around the door frame. *Be ready. Whatever's in the back of the picture frame, I've got to grab it and take it to Wally.*

"I'm so nervous!" said the woman in the blue jacket, and then there was the sound of glue pulling away from the wooden frame, and a thick white packet fell out.

Now! Caroline thought.

Like a racehorse from the starting gate, she tore into the room. The women gave startled cries, turning to stare wildly at her. Caroline snatched up the white packet, and with a "Sorry, not for sale," she went streaking out again and down the stairs.

The women shrieked. There was the sound of footsteps coming down the hall after her, then down the stairs. Caroline didn't stop.

"Catch her!" screamed one of the women, but Caroline was out the door and down the steps, the two women thundering along behind.

Down the street she ran, around a corner, through an alley. On the women came. She had to hide. She could probably outrun them if she really tried, but she was getting out of breath. She turned a corner and saw a gas station up ahead. Making a sharp turn beyond the station, she ran along one side into the rest room and locked the door behind her.

Breathing hard, Caroline listened for the women's footsteps, and it wasn't long before she heard them coming. They came around the corner, then slowed, and finally stopped not far from the rest room door.

"Where did she *go*?" one woman cried.

"Who *was* she?" asked the other, panting. "Never on this earth have I—"

"The little thief!"

"She must have known all along what we were after."

"How could she? *We* don't even know what was in there!"

Caroline leaned against the wall in the rest room, her heart thumping painfully. Then slowly, silently, she looked at the white packet in her hands. It appeared to be thin cloth, old cotton, perhaps, and gently she began to unfold it. Layer after layer began to fall away until finally, there in her hands, Caroline found a pair of old-fashioned underpants that reached from the waist all the way down to the ankles, with elastic at the top and bottoms.

Caroline stared. Jenny Bloomer had contributed a picture frame with a pair of women's underpants hidden in the back? Was this a joke or what?

She didn't know. All she knew was that the two women had wanted what was in that picture frame very badly. So whoever these underpants belonged to, they must be very valuable, and it was Caroline's job to see that they were returned to their rightful owner. If she went outside and the women were still there, they would snatch them away from her, she was sure.

Suddenly Caroline knew what to do. She thrust her left foot into the left leg of the underpants. Then she thrust her right foot into the right leg. She pulled the garment up under her sundress and tugged at the elastic around the ankles until the material had bunched up to her knees. Then, the strange underpants swishing against her legs, she opened the door a crack and peered out. The women were walking back toward Mrs. Ritter's Bed and Breakfast, talking and gesturing wildly.

Slowly Caroline emerged. Slowly, stiffly, she walked back along College Avenue to the Hatfords' house as more cheering came from the baseball field. Her hair was wet with sweat, her face flushed. One strap of her sundress had slipped down off her shoulder, and one shoe was untied.

Wally saw her coming. He and Mrs. Larson took a few steps forward.

"Gracious! What excitement!" Mrs. Larson exclaimed. "Those two women had no right coming in here and taking that picture! Jenny Bloomer wanted us to have it for our sale, and everyone should have an equal chance to buy it."

"Did you find out why they wanted it? Did you get what they were after?" asked Wally.

Caroline nodded, and while Wally and Mrs. Larson stared, she simply hiked up her sundress to show the long cotton underpants bunched around her knees.

Nineteen

■

Amelia B.

Wally saw his opportunity. He raised the Polaroid camera and took a picture. Then he started to laugh.

Caroline's face reddened even more as she dropped her dress.

"That?" Wally guffawed as Mrs. Larson kept staring. "*That's* what was hidden in the picture frame? Somebody's old-fashioned underpants?"

"Let me see those!" said Mrs. Larson, going over. She reached down and felt the material that was sticking out below Caroline's sundress. "That is old muslin if I ever saw it. Why, I haven't seen cotton like that since I don't know when. It looks like something out of my grandmother's trunk."

Seeing that they might be valuable, Caroline stepped out of the underpants carefully and held them out for closer inspection.

"What have we here?" Mrs. Larson cried, pointing

to a hand-stitched label on the inside. "Oh, my stars! Look what it says! Amelia Bloomer! Caroline, you have just stepped out of the bloomers of the famous suffragette herself, Amelia Bloomer! Why, these belong in a museum!"

"Those are called bloomers?" Wally asked, putting two and two together.

"Indeed they are!" said Mrs. Larson. "These were Amelia's trademark, you might say. She wore loose trousers like this everywhere she went, sticking out of the bottom of her dress, and they were called bloomers after her. Our very own Jenny Bloomer is related, you know."

"Why would Amelia Bloomer want to wear things like that?" asked Caroline.

"Because she felt that women should be able to do much more than they were allowed to do back then. She wanted them to be able to vote, to hold any jobs they liked, and to wear clothes that let them be more active. She designed her clothes herself."

Another cheer went up from the baseball field, and at that very moment a car drove up and Jenny Bloomer got out.

"I knew I ought to get back before people started arriving, but I hated to leave. The score was tied," she said. "Anyway, I'm here, so what can I do to help?"

"You can explain these," said Mrs. Larson with a smile, and held out the folded bloomers.

"What's this?" asked Jenny.

"These were sealed in the back of the framed photograph you gave to the sale. And look on the inside."

When Jenny Bloomer saw the embroidered name of her distant relative, she gasped. "I knew we were related, but I had no idea I had her bloomers! I didn't even know who those people in the photograph were, we've had it so long. We're moving to a smaller house and I just wanted to sort through some things."

"Well, they certainly made for an exciting morning for us!" said Mrs. Larson loudly. "Tell her, Wally."

"Two women came to the sale early—the same women who wanted to look at our sale stuff before," said Wally. "One of them wanted the picture you donated, but I wouldn't sell it to them, so she just put a twenty-dollar bill down and made off with the picture."

"And I followed them to Mrs. Ritter's Bed and Breakfast and snatched the bloomers away as soon as they fell out the back of the frame," said Caroline.

Jenny Bloomer stared at Caroline. "Was one of those women dark-haired and the other blond?"

"Yes," said Wally and Caroline together.

"Was one of those women short and the other tall?"

"Yes," said Wally and Caroline together.

"And one wore red, red polish on her toenails," offered Caroline.

"Those are my cousins, Dorothy and Marva!" cried Jenny. "Ever since Mother died, they have been pestering me to find out if she left them anything in her will.

That just seemed so greedy to me, because they didn't visit her or write to her when she was sick. So I didn't offer them any of the things I was giving away, just some boxes of letters between their mother and mine. I'll bet one of those letters mentioned something valuable hidden in one of my pictures."

"They did say something about a letter," said Caroline.

"Oh, I know I should have read that correspondence before I gave it away, but I had so many things to sort. I felt I had to give my cousins at least something, though. They probably thought there was money hidden in that picture frame. It wouldn't surprise me if they had used Amelia's bloomers for a dust cloth."

Another cheer came from the direction of the ball field, and a few seconds later, still another. And then one terrific roar, followed by clapping. A few horns began to blow.

"Well, it must be over," said Wally. "I wonder who won."

A few minutes later Peter came running up the sidewalk, followed by the rest of the Hatfords, and everyone was smiling.

"We won!" Peter cried delightedly. "The Buckman Badgers did it!"

The Malloys came up the sidewalk after them.

"Eddie's last hit brought in the winning run!" Beth called.

"And Jake struck out the last batter on Grafton's team!" said Eddie.

"It was a close game," said Coach Malloy, "but I must say, this was one of the best ball games by any sixth graders that I've ever seen."

"Same here," said Mr. Hatford. "I think Buckman will remember this one for a long, long time."

"Well, let the sale begin!" said Mrs. Hatford, looking around.

"It already has," said Wally.

His mother looked at him. "I thought I told you not to sell anything until we opened at noon."

"Well, we had a little excitement while you were at the game," said Mrs. Larson. "Two women came by and walked off with our prize offering."

"What?" cried Mrs. Hatford.

"Close your eyes," Mrs. Larson said.

Everyone closed their eyes. After a moment, Mrs. Larson said, "Now open." Everyone did.

Mrs. Larson was holding the pair of bloomers against her body. The legs came down almost to her ankles.

"What?" cried Mrs. Hatford and Mrs. Malloy together, while the men only stared.

"These bloomers were made famous by Amelia Bloomer herself!" Mrs. Larson declared, showing them the embroidered label on the inside, and the story had to be told all over again.

At the most dramatic moment, Wally triumphantly held up the picture he had taken of Caroline, sweaty and red-faced, one shoelace untied, with her dress hiked up to her waist and the long muslin bloomers below. Caroline tried to grab the picture away, but Wally held it just out of reach.

"Caroline, you look ravishing!" Beth joked.

Another woman arrived from the auxiliary with a basket of sandwiches for all the helpers, and while they ate, Jenny Bloomer talked some more about her cousins.

"I wondered why they called me and were so anxious to know if I still had all of Mother's things. They asked if I had given away any old photographs, and I said I had—that I had already taken the sale items to the Hatfords—and I guess that's when the trouble began. If they had been honest with me and told me about the letter, I would have shared whatever was inside the picture frame. Instead, they must have come to Buckman, rented a room, and tried every way they could to get that picture without my knowing. I don't think they deserve those bloomers, do you?"

"I think they belong to you, Jenny," said Mrs. Hatford. "And you may do whatever you like with them."

"In that case, I would like to donate them to the museum here in Buckman," said Jenny. "If my cousins show up, we will gladly refund their money, provided they return the photograph, of course. My guess is they will hightail it out of Buckman and the auxiliary will keep the twenty. We can certainly put it to good use at the fire department."

The Hatfords and the Malloys spent the afternoon helping out at the sale. Jake and Josh put customers' purchases in bags for them, Eddie helped carry things out to cars, Beth and her mother made change, Mr. Hatford and Coach Malloy kept their eyes on the customers to see that nothing else was taken, and Wally and Caroline kept one eye out for the two cousins of Jenny Bloomer, but they did not come back. They were probably already on the road, far out of town.

When the sale was over, the tables dismantled, and the leftover items taken away in a pickup truck, the four Hatford boys and the three Malloy girls sat down on the back steps of the Hatford house. Josh and Jake and Peter were still laughing at the photo Wally had taken of Caroline.

"Please give it to me, Wally," Caroline begged.

"Yeah? You want to trade?" asked Jake. "Don't you have some pictures of us?"

"Not on your life!" said Eddie. "You think we should turn over all those pictures of you for only one in return?"

Wally looked quickly at Caroline. Was this the way it was going to be? He wouldn't get those pictures back after all?

"So what else do you want?" asked Josh.

Beth looked at Eddie and Eddie looked at Caroline.

"Quit calling us the Whomper, the Weirdo, and the

Crazie," said Beth, and Eddie nodded. "But it's still not an even trade."

"Well, you'd better make up your mind, because we just might send Caroline's picture to the newspaper. They might like to print it along with the story of how Amelia Bloomer's bloomers got to be in the Buckman Museum," Jake said.

Wally grinned at Caroline, satisfied that for once the boys had the upper hand. But his face fell when Caroline suddenly brightened and said, "Oh, *would* you? *Please?* I'd love to have that picture in the paper. Maybe a talent scout will see it and he'll be looking for someone to play the part of an old-fashioned girl in the eighteen hundreds who has to work in a garment factory, and she steals the bloomers she's been sewing all week to buy food for her little sisters and—"

"Forget it," said Wally. Caroline *wanted* her picture shown around. Caroline *liked* to be seen in bloomers. Caroline was nuts. Caroline was Caroline. He gave up. "For you," he said, and handed her the picture.

The girls looked at him, then at each other.

"You won't call us the Whomper, the Weirdo, and the Crazie anymore?" asked Eddie.

"No," said Josh.

"Deal?"

"Deal." They all put their hands together, one on top of the other, and Eddie went home and returned with the photo album.

"For you," she said, and handed it to Jake.

Jake leafed through the pages quickly to see if all the pictures were there.

This was a little too easy! Wally thought. "How do we know you haven't shown them to people already?" he asked.

"Well, we haven't," said Eddie. "You'll just have to trust us."

"How do we know you haven't made copies and aren't still planning to blackmail us?" asked Josh.

"We aren't," said Beth.

"How do we know you won't go around *telling* people about them?" asked Wally.

"You don't," said Caroline. "So I guess you'll just have to stay on your best behavior."

"Uh . . . not so fast," said Jake. "Maybe *you'll* have to stay on *your* best behavior too!" With that, he pulled something out of his back pocket. "Unless you want these strung up the flagpole at school on Monday."

"What *is* it?" asked Caroline, staring as Jake unfolded it.

"*More* bloomers!" chortled Peter. "Eddie's underpants!"

The Malloy girls stared in horror. Eddie's cheeks turned from pale peach to rosy pink to tomato red.

"Let's play ball!" yelped Josh, pointing to the lines of print going this way and that all over the fabric.

"They're . . . full of holes!" gasped Beth. "Where did you get those?"

"I guess Peter thought they were a dishcloth when

you invited him to stay at your house for dinner," said Wally.

Eddie covered her face in humiliation. "I wish Mother wouldn't use our stuff!" she wailed.

"Okay," said Caroline. "What do we have to do to get them back?"

Wally and his brothers exchanged satisfied smiles. Oh, life was sweet, Wally decided. Life, for a change, was wonderful.

"Well," said Josh, "I suppose you could scrub our toilets for a week, make our beds, and clean out our closets."

The girls could only stare.

"Or maybe you could bow down when you see us coming and call us lord and master," said Jake.

"Never!" said Eddie.

"Or bake us cookies!" said Peter hopefully.

"How about this?" said Wally. "We give them back, but if you ever breathe one word about the pictures in that album, we'll tell everyone we know about Eddie's underpants with all the holes and the *Let's play ball!* messages on them."

"We promise we won't!" said the three Malloy girls together.

"But if *you* go around telling about the underpants, we get to tell about the pictures," said Beth. "Understood?"

"Okay," said Jake and Josh and Wally and Peter.

With that, Jake whirled the underpants once again,

but this time Eddie caught them. And as the girls headed home, Wally heard Eddie say, "Mom won't get any more of *these* for her rag bag, that's for sure!"

"Hey! Good game, Eddie!" Jake called after her.

"You didn't play so bad yourself," said Eddie.

■ ■ ■ ■ ■ ■ ■ ■ ■ ■ ■ ■ ■

Twenty

■

Dear Bill . . .

Dear Bill (and Danny and Steve and Tony and Doug):

Well, we got the pictures back. I don't think the girls are going to tell anyone about them, because we have some blackmail material of our own if they do. (And wouldn't you just like to know what!) Sorry, we can't tell, but man, did we ever luck out!

Not only that, but the Buckman Badgers won the championship. I could hear the cheering from way back here at the house. They say Eddie hit a scorching double in the eighth inning that brought home two runs and won the game. Then, with Jake pitching, Grafton didn't get a single hit in the ninth.

I wasn't at the game, though, and you know why: the Women's Auxiliary yard sale. But we had plenty of excitement of our own. Two women walked off with a framed photograph even after I said the sale hadn't started yet. But I told Caroline to follow them and bring back whatever she could. Well, she did, and you will never guess what was sealed behind the paper on the back of the frame. A pair of underpants! Yep! In case you don't know who Amelia Bloomer was—and these underpants are called bloomers—go to the encyclopedia and look her up.

We still don't know if the Malloys are going back to Ohio or not, but they'll be here for the next few months anyway. We might take them up Indian Knob, or show them the old coal mine.

Right now things are going pretty good, but maybe it's time we found out who really belongs here in Buckman—the Hatfords or the Malloys. Just in case you guys come back, I mean, and the Malloys stay. Just in case they think they can boss us around. I don't mean we'd be enemies or anything. But Caroline always wants to be queen of something, and she just might decide she wants to be queen of us.

Anyway, best wishes from Buckman's winning Badgers and Amelia Bloomer's bloomers.

Wally (and Jake and Josh and Peter)

About the Author

Readers of Phyllis Reynolds Naylor's boys-versus-girls books often want to know who's finally going to win the war. Well, says Naylor, she herself is a girl, but she raised two sons, so she knows how boys feel as well. Readers will just have to wait to see what the Hatfords and the Malloys have in mind.

The town of Buckman in the stories is really Buckhannon, West Virginia, where Naylor's husband spent most of his growing-up years. There are now nine books in the series—*The Boys Start the War, The Girls Get Even, Boys Against Girls, The Girls' Revenge, A Traitor Among the Boys, A Spy Among the Girls, The Boys Return, The Girls Take Over,* and *Boys in Control.*

Phyllis Reynolds Naylor is the author of more than a hundred books, including the Newbery Award–winning *Shiloh* and the other two books in the Shiloh trilogy, *Shiloh Season* and *Saving Shiloh.* She and her husband live in Bethesda, Maryland.

Read all about the Hatford boys and the Malloy girls.

The Boys Start the War

Just when the Hatford brothers are expecting three boys to move into the house across the river, where their best friends used to live, the Malloy girls arrive instead. Wally and his brothers decide to make Caroline and her sisters so miserable that they'll want to go back to Ohio, but they haven't counted on the ingenuity of the girls. From dead fish to dead bodies, floating cakes to floating heads, the pranks continue—first by the boys, then by the girls—until someone is taken prisoner!

The Girls Get Even

Still smarting from the boys' latest trick, the girls are determined to get even. Caroline is thrilled to play the part of Goblin Queen in the school play, especially since Wally Hatford has to be her footman. The boys, however, have a creepy plan for Halloween night. They're certain the girls will walk right into their trap. Little do the boys know what the Malloy sisters have in store.

Boys Against Girls

Abaguchie mania! Caroline Malloy shivers happily when her on-again, off-again enemy Wally Hatford tells her that the remains of a strange animal known as the abaguchie have been spotted in their area. Wally swears Caroline to secrecy and warns her not to search by herself. But Caroline will do anything to find the secret of the bones.

The Girls' Revenge

Christmas is coming, but Caroline Malloy and Wally Hatford aren't singing carols around the tree. Instead, these sworn enemies must interview each other for the dreaded December class project. Caroline, as usual, has a trick up her sleeve that's sure to shock Wally. In the meantime, Wally and his brothers find a way to spy on the Malloy girls at home. The girls vow to get revenge on those sneaky Hatfords with a trap the boys won't soon forget.

A Traitor Among the Boys

The Hatford boys make a New Year's resolution to treat the Malloy girls like sisters. But who says you can't play tricks on sisters? The girls will need to stay one step ahead of the boys and are willing to pay big-time for advance information. Homemade cookies should be all it takes to make a traitor spill the beans. In the meantime, Caroline is delighted with her role in the town play. Don't ask how Beth, Josh, and Wally get roped into it—just wait until show time, when Caroline pulls her wildest stunt yet!

A Spy Among the Girls

Valentine's Day is coming up, and love is in the air for Beth Malloy and Josh Hatford. When they're spotted holding hands, Josh tells his teasing brothers that he's simply spying on the girls to see what they're plotting next. At the same time, Caroline Malloy, the family actress, decides she must know what it's like to fall in love. Poor Wally Hatford is in for it when she chooses him as the object of her affection!

The Boys Return

It's spring break, and the only assignment Wally Hatford and Caroline Malloy have is to do something they've never done before. Wally's sure that will be a cinch, because the mighty Benson brothers are coming. It will be nonstop action all the way. For starters, the nine Benson and Hatford boys plan to scare the three Malloy sisters silly by convincing them that their house is haunted. Meanwhile, everyone in town has heard that there's a hungry cougar on the prowl. When the kids decide to take a break from their tricks and join forces to catch the cougar, guess who gets stuck with the scariest job?

The Girls Take Over

The Hatford boys and the Malloy girls are ready to outdo each other again. Eddie is the first girl ever to try out for the school baseball team. Now she and Jake are vying for the same position, while Caroline and Wally compete to become class spelling champ. As if that's not enough, the kids decide to race bottles down the rising Buckman River to see whose will travel farthest by the end of the month. Of course, neither team trusts the other, and when the girls go down to the river to capture the boys' bottles, well . . . it looks as if those Malloy girls may be in over their heads this time!

army raised by the utmost exercise of his feudal power to defend those estates in France which after the loss of Normandy still pertained to the English Crown. Hubert could not control this, but the transporting of the expedition lay apparently in his department. The King found no ships, or few, awaiting him; no supplies, no money, for his oversea venture. He flew into a rage. Although usually mild, affable, scholarly and artistic, he drew his sword and rushed upon the Justiciar, reproaching him with having betrayed his trust and being bribed by France. It certainly was a very unpleasant and awkward situation, the Army wishing to fight abroad, and the Navy and the Treasury unable or unwilling to carry them thither. The quarrel was smoothed down; the King recovered his temper; the expedition sailed in the following year and Hubert retained his place. But not for long. In 1232 he was driven from power by a small palace clique. Threatened in his life, he took sanctuary at Brentwood. He was dragged from this asylum, but the common, humble blacksmith who was ordered to put the fetters on him declared he would die any death rather than do so; and he is said to have used the words which historians have deemed to be the true monument of Hubert de Burgh: "Is he not that most faithful Hubert who so often saved England from the devastation of foreigners and restored England to England?"

* * * * *

During John's reign one of the most cruel tragedies of world history had run its course in Southern France. In the domains of Raymond VI, Count of Toulouse, there had grown up during several generations a heresy, sombre and austere in theory, but genial in practice. The Albigenses, or Cathares, "the Purified," as they were called, dismissed altogether from the human mind the resurrection of the body, Purgatory, and Hell. In their view life on earth in the flesh was the work of Satan. The material phase would soon pass and the soul, freed from its accursed encumbrance, would be resumed in eternal bliss into the Godhead. The "Perfects" of this cult practised chastity and abstinence, and professed in principle a sincere wish for death; but the mass of the population, relieved from the oppression of supernatural terror, developed, we are assured, in the delicious climate of those regions, easy morals and merry character. The thrilling sensation of being raised above the vicissitudes of this world and at the same time freed from the menaces of the next produced a great happiness in these regions, in which all classes joined, and from it sprang culture of manners and fervour of conviction.

This casting off of all spiritual chains was, naturally, unwelcome to the Papacy. The whole moral scheme of the Western world was based, albeit precariously, upon Original Sin, Redemption by Grace, and a Hell of infinite torment and duration, which could only be avoided through the ministrations of the clergy. It was some time before the Papacy realised the deadlines and the magnitude of the novel sin which was spreading in what we now call Southern France. Once the gravity of the challenge was understood it superseded even the rescue of the Holy Sepulchre from the infidel. In 1209 a Crusade for a different purpose was set on foot, and all temporal forces at the disposal of Rome were directed upon the Albigenses, under the leadership of Philip of France. At this time the burning of heretics and other undesirables, which had been practised sporadically in France, received the formal sanction of law. The process of blotting out the new heresy by the most atrocious cruelties which the human mind can conceive occupied nearly a generation. The heretics, led by the "Perfects," fought like tigers, regarding death as a final release from the curse of the body. But the work was thoroughly done. The Albigensian heresy was burned out at the stake. Only poor, hungry folk in the forests and mountains, which happily abound in these parts, still harboured those doubts about approaching damnation upon which so much of the discipline and responsibility of human beings and the authority and upkeep of the Church depended.

Of all the leaders in this Crusade none surpassed a certain Simon de Montfort, "a minor lord of the Paris region." He rose to commanding control in this war, and was acclaimed the effective leader. He was made Viscount of Béziers and Carcassonne "at the instance of the barons of God's army, the legates and the priests present." This capable, merciless man accomplished the bloody task, and when he fell at the siege of Toulouse he left behind him a son who bore his name, succeeded to his high station among the nobility of the age, and became associated with an idea which has made him for ever famous.

*   *   *   *   *

De Burgh's conduct had been far from blameless, but his fall had been deliberately engineered by men whose object was not to reform administration but to gain power. The leader of this intrigue was his former rival Peter des Roches, the Bishop of Winchester. Des Roches himself kept in the background, but at the Christmas Council of 1232 nearly every post of consequence in the administration was conferred upon his friends, most of them, like him, Poitevins. More was involved in the defeat of de Burgh than the triumph of des Roches and his party. De Burgh was the last of the great Justiciars who had wielded plenary and at times almost sovereign power. Henceforward the Household offices like the Wardrobe, largely dependent upon the royal will and favour, began to overshadow the great "national" offices, like the Justiciarship, filled by the baronial magnates. As they came to be occupied increasingly by foreign intruders, Poitevins,

Savoyards, Provençals, the national feeling of the baronage became violently hostile. Under the leadership of Richard the Marshal, a second son of the great William, the barons began to growl against the foreigners. Des Roches retorted that the King had need of foreigners to protect him against the treachery of his natural subjects; and large numbers of Poitevin and Breton mercenaries were brought over to sustain this view. But the struggle was short. In alliance with Prince Llewellyn the young Marshal drove the King among the Welsh marches, sacked Shrewsbury, and harried des Roches's lands. In the spring of 1234 Henry was forced to accept terms, and, although the Marshal was killed in April, the new Archbishop, Edmund Rich, insisted on the fulfilment of the treaty. The Poitevin officials were dismissed, des Roches found it convenient to go on a journey to Italy, and de Burgh was honourably restored to his lands and possessions.

The Poitevins were the first of the long succession of foreign favourites whom Henry III gathered round him in the middle years of his reign. Hatred of the aliens, who dominated the King, monopolised the offices, and made scandalous profits out of a country to whose national interests they were completely indifferent, became the theme of baronial opposition. The King's affection was reserved for those who flattered his vanity and ministered to his caprices. He developed a love for extravagant splendour, and naturally preferred to his morose barons the brilliant adventurers of Poitou and Provence. The culture of medieval Provence, the home of the troubadours and the creed of chivalry, fascinated Henry. In 1236 he married Eleanor, the daughter of Raymond of Provence. With Eleanor came her numerous and needy kinsmen, chief among them her four uncles. A new wave of foreigners descended upon the profitable wardships, marriages, escheats, and benefices, which the disgusted baronage regarded as their own.

The King delighted to shower gifts upon his charming relations, and the responsibility for all the evils of his reign was laid upon their shoulders. It is the irony of history that not the least unpopular was this same Simon de Montfort, son of the repressor of the Albigenses.

An even more copious source of discontent in England was the influence of the Papacy over the grateful and pious King. Pope Gregory IX, at desperate grips with the Holy Roman Emperor Frederick II, made ever greater demands for money, and his Legate, Otto, took an interest in English Church Reform. Otto's demand in 1240 for one-fifth of the clergy's rents and movables raised a storm. The rectors of Berkshire published a manifesto denying the right of Rome to tax the English Church, and urging that the Pope, like other bishops, should "live of his own." Nevertheless, early in 1241 Otto returned to Rome with a great treasure; and the Pope rewarded the loyalty of the Italian clergy by granting them the next three hundred vacant English benefices. The election of Innocent IV in 1243 led to renewed demands. In that year the Papal envoy forbade bishops in England to appoint to benefices until the long list of Papal nominees had been exhausted. Robert Grosseteste, scholar, scientist, and saint, a former Master of the Oxford Schools and since 1235 Bishop of Lincoln, led the English clergy in evasion or refusal of Papal demands. He became their champion. Although he still believed that the Pope was absolute, he heralded the attacks which Wyclif was more than a century later to make upon the exactions and corruption of the Roman Court.

The Church, writhing under Papal exaction, and the baronage, offended by Court encroachments, were united in hatred of foreigners. A crisis came in 1244, when a baronial commission was appointed to fix the terms of a money grant to the King. The barons insisted that the Justiciar, Chancellor, and Treasurer, besides certain judges, should be elected by the Great Council, on which they were strongly represented. Four of the King's Council were to be similarly elected, with power to summon the Great Council. The King turned in his distress to the already mulcted Church, but his appeal was rejected through the influence of Grosseteste. In 1247 the voracious Poitevins encouraged the King in despotic ideas of government. To their appetites were now added those of the King's three half-brothers, the Lusignans, the sons of John's Queen, Isabella, by her second marriage. Henry adopted a new tone. "Servants do not judge their master," he said in 1248. "Vassals do not judge their prince or bind him by conditions. They should put themselves at his disposal and be submissive to his will." Such language procured no money; and money was the pinch. Henry was forced to sell plate and jewels and give new privileges or new grants of old rights to those who would buy them. Salaries were unpaid, forced gifts extracted; the forest courts were exploited and extortion condoned. In 1252 the King, on the pretext of a Crusade, demanded a tithe of ecclesiastical rents and property for three years. On Grosseteste's advice the clergy refused this grant, because the King would not on his part confirm Magna Carta. Next year Grosseteste died, indomitable to the last against both Papal and royal exactions.

Meanwhile Henry had secretly accepted greater Continental obligations. The death of the Holy Roman Emperor Frederick in 1250 revived at Rome the old plan of uniting Sicily, over which he had ruled, to the Papal dominions. In 1254 Henry III accepted the Papal offer of the Sicilian Crown for his younger son Edmund. This was a foolish step, and the conditions attached to the gift raised it to the very height of folly. The English King was to provide an army, and he stood surety for a mass of Papal debts amounting to the vast sum in those days of about £90,000. When the King's acceptance of the Papal offer became known a storm of indignation broke over his head. Both the Great Council and the clergy refused financial aid. As if this were not enough, at the Imperial election of 1257 the King's brother, Richard of Cornwall, offered himself as Emperor, and Henry spent lavishly to secure his election. The final stroke was the King's complete failure to check the successes of Llewellyn, who in 1256 had swept the English out of Wales and intrigued to overthrow the English faction in Scotland. Despised, discredited, and frightened, without money or men, the King faced an angered and powerful opposition.

*   *   *   *   *

In the last years of Grosseteste's life he had come to hope great things of his friend, Simon de Montfort. Simon had married the King's sister and had inherited the Earldom of Leicester. He had been governor of the English lands in Gascony for four years. Strong and energetic, he had aroused the jealousy and opposition of the King's favourites; and as a result of their intrigues he had been brought to trial in 1252. The commission acquitted him; but in return for a sum of money from the King he unwillingly agreed to vacate his office. Friendship between him and the King was at an end; on the one side was contempt, on the other suspicion. In this way, from an unexpected quarter, appeared the leader whom the baronial and national opposition had long lacked.

There were many greater notables in England, and his relationship to the King was aspersed by the charge that he had seduced his bride before he married her. None the less there he stood with five resolute sons, an alien leader, who was to become the brain and driving force of the English aristocracy. Behind him gradually ranged themselves most of the great feudal chiefs, the whole strength of London as a corporate entity, all the lower clergy, and the goodwill of the nation. A letter of a Court official, written in July 1258, has been preserved. The King, so it says, had yielded to what he felt was overwhelming pressure. A commission for reform of government was set up; it was agreed that "public offices should only be occupied by the English," and that "the emissaries of Rome and the foreign merchants and bankers should be reduced to their proper station." Grants of land to foreigners, the position of the King's Household, the custody of the fortresses, were all called in question. "The barons," writes our civil servant, "have a great and difficult task which cannot be carried out easily or quickly. They are proceeding . . . *ferociter*. May the results be good!"

The Mother of Parliaments

THE later years of Henry III's troubled reign were momentous in their consequences for the growth of English institutions. This may perhaps be called the seed-time of our Parliamentary system, though few participants in the sowing could have foreseen the results that were eventually to be achieved. The commission for reform set about its work seriously, and in 1258 its proposals were embodied in the Provisions of Oxford, supplemented and extended in 1259 by the Provisions of Westminster. This baronial movement represented something deeper than dislike of alien counsellors. For the two sets of Provisions, taken together, represent a considerable shift of interest from the standpoint of Magna Carta. The Great Charter was mainly concerned to define various points of law, whereas the Provisions of Oxford deal with the overriding question of by whose advice and through what officials royal government should be carried on. Many of the clauses of the Provisions of Westminster moreover mark a limitation of baronial rather than of royal jurisdiction. The fruits of Henry II's work were now to be seen; the nation was growing stronger, more self-conscious and self-confident. The notable increase in judicial activity throughout the country, the more frequent visits of the judges and officials—all of them dependent upon local co-operation—educated the country knights in political responsibility and administration. This process, which shaped the future of English institutions, had its first effects in the thirteenth century.

The staple of the barons' demand was that the King in future should govern by a Council of Fifteen, to be elected by four persons, two from the baronial party and two from the royal. It is significant that the King's proclamation accepting the arrangement in English as well as French is the first public document to be issued in both languages since the time of William the Conqueror. For a spell this Council, animated and controlled by Simon de Montfort governed the land. They held each other in proper check, sharing among themselves the greater executive offices and entrusting the actual administration to "lesser men," as was then widely thought to be desirable. The magnates, once their own class interests were guarded, and their rights—which up to a certain point were the rights of the nation—were secure, did not wish to put the levers of power in the hands of one or two of their number. This idea of a Cabinet of politicians, chosen from the patriciate, with their highly trained functionaries of no political status operating under them, had in it a long vitality and many resurrections.

It is about this time that the word "Parlement"—Parliament—began to be current. In 1086 William the Conqueror had "deep speech" with his wise men before launching the Domesday inquiry. In Latin this would have appeared as *colloquium;* and "colloquy" is the common name in the twelfth century for the consultations between the King and his magnates. The occasional colloquy "on great affairs of the Kingdom" can at this point be called a Parliament. But more often the word means the permanent Council of officials and judges which sat at Westminster to receive petitions, redress grievances, and generally regulate the course of the law. By the thirteenth century Parliament establishes itself as the name of two quite different, though united, institutions.

If we translate their functions into modern terms we may say that the first of these assemblies deals with policy, the second with legislation and administration. The debate on the Address at the beginning of a session is very like a colloquy, while the proceedings of "Parliament" have their analogue in the committee stage of a Bill. In the reign of Henry III, and even of Edward I, it was by no means a foregone conclusion that the two assemblies would be amalgamated. Rather did it look as if the English Constitution would develop as did the French Constitution, with a King in Council as the real Government, with the magnates reduced to a mere nobility, and "Parlement" only a clearinghouse for legal business. Our history did not take this course. In the first place the magnates during the century that followed succeeded in mastering the Council and identifying their interests with it. Secondly, the English counties had a life of their own, and their representatives at Westminster were to exercise increasing influence. But without the powerful impulse of Simon de Montfort these forces might not have combined to shape a durable legislative assembly.

* * * * *

The King, the Court party, and the immense foreign interests associated therewith had no intention of submitting indefinitely to the thraldom of the Provisions. Every preparation was made to recover the lost ground. In 1259 the King returned with hopes of foreign aid from Paris, where he had been to sign a treaty of peace with the French. His son Edward was already the rising star of all who wished to see a strong monarchy. Supporters of this cause appeared among the poor and turbulent elements in London and the towns.

The enthusiasm of the revolution—for it was nothing less—had not been satisfied by a baronial victory. Ideas were afoot which would not readily be put to sleep. It is the merit of Simon de Montfort that he did not rest content with a victory by the barons over the Crown. He turned at once upon the barons themselves. If the King should be curbed, so also must they in their own spheres show respect for the general interest. Upon these issues the claims of the middle classes, who had played a great part in carrying the barons to supremacy, could not be disregarded. The "apprentice" or bachelor knights, who may be taken as voicing the wishes of the country gentry, formed a virile association of their own entitled "the Community of the Bachelors of England." Simon de Montfort became their champion. Very soon he began to rebuke great lords for abuse of their privileges. He wished to extend to the baronial estates the reforms already undertaken in the royal administration. He addressed himself pointedly to Richard, Earl of Gloucester, who ruled wide estates in the South-West and in South Wales. He procured an ordinance from the Council making it plain that the great lords were under the royal authority, which was again—though this he did not stress—under the Council. Here was dictatorship in a new form. It was a dictatorship of the Commonwealth, but, as so often happens to these bold ideas, it expressed itself inevitably through a man and a leader. These developments split the baronial party from end to end; and the King and his valiant son Edward, striking in with all their own resources upon their divided opponents, felt they might put the matter to the proof.

At Easter in 1261 Henry, freed by the Pope from his oath to accept the Provisions of Oxford and Westminster, deposed the officials and Ministers appointed by the barons. There were now two Governments with conflicting titles, each interfering with the other. The barons summoned the representatives of the shires to meet them at St Albans; the King summoned them to Windsor. Both parties competed for popular support. The barons commanded greater sympathy in the country, and only Gloucester's opposition to de Montfort held them back from sharp action. After the death of Gloucester in July 1262 the baronial party rallied to de Montfort's drastic policy. Civil war broke out, and Simon and his sons, all of whom played vigorous parts, a moiety of barons, the middle class, so far as it had emerged, and powerful allies in Wales together faced in redoubtable array the challenge of the Crown.

Simon de Montfort was a general as well as a politician. Nothing in his upbringing or circumstances would naturally have suggested to him the course he took. It is ungratefully asserted that he had no real conception of the ultimate meaning of his actions. Certainly he builded better than he knew. By September 1263 a reaction against him had become visible: he had succeeded only too well. Edward played upon the discontent among the barons, appealed to their feudal and selfish interest, fomented their jealousy of de Montfort, and so built up a strong royalist party. At the end of the year de Montfort had to agree to arbitration by Louis IX, the French king. The decision went against him. Loyal to his monarchial rank, the King of France defended the prerogative of the King of England and declared the Provisions to be illegal. As Louis was accepted as a saint in his own lifetime this was serious. Already however the rival parties had taken up arms. In the civil war that followed the feudal party more or less supported the King. The people, especially the towns, and the party of ecclesiastical reform, especially the Franciscans, rallied to de Montfort. New controls were improvised in many towns to defeat the royalist sympathies of the municipal oligarchies. In the summer of 1264 de Montfort once again came South to relieve the pressure which Henry and Edward were exerting on the Cinque Ports.

The King and Prince Edward met him in Sussex with a superior power. At Lewes a fierce battle was fought. In some ways it was a forerunner of Edgehill. Edward, like Rupert four hundred years later, conquered all before him, pursued incontinently, and returned to the battlefield only to find that all was lost. Simon had, with much craft and experience of war, laid a trap to which the peculiar conditions of the ground lent themselves, whereby when his centre had been pierced his two wings of armoured cavalry fell upon the royal main body from both flanks and crushed all resistance. He was accustomed at this time owing to a fall from his horse to be carried with the army in a sumptuous and brightly decorated litter, like the coach of an eighteenth-century general. In this he placed two or three hostages for their greater security, and set it among the Welsh in the centre, together with many banners and emblems suggesting his presence. Prince Edward, in his charge, captured this trophy, and killed the unlucky hostages from his own party who were found therein. But meanwhile the King and all his Court and principal supporters were taken prisoners by de Montfort, and the energetic prince returned only to share their plight.

Simon de Montfort was now in every respect master of England, and if he had proceeded in the brutal manner of modern times in several European countries by the wholesale slaughter of all who were in his power he might long have remained so. In those days however, for all their cruelty in individual cases, nothing was pushed to the last extreme. The influences that counted with men in contest for power at the peril of their lives were by no means only brutal. Force, though potent, was not sovereign. Simon made a treaty with the captive

King and the beaten party, whereby the rights of the Crown were in theory respected, though in practice the King and his son were to be subjected to strict controls. The general balance of the realm was preserved, and it is clear from Simon's action not only that he felt the power of the opposing forces, but that he aimed at their ultimate unification. He saw himself, with the King in his hands, able to use the authority of the Crown to control the baronage and create the far broader and better political system which, whether he aimed at it or not, must have automatically followed from his success. Thus he ruled the land, with the feeble King and the proud Prince Edward prisoners in his hands. This opens the third and final stage in his career.

*   *   *   *   *

All the barons, whatever party they had chosen, saw themselves confronted with an even greater menace than that from which they had used Simon to deliver them. The combination of Simon's genius and energy with the inherent powers of a Plantagenet monarchy and the support of the middle classes, already so truculent, was a menace to their class privileges far more intimate and searching than the misgovernment of John or the foreign encumbrances of Henry III. Throughout these struggles of lasting significance the English barony never deviated from their own self-interest. At Runnymede they had served national freedom when they thought they were defending their own privilege. They had now no doubt that Simon was its enemy. He was certainly a despot, with a king in his wallet and the forces of social revolution at his back. The barons formed a hard confederacy among themselves, and with all the forces of the Court not in Simon's hands schemed night and day to overthrow him.

For the moment de Montfort was content that the necessary steps should be taken by a council of nine who controlled expenditure and appointed officials. Any long-term settlement could be left until the Parliament which he had summoned for 1265. The Earl's autocratic position was not popular, yet the country was in such a state of confusion that circumstances seemed to justify it. In the North and along the Welsh Marches the opposition was still strong and reckless; in France the Queen and the earls Hugh Bigod and Warenne intrigued for support; the Papacy backed the King. De Montfort kept command of the Narrow Seas by raising a fleet in the Cinque Ports and openly encouraging privateering. In the West however he lost the support of Gilbert de Clare, Earl of Gloucester and the son of his former rival Richard de Clare. Without openly joining the royalists Clare conspired with them and revived his father's quarrel with de Montfort. Summoned to the Parliament of 1265, he replied by accusing the Earl of appropriating for himself and his sons the revenues of the Crown and the confiscated property of the opposition nobles. There was some truth in these accusations, but Clare's main objection appears to have been that he did not share the spoils.

In January 1265 a Parliament met in London to which Simon summoned representatives both from the shires and from the towns. Its purpose was to give an appearance of legality to the revolutionary settlement, and this, under the guidance of de Montfort, it proceeded to do. Its importance lay however more in its character as a representative assembly than in its work. The constitutional significance which was once attached to it as the first representative Parliament in our history is somewhat discounted by modern opinion. The practical reason for summoning the strong popular element was de Montfort's desire to weight the Parliament with his own supporters: among the magnates only five earls and eighteen barons received writs of summons. Again he fell back upon the support of the country gentry and the burgesses against the hostility or indifference of the magnates. In this lay his message and his tactics.

The Parliament dutifully approved of de Montfort's actions and accepted his settlement embodied in the Provisions. But Clare's withdrawal to the West could only mean the renewal of war. King Henry III abode docilely in Simon's control, and was treated all the time with profound personal respect. Prince Edward enjoyed a liberty which could only have been founded upon his parole not to escape. However, as the baronial storm gathered and many divisions occurred in Simon's party, and all the difficulties of government brought inevitable unpopularity in their train, he went out hunting one day with a few friends, and forgot to return as in honour bound. He galloped away through the woodland, first after the stag and then in quest of larger game. He at once became the active organising head of the most powerful elements in English life, to all of which the destruction of Simon de Montfort and his unheard-of innovations had become the supreme object. By promising to uphold the Charters, to remedy grievances and to expel the foreigners, Edward succeeded in uniting the baronial party and in cutting away the ground from under de Montfort's feet. The Earl now appeared as no more than the leader of a personal faction, and his alliance with Llewellyn, by which he recognised the claims of the Welsh prince to territory and independence, compromised his reputation. Out-manœuvred politically by Edward, he had also placed himself at a serious military disadvantage. While Edward and the Marcher barons, as they were called, held the Severn valley de Montfort was penned in, his retreat to the east cut off, and his forces driven back into South Wales. At the beginning of August he made another attempt to cross the river and to join the forces which his son, Simon, was bringing up from the south-east. He succeeded in passing by a ford near Worcester, but his son's forces were trapped by Edward near Kenilworth and routed. Unaware of this disaster, the Earl was caught in turn at Evesham; and here on August 4 the final battle took place.

It was fought in the rain and half-darkness of a sudden storm. The Welsh broke before Edward's heavy horse, and the small group around de Montfort were left to fight desperately until sheer weight of numbers overwhelmed them. De Montfort died a hero on the field. The Marchers massacred large numbers of fugitives and prisoners and mutilated the bodies of the dead. The old King, a pathetic figure, who had been carried by the Earl in all his wanderings, was wounded by his son's followers, and only escaped death by revealing his identity with the cry, "Slay me not! I am Henry of Winchester, your King."

*   *   *   *   *

The great Earl was dead, but his movement lived widespread and deep throughout the nation. The ruthless, haphazard granting away of the confiscated lands after Evesham provoked the bitter opposition of the disinherited. In isolated centres at Kenilworth, Axholme, and Ely the followers of de Montfort held out, and pillaged the countryside in sullen despair. The Government was too weak to reduce them. The whole country suffered from confusion and unrest. The common folk did not conceal their partisanship for de Montfort's cause, and rebels and outlaws beset the roads and forests. Foreign merchants were forbidden in the King's name to come to England because their safety could not be guaranteed. A reversion to feudal independence and consequent anarchy appeared imminent. In these troubles Pope Clement IV and his Legate Ottobon enjoined moderation; and after a sixmonths unsuccessful siege of Kenilworth Edward realised that this was the only policy. There was strong opposition from those who had benefited from the confiscations. The Earl of

Gloucester had been bitterly disillusioned by Edward's repudiation of his promises of reform. Early in 1267 he demanded the expulsion of the aliens and the re-enactment of the Provisions. To enforce his demands he entered London with general acceptance. His action and the influence of the Legate secured pardon and good terms for the disinherited on the compromise principle of "No disinheritance, but repurchase." Late in 1267 the justices were sent out through the country to apply these terms equitably. The records testify to the widespread nature of the disturbances and to the fact that locally the rebellion had been directed against the officials, that it had been supported by the lower clergy, with not a few abbots and priors, and that a considerable number of the country gentry not bound to the baronial side by feudal ties had supported de Montfort.

In the last years of his life, with de Montfort dead and Edward away on Crusade, the feeble King enjoyed comparative peace. More than half a century before, at the age of nine, he had succeeded to the troubled inheritance of his father in the midst of civil war. At times it had seemed as if he would also die in the midst of civil war. At last however the storms were over: he could turn back to the things of beauty that interested him far more than political struggles. The new Abbey of Westminster, a masterpiece of Gothic architecture, was now dedicated; its consecration had long been the dearest object of Henry III's life. And here in the last weeks of 1272 he was buried.

The quiet of these last few years should not lead us to suppose that de Montfort's struggle and the civil war had been in vain. Among the common people he was for many years worshipped as a saint, and miracles were worked at his tomb. Their support could do nothing for him at Evesham, but he had been their friend, he had inspired the hope that he could end or mend the suffering and oppression of the poor; for this they remembered him when they had forgotten his faults. Though a prince among administrators, he suffered as a politician from over-confidence and impatience. He trampled upon vested interests, broke with all traditions, did violence to all forms, and needlessly created suspicion and distrust. Yet de Montfort had lighted a fire never to be quenched in English history. Already in 1267 the Statute of Marlborough had re-enacted the chief of the Provisions of Westminster. Not less important was his influence upon his nephew, Edward, the new King, who was to draw deeply upon the ideas of the man he had slain. In this way de Montfort's purposes survived both the field of Evesham and the reaction which succeeded it, and in Edward I the great Earl found his true heir.

King Edward I

FEW princes had received so thorough an education in the art of rulership as Edward I when at the age of thirty-three his father's death brought him to the crown. He was an experienced leader and a skilful general. He had carried his father on his shoulders; he had grappled with Simon de Montfort, and, while sharing many of his views, had destroyed him. He had learned the art of war by tasting defeat. When at any time in the closing years of King Henry III he could have taken control he had preferred a filial and constitutional patience, all the more remarkable when his own love of order and reform is contrasted with his father's indolence and incapacity and the general misgovernment of the realm.

Of elegant build and lofty stature, a head and shoulders above the height of the ordinary man, with hair always abundant, which, changing from yellow in childhood to black in manhood and snow-white in age, marked the measured progress of his life, his proud brow and regular features were marred only by the drooping left eyelid which had been characteristic of his father. If he stammered he was also eloquent. There is much talk of his limbs. His sinewy, muscular arms were those of a swordsman; his long legs gave him a grip of the saddle, and the nickname of "Longshanks." The Dominican chronicler Nicholas Trivet, by whom these traits are recorded, tells us that the King delighted in war and tournaments, and especially in hawking and hunting. When he chased the stag he did not leave his quarry to the hounds, nor even to the hunting spear; he galloped at breakneck speed to cut the unhappy beast to the ground.

All this was typical of his reign. He presents us with qualities which are a mixture of the administrative capacity of Henry II and the personal prowess and magnanimity of Cœur de Lion. No English king more fully lived up to the maxim he chose for himself: "To each his own." He was animated by a passionate regard for justice and law, as he interpreted them, and for the rights of all groups within the community. Injuries and hostility roused, even to his last breath, a passionate torrent of resistance. But submission, or a generous act, on many occasions earned a swift response and laid the foundation of future friendship.

Edward was in Sicily when his father died, but the greatest magnates in the realm, before the tomb had closed upon the corpse of Henry III, acclaimed him King, with the assent of all men. It was two years before he returned to England for his coronation. In his accession the hereditary and elective principles flowed into a common channel, none asking which was the stronger. His conflicts with Simon de Montfort and the baronage had taught him the need for the monarchy to stand on a national footing. If Simon in his distresses had called in the middle class to aid him alike against Crown and arrogant nobles, the new King of his own free will would use this force in its proper place from the outset. Proportion is the keynote of his greatest years. He saw in the proud, turbulent baronage and a rapacious Church checks upon the royal authority; but he also recognised them as oppressors of the mass of his subjects; and it was by taking into account to a larger extent than had occurred before the interests of the middle class, and the needs of the people as a whole, that he succeeded in producing a broad, well-ordered foundation upon which an active monarchy could function in the general interest. Thus inspired, he sought a national kingship, an extension of his mastery throughout the British Isles, and a preponderant influence in the councils of Europe.

His administrative reforms in England were not such as to give satisfaction to any one of the strong contending forces, but rather to do justice to the whole. If the King resented the fetters which the Charter had imposed upon his grandfather, if he desired to control the growing opulence and claims of the Church, he did not himself assume the recaptured powers, but reposed them upon a broader foundation. When in his conflicts with the recent past he took away privileges which the Church and the baronage had gained he acted always in what was acknowledged to be the interest of the whole community. Throughout all his legislation, however varied its problems, there runs a common purpose: "We must find out what is ours and due to us, and others what is theirs and due to them."

Here was a time of setting in order. The reign is memorable, not for the erection of great new landmarks, but because the beneficial tendencies of the three preceding reigns were extracted from error and confusion and organised and consolidated in a permanent structure. The framework and policies of the nation, which we have seen shaping themselves with many fluctuations, now set and hardened into a form which, surviving the tragedies of the Black Death, the Hundred Years War with France, and the Wars of the Roses, endured for the remainder of the Middle Age, and some of them for longer. In this period we see a knightly and bourgeois stage of society increasingly replacing pure feudalism. The organs of government, land tenure, the military and financial systems, the relations of Church and State, all reach definitions which last nearly till the Tudors.

*   *   *   *   *

The first eighteen years of the reign witnessed an outburst of legislative activity for which there was to be no parallel for centuries. Nearly every year was marked by an important statute. Few of these were original, most were conservative in tone, but their cumulative effect was revolutionary. Edward relied upon his Chancellor, Robert Burnell, Bishop of Bath and Wells, a man of humble birth, who had risen through the royal chancery and household to his bishopric, and until his death in 1292 remained the King's principal adviser. Burnell's whole life had been spent in the service of the Crown; all his policy was devoted to the increase of its power at the expense of feudal privilege and influence. He had not been Chancellor for more than three weeks, after Edward's return to England in 1274, before a searching inquiry into the local administration was begun. Armed with a list of forty questions, commissioners were sent throughout the land to ask what were the rights and possessions of the King, what encroachments had been made upon them, which officials were negligent or corrupt, which sheriffs "for prayer, price, or favour" concealed felonies, neglected their duties, were harsh or bribed. Similar inquests had been made before; none was so thorough or so fertile. "Masterful, but not tyrannical," the King's policy was to respect all rights and overthrow all usurpations.

The First Statute of Westminster in the Parliament of 1275 dealt with the administrative abuses exposed by the commissioners. The Statute of Gloucester in 1278 directed the justices to inquire by writs of *Quo Warranto* into the rights of feudal magnates to administer the law by their own courts and officials within their demesnes, and ordained that those rights should be strictly defined. The main usefulness of the inquiry was to remind the great feudalists that they had duties as well as rights. In 1279 the Statute of Mortmain, *De Religiosis*, forbade gifts of land to be made to the Church, though the practice was allowed to continue under royal licence. In 1285 the Statute of Winchester attacked local disorder, and in the same year was issued the Second Statute of Westminster, *De Donis Conditionalibus,* which strengthened the system of entailed estates. The Third Statute of Westminster, *Quia Emptores,* dealt with land held, not upon condition, but in fee simple. Land held on these terms might be freely alienated, but it was stipulated for the future that the buyer must hold his purchase not from the seller, but from the seller's lord, and by the same feudal services and customs as were attached to the land before the sale. It thus called a halt to the growth of sub-infeudation, and was greatly to the advantage of the Crown, as overlord, whose direct tenants now increased in number.

The purpose of this famous series of laws was essentially conservative, and for a time their enforcement was efficient. But economic pressures were wreaking great changes in the propertied life of England scarcely less deep-cutting than those which had taken place in the political sphere. Land gradually ceased to be the moral sanction upon which national society and defence were based. It became by successive steps a commodity, which could in principle, like wool or mutton, be bought and sold, and which under certain restrictions could be either transferred to new owners by gift or testament or even settled under conditions of entail on future lives which were to be the foundation of a new aristocracy.

Of course only a comparatively small proportion of the land of England came into this active if rude market; but enough of a hitherto solid element was fluid to make a deep stir. In those days, when the greatest princes were pitifully starved in cash, there was already in England one spring of credit bubbling feebly. The Jews had unseen and noiselessly lodged themselves in the social fabric of that fierce age. They were there and they were not there; and from time to time they could be most helpful to high personages in urgent need of money; and to none more than to a king who did not desire to sue Parliament for it. The spectacle of land which could be acquired on rare but definite occasions by anyone with money led the English Jews into a course of shocking imprudence. Land began to pass into the hand of Israel, either by direct sale or more often by mortgage. Enough land came into the market to make both processes advantageous. In a couple of decades the erstwhile feudal lords were conscious that they had parted permanently for fleeting lucre with a portion of the English soil large enough to be noticed.

For some time past there had been growing a wrathful reaction. Small landowners oppressed by mortgages, spendthrift nobles who had made bad bargains, were united in their complaints. Italian moneylenders were now coming into the country, who could be just as useful in times of need to the King as the Jews. Edward saw himself able to conciliate powerful elements and escape from awkward debts, by the simple and well-trodden path of anti-Semitism. The propaganda of ritual murder and other dark tales, the commonplaces of our enlightened age, were at once invoked with general acclaim. The Jews, held up to universal hatred, were pillaged, maltreated, and finally expelled the realm. Exception was made for certain physicians without whose skill persons of consequence might have lacked due attention. Once again the sorrowful, wandering race, stripped to the skin, must seek asylum and begin afresh. To Spain or North Africa the melancholy caravan, now so familiar, must move on. Not until four centuries had elapsed was Oliver Cromwell by furtive contracts with a moneyed Israelite to open again the coasts of England to the enterprise of the Jewish race. It was left to a Calvinist dictator to remove the ban which a Catholic king had imposed. The bankers of Florence and Siena, who had taken the place of the Jews, were in their turn under Edward I's grandson to taste the equities of Christendom.

*   *   *   *   *

Side by side with the large statutory achievements of the reign the King maintained a ceaseless process of administrative reform. His personal inspections were indefatigable. He travelled continually about his domain, holding at every centre strict inquiry into abuses of all kinds, and correcting the excesses of local magnates with a sharp pen and a strong hand. Legality, often pushed into pedantic interpretations, was a weapon upon which he was ever ready to lay his hands. In every direction by tireless perseverance he cleansed the domestic government of the realm, and ousted private interests from spheres which belonged not only to himself but to his people.

Edward I was remarkable among medieval kings for the seriousness with which he regarded the work of administration and good government. It was natural therefore that he should place more reliance upon expert professional help than upon what has been neatly termed "the amateurish assistance of great feudalists staggering under the weight of their own dignity." By the end of the thirteenth century three departments of specialised administration were already at work. One was the Exchequer, established at Westminster, where most of the revenue was received and the accounts kept. The second was the Chancery, a general secretariat responsible for the writing and drafting of innumerable royal charters, writs, and letters. The third was the Wardrobe, with its separate secretariat, the Privy Seal, attached to the ever-moving royal household, and combining financial and secretarial functions, which might range from financing a Continental war to buying a pennyworth of pepper for the royal cook. Burnell was a typical product of the incipient Civil Service. His place after his death was taken by an Exchequer official, Walter Langton, the Treasurer, who, like Burnell, looked upon his see of Lichfield as a reward for skilful service rather than a spiritual office.

Though the most orthodox of Churchmen, Edward I did not escape conflict with the Church. Anxious though he was to pay his dues to God, he had a far livelier sense than his father of what was due to Cæsar, and circumstances more than once forced him to protest. The leader of the Church party was John Pecham, a Franciscan friar, Archbishop of Canterbury from 1279 to 1292. With great courage and skill Pecham defended what he regarded as the just rights of the Church and its independence against the Crown. At the provincial Council held at Reading in 1279 he issued a number of pronouncements which angered the King. One was a canon against plurality of clerical offices, which struck at the principal royal method of rewarding the growing Civil Service. Another was the order that a copy of the Charter, which Edward had sworn to uphold, should be publicly posted in every cathedral and collegiate church. All who produced royal writs to stop cases in ecclesiastical courts and all who violated Magna Carta were threatened with excommunication.

Pecham bowed to Edward's anger and waited his time. In 1281, when another provincial Council was summoned to Lambeth, the King, suspecting mischief, issued writs to its members forbidding them to "hold counsel concerning matters which appertain to our crown, or touch our person, our state, or the state of our Council." Pecham was undeterred. He revived almost verbatim the principal legislation of the Reading Council, prefaced it with an explicit assertion of ecclesiastical liberty, and a month later wrote a remarkable letter to the King, defending his action. "By no human constitution," he wrote, "not even by an oath, can we be bound to ignore laws which rest undoubtedly upon divine authority." "A fine letter" was the marginal comment of an admiring clerk who copied it into the Archbishop's register.

Pecham's action might well have precipitated a crisis comparable to the quarrel between Becket and Henry II, but Edward seems to have quietly ignored the challenge. Royal writs of prohibition continued to be issued. Yet moderation was observed, and in 1286 by a famous writ Edward wisely ordered his itinerant justices to act circumspectly in matters of ecclesiastical jurisdiction, and listed the kinds of case which should be left to Church courts. The dispute thus postponed was to outlive both Archbishop and King.

*   *   *   *   *

At the beginning of the reign relations between England and France were governed by the Treaty of Paris, which the baronial party had concluded in 1259. For more than thirty years peace reigned between the two countries, though often with an undercurrent of hostility. The disputes about the execution of the terms of the treaty and the quarrels between English, Gascon, and French sailors in the Channel, culminating in a great sea-fight off Saint-Mahé in 1293, need never have led to a renewal of war, had not the presence of the English in the South of France been a standing challenge to the pride of the French and a bar to their national integrity. Even when Philip the Fair, the French king, began to seek opportunities of provocation Edward was long-suffering and patient in his attempts to reach a compromise. Finally however the Parlement of Paris declared the Duchy of Gascony forfeit. Philip asked for the token surrender of the principal Gascon fortresses, as a recognition of his legal powers as overlord. Edward complied. But once Philip was in possession he refused to give them up again. Edward now realised that he must either fight or lose his French possessions.

By 1294 the great King had changed much from his early buoyant manhood. After the long stormy years of sustaining his father he had reigned himself for nearly a quarter of a century. Meanwhile his world had changed about him; he had lost his beloved wife Eleanor of Castile, his mother, Eleanor of Provence, and his two eldest infant sons. Burnell was now dead. Wales and Scotland presented grave problems; opposition was beginning to make itself heard and felt. Alone, perplexed and ageing, the King had to face an endless succession of difficulties.

In June 1294 he explained the grounds of the quarrel with the French to what is already called "a Parliament" of magnates in London. His decision to go to war was accepted with approval, as has often been the case in more regularly constituted assemblies.

The war itself had no important features. There were campaigns in Gascony, a good deal of coastal raiding in the Channel, and a prolonged siege by the English of Bordeaux. Any enthusiasm which had been expressed at the outset wore off speedily under the inevitable increases of taxation. All wool and leather, the staple items of the English export trade, were impounded, and could only be redeemed by the payment of a customs duty of 40s. on the sack instead of the half-mark (6s. 8d.) laid down by the Parliament of 1275. In September the clergy, to their great indignation, were ordered to contribute one-half of their revenues. The Dean of St Paul's, who attempted to voice their protests in the King's own terrifying presence, fell down in a fit and died. In November Parliament granted a heavy tax upon all movable property. As the collection proceeded a bitter and sullen discontent spread among all classes. In the winter of 1294 the Welsh revolted, and when the King had suppressed them he returned to find that Scotland had allied itself with France. From 1296 onward war with Scotland was either smouldering or flaring.

After October 1297 the French war degenerated into a series of truces which lasted until 1303. Such conditions involved expense little less than actual fighting. These were years of severe strain, both at home and abroad, and especially with Scotland. Although the King did not hesitate to recall recurrent Parliaments to Westminster and explained the whole situation to them, he did not obtain the support which he needed. Parliament was reluctant to grant the new taxes demanded of it.

The position of the clergy was made more difficult by the publication in 1296 of the Papal Bull *Clericis Laicos,* which forbade the payment of extraordinary taxation without Papal authority. At the autumn Parliament at Bury St Edmunds the clergy, under the leadership of Robert Winchelsea, the new Primate, decided after some hesitation that they were unable to make any contribution. Edward in his anger outlawed them and declared their lay fiefs forfeit. The Archbishop retaliated by threatening with excommunication any who should disobey the Papal Bull. For a time passion ran high, but eventually a calmer mood prevailed. By the following summer the quarrel was allayed, and the Pope by a new Bull, *Etsi de Statu,* had withdrawn his extreme claims.

Edward was the more prepared to come to terms with the Church because opposition had already broken out in another quarter. He proposed to the barons at Salisbury that a number of them should serve in Gascony while he conducted a campaign in Flanders. This was ill received. Humphrey de Bohun, Earl of Hereford and Constable of England, together with the Marshal, Roger Bigod, Earl of Norfolk, declared that their hereditary offices could only be exercised in the King's company. Such excuses deceived nobody. Both the Earls had personal grudges against the King, and—much more important—they voiced the resentment felt by a large number of the barons who for the past twenty years had steadily seen the authority of the Crown increased to their own detriment. The time was ripe for a revival of the baronial opposition which a generation before had defied Edward's father.

For the moment the King ignored the challenge. He pressed forward with his preparations for war, appointed deputies in place of Hereford and Norfolk, and in August sailed for Flanders. The opposition saw in his absence their long-awaited opportunity. They demanded the confirmation of those two instruments, Magna Carta and its extension, the Charter of the Forest, which were the final version of the terms extorted from John, together with six additional articles. By these no tallage or aid was to be imposed in future except with the consent of the community of the realm; corn, wool, and the like must not be impounded against the will of their owners; the clergy and laity of the realm must recover their ancient liberties; the two Earls and their supporters were not to be penalised for their refusal to serve in Gascony; the prelates were to read the Charter aloud in their cathedrals, and to excommunicate all who neglected it. In the autumn the two Earls, backed by armed forces, appeared in London and demanded the acceptance of these proposals. The Regency, unable to resist, submitted. The articles were confirmed, and in November at Ghent the King ratified them reserving however certain financial rights of the Crown.

These were large and surprising concessions. Both King and opposition attached great importance to them, and the King was suspected, perhaps with justice, of trying to withdraw from the promises he had given. Several times the baronial party publicly drew attention to these promises before Parliament, and finally in February 1301 the King was driven by the threats and arguments of a Parliament at Lincoln to grant a new confirmation of both charters and certain further articles in solemn form.

By this crisis and its manner of resolution, two principles had been established from which important consequences flowed. One was that the King had no right to despatch the feudal host wherever he might choose. This limitation sounded the death-knell of the feudal levy, and inexorably led in the following century to the rise of indentured armies serving for pay. The second point of principle now recognised was that the King could not plead "urgent necessity" as a reason for imposing taxation without consent. Other English monarchs as late as the seventeenth century were to make the attempt. But by Edward's failure a precedent had been set up, and a long stride had been taken towards the dependence of the Crown upon Parliamentary grants.

Edward to a greater extent than any of his predecessors had shown himself prepared to govern in the national interest and with some regard for constitutional form. It was thus ironical, and to the King exasperating, that he found the principles he had emphasised applied against himself. The baronial party had not resorted to war; they had acted through the constitutional machinery the King himself had taken so much pains to create. Thereby they had shifted their ground: they spoke no longer as the representatives of the feudal aristocracy, but as the leaders of a national opposition. So the Crown was once again committed solemnly and publicly to the principles of Magna Carta, and the concession was made all the more valuable because remedies of actual recent abuses of the royal prerogative powers had been added to the original charters. Here was a real constitutional advance.

*   *   *   *   *

In their fatal preoccupation with their possessions in France the English kings had neglected the work of extending their rule within the Island of Great Britain. There had been fitful interference both in Wales and Scotland, but the task of keeping the frontiers safe had fallen mainly upon the shoulders of the local Marcher lords. As soon as the Treaty of Paris had brought a generation's respite from Continental adventures it was possible to turn to the urgent problems of internal security. Edward I was the first of the English kings to put the whole weight of the Crown's resources behind the effort of national expansion in the West and North, and to him is due the conquest of the independent areas of Wales and the securing of the Western frontier. He took the first great step towards the unification of the Island. He sought to conquer where the Romans, the Saxons, and the Normans all in their turn had failed. The mountain fastnesses of Wales nursed a hardy and unsubdued race which, under the grandson of the great Llewellyn, had in the previous reign once again made a deep dint upon the politics of England. Edward, as his father's lieutenant, had experience of the Welsh. He had encountered them in war, with questionable success. At the same time he had seen, with disapproving eye, the truculence of the barons of the Welsh Marches, the Mortimers, the Bohuns, and in the South the Clares, with the Gloucester estates, who exploited their military privileges against the interests alike of the Welsh and English people. All assertions of Welsh independence were a vexation to Edward; but scarcely less obnoxious was a system of guarding the frontiers of England by a confederacy of robber barons who had more than once presumed to challenge the authority of the Crown. He resolved, in the name of justice and progress, to subdue the unconquered refuge of petty princes and wild mountaineers in which barbaric freedom had dwelt since remote antiquity, and at the same time to curb the privileges of the Marcher lords.

Edward I, utilising all the local resources which the barons of the Welsh Marches had developed in the chronic strife of many generations, conquered Wales in several years of persistent warfare, coldly and carefully devised, by land and sea. The forces he employed were mainly Welsh levies in his pay, reinforced by regular troops from Gascony and by one of the last appearances of the feudal levy; but above all it was by the terror of winter campaigns that he broke the power of the valiant Ancient Britons. By Edward's Statute of Wales the independent principality came to an end. The land of Llewellyn's Wales was transferred entirely to the King's dominions and organised into the shires of Anglesey, Carnarvon, Merioneth, Cardigan and Camarthen. The king's son Edward, born in Carnarvon, was proclaimed the first English Prince of Wales.

The Welsh wars of Edward reveal to us the process by which the military system of England was transformed from the age-long Saxon and feudal basis of occasional service to that of paid regular troops. We have seen how Alfred the Great suffered repeatedly from the expiry of the period for which the "fyrd" could be called out. Four hundred years had passed, and Norman feudalism still conformed to this basic principle. But how were campaigns to be conducted winter and summer for fifteen months at a time by such methods? How were Continental expeditions to be launched and pursued? Thus for several reigns the principle of scutage had been agreeable alike to barons who did not wish to serve and to sovereigns who preferred a money payment with which to hire full-time soldiers. In the Welsh wars both systems are seen simultaneously at work, but the old is fading. Instead of liege service Governments now required trustworthy mercenaries, and for this purpose money was the solvent.

At the same time a counter-revolution in the balance of warfare was afoot. The mailed cavalry which from the fifth century had eclipsed the ordered ranks of the legion were wearing out their long day. A new type of infantry raised from the common people began to prove its dominating quality. This infantry operated, not by club or sword or spear, or even by hand-flung missiles, but by an archery which, after a long development, concealed from Europe, was very soon to make an astonishing entrance upon the military scene and gain a dramatic ascendancy upon the battlefields of the Continent. Here was a prize taken by the conquerors from their victims. In South Wales the practice of drawing the long-bow had already attained an astonishing efficiency, of which one of the Marcher lords has left a record. One of his knights had been hit by an arrow which pierced not only the skirts of his mailed shirt, but his mailed breeches, his thigh, and the wood of his saddle, and finally struck deep into his horse's flank. This was a new fact in the history of war, which is also a part of the history of civilisation, deserving to be mentioned with the triumph of bronze over flint, or iron over bronze. For the first time infantry possessed a weapon which could penetrate the armour of the clanking age, and which in range and rate of fire was superior to any method ever used before, or ever used again until the coming of the modern rifle. The War Office has among its records a treatise written during the peace after Waterloo by a general officer of long experience in the Napoleonic wars recommending that muskets should be discarded in favour of the long-bow on account of its superior accuracy, rapid discharge, and effective range.

Thus the Welsh war, from two separate points of departure, destroyed the physical basis of feudalism, which had already, in its moral aspect, been outsped and outclassed by the extension and refinement of administration. Even when the conquest was completed the process of holding down the subdued regions required methods which were beyond the compass of feudal barons. Castles of stone, with many elaborations, had indeed long played a conspicuous part in the armoured age. But now the extent of the towered walls must be enlarged not only to contain more numerous garrisons, but to withstand great siege engines, such as trebuchets and mangonels, which had recently been greatly improved, and to hinder attackers from approaching to the foot of the inner walls. Now, moreover, not merely troops of steel-clad warriors will ride forth, spreading random terror in the countryside, but disciplined bodies of infantry, possessing the new power of long-range action, will be led by regular commanders upon a plan prescribed by a central command.

*   *   *   *   *

The great quarrel of Edward's reign was with Scotland. For long years the two kingdoms had dwelt in amity. In the year 1286 Alexander III of Scotland, riding his horse over a cliff in the darkness, left as his heir Margaret his granddaughter, known as the Maid of Norway. The Scottish magnates had been persuaded to recognise this princess of fourteen as his successor. Now the bright project arose that the Maid of Norway should at the same moment succeed to the Scottish throne and marry Edward, the King's son. Thus would be achieved a union of royal families by which the antagonism of England and Scotland might be laid to rest. We can measure the sagacity of the age by the acceptance of this plan. Practically all the ruling forces in England and Scotland were agreed upon it. It was a dream, and it passed as a dream. The Maid of Norway embarked in 1290 upon stormy seas only to die before reaching land, and Scotland was bequeathed the problem of a disputed succession, in the decision of which the English interest must be a heavy factor. The Scottish nobility were allied at many points with the English royal family, and from a dozen claimants, some of them bastards, two men stood clearly forth, John Balliol and Robert Bruce. Bruce asserted his aged father's closeness in relationship to the common royal ancestor; Balliol, a more distant descendant, the rights of primogeniture. But partisanship was evenly balanced.

Since the days of Henry II the English monarchy had intermittently claimed an overlordship of Scotland, based on the still earlier acknowledgment of Saxon overlordship by Scottish kings. King Edward, whose legal abilities were renowned, had already arbitrated in similar circumstances between Aragon and Anjou. He now imposed himself with considerable acceptance as arbitrator in the Scottish succession. Since the alternatives were the splitting of Scotland into rival kingships or a civil war to decide the matter, the Scots were induced to seek Edward's judgment; and he, pursuing all the time a path of strict legality, consented to the task only upon the prior condition of the reaffirmation of his overlordship, betokened by the surrender of certain Scottish castles. The English King discharged his function as arbitrator with extreme propriety. He rejected the temptation presented to him by Scottish baronial intrigues of destroying the integrity of Scotland. He pronounced in 1292 in favour of John Balliol. Later judgments have in no wise impugned the correctness of his decision. But, having regard to the deep division in Scotland, and the strong elements which adhered to the Bruce claim, John Balliol inevitably became not merely his choice, but his puppet. So thought King Edward I, and plumed himself upon a just and at the same time highly profitable decision. He had confirmed his overlordship of Scotland. He had nominated its king, who stood himself in his own land upon a narrow margin. But the national feeling of Scotland was pent up behind these barriers of legal affirmation. In their distress the Scottish baronage accepted King Edward's award, but they also furnished the new King John with an authoritative council of twelve great lords to overawe him and look after the rights of Scotland. Thus King Edward saw with disgust that all his fair-seeming success left him still confronted with the integrity of Scottish nationhood, with an independent and not a subject Government, and with a hostile rather than a submissive nation.

At this very moment the same argument of overlordship was pressed upon him by the formidable French king, Philip IV. Here Edward was the vassal, proudly defending feudal interests, and the French suzerain had the lawful advantage. Moreover, if England was stronger than Scotland, France was in armed power superior to England. This double conflict imposed a strain upon the financial and military resources of the English monarchy which it could by no means meet. The rest of Edward's reign was spent in a twofold struggle North and South, for the sake of which he had to tax his subjects beyond all endurance. He journeyed energetically to and fro between Flanders and the Scottish Lowlands. He racked the land for money. Nothing else mattered; and the embryonic Parliamentary system profited vastly by the repeated concessions he made in the hope of carrying opinion with him. He confirmed the bulk of the reforms wrung from John. With some exceptions among the great lords, the nation was with him in both of his external efforts, but though time and again it complied with his demands it was not reconciled to the crushing burden. Thus we see the wise law-giver, the thrifty scrutineer of English finances, the administrative reformer, forced to drive his people beyond their strength, and in this process to rouse oppositions which darkened his life and clouded his fame.

To resist Edward the Scots allied themselves with the French. Since Edward was at war with France he regarded this as an act of hostility. He summoned Balliol to meet him at Berwick. The Scottish nobles refused to allow their king to go, and from this moment war began. Edward struck with ruthless severity. He advanced on Berwick. The city, then the great emporium of Northern trade, was unprepared, after a hundred years of peace, to resist attack. Palisades were hurriedly raised, the citizens seized such weapons as were at hand. The English army, with hardly any loss, trampled down these improvised defences, and Berwick was delivered to a sack and slaughter which shocked even those barbaric times. Thousands were slain. The most determined resistance came from thirty Flemish merchants who held their depot, called the Red Hall, until it was burnt down. Berwick sank in a few hours from one of the active centres of European commerce to the minor seaport which exists to-day.

This act of terror quelled the resistance of the ruling classes in Scotland. Perth, Stirling, Edinburgh, yielded themselves to the King's march. Here we see how Edward I anticipated the teachings of Machiavelli; for to the frightfulness of Berwick succeeded a most gracious, forgiving spirit which welcomed and made easy submission in every form. Balliol surrendered his throne and Scotland was brought under English administration. But, as in Wales, the conqueror introduced not only an alien rule, but law and order, all of which were equally unpopular. The governing classes of Scotland had conspicuously failed, and Edward might flatter himself that all was over. It was only beginning. It has often been said that Joan of Arc first raised the standard of nationalism in the Western world. But over a century before she appeared an outlaw knight, William Wallace, arising from the recesses of South-West Scotland which had been his refuge, embodied, commanded, and led to

victory the Scottish nation. Edward, warring in France with
piebald fortune, was forced to listen to tales of ceaseless inroads and forays against his royal peace in Scotland, hitherto
deemed so sure. Wallace had behind him the spirit of a race
as stern and as resolute as any bred among men. He added
military gifts of a high order. Out of an unorganised mass of
valiant fighting men he forged, in spite of cruel poverty and
primitive administration, a stubborn, indomitable army, ready
to fight at any odds and mock defeat. The structure of this
army is curious. Every four men had a fifth man as leader;
every nine men a tenth; every nineteen men a twentieth, and so
on to every thousand; and it was agreed that the penalty for
disobedience to the leader of any unit was death. Thus from
the ground does freedom raise itself unconquerable.

Warenne, Earl of Surrey, was Edward's commander in the
North. When the depredations of the Scottish rebels had become intolerable he advanced at the head of strong forces
upon Stirling. At Stirling Bridge, near the Abbey of Cambus-
kenneth, in September 1297, he found himself in the presence
of Wallace's army. Many Scotsmen were in the English service. One of these warned him of the dangers of trying to deploy
beyond the long, narrow bridge and causeway which spanned
the river. This knight pleaded calculations worthy of a modern
staff officer. It would take eleven hours to move the army
across the bridge, and what would happen, he asked, if the
vanguard were attacked before the passage was completed? He
spoke of a ford higher up, by which at least a flanking force
could cross. But Earl Warenne would have none of these
things. Wallace watched with measuring eye the accumulation
of the English troops across the bridge, and at the right
moment hurled his full force upon them, seized the bridgehead, and slaughtered the vanguard of five thousand men.
Warenne evacuated the greater part of Scotland. His fortress

garrisons were reduced one after the other. The English could barely hold the line of the Tweed.

It was beyond the compass of King Edward's resources to wage war with France and face the hideous struggle with Scotland at the same time. He sought at all costs to concentrate on the peril nearest home. He entered upon a long series of negotiations with the French King which were covered by truces repeatedly renewed, and reached a final Treaty of Paris in 1303. Though the formal peace was delayed for some years, it was in fact sealed in 1294 by the arrangement of a marriage between Edward and Philip's sister, the young Princess Margaret, and also by the betrothal of Edward's son and heir, Edward of Carnarvon, to Philip's daughter Isabella. This dual alliance of blood brought the French war to an effective close in 1297, although through Papal complications neither the peace nor the King's marriage were finally and formally confirmed until 1299. By these diplomatic arrangements Edward from the end of 1297 onwards was able to concentrate his strength against the Scots.

Wallace was now the ruler of Scotland, and the war was without truce or mercy. A hated English official, a tax-gatherer, had fallen at the bridge. His skin, cut into suitable strips, covered Wallace's sword-belt for the future. Edward, forced to quit his campaign in France, hastened to the scene of disaster, and with the whole feudal levy of England advanced against the Scots. The Battle of Falkirk in 1298, which he conducted in person, bears a sharp contrast to Stirling Bridge. Wallace, now at the head of stronger powers, accepted battle in a withdrawn defensive position. He had few cavalry and few archers; but his confidence lay in the solid "schiltrons" (or circles) of spearmen, who were invincible except by actual physical destruction. The armoured cavalry of the English vanguard were hurled back with severe losses from the spear-points. But

Edward, bringing up his Welsh archers in the intervals between horsemen of the second line, concentrated a hail of
arrows upon particular points in the Scottish schiltrons, so that
there were more dead and wounded than living men in these
places. Into the gaps and over the carcasses the knighthood of
England forced their way. Once the Scottish order was broken
the spearmen were quickly massacred. The slaughter ended
only in the depths of the woods, and Wallace and the Scottish
army were once again fugitives, hunted as rebels, starving, suffering the worst of human privations, but still in arms.

The Scots were unconquerable foes. It was not until 1305
that Wallace was captured, tried with full ceremonial in Westminster Hall, and hanged, drawn, and quartered at Tyburn.
But the Scottish war was one in which, as a chronicler said,
"every winter undid every summer's work." Wallace was to
pass the torch to Robert Bruce.

*　　*　　*　　*　　*

In the closing years of Edward's life he appears as a lonely
and wrathful old man. A new generation had grown up around
him with whom he had slight acquaintance and less sympathy.
Queen Margaret was young enough to be his daughter, and
sided often with her step-children against their father. Few
dared to oppose the old King, but he had little love or respect
in his family circle.

With Robert Bruce, grandson of the claimant of 1290, who
had won his way partly by right of birth, but also by hard
measures, the war in Scotland flared again. He met the chief
Scotsman who represented the English interest in the solemn
sanctuary of the church in the Border town of Dumfries. The
two leaders were closeted together. Presently Bruce emerged
alone, and said to his followers, "I doubt me I have killed the
Red Comyn." Whereat his chief supporter, muttering "I'se
mak' siccar!" re-entered the sacred edifice. A new champion

of this grand Northern race had thus appeared in arms. King Edward was old, but his will-power was unbroken. When the news came south to Winchester, where he held his Court, that Bruce had been crowned at Scone his fury was terrible to behold. He launched a campaign in the summer of 1306 in which Bruce was defeated and driven to take refuge on Rathlin island, off the coast of Antrim. Here, according to the tale, Bruce was heartened by the persistent efforts of the most celebrated spider known to history. Next spring he returned to Scotland. Edward was now too ill to march or ride. Like the Emperor Severus a thousand years before, he was carried in a litter against this stern people, and like him he died upon the road. His last thoughts were on Scotland and on the Holy Land. He conjured his son to carry his bones in the van of the army which should finally bring Scotland to obedience, and to send his heart to Palestine with a band of a hundred knights to help recover the Sacred City. Neither wish was fulfilled by his futile and unworthy heir.

*   *   *   *   *

Edward I was the last great figure in the formative period of English law. His statutes, which settled questions of public order, assigned limits to the powers of the seigneurial courts, and restrained the sprawling and luxurious growth of judge-made law, laid down principles that remained fundamental to the law of property until the mid-nineteenth century. By these great enactments necessary bounds were fixed to the freedom of the Common Law which, without conflicting with its basic principles or breaking with the past, imparted to it its final form.

In the constitutional sphere the work of Edward I was not less durable. He had made Parliament—that is to say, certain selected magnates and representatives of the shires and boroughs—the associate of the Crown, in place of the old Court of Tenants-in-Chief. By the end of his reign this conception had been established. At first it lacked substance; only gradually did it take on flesh and blood. But between the beginning and the end of Edward's reign the decisive impulse was given. At the beginning anything or nothing might have come out of the experiments of his father's troubled time. By the end it was fairly settled in the customs and traditions of England that "sovereignty," to use a term which Edward would hardly have understood, would henceforward reside not in the Crown only, nor in the Crown and Council of the Barons, but in the Crown in Parliament.

Dark constitutional problems loomed in the future. The boundary between the powers of Parliament and those of the Crown was as yet very vaguely drawn. A statute, it was quickly accepted, was a law enacted by the King in Parliament, and could only be repealed with the consent of Parliament itself. But Parliament was still in its infancy. The initiative in the work of government still rested with the King, and necessarily he retained many powers whose limits were undefined. Did royal ordinances, made in the Privy Council on the King's sole authority, have the validity of law? Could the King in particular cases override a statute on the plea of public or royal expediency? In a clash between the powers of King and Parliament who was to say on which side right lay? Inevitably, as Parliament grew to a fuller stature, these questions would be asked; but for a final answer they were to wait until Stuart kings sat on the English throne.

Nevertheless the foundations of a strong national monarchy for a United Kingdom and of a Parliamentary Constitution had been laid. Their continuous development and success depended upon the King's immediate successor. Idle weaklings, dreamers, and adventurous boys disrupted the nascent unity of the Island. Long years of civil war, and despotism in reaction from anarchy, marred and delayed the development of its institutions. But when the traveller gazes upon the plain marble tomb at Westminster on which is inscribed, "Here lies Edward I, the Hammer of the Scots. Keep troth," he stands before the resting-place of a master-builder of British life, character, and fame.

Bannockburn

EDWARD II's reign may fairly be regarded as a melancholy appendix to his father's and the prelude to his son's. The force and fame which Edward I had gathered in his youth and prime cast their shield over the decline of his later years. We have seen him in his strength; we must see him in his weakness. Men do not live for ever, and in his final phase the bold warrior who had struck down Simon de Montfort, who had reduced the Welsh to obedience, and even discipline, who was "the Hammer of the Scots," who had laid the foundations of Parliament, who had earned the proud title of "the English Justinian" by his laws, was fighting a losing battle with a singularly narrow, embittered, and increasingly class-conscious nobility. This battle old age and death forced him to confide to his embarrassed son, who proved incapable of winning it.

A strong, capable King had with difficulty upborne the load. He was succeeded by a perverted weakling, of whom some amiable traits are recorded. Marlowe in his tragedy puts in his mouth at the moment of his death some fine lines:

> Tell Isabel the Queen I looked not thus
> When for her sake I ran at tilt in France,
> And there unhorsed the Duke of Cleremont.

Of this tribute history did not deprive the unfortunate King; but the available records say little of war or tournaments and dwell rather upon Edward's interest in thatching and ditching and other serviceable arts. He was addicted to rowing, swimming, and baths. He carried his friendship for his advisers beyond dignity and decency. This was a reign which by its weakness contributed in the long run to English strength. The ruler was gone, the rod was broken, and the forces of English nationhood, already alive and conscious under the old King, resumed their march at a quicker and more vehement step. In default of a dominating Parliamentary institution, the Curia Regis, as we have seen, seemed to be the centre from which the business of government could be controlled. On the death of Edward I the barons succeeded in gaining control of this mixed body of powerful magnates and competent Household officials. They set up a committee called "the Lords Ordainers," who represented the baronial and ecclesiastical interests of the State. Scotland and France remained the external problems confronting these new masters of government, but their first anger was directed upon the favourite of the King. Piers Gaveston, a young, handsome Gascon, enjoyed his fullest confidence. His decisions made or marred. There was a temper which would submit to the rule of a King, but would not tolerate the pretensions of his personal cronies. The barons' party attacked Piers Gaveston. Edward and his favourite tried to stave off opposition by harrying the Scots. They failed, and in 1311 Gaveston was exiled to Flanders. Thence he was so imprudent as to return, in defiance of the Lords Ordainers. Compelling him to take refuge in the North, they pursued him, not so much by war as by a process of establishing their authority, occupying castles, controlling the courts, and giving to the armed forces orders which were obeyed. Besieged in the castle of Scarborough, Gaveston made terms with his foes. His life was to be spared; and on this they took him under guard. But other nobles, led by the Earl of Warwick, one of the foremost Ordainers, who had not been present at the agreement of Scarborough, violated these conditions. They overpowered the escort, seized the favourite at Deddington in Oxfordshire, and hewed off his head on Blacklow Hill, near Warwick.

In spite of these successes by the Ordainers royal power remained formidable. Edward was still in control of Government, although he was under their restraint. Troubles in France and war in Scotland confronted him. To wipe out his setbacks at home he resolved upon the conquest of the Northern kingdom. A general levy of the whole power of England was set on foot to beat the Scots. A great army crossed the Tweed in the summer of 1314. Twenty-five thousand men, hard to gather, harder still to feed in those days, with at least three thousand armoured knights and men-at-arms, moved against the Scottish host under the nominal but none the less baffling command of Edward II. The new champion of Scotland, Robert the Bruce, now faced the vengeance of England. The Scottish army, of perhaps ten thousand men, was composed, as at Falkirk, mainly of the hard, unyielding spearmen who feared nought and, once set in position, had to be killed. But Bruce had pondered deeply upon the impotence of pikemen, however faithful, if exposed to the alternations of an arrow shower and an armoured charge. He therefore, with a foresight and skill which proves his military quality, took three precautions. First, he chose a position where his flanks were secured by impenetrable woods; secondly, he dug upon his front a large number of small round holes or "pottes," afterwards to be imitated by the archers at Crécy, and covered them with branches and turfs as a trap for charging cavalry; thirdly, he kept in his own hand his small but highly trained force of mounted knights to break up any attempt at planting archers upon his flank to derange his schiltrons. These dispositions made, he awaited the English onslaught.

The English army was so large that it took three days to

close up from rear to front. The ground available for deployment was little more than two thousand yards. While the host was massing itself opposite the Scottish position an incident took place. An English knight, Henry de Bohun, pushed his way forward at the head of a force of Welsh infantry to try by a surprise move to relieve Stirling Castle which was in English hands. Bruce arrived just in time to throw himself and some of his men between them and the castle walls. Bohun charged him in single combat. Bruce, though not mounted on his heavy war-horse, awaited his onset upon a well-trained hack, and, striking aside the English lance with his battle-axe, slew Bohun at a single blow before the eyes of all.

On the morning of June 24 the English advanced, and a dense wave of steel-clad horsemen descended the slope, splashed and scrambled through the Bannock Burn, and charged uphill upon the schiltrons. Though much disordered by the "pottes," they came to deadly grip with the Scottish spearmen. "And when the two hosts so came together and the great steeds of the knights dashed into the Scottish pikes as into a thick wood there rose a great and horrible crash from rending lances and dying horses, and there they stood locked together for a space." As neither side would withdraw the struggle was prolonged and covered the whole front. The strong corps of archers could not intervene. When they shot their arrows into the air, as William had done at Hastings, they hit more of their own men than of the Scottish infantry. At length a detachment of archers was brought round the Scottish left flank. But for this Bruce had made effective provision. His small cavalry force charged them with the utmost promptitude, and drove them back into the great mass waiting to engage, and now already showing signs of disorder. Continuous reinforcements streamed forward towards the English fighting line. Confusion steadily increased. At length the appearance on the hills to the English right of the camp-followers of Bruce's army, waving flags and raising loud cries, was sufficient to induce a general retreat, which the King himself, with his numerous personal guards, was not slow to head. The retreat speedily became a rout. The Scottish schiltrons hurled themselves forward down the slope, inflicting immense carnage upon the English even before they could re-cross the Bannock Burn. No more grievous slaughter of English chivalry ever took place in a single day. Even Towton in the Wars of the Roses was less destructive. The Scots claimed to have slain or captured thirty thousand men, more than the whole English army, but their feat in virtually destroying an army of cavalry and archers mainly by the agency of spearmen must nevertheless be deemed a prodigy of war.

*　　*　　*　　*　　*

In the long story of a nation we often see that capable rulers by their very virtues sow the seeds of future evil and weak or degenerate princes open the pathway of progress. At this time the unending struggle for power had entered upon new ground. We have traced the ever-growing influence, and at times authority, of the permanent officials of the royal Household. This became more noticeable, and therefore more obnoxious, when the sovereign was evidently in their hands, or not capable of overtopping them in policy or personality. The feudal baronage had striven successfully against kings. They now saw in the royal officials agents who stood in their way, yet at the same time were obviously indispensable to the widening aspects of national life. They could no more contemplate the abolition of these officials than their ancestors the destruction of the monarchy. The whole tendency of their movement was therefore in this generation to acquire control of an invaluable machine. They sought to achieve in the fourteenth century that power of choosing, or at least of supervis-

THE BIRTH OF BRITAIN

ing, the appointments to the key offices of the Household which the Whig nobility under the house of Hanover actually won.

The Lords Ordainers, as we have seen, had control of the Curia Regis; but they soon found that many of the essentials of power still eluded their grasp. In those days the King was expected to rule as well as to reign. The King's sign manual, the seal affixed to a document, a writ or warrant issued by a particular officer, were the facts upon which the courts pronounced, soldiers marched, and executioners discharged their functions. One of the main charges brought against Edward II at his deposition was that he had failed in his task of government. From early in his reign he left too much to his Household officials. To the Lords Ordainers it appeared that the high control of government had withdrawn itself from the Curia Regis, into an inner citadel described as "the King's Wardrobe." There was the King, in his Wardrobe, with his favourites and indispensable functionaries, settling a variety of matters from the purchase of the royal hose to the waging of a Continental war. Outside this select, secluded circle the rugged, arrogant, virile barons prowled morosely. The process was exasperating; like climbing a hill where always a new summit appears. Nor must we suppose that such experiences were reserved for this distant age alone. It is the nature of supreme executive power to withdraw itself into the smallest compass; and without such contraction there is no executive power. But when this exclusionary process was tainted by unnatural vice and stained by shameful defeat in the field it was clear that those who beat upon the doors had found a prosperous occasion, especially since many of the Ordainers had prudently absented themselves from the Bannockburn campaign and could thus place all the blame for its disastrous outcome upon the King.

The forces were not unequally balanced. To do violence to the sacred person of the King was an awful crime. The Church by its whole structure and tradition depended upon him. A haughty, self-interested aristocracy must remember that in most parts of the country the common people, among whom bills and bows were plentiful, had looked since the days of the Conqueror to the Crown as their protector against baronial oppression. Above all, law and custom weighed heavily with all classes, rich and poor alike, when every district had a life of its own and very few lights burned after sundown. The barons might have a blasting case against the King at Westminster, but if he appeared in Shropshire or Westmorland with his handful of guards and the royal insignia he could tell his own tale, and men, both knight and archer, would rally to him.

In this equipoise Parliament became of serious importance to the contending interests. Here at least was the only place where the case for or against the conduct of the central executive could be tried before something that resembled, however imperfectly, the nation. Thus we see in this ill-starred reign both sides operating in and through Parliament, and in this process enhancing its power. Parliament was called together no fewer than twenty-five times under King Edward II. It had no share in the initiation or control of policy. It was of course distracted by royal and baronial intrigue. Many of its knights and burgesses were but the creatures of one faction or the other. Nevertheless it could be made to throw its weight in a decisive manner from time to time. This therefore was a period highly favourable to the growth of forces in the realm which were to become inherently different in character from either the Crown or the barons.

Thomas of Lancaster, nephew to Edward I, was the forefront of the baronial opposition. Little is known to his credit. He had long been engaged in treasonable practices with the

Scots. As leader of the barons he had pursued Gaveston to his death, and, although not actually responsible for the treachery which led to his execution, he bore henceforward upon his shoulders the deepest hate of which Edward II's nature was capable. Into the hands of Thomas and his fellow Ordainers Edward was now thrown by the disaster of Bannockburn, and Thomas for a while became the most important man in the land. Within a few years however the moderates among the Ordainers became so disgusted with Lancaster's incompetence and with the weakness into which the process of Government had sunk that they joined with the royalists to edge him from power. The victory of this middle party, headed by the Earl of Pembroke, did not please the King. Aiming to be more efficient than Lancaster, Pembroke and his friends tried to enforce the Ordinances more effectively, and carried out a great reform of the royal Household.

Edward, for his part, began to build up a royalist party, at the head of which were the Despensers, father and son, both named Hugh. These belonged to the nobility, and their power lay on the Welsh border. By a fortunate marriage with the noble house of Clare, and by the favour of the King, they rose precariously amid the jealousies of the English baronage to the main direction of affairs. Against both of them the hatreds grew, because of their self-seeking and the King's infatuation with the younger man. They were especially unpopular among the Marcher lords, who were disturbed by their restless ambitions in South Wales. In 1321 the Welsh Marcher lords and the Lancastrian party joined hands with intent to procure the exile of the Despensers. Edward soon recalled them, and for once showed energy and resolution. By speed of movement he defeated first the Marcher lords and then the Northern barons under Lancaster at Boroughbridge in Yorkshire in the next year. Lancaster was beheaded by the King. But by some perversity of popular sentiment miracles were reported at his grave, and his execution was adjudged by many of his contemporaries to have made him a martyr to royal oppression.

The Despensers and their King now seemed to have attained a height of power. But a tragedy with every feature of classical ruthlessness was to follow. One of the chief Marcher lords, Roger Mortimer, though captured by the King, contrived to escape to France. In 1324 Charles IV of France took advantage of a dispute in Gascony to seize the duchy, except for a coastal strip. Edward's wife, Isabella, "the she-wolf of France," who was disgusted by his passion for Hugh Despenser, suggested that she should go over to France to negotiate with her brother Charles about the restoration of Gascony. There she became the lover and confederate of the exiled Mortimer. She now hit on the stroke of having her son, Prince Edward, sent over from England to do homage for Gascony. As soon as the fourteen-year-old prince, who as heir to the throne could be used to legitimise opposition to King Edward, was in her possession she and Mortimer staged an invasion of England at the head of a large band of exiles. So unpopular and precarious was Edward's Government that Isabella's triumph was swift and complete, and she and Mortimer were emboldened to depose him. The end was a holocaust. In the furious rage which in these days led all who swayed the Government of England to a bloody fate the Despensers were seized and hanged. For the King a more terrible death was reserved. He was imprisoned in Berkeley Castle, and there by hideous methods, which left no mark upon his skin, was slaughtered. His screams as his bowels were burnt out by red-hot irons passed into his body were heard outside the prison walls, and awoke grim echoes which were long unstilled.

Scotland and Ireland

THE failures of the reign of Edward II had permanent effects on the unity of the British Isles. Bannockburn ended the possibility of uniting the English and Scottish Crowns by force. Across the Irish Sea the dream of a consolidated Anglo-Norman Ireland also proved vain. Centuries could scarcely break down the barrier that the ruthless Scottish wars had raised between North and South Britain. From Edward I's onslaught on Berwick, in 1296, the armed struggle had raged for twenty-seven years. It was not until 1323 that Robert the Bruce at last obliged Edward II to come to terms. Even then Bruce was not formally recognised as King of Scots. This title, and full independence for his country, he gained by the Treaty of Northampton signed in 1328 after Edward's murder. A year later the saviour of Scotland was dead.

One of the most famous stories of medieval chivalry tells how Sir James, the "Black" Douglas, for twenty years the faithful sword-arm of the Bruce, took his master's heart to be buried in the Holy Land, and how, touching at a Spanish port, he responded to a sudden call of chivalry and joined the hard-pressed Christians in battle with the Moors. Charging the heathen host, he threw far into the *mêlée* the silver casket containing the heart of Bruce. "Forward, brave heart, as thou wert wont. Douglas will follow thee or die!" He was killed in the moment of victory. So Froissart tells the story in prose and Aytoun in stirring verse, and so, in every generation, Scottish children have been thrilled by the story of "the Good Lord James."

While the Bruce had lived his great prestige, and the loyalty of his lieutenants, served as a substitute for the institutions and traditions that united England. His death left the throne to his son, David II, a child of six, and there ensued one of those disastrous minorities that were the curse of Scotland. The authority of the Scottish kings had often been challenged by the great magnates of the Lowlands and by the Highland chiefs. To this source of weakness were now added others. The kin of the "Red" Comyn, never forgiving his assassination by Bruce, were always ready to lend themselves to civil strife. And the barons who had supported the cause of Balliol, and lost their Scottish lands to the followers of Bruce, constantly dreamt of regaining them with English help. David II reigned for forty-two years, but no less than eighteen of them were spent outside his kingdom. For a long spell during the wars of his Regents with the Balliol factions he was a refugee in France. On his return he showed none of his father's talents. Loyalty to France led him to invade England. In 1346, the year of Crécy, he was defeated and captured at Neville's Cross in County Durham. Eleven years of imprisonment followed before he was ransomed for a sum that sorely taxed Scotland. David II was succeeded by his nephew Robert the High Steward, first king of a line destined to melancholy fame.

For many generations the Stuarts, as they came euphoniously to be called, had held the hereditary office from which they took their name. Their claim to the throne was legitimate but they failed to command the undivided loyalty of the Scots. The first two Stuarts, Robert II and Robert III, were both elderly men of no marked strength of character. The affairs of the kingdom rested largely in the hands of the magnates, whether assembled in the King's Council or dispersed about their estates. For the rest of the fourteenth century, and throughout most of the fifteenth, Scotland was too deeply divided to threaten England, or be of much help to her old ally France. A united England, free from French wars, might have taken advantage of the situation, but by the mid-fifteenth century England was herself tormented by the Wars of the Roses.

Union of the Crowns was the obvious and natural solution. But after the English attempts, spread over several reigns, had failed to impose union by force, the re-invigorated pride of Scotland offered an insurmountable obstacle. Hatred of the English was the mark of a good Scot. Though discontented nobles might accept English help and English pay, the common people were resolute in their refusal to bow to English rule in any form. The memory of Bannockburn kept a series of notable defeats at the hands of the English from breeding despair or thought of surrender.

It is convenient to pursue Scottish history further at this stage. Destiny was adverse to the House of Stuart. Dogged by calamity, they could not create enduring institutions comparable to those by whose aid the great Plantagenets tamed English feudalism. King Robert III sent his son later James I to be schooled in France. Off Flamborough Head in 1406 he was captured by the English, and taken prisoner to London. He was twelve years old. In the following month, King Robert died, and for eighteen years Scotland had no monarch. The English government was at last prepared to let King James I be ransomed and return to his country. Captivity had not daunted James. He had conceived a justfiable admiration for the English monarch's position and powers, and on his arrival in Scotland he asserted his sovereignty with vigour. During his effective reign of thirteen years he ruthlessly disciplined the Scottish baronage. It was not an experience they enjoyed. James put down his cousins of the House of Albany, whose family had been regents during his absence. He quelled the pretensions to independence of the powerful Lord of the Isles, who controlled much of the Northern mainland as well as the Hebrides. All this was accompanied by executions and widespread confiscations of great estates. At length a party of infuriated lords decided on revenge; in 1437 they found the opportunity to slay James by the sword. So died, and before his task had been accomplished, one of the most forceful of Scottish kings.

The throne once more descended to a child, James II, aged seven. After the inevitable tumults of his minority the boy grew into a popular and vigorous ruler. He had need of his gifts for the "Black" Douglases, descendants of Bruce's faithful knight, had now become over-mighty subjects and constituted a heavy menace to the Crown. Enriched by estates confiscated from Balliol supporters, they were the masters of South-West Scotland. Large territories in the East were held by their kin, the "Red" Douglases, and they also made agile use of their alliances with the clans and confederacies of the North. Moreover, they had a claim, acceptable in the eyes of some, to the throne itself.

For more than a century the Douglases had been among the foremost champions of Scotland; one of them had been the hero of the Battle of Otterburn, celebrated in the ballad of Chevy Chase. Their continual intrigues, both at home and at the English court, with which they were in touch, incensed the young and high-spirited King. In 1452, when he had not long turned twenty-one, James invited the "Black" Douglas to Stirling. Under a safe-conduct he came; and there the King himself in passion stabbed him with his own hand. The King's attendants finished his life. But to cut down the chief of the Douglases was not to stamp out the family. James found himself sorely beset by the Douglas's younger brother and by his kin. Only in 1455 did he finally succeed, by burning their castles and ravaging their lands, in driving the leading Douglases over the

Border. In England they survived for many years to vex the House of Stuart with plots and conspiracies, abetted by the English Crown.

James II was now at the height of his power, but fortune seldom favoured the House of Stuart for very long. Taking advantage of the English civil wars, James in 1460 set siege to the castle of Roxburgh, a fortress that had remained in English hands. One of his special interests was cannon and fire-power. While inspecting one of his primitive siege-guns, the piece exploded, and he was killed by a flying fragment. James II was then in his thirtieth year. For the fourth time in little more than a century a minor inherited the Scottish Crown. James III was a boy of nine. As he grew up, he showed some amiable qualities; he enjoyed music and took an interest in architecture. But he failed to inherit the capacity for rule displayed by his two predecessors. His reign, which lasted into Tudor times, was much occupied by civil wars and disorders, and its most notable achievement was the rounding off of Scotland's territories by the acquisition, in lieu of a dowry, of Orkney and Shetland from the King of Denmark whose daughter James married.

*   *   *   *   *

The disunity of the kingdom, fostered by English policy and perpetuated by the tragedies that befell the Scottish sovereigns, was not the only source of Scotland's weakness. The land was divided, in race, in speech, and in culture. The rift between Highlands and Lowlands was more than a geographical distinction. The Lowlands formed part of the feudal world, and, except in the South-West, in Galloway, English was spoken. The Highlands preserved a social order much older than feudalism. In the Lowlands the King of Scots was a feudal magnate, in the Highlands he was the chief of a loose federation of clans. He had, it is true, the notable advantage of blood kinship both with the new Anglo-Norman nobility and with the ancient Celtic kings. The Bruces were undoubted descendants of the family of the first King of Scots in the ninth century, Kenneth MacAlpin, as well as of Alfred the Great; the Stuarts claimed, with some plausibility, to be the descendants of Macbeth's contemporary, Banquo. The lustre of a divine antiquity illumined princes whose pedigree ran back into the Celtic twilight of Irish heroic legend. For all Scots, Lowland and Highland alike, the royal house had a sanctity which commanded reverence through periods when obedience and even loyalty were lacking; and much was excused those in whom royal blood ran.

But reverence was not an effective instrument of government. The Scottish Estates did not create the means of fusion of classes that were provided by the English Parliament. In law and fact feudal authority remained far stronger than in England. The King's justice was excluded from a great part of Scottish life, and many of his judges were ineffective competitors with the feudal system. There was no equivalent of the Justice of the Peace or of the Plantagenet Justices in Eyre.

Over much of the kingdom feudal justice itself fought a doubtful battle with the more ancient clan law. The Highland chiefs might formally owe their lands and power to the Crown and be classified as feudal tenants-in-chief, but their real authority rested on the allegiance of their clansmen. Some clan chiefs, like the great house of Gordon, in the Highlands, were also feudal magnates in the neighbouring Lowlands. In the West, the rising house of Campbell played either rôle as it suited them. They were to exercise great influence in the years to come.

Meanwhile the Scots peasant farmer and the thrifty burgess, throughout these two hundred years of political strife, pursued their ways and built up the country's real strength, in spite of the numerous disputes among their lords and masters. The

Church devoted itself to its healing mission, and many good bishops and divines adorn the annals of medieval Scotland. In the fifteenth century three Scots universities were founded, St. Andrew's, Glasgow and Aberdeen—one more than England had until the nineteenth century.

* * * * *

Historians of the English-speaking peoples have been baffled by medieval Ireland. Here in the westernmost of the British Isles dwelt one of the oldest Christian communities in Europe. It was distinguished by missionary endeavours and monkish scholarship while England was still a battlefield for heathen Germanic invaders. Until the twelfth century however Ireland had never developed the binding feudal institutions of state that were gradually evolving elsewhere. A loose federation of Gaelic-speaking rural principalities was dominated by a small group of clan patriarchs who called themselves "kings." Over all lay the shadowy authority of the High King of Tara, which was not a capital city but a sacred hill surmounted by earthworks of great antiquity. Until about the year 1000 the High King was generally a member of the powerful northern family of O'Neill. The High Kings exercised no real central authority, except as the final arbiters of genealogical disputes, and there were no towns of Irish founding from which government power could radiate.

When the long, sorrowful story began of English intervention in Ireland, the country had already endured the shock and torment of Scandinavian invasion. But although impoverished by the ravages of the Norsemen, and its accepted order of things greatly disturbed, Ireland was not remade. It was the Norsemen who built the first towns—Dublin, Waterford, Limerick and Cork. The High Kingship had been in dispute since the great Brian Boru, much lamented in song, had broken the

O'Neill succession, only himself to be killed in his victory over the Danes at Clontarf in 1014. A century and a half later, one of his disputing successors, the King of Leinster, took refuge at the court of Henry II in Aquitaine. He secured permission to raise help for his cause from among Henry's Anglo-Norman knights. It was a fateful decision for Ireland. In 1169 there arrived in the country the first progenitors of the Anglo-Norman ascendancy.

Led by Richard de Clare, Earl of Pembroke and known as "Strongbow," the invaders were as much Welsh as Norman; and with their French-speaking leaders came the Welsh rank and file. Even to-day some of the commonest Irish names suggest a Welsh ancestry. Others of the leaders were of Flemish origin. But all represented the high, feudal society that ruled over Western Europe, and whose conquests already ranged from Wales to Syria. Irish military methods were no match for the newcomers, and "Strongbow," marrying the daughter of the King of Leinster, might perhaps have set up a new feudal kingdom in Ireland, as had been done by William the Conqueror in England, by Roger in Sicily, and by the Crusading chiefs in the Levant. But "Strongbow" was doubtful both of his own strength and of the attitude of his vigilant superior, Henry II. So the conquests were proffered to the King, and Henry briefly visited this fresh addition to his dominions in 1171 in order to receive the submission of his new vassals. The reviving power of the Papacy had long been offended by the traditional independence of the Irish Church. By Papal Bull in 1155 the overlordship of Ireland had been granted to the English king. The Pope at the time was Adrian IV, an Englishman and the only Englishman ever to be Pope. Here were foundations both spiritual and practical. But the Lord of England and of the greater part of France had little time for Irish problems.

He left the affairs of the island to the Norman adventurers, the "Conquistadores" as they have been called. It was a pattern often to be repeated.

The century that followed Henry II's visit marked the height of Anglo-Norman expansion. More than half the country was by now directly subjected to the knightly invaders. Among them was Gerald of Windsor, ancestor of the Fitzgerald family, the branches of which, as Earls of Kildare and Lords of much else, were for long to control large tracts of southern and central Ireland. There was also William de Burgh, brother of the great English Justiciar, and ancestor of the Earls of Ulster; and Theobald Walter, King John's butler, founder of the powerful Butler family of Ormond which took their name from his official calling. But there was no organised colonisation and settlement. English authority was accepted in the Norse towns on the Southern and Eastern coasts, and the King's writ ran over a varying area of country surrounding Dublin. This hinterland of the capital was significantly known as "The Pale," which might be defined as a defended enclosure. Immediately outside lay the big feudal lordships, and beyond these were the "wild" unconquered Irish of the west. Two races dwelt in uneasy balance, and the division between them was sharpened when a Parliament of Ireland evolved towards the end of the thirteenth century. From this body the native Irish were excluded; it was a Parliament in Ireland of the English only.

* * * * *

Within a few generations of the coming of the Anglo-Normans, however, the Irish chieftains began to recover from the shock of new methods of warfare. They hired mercenaries to help them, originally in large part recruited from the Norse-Celtic stock of the Scottish western isles. These were the terrible "galloglasses," named from the Irish words for "foreign henchmen." Supported by these ferocious axe-bearers, the clan chiefs regained for the Gaelic-speaking peoples wide regions of Ireland, and might have won more, had they not incessantly quarrelled among themselves.

Meanwhile a change of spirit had overtaken many of the Anglo-Norman Irish barons. These great feudatories were constantly tempted by the independent rôle of the Gaelic clan chief that was theirs for the taking. They could in turn be subjects of the English King or petty kings themselves, like their new allies, with whom they were frequently united by marriage. Their stock was seldom reinforced from England, except by English lords who wedded Irish heiresses, and then became absentee landlords. Gradually however a group of Anglo-Irish nobles grew up, largely assimilated to their adopted land, and as impatient as their Gaelic peasants of rule from London.

If English kings had regularly visited Ireland, or regularly appointed royal princes as resident lieutenants the ties between the two countries might have been closely and honourably woven together. As it was, when the English King was strong, English laws generally made headway; otherwise a loose Celtic anarchy prevailed. King John, in his furious fitful energy, twice went to Ireland and twice brought the quarrelsome Norman barons and Irish chiefs under his suzerainty. Although Edward I never landed in Ireland, English authority was in the ascendant. Thereafter, the Gaels revived. The shining example of Scotland was not lost upon them. The brother of the victor of Bannockburn, Edward Bruce, was called in by his relations among the Irish chiefs with an army of Scottish veterans. He was crowned King of Ireland in 1316, but after a temporary triumph and in spite of the aid of his brother was defeated and slain at Dundalk.

Thus Ireland did not break loose from the English crown and gain independence under a Scottish dynasty. But the victory of English arms did not mean a victory for English law, custom or speech. The Gaelic reaction gathered force. In Ulster the O'Neills gradually won the mastery of Tyrone. In Ulster and Connaught the feudal trappings were openly discarded when the line of the de Burgh Earls of Ulster ended in 1333 with a girl. According to feudal law, she succeeded to the whole inheritance, and was the King's ward to be married at his choice. In fact she was married to Edward III's second son, Lionel of Clarence. But in Celtic law women could not succeed to the chieftainship. The leading male members of the cadet branches of the de Burgh family accordingly "went Irish," snatched what they could of the inheritance and assumed the clan names of Burke or, after their founder, Mac-William. They openly defied the Government in Ulster and Connaught; in the Western province both French and Irish were spoken but not English, and English authority vanished from these outer parts.

To preserve the English character of the Pale and of its surrounding Anglo-Norman lordships, a Parliament was summoned in the middle of the fourteenth century. Its purpose was to prevent the English from "going Irish" and to compel men of Irish race in the English-held parts of Ireland to conform to English ways. But its enactments had little effect. In the Pale the old Norman settlers clung to their privileged position and opposed all attempts by the representatives of the Crown to bring the "mere Irish" under the protection of English laws and institutions. Most of Ireland by now lay outside the Pale, either under native chiefs who had practically no dealings with the representatives of the English kings, or controlled by Norman dynasts such as the two branches of the Fitzgeralds, who were earls or clan chiefs, as suited them best. English authority stifled the creation of either a native or a "Norman" centre of authority, and the absentee "Lord of Ireland" in London could not provide a substitute, nor even prevent his own colonists from intermingling with the population. By Tudor times anarchic Ireland lay open to reconquest, and to the tribulations of re-imposing English royal authority was to be added from Henry VIII's Reformation onwards the fateful divisions of religious belief.

The Long-Bow

IT SEEMED that the strong blood of Edward I had but
slumbered in his degenerate son, for in Edward III England once more found leadership equal to her steadily growing
strength. Beneath the squalid surface of Edward II's reign there
had none the less proceeded in England a marked growth of
national strength and prosperity. The feuds and vengeances of
the nobility, the foppish vices of a weak King, had been confined to a very limited circle. The English people stood at this
time possessed of a commanding weapon, the qualities of which
were utterly unsuspected abroad. The long-bow, handled by the
well-trained archer class, brought into the field a yeoman type
of soldier with whom there was nothing on the Continent to
compare. An English army now rested itself equally upon the
armoured knighthood and the archers.

The power of the long-bow and the skill of the bowmen had
developed to a point where even the finest mail was no certain
protection. At two hundred and fifty yards the arrow hail produced effects never reached again by infantry missiles at such
a range until the American civil war. The skilled archer was a
professional soldier, earning and deserving high pay. He went
to war often on a pony, but always with a considerable transport for his comfort and his arrows. He carried with him a
heavy iron-pointed stake, which, planted in the ground,
afforded a deadly obstacle to charging horses. Behind this
shelter a company of archers in open order could deliver a
discharge of arrows so rapid, continuous, and penetrating as to

annihilate the cavalry attack. Moreover, in all skirmishing and patrolling the trained archer brought his man down at ranges which had never before been considered dangerous in the whole history of war. Of all this the Continent, and particularly France, our nearest neighbour, was ignorant. In France the armoured knight and his men-at-arms had long exploited their ascendancy in war. The foot-soldiers who accompanied their armies were regarded as the lowest type of auxiliary. A military caste had imposed itself upon society in virtue of physical and technical assertions which the coming of the long-bow must disprove. The protracted wars of the two Edwards in the mountains of Wales and Scotland had taught the English many hard lessons, and although European warriors had from time to time shared in them they had neither discerned nor imparted the slumbering secret of the new army. It was with a sense of unmeasured superiority that the English looked out upon Europe towards the middle of the fourteenth century.

The reign of King Edward III passed through several distinct phases. In the first he was a minor, and the land was ruled by his mother and her lover, Roger Mortimer. This Government, founded upon unnatural murder and representing only a faction in the nobility, was condemned to weakness at home and abroad. Its rule of nearly four years was marked by concession and surrender both in France and in Scotland. For this policy many plausible arguments of peace and prudence might be advanced. The guilty couple paid their way by successive abandonments of English interests. A treaty with France in March 1327 condemned England to pay a war indemnity, and restricted the English possessions to a strip of land running from Saintes in Saintonge and Bordeaux to Bayonne, and to a defenceless enclave in the interior of Gascony. In May 1328 the "Shameful Treaty of Northampton," as it was called at the time, recognised Bruce as King north of the Tweed, and implied the abandonment of all the claims of Edward I in Scotland.

The anger which these events excited was widespread. The régime might however have maintained itself for some time but for Mortimer's quarrel with the barons. After the fall of the Despensers Mortimer had taken care to put himself in the advantageous position they had occupied on the Welsh border, where he could exercise the special powers of government appropriate to the Marches. This and his exorbitant authority drew upon him the jealousies of the barons he had so lately led. His desire to make his position permanent led him to seek from a Parliament convened in October at Salisbury the title of Earl of March, in addition to the office he already held of Justice of Wales for life. Mortimer attended, backed by his armed retainers. But it then appeared that many of the leading nobles were absent, and among them Henry, Earl of Lancaster, son of the executed Thomas and cousin of the King, who held a counter-meeting in London. From Salisbury Mortimer, taking with him the young King, set forth in 1328 to ravage the lands of Lancaster, and in the disorders which followed he succeeded in checking the revolt.

It was plain that the barons themselves were too much divided to overthrow an odious but ruthless Government. But Mortimer made an overweening mistake. In 1330 the King's uncle, the Earl of Kent, was deceived into thinking that Edward II was still alive. Kent made an ineffective attempt to restore him to liberty, and was executed in March of that year. This event convinced Henry of Lancaster and other magnates that it might be their turn to suffer next at Mortimer's hands. They decided to get their blow in first by joining Edward III. All eyes were therefore turned to the young King. When seventeen in 1329 he had been married to Philippa of Hainault. In

June 1330 a son was born to him; he felt himself now a grown man who must do his duty by the realm. But effective power still rested with Mortimer and the Queen-Mother. In October Parliament sat at Nottingham. Mortimer and Isabella, guarded by ample force, were lodged in the castle. It is clear that very careful thought and preparation had marked the plans by which the King should assert his rights. Were he to succeed, Parliament was at hand to acclaim him. Mortimer and Isabella did not know the secrets of the castle. An underground passage led into its heart. Through this on an October night a small band of resolute men entered, surprised Mortimer in his chamber, which as usual was next to the Queen's, and, dragging them both along the subterranean way, delivered them to the King's officers. Mortimer, conducted to London, was brought before the peers, accused of the murder in Berkeley Castle and other crimes, and, after condemnation by the lords, hanged on November 29. Isabella was consigned by her son to perpetual captivity. Three thousand pounds a year was provided for her maintenance at Castle Rising, in Norfolk, and Edward made it his practice to pay her a periodic visit. She died nearly thirty years later.

Upon these grim preliminaries the long and famous reign began.

*   *   *   *   *

The guiding spirit of the new King was to revive the policy, assert the claims, and restore the glories of his grandfather. The quarrel with Scotland was resumed. Since Bannockburn Robert Bruce had reigned unchallenged in the North. His triumph had been followed inevitably by the ruin and expulsion of the adherents of the opposite Scottish party. Edward, the son of John Balliol, the nominee of Edward I, had become a refugee at the English Court, which extended them the same kind of patronage afterwards vouchsafed by Louis XIV to the

Jacobite exiles. No schism so violent as that between Bruce and Balliol could fail to produce rankling injuries. Large elements in Scotland, after Bruce's death in 1329, looked to a reversal of fortune, and the exiles, or "disinherited," as they were termed, maintained a ceaseless intrigue in their own country and a constant pressure upon the English Government. In 1332 an endeavour was made to regain Scotland. Edward Balliol rallied his adherents and, with the secret support of Edward III, sailed from Ravenspur to Kinghorn in Fife. Advancing on Perth, he met and defeated the infant David's Regent at Dupplin Moor. Balliol received the submission of many Scottish magnates, and was crowned at Scone.

Henceforward fortune failed him. Within two months he and his supporters were driven into England. Edward III was now able to make what terms he liked with the beaten Balliol. He was recognised by Balliol as his overlord and promised the town and shire of Berwick. In 1333 therefore Edward III advanced to besiege Berwick, and routed the Scots at Halidon Hill. Here was a battle very different in character from Bannockburn. The power of the archers was allowed to play its part, the schiltrons were broken, and the exiled party reestablished for a while their authority in their native land. There was a price to pay. Balliol, as we have seen, had to cede to the English King the whole of South-Eastern Scotland. In exacting this concession Edward III had overshot the mark; he had damned Balliol's cause in the eyes of all Scots. Meanwhile the descendants and followers of Robert Bruce took refuge in France. The contacts between Scotland and France, and the constant aid given by the French Court to the Scottish enemies of England, roused a deep antagonism. Thus the war in Scotland pointed the path to Flanders.

Here a new set of grievances formed a substantial basis for a conflict. The loss of all the French possessions, except Gascony, and the constant bickering on the Gascon frontiers, had been endured perforce since the days of John. Successive English kings had done homage in Paris for domains of which they had in large part long since been deprived. But in 1328 the death of Charles IV without a direct heir opened a further issue. Philip of Valois assumed the royal power and demanded homage from Edward, who made difficulties. King Edward III, in his mother's right—if indeed the female line was valid— had a remote claim to the throne of France. This claim, by and with the assent and advice of the Lords Spiritual and Temporal, and of the Commons of England, he was later to advance in support of his campaigns.

The youthful Edward was less drawn to domestic politics than to foreign adventure and the chase. He was conscious moreover from the first of the advantage to be gained by diverting the restless energies of his nobles from internal intrigues and rivalries to the unifying purpose of a foreign war. This was also in harmony with the temper of his people. The wars of John and Henry III on the mainland disclose a perpetual struggle between the King and his nobles and subjects to obtain men and money. European adventure was regarded as a matter mainly of interest to a prince concerned with his foreign possessions or claims. Now we see the picture of the Estates of the Realm becoming themselves ardently desirous of foreign conquests. Edward III did not have to wring support from his Parliament for an expedition to France. On the contrary, nobles, merchants, and citizens vied with one another in pressing the Crown to act.

The dynastic and territorial disputes were reinforced by a less sentimental but none the less powerful motive, which made its appeal to many members of the Houses of Parliament. The wool trade with the Low Countries was the staple of English exports, and almost the sole form of wealth which rose above the resources of agriculture. The Flemish towns had attained a high economic development, based upon the art of weaving cloth, which they had brought to remarkable perfection. They depended for their prosperity upon the wool of England. But the aristocracy under the Counts of Flanders nursed French sympathies which recked little of the material well-being of the burghers, regarding them as dangerous and subversive folk whose growth in wealth and power conflicted with feudal ascendancy. There was therefore for many years a complete divergence—economic, social, and political—between the Flemish towns and the nobility of the Netherlands. The former looked to England, the latter to France. Repeated obstructions were placed by the Counts of Flanders upon the wool trade, and each aroused the anger of those concerned on both sides of the narrow sea. The mercantile element in the English Parliament, already inflamed by running sea-fights with the French in the Channel, pleaded vehemently for action.

In 1336 Edward was moved to retaliate in a decisive manner. He decreed an embargo on all exports of English wool, thus producing a furious crisis in the Netherlands. The townspeople rose against the feudal aristocracy, and under Van Arteveldt, a war-like merchant of Ghent, gained control, after a struggle of much severity, over a large part of the country. The victorious burghers, threatened by aristocratic and French revenge, looked to England for aid, and their appeals met with a hearty and deeply interested response. Thus all streams of profit and ambition flowed into a common channel at a moment when the flood-waters of conscious military strength ran high, and in 1337, when Edward repudiated his grudging homage to Philip VI, the Hundred Years War began. It was never to be concluded; no general peace treaty was signed, and not until the Peace of Amiens in 1802, when France was a Republic and the French Royal heir a refugee within these isles, did the English sovereign formally renounce his claims to the throne of the Valois and the Bourbons.

*   *   *   *   *

Edward slowly assembled the expeditionary army of England. This was not a feudal levy, but a paid force of picked men. Its backbone consisted of indentured warriors, recruited where and how their captains pleased. In consequence, far less than the legal quota of unreliable militia needed to be drawn from every shire. Both knights and archers embodied the flower of the nation, and the men who gathered in the Cinque Ports formed one of the most formidable and efficient invading armies history had yet seen. These preparations were well known in France, and the whole strength of the monarchy was bent to resist them.

Philip VI looked first to the sea. For many years there had been a warfare of privateers, and bitter hatred ruled between the maritime populations on both sides of the Channel. All the resources of the French marine were strained to produce a fleet; even hired Genoese galleys appeared in the French harbours. In Normandy plans were mooted for a counter-invasion which should repeat the exploits of William the Conqueror. But Edward had not neglected his sea-power. His interest in the Navy won him from Parliament early in his reign the title of "King of the Sea." He was able to marshal a fleet equal in vessels and superior in men. A great sea battle was necessary before the transport of the English army to France and its maintenance there was feasible. In the summer of 1340 the hostile navies met off Sluys, and a struggle of nine hours ensued. "This battle," says Froissart, "was right furious and horrible, for battles by sea are more dangerous and fiercer than battles by land, for at sea there is no retreat or fleeing; there is no remedy but to fight and abide the fortune." The French admirals had been ordered, under pain of death, to prevent the invasion, and both sides fought well; but the French fleet was decisively beaten and the command of the Channel passed into the hands of the invading Power. The seas being now open, the army crossed to France. At Cadzand the landing was opposed. Large bodies of Genoese cross-bowmen and men-at-arms awaited the disembarkation. But the English archers, shooting from the ships at long range, cleared the shores and covered the invading troops.

Joined with the revolted Flemings, Edward's numbers were greatly augmented, and this combined force, which may have exceeded twenty thousand, undertook the first Anglo-Flemish siege of Tournai. The city was stubbornly defended, and as the grip of famine tightened upon the garrison the horrible spectacle was presented of the "useless mouths" being driven forth into No Man's Land to perish by inches without pity or relief. But the capture of this fortress was beyond Edward's resources in money and supplies. The power of the archers did not extend to stone walls; the first campaign of what was a great European war yielded no results, and a prolonged truce supervened.

This truce was imposed upon the combatants through lack of money, and carried with it no reconciliation. On the contrary, both sides pursued their quarrel in secondary ways. The French wreaked their vengeance on the burghers of the Netherlands, whom they crushed utterly, and Van Artevelde met his death in a popular tumult at Ghent. The English retaliated as best they could. There was a disputed succession in Brittany, which they fomented with substantial aids. The chronic warfare on the frontiers of Gascony continued. Both sides looked forward to a new trial of strength. Well-trained men, eager to fight, there were in plenty, but to maintain them in the field required funds, which to us seem pitifully small, but without which all was stopped. How could these resources be obtained?

The Jews had been exploited, pillaged, and expelled in 1290. The Florentine bankers, who had found the money for the first invasion, had been ruined by royal default. The main effort, not only of the Court but of Parliament, was to secure the modest sums of ready money without which knights could not ride nor archers draw their bows. But here a fertile source was at hand. The wealthier and best-organised commercial interest in England was the wool trade, eager to profit from war. A monopoly of wool merchants was created, bound to export only through a particular town to be prescribed by the King from time to time in accordance with his needs and judgment. This system, which was called the Staple, gave the King a convenient and flexible control. By taxing the wool exports which passed through his hands at the Staple port he was assured of an important revenue independent of Parliament. Moreover, the wool merchants who held the monopoly formed a corporation interested in the war, dependent on the King, and capable of lending him money in return for considerate treatment. This development was not welcomed by Parliament, where the smaller wool merchants were increasingly represented. They complained of the favor shown to the monopolists of the Staple, and they also pointed to the menace to Parliamentary power involved in the King's independent resources.

By the spring of 1346 Parliament had at length brought itself to the point of facing the taxation necessary to finance a new invasion. The army was reconstituted, more efficiently than before, its old elements were refreshed with carefully chosen levies. In one wave 2,400 cavalry, twelve thousand archers, and other infantry sailed, and landed unopposed at St. Vaast in Normandy on July 12, 1346. Their object this time was no less than the capture of Paris by a sudden dash. The secret was well kept; even the English army itself believed it was going to Gascony. The French could not for some time collect forces sufficient to arrest the inroad. Caen fell, and Edward advanced, burning and laying waste the country, to the very walls of Paris. But by this time the whole power of the French monarchy had gathered against him. A huge force which comprised all the chivalry of France and was probably three times as big as Edward's army assembled in the neighbourhood of St. Denis. Against such opposition, added to the walls of a fortified city, Edward's resources could not attempt to prevail. King Philip grimly invited him to choose upon which bank of the Seine he would fight a pitched battle.

The thrust had failed and retreat imposed itself upon the army. The challenger was forced to quit the lists at a pace which covered sixty miles in four days. The French army moved on a parallel line to the southward and denied the Seine valley to the retreating English. They must now make for the Somme, and hope to cross between Amiens and the sea. Our generation has become familiar with this stretch of the river, which flows through broad morasses, in those days quite undrained and passable only by lengthy causeways and bridges. All these were broken or held by the levies of Picardy. Four separate attempts to find a passage failed. The vanguard of the French main army was already at Amiens. Edward and the English host, which had tried so audacious, even foolhardy, a spring, now seemed penned in a triangle between the Somme, the seashore, and the French mass. No means had been found to bring the fleet and its transports to any suitable harbour. To cross the Somme near the mouth was a desperate enterprise. The ford was very lengthy, and the tides, violent and treacherous, offered only a few precarious hours in any day.

Moreover, the passage was defended by strong forces popularly estimated to have been upwards of twelve thousand men. "The King of England," says Froissart, "did not sleep much that night, but, rising at midnight, ordered his trumpet to sound. Very soon everything was ready; and, the baggage being loaded, they set out about daybreak, and rode on until they came to the ford at sunrise: but the tide was at that time so full they could not cross." By the afternoon, at the ebb, the enemy's strength was manifest. But since to pause was to perish the King ordered his marshals to plunge into the water and fight their way across. The French resistance was spirited. The knighthood of Picardy rode out and encountered the English on the treacherous sands in the rising waters. "They appeared to be as fond of tilting in the water as upon dry land." By hard fighting, under conditions most deadly to men encased in mail, the passage was forced. At the landing the Genoese cross-bowmen inflicted losses and delayed the deployment until the long-bow asserted its mastery. Thus did King Edward's army escape.

Philip, at the head of a host between thirty and forty thousand strong, was hard upon the track. He had every hope of bringing the insolent Islanders to bay with their backs to the river, or catching them in transit. When he learned that they were already over he called a council of war. His generals advised that, since the tide was now in, there was no choice but to ascend to Abbeville and cross by the bridge which the French held there. To Abbeville they accordingly moved, and lay there for the night.

Edward and his army were intensely convinced of the narrowness of their deliverance. That night they rejoiced; the countryside was full of food; the King gathered his chiefs to supper and afterwards to prayer. But it was certain that they could not gain the coast without a battle. No other resolve was open than to fight at enormous odds. The King and the Prince of Wales, afterwards famous as the Black Prince, received all the offices of religion, and Edward prayed that the impending battle should at least leave him unstripped of honour. With the daylight he marshalled about eleven thousand men in three divisions. Mounted upon a small palfrey, with a white wand in his hand, with his splendid surcoat of crimson and gold above his armour, he rode along the ranks, "encouraging and entreating the army that they would guard his honour and defend his right." "He spoke this so sweetly and with such a cheerful countenance that all who had been dispirited were directly comforted by seeing and hearing him. . . . They ate and drank at their ease . . . and seated themselves on the ground, placing their helmets and bows before them, that they might be the fresher when their enemies should arrive." Their position on the open rolling downs enjoyed few advantages, but the forest of Crécy on their flanks afforded protection and the means of a final stand.

King Philip at sunrise on this same Saturday, August 26, 1346, heard Mass in the monastery of Abbeville, and his whole army, gigantic for those times, rolled forward in their long pursuit. Four knights were sent forth to reconnoitre. About midday the King, having arrived with large masses on the farther bank of the Somme, received their reports. The English were in battle array and meant to fight. He gave the sage counsel to halt for the day, bring up the rear, form the battle-line, and attack on the morrow. These orders were carried by famous chiefs to all parts of the army. But the thought of leaving, even for a day, this hated foe, who had for so many marches fled before overwhelming forces, and was now compelled to come to grips, was unendurable to the French army. What surety had they that the morrow might not see their enemies decamped and the field bare? It became impossible to control the forward movement. All the roads and tracks from Abbeville to Crécy were black and glittering with the marching columns. King Philip's orders were obeyed by some, rejected by most. While many great bodies halted obediently, still larger masses poured forward, forcing their way through the stationary or withdrawing troops, and at about five in the afternoon came face to face with the English army lying in full view on the broad slopes of Crécy. Here they stopped.

King Philip, arriving on the scene, was carried away by the ardour of the throng around him. The sun was already low; nevertheless all were determined to engage. There was a corps of six thousand Genoese cross-bowmen in the van of the army. These were ordered to make their way through the masses of horsemen, and with their missiles break up the hostile array in preparation for the cavalry attacks. The Genoese had marched eighteen miles in full battle order with their heavy weapons and store of bolts. Fatigued, they made it plain that they were in no condition to do much that day. But the Count d'Alençon, who had covered the distance on horseback, did not accept this remonstrance kindly. "This is what one gets," he exclaimed, "by employing such scoundrels, who fall off when there is anything for them to do." Forward the Genoese! At this moment, while the cross-bowmen were threading their way to the front under many scornful glances, dark clouds swept across the sun and a short, drenching storm beat upon the hosts. A large flight of crows flew cawing through the air above the French in gloomy presage. The storm, after wetting the bow-strings of the Genoese, passed as quickly as it had come, and the setting sun shone brightly in their eyes and on the backs of the English. This, like the crows, was adverse, but it was more material. The Genoese, drawing out their array, gave a loud shout, advanced a few steps, shouted again, and a third time advanced, "hooted," and discharged their bolts. Unbroken silence had wrapped the English lines, but at this the archers, six or seven thousand strong, ranged on both flanks in "portcullis" formation, who had hitherto stood motionless, advanced one step, drew their bows to the ear, and came into action. They "shot their arrows with such force and quickness," says Froissart, "that it seemed as if it snowed."

The effect upon the Genoese was annihilating; at a range which their own weapons could not attain they were in a few minutes killed by thousands. The ground was covered with feathered corpses. Reeling before this blast of missile destruction, the like of which had not been known in war, the survivors recoiled in rout upon the eager ranks of the French chivalry and men-at-arms, which stood just out of arrow-shot. "Kill me those scoundrels," cried King Philip in fury, "for they stop up our road without any reason." Whereupon the front line of the French cavalry rode among the retreating Genoese, cutting them down with their swords. In doing so they came within the deadly distance. The arrow snowstorm beat upon them, piercing their mail and smiting horse and man. Valiant squadrons from behind rode forward into the welter, and upon all fell the arrow hail, making the horses caper, and strewing the field with richly dressed warriors. A hideous disorder reigned. And now Welsh and Cornish light infantry, slipping through the chequered ranks of the archers, came forward with their long knives and, "falling upon earls, barons, knights, and squires, slew many, at which the King of England was afterwards exasperated." Many a fine ransom was cast away in those improvident moments.

In this slaughter fell King Philip's ally, the blind King of Bohemia, who bade his knights fasten their bridles to his in order that he might strike a blow with his own hand. Thus entwined, he charged forward in the press. Man and horse they fell, and the next day their bodies were found still linked. His son, Prince Charles of Luxembourg, who as Emperor-elect of the Holy Roman Empire signed his name as King of the Romans, was more prudent, and, seeing how matters lay, departed with his following by an unnoticed route. The main attack of the French now developed. The Count d'Alençon and the Count of Flanders led heavy cavalry charges upon the English line. Evading the archers as far as possible, they sought the men-at-arms, and French, German, and Savoyard squadrons actually reached the Prince of Wales's division. The enemy's numbers were so great that those who fought about the Prince sent to the windmill, whence King Edward directed the battle, for reinforcements. But the King would not part with his reserves, saying, "Let the boy win his spurs"—which in fact he did.

Another incident was much regarded. One of Sir John of Hainault's knights, mounted upon a black horse, the gift that day of King Philip, escaping the arrows, actually rode right through the English lines. Such was their discipline that not a man stirred to harm him, and, riding round the rear, he returned eventually to the French army. Continuous cavalry charges were launched upon the English front, until utter darkness fell upon the field. And all through the night fresh troops of brave men, resolved not to quit the field without striking their blow, struggled forward, groping their way. All these were slain, for "No quarter" was the mood of the English, though by no means the wish of their King.

When night had fallen Philip found himself with no more than sixty knights in hand. He was slightly wounded by one arrow, and his horse had been shot under him by another. Sir John Hainault, mounting him again, seized his bridle and forced him from the field upon the well-known principle which, according to Froissart, he exactly expounded, of living to fight another day. The King had but five barons with him on reaching Amiens the next morning.

"When on this Saturday night the English heard no more hooting or shouting, nor any more crying out to particular lords, or their banners, they looked upon the field as their own and their enemies as beaten. They made great fires, and lighted torches because of the obscurity of the night. King Edward who all that day had not put on his helmet, then came down from his post, and, with his whole battalion, advanced to the Prince of Wales, whom he embraced in his arms and kissed, and said, 'Sweet son, God give you good perseverance. You are my son, for most loyally have you acquitted yourself this day. You are worthy to be a sovereign.' The Prince bowed down very low, and humbled himself, giving all honour to the King his father."

On the Sunday morning fog enshrouded the battlefield, and the King sent a strong force of five hundred lancers and two thousand archers to learn what lay upon his front. These met the columns of the French rear, still marching up from Rouen to Beauvais in ignorance of the defeat, and fell upon them. After this engagement the bodies of 1,542 knights and esquires were counted on the field. Later this force met with the troops of the Archbishop of Rouen and the Grand Prior of France, who were similarly unaware of the event, and were routed with much slaughter. They also found very large numbers of stragglers and wandering knights, and "put to the sword all they met." "It has been assured to me for fact," says Froissart, "that of foot-soldiers, sent from the cities, towns, and municipalities, there were slain, this Sunday morning, four times as many as in the battle of the Saturday." This astounding victory of Crécy ranks with Blenheim, Waterloo, and the final advance in the last summer of the Great War as one of the four supreme achievements.[1]

*　　*　　*　　*　　*

Edward III marched through Montreuil and Blangy to Boulogne, passed through the forest of Hardelot, and opened the siege of Calais. Calais presented itself to English eyes as

[1] Written in 1939.

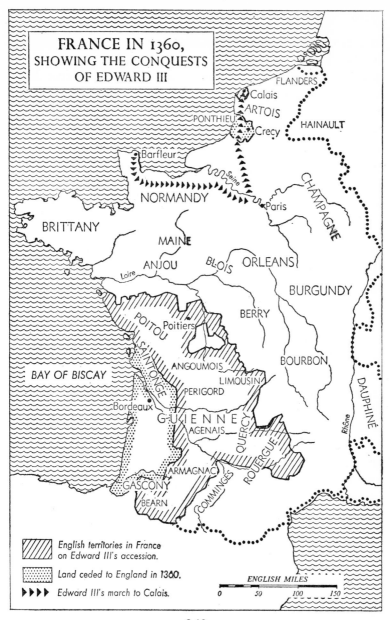

FRANCE IN 1360,
SHOWING THE CONQUESTS
OF EDWARD III

FLANDERS

Calais
ARTOIS
PONTHIEU
Crecy
HAINAULT

Barfleur

Seine

NORMANDY
Paris
CHAMPAGNE

BRITTANY

MAINE

ANJOU
BLOIS
ORLEANS

Loire

BERRY
BURGUNDY

POITOU

Poitiers

BAY OF BISCAY

ANGOUMOIS
LIMOUSIN
BOURBON

SAINTONGE

PERIGORD

Bordeaux

GUIENNE
AGENAIS
QUERCY
ROUERGUE
DAUPHINÉ

Rhône

ARMAGNAC
COMMINGES

GASCONY
BEARN

English territories in France
on Edward III's accession.

Land ceded to England in 1360.

Edward III's march to Calais.

ENGLISH MILES

0   50   100   150

· 349 ·

the hive of that swarm of privateers who were the endless curse of the Channel. Here on the nearest point of the Continent England had long felt a festering sore. Calais was what Dunkirk was to become three centuries later. The siege lasted for nearly a year. Every new art of war was practised by land; the bombards flung cannon-balls against the ramparts with terrifying noise. By sea elaborate barriers of piles stopped the French light craft, which sought to evade the sea blockade by creeping along the coast. All reliefs by sea and land failed. But the effort of maintaining the siege strained the resources of the King to an extent we can hardly conceive. When the winter came his soldiers demanded to go home, and the fleet was on the verge of mutiny. In England everyone complained, and Parliament was morose in demeanour and reluctant in supply. The King and his army lived in their hutments, and he never recrossed the Channel to his kingdom. Machiavelli has profoundly observed that every fortress should be victualled for a year, and this precaution has covered almost every case in history.

Moreover, the siege had hardly begun when King David of Scotland, in fulfilment of the alliance with France, led his army across the Border. But the danger was foreseen, and at Neville's Cross, just west of the city of Durham, the English won a hard-fought battle. The Scottish King himself was captured, and imprisoned in the Tower. He remained there, as we have seen, for ten years until released under the Treaty of Berwick for an enormous ransom. This decisive victory removed the Scottish danger for a generation, but more than once, before and after Flodden, the French alliance was to bring disaster to this small and audacious nation.

Calais held out for eleven months, and yet this did not suffice. Famine at length left no choice to the besieged. They sued for terms. The King was so embittered that when at his demand six of the noblest citizens presented themselves in their shirts, barefoot, emaciated, he was for cutting off their heads. The warnings of his advisers that his fame would suffer in history by so cruel a deed left him obdurate. But Queen Philippa, great with child, who had followed him to the war, fell down before him in an edifying, and perhaps prearranged, tableau of Mercy pleading with Justice. So the burghers of Calais who had devoted themselves to save their people were spared, and even kindly treated. Calais, then, was the fruit, and the sole territorial fruit so far, of the exertions, prodigious in quality, of the whole power of England in the war with France. But Crécy had a longer tale to tell.

The Black Death

WHILE feats of arms and strong endeavours held the
English mind a far more deadly foe was marching
across the continents to their doom. Christendom has no
catastrophe equal to the Black Death. Vague tales are told of
awful events in China and of multitudes of corpses spreading
their curse afar. The plague entered Europe through the
Crimea, and in the course of twenty years destroyed at least
one-third of its entire population. The privations of the people,
resulting from ceaseless baronial and dynastic wars, presented
an easy conquest to disease. The records in England tell more
by their silence than by the shocking figures which confront
us wherever records were kept. We read of lawsuits where all
parties died before the cases could be heard; of monasteries
where half the inmates perished; of dioceses where the surviving clergy could scarcely perform the last offices for their
flocks and for their brethren; of the Goldsmiths' Company,
which had four Masters in a year. These are detailed indica-
tions. But far more convincing is the gap which opens in all
the local annals of the nation. A whole generation is slashed
through by a hideous severance.

The character of the pestilence was appalling. The disease
itself, with its frightful symptoms, the swift onset, the blotches,
the hardening of the glands under the armpit or in the groin,
these swellings which no poultice could resolve, these tumours
which, when lanced, gave no relief, the horde of virulent car-
buncles which followed the dread harbingers of death, the
delirium, the insanity which attended its triumph, the blank

spaces which opened on all sides in human society, stunned and for a time destroyed the life and faith of the world. This affliction, added to all the severities of the Middle Ages, was more than the human spirit could endure. The Church, smitten like the rest in body, was wounded grievously in spiritual power. If a God of mercy ruled the world, what sort of rule was this? Such was the challenging thought which swept upon the survivors. Weird sects sprang into existence, and plague-haunted cities saw the gruesome procession of flagellants, each lashing his forerunner to a dismal dirge, and ghoulish practices glare at us from the broken annals. It seemed to be the death-rattle of the race.

But at length the plague abated its force. The tumours yielded to fomentations. Recoveries became more frequent; the resistant faculties of life revived. The will to live triumphed. The scourge passed, and a European population, too small for its clothes, heirs to much that had been prepared by more numerous hands, assuaging its griefs in their universality, turned with unconquerable hope to the day and to the morrow.

Philosophers might suggest that there was no need for the use of the destructive mechanism of plague to procure the changes deemed necessary among men. A more scientific reagent was at hand. Gunpowder, which we have seen used in the puny bombards which, according to some authorities, Edward had fired at Crécy and against Calais, was soon decisively to establish itself as a practical factor in war and in human affairs based on war. If cannon had not been invented the English mastery of the long-bow might have carried them even farther in their Continental domination. We know no reason why the yeoman archer should not have established a class position similar in authority to that of the armoured knights, but upon a far broader foundation.

The early fifteenth century was to see the end of the rule of the armoured men. Breastplates and backplates might long be worn as safeguards to life, but no longer as the instrument and symbol of power. If the archers faded it was not because they could not master chivalry; a more convenient agency was at hand which speedily became the common property of all nations. Amid jarring booms and billowing smoke which frequently caused more alarm to friends than foes, but none the less arrested all attention, a system which had ruled and also guided Christendom for five hundred years, which had in its day been the instrument of an immense advance in human government and stature, fell into ruins which were painfully carted away to make room for new building.

*   *   *   *   *

The calamity which fell upon mankind reduced their numbers and darkened their existence without abating their quarrels. The war between England and France continued in a broken fashion, and the Black Prince, the most renowned warrior in Europe, became a freebooter. Grave reasons of State had been adduced for Edward's invasion of France in 1338, but the character of the Black Prince's forays in Aquitaine can vaunt no such excuses. Nevertheless they produced a brilliant military episode.

In 1355 King Edward obtained from Parliament substantial grants for the renewal of active war. An ambitious strategy was adopted. The Black Prince would advance northward from the English territories of Gascony and Aquitaine towards the Loire. His younger brother, John of Gaunt, Duke of Lancaster, struck in from Brittany. The two forces were to join for a main decision. But all this miscarried, and the Black Prince found himself, with forces shrunk to about four thousand men, of whom however nearly a half were the dreaded archers, forced to retire with growing urgency before the advance of a French royal army twenty thousand strong. So grim were his straits that he proposed, as an accommodation, that he and the army should be allowed to escape to England. These terms were rejected by the Franch, who once again saw their deeply hated foe in their grasp. At Poitiers the Prince was brought to bay. Even on the morning of his victory his vanguard was already marching southwards in retreat. But King John of France was resolved to avenge Crécy and finish the war at a stroke. Forced against all reason and all odds to fight, the haggard band of English marauders who had carried pillage and arson far and wide were drawn up in array and position chosen by consummate insight. The flanks were secured by forests; the archers lined a hedgerow and commanded the only practicable passage.

Ten years had passed since Crécy, and French chivalry and high command alike had brooded upon the tyranny of that event. They had been forced to accept the fact that horses could not face the arrow storm. King Edward had won with an army entirely dismounted. The confusion wrought by English archery in a charging line of horses collapsing or driven mad through pain was, they realised, fatal to the old forms of warfare. King John was certain that all must attack on foot, and he trusted to overwhelming numbers. But the great merit of the Black Prince is that he did not rest upon the lessons of the past or prepare himself to repeat the triumphs of a former battle. He understood that the masses of mail-clad footmen who now advanced upon him in such towering numbers would not be stopped as easily as the horses. Archery alone, however good the target, would not save him. He must try the battle of manœuvre and counter-attack. He therefore did the opposite to what military convention, based upon the then known facts, would have pronounced right.

The French nobility left their horses in the rear. The Black Prince had all his knights mounted. A deadly toll was taken by the archers upon the whole front. The French chivalry, encumbered by their mail, plodded ponderously forward amid vineyards and scrub. Many fell before the arrows, but the arrows would not have been enough at the crisis. It was the English spear and axe men who charged in the old style upon ranks disordered by their fatigue of movement and the accidents of the ground. At the same time, in admirable concert, a strong detachment of mounted knights, riding round the French left flank, struck in upon the harassed and already disordered attack. The result was a slaughter as large and a victory as complete as Crécy, but with even larger gains. The whole French army was driven into ruin. King John and the flower of his nobility were captured or slain. The pillage of the field could not be gathered by the victors; they were already overburdened with the loot of four provinces. The Black Prince, whose record is dinked by many cruel acts of war, showed himself a paladin of the age when, in spite of the weariness and stresses of the desperate battle, he treated the captured monarch with all the ceremony of his rank, seated him in his own chair in the camp, and served him in person with such fare as was procurable. Thus by genius, valour, and chivalry he presents himself in a posture which history has not failed to salute.

King John was carried to London. Like King David of Scotland before him, he was placed in the Tower, and upon this personal trophy, in May 1360, the Treaty of Brétigny was signed. By this England acquired, in addition to her old possession of Gascony, the whole of Henry II's possessions in Aquitaine in full sovereignty, Edward I's inheritance of Ponthieu, and the famous port and city of Calais, which last was held for nearly two hundred years. A ransom was fixed for King John at three million gold crowns, and equivalent of

£ 500,000 sterling. This was eight times the annual revenue of the English Crown in time of peace.

At Crécy France had been beaten on horseback; at Poitiers she was beaten on foot. These two terrible experiments against the English bit deep into French thought. A sense of hopelessness overwhelmed the French Court and army. How could these people be beaten or withstood? A similar phase of despair had swept across Europe a century earlier after the menacing battles of the Mongol invasions. But, as has been wisely observed, the trees do not grow up to the sky. For a long spell the French avoided battles; they became as careful in fighting the England of King Edward III as in the days of Marlborough they fought the England of Queen Anne. But a great French hero appeared in Bertrand du Guesclin, who, like Fabius Cunctator against Hannibal, by refusing battle and acting through sieges and surprises, rallied the factor of time to the home side. The triumph and the exhaustion of England were simultaneously complete. It was proved that the French army could not beat the English, and at the same time that England could not conquer France. The main effort of Edward III, though crowned with all the military laurels, had failed.

*　　*　　*　　*　　*

The years of the war with France are important in the history of Parliament. The need for money drove the Crown and its officials to summoning it frequently. This led to rapid and important developments. One of the main functions of the representatives of the shires and boroughs was to petition for the redress of grievances, local and national, and to draw the attention of the King and his Council to urgent matters. The stress of war forced the Government to take notice of these petitions of the Commons of England, and during the reign of Edward III the procedure of collective petition, which had

· 357 ·

started under Edward II, made progress. The fact that the Commons now petitioned as a body in a formal way, and asked, as they did in 1327, that these petitions should be transformed into Parliamentary statutes, distinguishes the lower House from the rest of Parliament. Under Edward I the Commons were not an essential element in a Parliament, but under Edward III they assumed a position distinct, vital, and permanent. They had their own clerk, who drafted their petitions and their rejoinders to the Crown's replies. The separation of the Houses now appears. The Lords had come to regard themselves not only as the natural counsellors of the Crown, but as enjoying the right of separate consultation within the framework of Parliament itself. In 1343 the prelates and magnates met in the White Chamber at Westminster, and the knights and burgesses adjourned to the Painted Chamber to discuss the business of the day. Here, in this Parliament, for the first time, the figure of a Speaker emerged. He was not on this occasion a Member of the House, and for some time to come the Commons generally spoke through an appointed deputation. But by the end of the reign the rôle of the Speaker was recognised, and the Crown became anxious to secure its own nominees for this important and prominent office.

The concessions made by Edward III to the Commons mark a decisive stage. He consented that all aids should be granted only in Parliament. He accepted the formal drafts of the Commons' collective petitions as the preliminary bases for future statutes, and by the time of his death it was recognized that the Commons had assumed a leading part in the granting of taxes and the presentation of petitions. Naturally the Commons stood in awe of the Crown. There was no long tradition of authority behind them. The assertions of the royal prerogative in the days of Edward I still echoed in their minds, and there was no suggestion that either they or Parliament as a whole had any right of control or interference in matters of administration and government. They were summoned to endorse political settlements reached often by violence, to vote money and to voice grievances. But the permanent acceptance of Parliament as an essential part of the machinery of government and of the Commons as its vital foundation is the lasting work of the fourteenth century.

Against Papal agents feeling was strong. The interventions of Rome in the days of John, the submissiveness of Henry III to the Church, the exactions of the Papal tax-collectors, the weight of clerical influence within the Household and the Council, all contributed to the growing criticism and dislike of the Church of England. The reign of Edward III brought the climax of this mood. The war with France had stimulated and embittered national sentiment, which resented the influence of an external institution whose great days were already passing. Moreover, this declining power had perforce abandoned its sacred traditional seat in Rome, and was now installed under French influence in enemy territory at Avignon. During these years Parliament passed statutes forbidding appeals to be carried to the Papal Curia for matters cognisable in the royal courts and restricting its power to make appointments in the Church of England. It is true that these statutes were only fitfully enforced, as dictated by diplomatic demands, but the drain of the war left little money for Rome, and the Papal tax-collectors gleaned the country to little avail during the greater part of the reign.

The renewal in 1369 of serious fighting in Aquitaine found England exhausted and disillusioned. The clergy claimed exemption from taxation, though not always successfully, and they could often flaunt their wealth in the teeth of poverty and economic dislocation. Churchmen were ousting the nobility from public office and anti-clerical feeling grew in Parliament.

The King was old and failing, and a resurgence of baronial power was due. John of Gaunt set himself to redress the balance in favour of the Lords by a carefully planned political campaign against the Church. Ready to his hand lay an unexpected weapon. In the University of Oxford, the national centre of theological study and learning, criticism of Papal pretensions and power raised its voice. The arguments for reform set forth by a distinguished Oxford scholar named Wyclif attracted attention. Wyclif was indignant at the corruption of the Church, and saw in its proud hierarchy and absolute claims a distortion of the true principles of Christianity. He declared that dominion over men's souls had never been delegated to mortals. The King, as the Vicar of God in things temporal, was as much bound by his office to curb the material lavishness of the clergy as the clergy to direct the spiritual life of the King. Though Pope and King was each in his sphere supreme, every Christian held not "in chief" of them, but rather of God. The final appeal was to Heaven, not to Rome.

Wyclif's doctrine could not remain the speculations of a harmless schoolman. Its application to the existing facts of Church and State opened deep rifts. It involved reducing the powers of the Church temporal in order to purify the Church spiritual. John of Gaunt was interested in the first, Wyclif in the second. The Church was opposed to both. Gaunt and Wyclif in the beginning each hoped to use the other for his special aim. In 1377 they entered into alliance. Gaunt busied himself in packing the new Parliament, and Wyclif lent moral support by "running about from church to church preaching against abuses." But counter-forces were also aroused. Wyclif's hopes of Church reform were soon involved in class and party prejudices, and Gaunt by his alliance with the revolutionary theologian consolidated the vested interest of the Episcopate against himself. Thus both suffered from their union. The bishops, recognising in Wyclif Gaunt's most dangerous supporter, arraigned him on charges of heresy at St. Paul's. Gaunt, coming to his aid, encountered the hostility of the London mob. The ill-matched partnership fell to pieces and Wyclif ceased to count in high politics.

It was at this same point that his enduring influence began. He resolved to appeal to the people. Church abuses and his own reforming doctrines had attracted many young students around him. He organised his followers into bands of poor preachers, who, like those of Wesley in a later century, spread the doctrines of poverty and holiness for the clergy throughout the countryside. He wrote English tracts, of which the most famous was *The Wicket,* which were passed from hand to hand. Finally, with his students he took the tremendous step of having the Bible translated into English.

"Cristen men and wymmen, olde and yonge, shulden studie fast in the Newe Testament, for it is of ful autorite, and opyn to undirstonding of simple men, as to the poyntis that be moost nedeful to salvacioun. . . . Each place of holy writ, both opyn and derk, techith mekenes and charite; and therfore he that kepith mekenes and charite hath the trewe undirstondyng and perfectioun of al holi writ. . . . Therefore no simple man of wit be aferd unmesurabli to studie in the text of holy writ . . . and no clerk be proude of the verrey undirstondyng of holy writ, for why undirstonding of hooly writ with outen charite that kepith Goddis [be]heestis, makith a man depper dampned . . . and pride and covetise of clerkis is cause of her blindnes and eresie, and priveth them fro verrey undirstondyng of holy writ."

The spirit of early Christianity now revived the English countryside with a keen, refreshing breeze after the weariness of sultry days. But the new vision opened to rich and poor alike profoundly disturbed the decaying society to which it was vouchsafed. The powers of Church and State were soon to realise their danger.

* * * * *

The long reign had reached its dusk. The glories of Crécy and Poitiers had faded. The warlike King, whose ruling passions were power and fame, who had been willing to barter many prerogatives for which his ancestors had striven in order to obtain money for foreign adventure, was now in old age a debtor to time and fortune. Harsh were the suits they laid against him. He saw the wide conquests which his sword and his son had made in France melt like snow at Easter. A few coastal towns alone attested the splendour of victories long to be cherished in the memories of the Island race. Queen Philippa, his loving wife, had died of plague in 1369. Even before her death the old King had fallen under the consoling thrall of Alice Perrers, a lady of indifferent extraction, but of remarkable wit and capacity, untrammelled by scruple or by prudence. The spectacle of the famous King in his sixties, infatuated by an illicit love, jarred upon the haggard yet touchy temper of the times. Here was something less romantic than the courtly love that had been symbolised in 1348 by the founding of the Order of the Garter. Nobles and people alike would not extend to the mistress of the King's old age the benefits of the commanding motto of the Order, *Honi soit qui mal y pense.* Alice not only enriched herself with the spoils of favour, and decked herself in some at least of the jewels of Queen Philippa, but played high politics with lively zest. She even took her seat with the judges on the bench trying cases in which she was concerned. The movement of the nobility and the Commons was therefore united against her.

The King, at length worn down by war, business, and pleasure, subsided into senility. He had reached the allotted span. He celebrated the jubilee of his reign. The last decade was disparaging to his repute. Apart from Alice, he concentrated his remaining hopes upon the Black Prince; but this great soldier, renowned throughout Europe, was also brought low by the fatigues of war, and was sinking fast in health. In 1376 the Black Prince expired, leaving a son not ten years old as heir apparent to the throne. King Edward III's large share of life narrowed sharply at its end. Mortally stricken, he retired to Sheen Lodge, where Alice, after the modern fashion, encouraged him to dwell on tournaments, the chase, and wide plans when he should recover. But hostile chroniclers have it that when the stupor preceding death engulfed the King she took the rings from his fingers and other movable property in the house and departed for some time to extreme privacy. We have not heard her tale, but her reappearance in somewhat buoyant situations in the new reign seems to show that she had one to tell. All accounts, alas! confirm that King Edward died deserted by all, and that only the charity of a local priest procured him the protection and warrant of the Church in his final expedition.

The Black Prince's son was recognised as King by general assent on the very day his grandfather died, no question of election being raised, and the crown of England passed to a minor.

BOOK THREE

THE END OF THE
FEUDAL AGE

King Richard II and the Social Revolt

JOHN OF GAUNT, Duke of Lancaster, younger brother of the Black Prince, uncle of the King, was head of the Council of Regency and ruled the land. Both the impact and the shadow of the Black Death dominated the scene. A new fluidity swept English society. The pang of almost mortal injury still throbbed, but with it crept a feeling that there was for the moment more room in the land. A multitude of vacant places had been filled, and many men in all classes had the sense of unexpected promotion and enlargement about them. A community had been profoundly deranged, reduced in collective strength, but often individually lifted.

The belief that the English were invincible and supreme in war, that nothing could stand before their arms, was ingrained. The elation of Crécy and Poitiers survived the loss of all material gains in France. The assurance of being able to meet the French or the Scots at any time upon the battlefield overrode inquiries about the upshot of the war. Few recognised the difference between winning battles and making lasting conquests. Parliament in its youth was eager for war, improvident in preparation, and resentful in paying for it. While the war continued the Crown was expected to produce dazzlings results, and at the same time was censured for the burden of taxation and annoyance to the realm. A peace approached inexorably which would in no way correspond to the sensation of overwhelming victory in which the English indulged themselves. This ugly prospect came to Richard II as a prominent part of his inheritance.

In the economic and social sphere there arose a vast tumult. The Black Death had struck a world already in movement. Ever since the Crown had introduced the custom of employing wage-earning soldiers instead of the feudal levy the landed tie had been dissolving. Why should not the noble or knight follow the example of his liege lord? Covenants in which a small landowner undertook to serve a powerful neighbour, "except against the King," became common. The restriction would not always be observed. The old bonds of mutual loyalty were disappearing, and in their place grew private armies, the hired defenders of property, the sure precursors of anarchy.

In medieval England the lords of the manors had often based their prosperity on a serf peasantry, whose status and duties were enjoined by long custom and enforced by manorial courts. Around each manor a closely bound and self-sufficient community revolved. Although there had been more movement of labour and interchange of goods in the thirteenth and early fourteenth centuries than was formerly supposed, development had been relatively slow and the break-up of the village community gradual. The time had now come when the compartments of society and toil could no longer preserve their structure. The convulsion of the Black Death violently accelerated this deep and rending process. Nearly one-third of the population being suddenly dead, a large part of the land passed out of cultivation. The survivors turned their ploughs to the richest soils and quartered their flocks and herds on the fairest pastures. Many landowners abandoned ploughs and enclosed, often by encroachment, the best grazing. At this time, when wealth-getting seemed easier and both prices and profits ran high, the available labour was reduced by nearly a half. Small-holdings were deserted, and many manors were denuded of the peasantry who had served them from time immemorial. Ploughmen and labourers found themselves in high demand, and were competed for on all sides. They in their turn sought to better themselves, or at least to keep their living equal with the rising prices. The poet Langland gives an unsympathetic but interesting picture in *Piers Plowman:*

> Labourers that have no land, to live on but their hands,
> Deigned not to dine a day, on night-old wortes.
> May no penny ale him pay, nor a piece of bacon,
> But it be fresh flesh or fish, fried or baked,
> And that chaud and plus-chaud, for chilling of their maw,
> But he be highly-hired, else will he chide.

But their masters saw matters differently. They repulsed fiercely demands for increased wages; they revived ancient claims to forced or tied labour. The pedigrees of villagers were scrutinised with a care hitherto only bestowed upon persons of quality. The villeins who were declared serfs were at least free from new claims. Assertions of long-lapsed authority, however good in law, were violently resisted by the country folk. They formed unions of labourers to guard their interests. There were escapes of villeins from the estates, like those of the slaves from the Southern states of America in the 1850's. Some landlords in their embarrassment offered to commute the labour services they claimed and to procure obedience by granting leases to small-holders. On some manors the serfs were enfranchised in a body and a class of free tenants came into being. But this feature was rare. The greatest of all land-lords was the Church. On the whole the Spiritual Power stood up successfully against the assault of this part of its flock. When a landlord was driven, as was the Abbot of Battle, on the manor of Hutton, to lease vacant holdings this was done on the shortest terms, which at the first tactical opportunity were reduced to a yearly basis. A similar attempt in eighteenth-century France to revive obsolete feudal claims aroused the spirit of revolution.

The turmoil through which all England passed affected the daily life of the mass of the people in a manner not seen again in our social history till the Industrial Revolution of the nineteenth century. Here was a case in which a Parliament based upon property could have a decided opinion. In England, as in Frnace, the Crown had more than once in the past interfered with the local regulation of wages, but the Statute of Labourers (1351) was the first important attempt to fix wages and prices for the country as a whole. In the aggravated conditions following the pestilence Parliament sought to enforce these laws as fully as it dared. "Justices of labour," drawn from the rural middle classes and with fixed salaries, were appointed to try offenders. Between 1351 and 1377 nine thousand cases of breach of contract were tried before the Common Pleas. In many parts the commissioners, who were active and biased, were attacked by the inhabitants. Unrest spread wide and deep.

Still, on the morrow of the plague there was an undoubted well-being among the survivors. Revolts do not break out in countries depressed by starvation. Says Froissart, "The peasants' rebellion was caused and incited by the great ease and plenty in which the meaner folk of England lived." The people were not without the means of protesting against injustice, nor without the voice to express their discontent. Among the lower clergy the clerks with small benefices had been severely smitten by the Black Death. In East Anglia alone eight hundred priests had died. The survivors found that their stipends remained unaltered in a world of rising prices, and that the higher clergy were completely indifferent to this problem of the ecclesiastical proletarian. For this atonement was to be exacted. The episcopal manors were marked places of attack in the rising. At the fairs, on market-day, agitators, especially among the friars, collected and stirred crowds. Langland voiced the indignation of the established order against these Christian communists:

> They preach men of Plato and prove it by Seneca
> That all things under heaven ought to be in common:
> And yet he lies, as I live, that to the unlearned so preacheth.

Many vehement agitators, among whom John Ball is the best known, gave forth a stream of subversive doctrine. The country was full of broken soldiers, disbanded from the war, and all knew about the long-bow and its power to kill nobles, however exalted and well armed. The preaching of revolutionary ideas was widespread, and a popular ballad expressed the response of the masses:

> When Adam delved, and Eve span,
> Who was then a gentleman?

This was a novel question for the fourteenth century, and awkward at any time. The rigid, time-enforced framework of medieval England trembled to its foundations.

These conditions were by no means confined to the Island. Across the Channel a radical and democratic movement, with talk much akin to that of our own time, was afoot. All this rolled forward in England to the terrifying rebellion of 1381. It was a social upheaval, spontaneous and widespread, arising in various parts of the country from the same causes, and united by the same sentiments. That all this movement was the direct consequence of the Black Death is proved by the fact that the revolt was most fierce in those very districts of Kent and the East Midlands where the death-rate had been highest and the derangement of custom the most violent. It was a cry of pain and anger from a generation shaken out of submissiveness by changes in their lot, which gave rise alike to new hope and new injustice.

*　　*　　*　　*　　*

Throughout the summer of 1381 there was a general ferment. Beneath it all lay organisation. Agents moved round the villages of Central England, in touch with a "Great Society" which was said to meet in London. In May violence broke out in Essex. It was started by an attempt to make a second and more stringent collection of the poll-tax which had been levied in the previous year. The turbulent elements in London took fire, and a band under one Thomas Faringdon marched off to join the rebels. Walworth, the mayor, faced a strong municipal opposition which was in sympathy and contact with the rising. In Kent, after an attack on Lesnes Abbey, the peasants marched through Rochester and Maidstone, burning manorial and taxation records on their way. At Maidstone they released the agitator John Ball from the episcopal prison, and were joined by a military adventurer with gifts and experience of leadership, Wat Tyler.

The royal Council was bewildered and inactive. Early in June the main body of rebels from Essex and Kent moved on London. Here they found support. John Horn, fishmonger, invited them to enter; the alderman in charge of London Bridge did nothing to defend it, and Aldgate was opened treacherously to a band of Essex rioters. For three days the city was in confusion. Foreigners were murdered; two members of the Council, Simon Sudbury, the Archbishop of Canterbury and Chancellor, and Sir Robert Hales, the Treasurer, were dragged from the Tower and beheaded on Tower Hill; the Savoy palace of John of Gaunt was burnt; Lambeth and Southwark were sacked. This was the time for paying off old scores. Faringdon had drawn up proscription lists, and the extortionate financier Richard Lyons was killed. All this has a modern ring. But the loyal citizen body rallied round the mayor, and at Smithfield the King faced the rebel leaders. Among the insurgents there seems to have been a general loyalty to the sovereign. Their demands were reasonable but disconcerting. They asked for the repeal of oppressive statutes, for the abolition of villeinage, and for the division of Church property. In particular they asserted that no man ought to be a serf or do labour services to a *seigneur*, but pay fourpence an acre a year for his land and not have to serve any man against his will, but only by agreement. While the parley was going on Tyler was first wounded by Mayor Walworth and then smitten to death by one of the King's squires. As the rebel leader rolled off his horse, dead in the sight of the great assembly, the young King met the crisis by riding forward alone with the cry, "I will be your leader. You shall have from me all you seek. Only follow me to the fields outside." But the death of Tyler proved a signal for the wave of reaction. The leaderless bands wandered home and spread a vulgar lawlessness through their counties. They were pursued by reconstructed authority. Vengeance was wreaked.

The rising had spread throughout the South-West. There were riots in Bridgewater, Winchester, and Salisbury. In Hertfordshire the peasants rose against the powerful and hated Abbey of St Albans, and marched on London under Jack Straw. There was a general revolt in Cambridgeshire, accompanied by burning of rolls and attacks on episcopal manors. The Abbey of Ramsey, in Huntingdonshire, was attacked, though the burghers of Huntingdon shut their gates against the rioters. In Norfolk and Suffolk, where the peasants were richer and more independent, the irritation against legal villeinage was stronger. The Abbey of Bury St Edmunds was a prominent object of hatred, and the Flemish woollen-craftsmen were murdered in Lynn. Waves of revolt rippled on as far north as Yorkshire and Cheshire, and to the west in Wiltshire and Somerset.

But after Tyler's death the resistance of the ruling classes was organised. Letters were sent out from Chancery to the royal officials commanding the restoration of order, and justices under Chief Justice Tresilian gave swift judgment upon insurgents. The King, who accompanied Tresilian on the punitive circuit, pressed for the observance of legal forms in the punishment of rebels. The warlike Bishop le Despenser, of Norwich, used armed force in the Eastern Counties in defence of Church property, and a veritable battle was fought at North Walsham. Nevertheless the reaction was, according to modern examples, very restrained. Not more than a hundred and fifty executions are recorded in the rolls. There was nothing like the savagery we have seen in many parts of Europe in our own times. Law re-established ruled by law. Even in this furious class reaction no men were hanged except after trial by jury. In January 1382 a general amnesty, suggested by Parliament, was proclaimed. But the victory of property was won, and there followed the unanimous annulment of all concessions and a bold attempt to re-create intact the manorial system of the early part of the century. Yet for generations the upper classes lived in fear of a popular rising and the labourers continued to combine. Servile labour ceased to be the basis of the system. The legal aspect of serfdom became of little importance, and the development of commutation went on, speaking broadly, at an accelerated pace after 1349. Such were the more enduring legacies of the Black Death. The revolt, which to the historian is but a sudden flash of revealing light on medieval conditions among the poorer classes, struck with lasting awe the imagination of its contemporaries. It left a hard core of bitterness among the peasantry, and called forth a vigorous and watchful resistance from authority. Henceforth a fixed desire for the division of ecclesiastical property was conceived. The spread of Lollardy after the revolt drew upon it the hostility of the intimidated victors. Wyclif's "poor preachers" bore the stigma of having fomented the troubles, and their presecution was the revenge of a shaken system.

In the charged, sullen atmosphere of the England of the 1380's Wyclif's doctrines gathered wide momentum. But, faced by social revolution, English society was in no mood for Church reform. All subversive doctrines fell under censure, and although Wyclif was not directly responsible or accused of seditious preaching the result was disastrous to his cause. The landed classes gave silent assent to the ultimate suppression of the preacher by the Church. This descended swiftly and effectively. Wyclif's old opponent, Courtenay, had become Archbishop after Sudbury's murder. He found Wyclif's friends in control of Oxford. He acted with speed. The doctrines of the reformer were officially condemned. The bishops were instructed to arrest all unlicensed preachers, and the Archbishop himself rapidly became the head of a system of Church discipline; and this, with the active support of the State in Lancastrian days, eventually enabled the Church to recover from the attack of the laity. In 1382 Courtenay descended upon Oxford and held a convocation where Christ Church now stands. The chief Lollards were sharply summoned to recant. The Chancellor's protest of university privilege was brushed aside. Hard censure fell upon Wyclif's followers. They blenched and bowed. Wyclif found himself alone. His attack on Church doctrine as distinct from Church privilege had lost him the support of Gaunt. His popular preachers and the first beginnings of Bible-reading could not build a solid party against the dominant social forces.

Wyclif appealed to the conscience of his age. Baffled, though not silenced, in England, his inspiration stirred a distant and little-known land, and thence disturbed Europe. Students from Prague had come to Oxford, and carried his doctrines, and indeed the manuscripts of his writings, to Bohemia. From this sprang the movement by which the fame of John Huss eclipsed that of his English master and evoked the enduring national consciousness of the Czech people.

By his frontal attack on the Church's absolute authority over men in this world, by his implication of the supremacy of the individual conscience, and by his challenge to ecclesiastical dogma Wyclif had called down upon himself the thunderbolts of repression. But his protest had led to the first of the Oxford Movements. The cause, lost in his day, impelled the tide of the Reformation. Lollardy, as the Wyclif Movement came to be called, was driven beneath the surface. The Church, strengthening its temporal position by alliance with the State, brazenly repelled the first assault; but its spiritual authority bore henceforward and scars and enfeeblement resulting from the conflict.

Fuller, the seventeenth-century writer, wrote of Wyclif's preachers, "These men were sentinels against an army of enemies until God sent Luther to relieve them." In Oxford Wyclifite tradition lingered in Bible study until the Reformation, to be revived by Colet's lectures of 1497–98. In the country Lollardy became identified with political sedition, though this was not what Wyclif had taught. Its ecclesiastical opponents were eager to make the charge, and the passionate, sometimes ignorant, invective of the Lollard preachers, often laymen, supplied a wealth of evidence. Cruel days lay ahead. The political tradition was to be burned out in the misery of Sir John Oldcastle's rebellion under Henry V. But a vital element of resistance to the formation of a militant and triumphant Church survived in the English people. A principle had been implanted in English hearts which shaped the destiny of the race. Wyclif's failure in his own day was total, and the ray of his star faded in the light of the Reformation dawn. "Wyclif," wrote Milton in *Areopagitica,* "was a man who wanted, to render his learning consummate, nothing but his living in a happier age."

The stubborn wish for practical freedom was not broken in England, and the status and temper of the people stand in favourable contrast to the exhausted passivity of the French peasant, bludgeoned to submission by war, famine, and the brutal suppressions of the Jacquerie.

"It is cowardise and lack of hartes and corage," wrote Sir John Fortescue, the eminent jurist of Henry VI's reign, "that kepeth the Frenchmen from rysyng, and not povertye; which corage no Frenche man hath like to the English man. It hath ben often seen in Englond that iij or iv thefes, for povertie, hath sett upon vij or viij true men, and robbyd them al. But it had not been seen in Fraunce, that vij or viij thefes have ben hardy to robbe iij or iv true men. Wherefor it is right seid that few Frenchmen be hangyd for robbery, for that they have no hertys to do so terryble an acte. There be therefor mo men hangyd in Eglnd, in a yere, for robberye and manslaughter, than ther be hangid in Fraunce for such cause of crime in vij yers."

*   *   *   *   *

The King was now growing up. His keen instincts and precocious abilities were sharpened by all that he had seen and done. In the crisis of the Peasants' Revolt the brunt of many things had fallen upon him, and by his personal action he had saved the situation on a memorable occasion. It was the King's

Court and the royal judges who had restored order when the feudal class had lost their nerve. Yet the King consented to a prolonged tutelage. John of Gaunt, Viceroy of Aquitaine, quitted the realm to pursue abroad interests which included claims to the kingdom of Castile. He left behind him his son, Henry, a vigorous and capable youth, to take charge of his English estates and interests.

It was not till he was twenty that Richard determined to be complete master of his Council, and in particular to escape from the control of his uncles. No King had been treated in such a way before. His grandfather had been obeyed when he was eighteen. Richard at sixteen had played decisive parts. His Household and the Court around it were deeply interested in his assumption of power. This circle comprised the brains of the Government, and the high Civil Service. Its chiefs were the Chancellor, Michael de la Pole, Chief Justice Tresilian, and Alexander Neville, Archbishop of York. Behind them Simon Burley, Richard's tutor and close intimate, was probably the guide. A group of younger nobles threw in their fortunes with the Court. Of these the head was Robert de Vere, Earl of Oxford, who now played a part resembling that of Gaveston under Edward II, and in one aspect foreshadowed that of Strafford in a future generation. The King, the fountain of honour, spread his favours among his adherents, and de Vere was soon created Duke of Ireland. This was plainly a political challenge to the magnates of the Council. Ireland was a reservoir of men and supplies, beyond the control of Parliament and the nobility, which could be used for the mastery of England.

The accumulation of Household and Government offices by the clique around the King and his effeminate favourite affronted the feudal party, and to some extent the national spirit. As so often happens, the opposition found in foreign affairs a vehicle of attack. Lack of money, fear of asking for it, and above all no military leadership, had led the Court to pacific courses. The nobility were at one with the Parliament in decrying the unmartial Chancellor Pole and the lush hedonism of the Court. "They were," they jeered, "rather knights of Venus than of Bellona." War must be waged with France; and on this theme in 1386 a coherent front was formed against the Crown. Parliament was led to appoint a commission of five Ministers and nine lords, of whom the former Councillors of Regency were the chiefs. The Court bent before the storm of Pole's impeachment. A purge of the Civil Service, supposed to be the source alike of the King's errors and of his strength, was instituted; and we may note that Geoffrey Chaucer, his equerry, but famous for other reasons, lost his two posts in the Customs.

When the commissioners presently compelled the King to dismiss his personal friends Richard in deep distress withdrew from London. In North Wales he consorted with the new Duke of Ireland, at York with Archbishop Neville, and at Nottingham with Chief Justice Tresilian. He sought to marshal his forces for civil war at the very same spot where Charles I would one day unfurl the royal standard. Irish levies, Welsh pikemen, and above all Cheshire archers from his own earldom, were gathering to form an army. Upon this basis of force Tresilian and four other royal judges pronounced that the pressure put upon him by the Lords Appellant, as they were now styled, and the Parliament was contrary to the laws and Constitution of England. This judgment, the legal soundness of which is undoubted, was followed by a bloody reprisal. The King's uncle, Gloucester, together with other heads of the baronial oligarchy, denounced the Chief Justice and those who had acted with him, including de Vere and the other royal advisers, as traitors to the realm. The King—he was but twenty

—had based himself too bluntly upon his royal authority. The lords of the Council were still able to command the support of Parliament. They resorted to arms. Gloucester, with an armed power, approached London. Richard, arriving there first, was welcomed by the people. They displayed his red and white colours, and showed attachment to his person, but they were not prepared to fight the advancing baronial army. In Westminster Hall the three principal Lords Appellant, Gloucester, Arundel, and Warwick, with an escort outside of three hundred horsemen, bullied the King into submission. He could do no more than secure the escape of his supporters.

De Vere retired to Chester and raised an armed force to secure the royal rights. With this, in December 1387, he marched towards London. But now appeared in arms the Lords Appellant, and also Gaunt's son Henry. At Radcot Bridge, in Oxfordshire, Henry and they defeated and broke de Vere. The favourite fled overseas. The King was now at the mercy of the proud faction which had usurped the rights of the monarchy. They disputed long among themselves whether or not he should be deposed and killed. The older men were for the extreme course; the younger restrained them. Richard was brutally threatened with the fate of his great-grandfather, Edward II. So severe was the discussion that only two of the Lords Appellant consented to remain with him for supper. It was Henry, the young military victor, who pleaded for moderation, possibly because his father's claim to the throne would have been overridden by the substitution of Gloucester for Richard.

The Lords Appellant, divided as they were, shrank from deposing and killing the King; but they drew the line at nothing else. They forced him to yield at every point. Cruel was the vengeance that they wreaked upon the upstart nobility of his circle and his legal adherents. The Estates of the Realm were summoned to give countenance to the new régime. On the appointed day the five Lords Appellant, in golden clothes, entered Westminster Hall arm-in-arm. "The Merciless Parliament" opened its session. The most obnoxious opponents were the royal judges, headed by Tresilian. He had promulgated at Nottingham the doctrine of the Royal Supremacy, with its courts and lawyers, over the nobles who held Parliament in their hand. To this a solemn answer was now made, which, though, as so often before, it asserted the fact of feudal power, also proclaimed the principle of Parliamentary control. The fact vanished in the turbulence of those days, but the principle echoed down into the seventeenth century.

Chief Justice Tresilian and four of the other judges responsible for the Nottingham declaration were hanged, drawn, and quartered at Tyburn. The royal tutor, Burley, was not spared. The victory of the old nobility was complete. Only the person of the King was respected, and that by the narrowest of margins. Richard, forced not only to submit but to assent to the slaughter of his friends, buried himself as low as he could in retirement.

We must suppose that this treatment produced a marked impression upon his mind. It falls to the lot of few mortals to endure such ordeals. He brooded upon his wrongs, and also upon his past mistakes. He saw in the triumphant lords men who would be tyrants not only over the King but over the people. He laid his plans for revenge and for his own rights with far more craft than before. For a year there was a sinister lull.

* * * * *

On May 3, 1389, Richard took action which none of them had foreseen. Taking his seat at the Council, he asked blandly to be told how old he was. On being answered that he was three-and-twenty he declared that he had certainly come of age, and that he would no longer submit to restrictions upon his rights which none of his subjects would endure. He would manage the realm himself; he would choose his own advisers; he would be King indeed. This stroke had no doubt been prepared with the uncanny and abnormal cleverness which marked many of Richard's schemes. It was immediately successful. Bishop Thomas, the Earl of Arundel's brother, and later Archbishop of Canterbury, surrendered the Great Seal at his demand. Bishop Gilbert quitted the Treasury, and the King's sympathisers, William of Wykeham and Thomas Brantingham, were restored to their posts as Chancellor and Treasurer. King's nominees were added to those of the Appellants on the judicial bench. Letters from the King to the sheriffs announced that he had assumed the government, and the news was accepted by the public with an unexpected measure of welcome.

Richard used his victory with prudence and mercy. In October 1389 John of Gaunt returned from Spain, and his son, Henry, now a leading personage, was reconciled to the King. The terrible combination of 1388 had dissolved. The machinery of royal government, triumphant over faction, resumed its sway, and for the next eight years Richard governed England in the guise of a constitutional and popular King.

This was an age in which the masses were totally excluded from power, and when the ruling classes, including the new middle class, even in their most deadly quarrels, always united to keep them down. Richard has been judged and his record declared by the socially powerful elements which overthrew him; but their verdict upon his character can only be accepted under reserve. That he sought to subvert and annul the constitutional rights which the rivalries of factions and of Church and baronage had unconsciously but resolutely built up cannot be denied; but whether this was for purposes of personal satisfaction or in the hope of fulfilling the pledge which he had made in the crisis of the Peasants' Revolt, "I will be your leader," is a question not to be incontinently brushed aside. It is true that to one deputation of rebels in 1381 he had testily replied, "Villeins ye are still, and villeins ye shall remain," adding that pledges made under duress went for nothing. Yet by letters patent he freed many peasants from their feudal bonds. He had solemnly promised the abolition of serfdom. He had proposed it to Parliament. He had been overruled. He had a long memory for injuries. Perhaps also it extended to his obligations.

The patience and skill with which Richard accomplished his revenge are most striking. For eight years he tolerated the presence of Arundel and Gloucester, not, as before, as the governors of the country, but still in high positions. There were moments when his passion flared. In 1394, when Arundel was late for the funeral of the Queen, Anne of Bohemia, and the whole procession was delayed, he snatched a steward's wand, struck him in the face and drew blood. The clergy raised a cry that the Church of Westminster had been polluted. Men raked up an old prophecy that God's punishment for the murder of Thomas à Becket would not be exacted from the nation until blood was shed in that sacred nave. Yet after a few weeks we see the King apparently reconciled to Arundel and all proceeding under a glittering mask.

While the lords were at variance the King sought to strengthen himself by gathering Irish resources. In 1394 he went with all the formality of a Royal Progress to Ireland, and for this purpose created an army dependent upon himself, which was to be useful later in overawing opposition in England. When he returned his plans for subduing both the baronage and the Estates to his authority were far advanced. To free himself from the burden of war, which would make him directly dependent upon the favours of Parliament, he made a settlement with France. After the death of his first wife, Anne, he had married in 1396 the child Isabelle, daughter of Charles VI of France. Upon this a truce or pact of amity and non-aggression for thirty years was concluded. A secret clause laid down that if Richard were in future to be menaced by any of his subjects the King of France would come to his aid. Although the terms of peace were the subject of complaint the King gained immensely by his liberation from the obligation of making a war, which he could only sustain by becoming the beggar and drudge of Parliament. So hard had the Estates pressed the royal power, now goading it on and now complaining of results, that we have the unique spectacle of a Plantagenet king lying down and refusing to pull the wagon farther over such stony roads. But this did not spring from lack of mental courage or from narrowness of outlook. It was a necessary feature in the King's far-reaching designs. He wished beyond doubt to gain absolute power over the nobility and Parliament. Whether he also purposed to use this dictatorship in the interests of the humble masses of his subjects is one of the mysteries, but also the legend, long linked with his name. His temperament, the ups and downs of his spirits, his sudden outbursts, the almost superhuman refinements of his calculations, have all been abundantly paraded as the causes of his ruin. But the common people thought he was their friend. He would, they imagined, had he the power, deliver them from the hard oppression of their masters, and long did they cherish his memory.

*   *   *   *   *

The Irish expedition had been the first stage towards the establishment of a despotism; the alliance with France was the second. The King next devoted himself to the construction of a compact, efficient Court party. Both Gaunt and his son and Mowbray, Earl of Norfolk, one of the former Appellants, were now rallied to his side, partly in loyalty to him and partly in hostility to Arundel and Gloucester. New men were brought into the Household. Sir John Bushy and Sir Henry Greene represented local county interests and were unquestioning servants of the Crown. Drawn from the Parliamentary class, the inevitable arbiter of the feuds between Crown and aristocracy, they secured to the King the influence necessary to enable him to face the Estates of the Realm. In January 1397 the Estates were summoned to Westminster, where under deft and at the same time resolute management they showed all due submission. Thus assured, Richard decided at last to strike.

Arundel and Gloucester, though now somewhat in the shade, must have considered themselves protected by time and much friendly intercourse from the consequences of what they had done in 1388. Much had happened since then, and Chief Justice Tresilian, the tutor Burley, and other victims of that blood-bath seemed distant memories. It was with amazement that they saw the King advancing upon them in cold hatred rarely surpassed among men. Arundel and some others of his associates were declared traitors and accorded only the courtesy of decapitation. Warwick was exiled to the Isle of Man. Gloucester, arrested and taken to Calais, was there murdered by Richard's agents; and this deed, not being covered by constitutional forms, bred in its turn new retributions. A stigma rested henceforward on the King similar to that which had marked John after the murder of Arthur. But for the moment he was supreme as no King of all England had been before, and still his wrath was unassuaged.

Parliament was called only to legalise these events. It was found to be so packed and so minded that there was nothing they would not do for the King. Never has there been such a Parliament. With ardour pushed to suicidal lengths, it suspended almost every constitutional right and privilege gained in the preceding century. It raised the monarchy upon a foundation more absolute than even William the Conqueror, war-leader of his freebooting lieutenants, had claimed. All that had been won by the nation through the crimes of John and the degeneracy of Edward II, all that had been conceded or established by the two great Edwards, was relinquished. And the Parliament, having done its work with this destructive thoroughness, ended by consigning its unfinished business to the care of a committee of eighteen persons. As soon as Parliament had dispersed Richard had the record altered by inserting words that greatly enlarged the scope of the committee's work. If his object was not to do away with Parliament, it was at least to reduce it to the rôle it had played in the early days of Edward I, when it had been in fact as well as in name the "King's Parliament."

The relations between Gaunt's son, Henry, the King's cousin and contemporary, passed through drama into tragedy. Henry believed himself to have saved the King from being deposed and murdered by Gloucester, Arundel, and Warwick in the crisis of 1388. Very likely this was true. Since then he had dwelt in familiarity and friendship with Richard; he represented a different element from the old nobility who had challenged the Crown. These two young men had lived their lives in fair comradeship; the one was King, the other, as son of John of Gaunt, stood near the throne and nearer to the succession.

A quarrel arose between Henry and Thomas Mowbray, now Duke of Norfolk. Riding back from Brentford to London, Mowbray voiced his uneasiness. The King, he said, had never forgiven Radcot Bridge nor the former Appellant party, to which he and his companion had both belonged. They would be the next victims. Henry accused Mowbray of treasonable

language. Conflicting reports of what had been said were laid
before Parliament. Each, when challenged, gave the lie to the
other. Trial by battle appeared the correct solution. The
famous scene took place in September 1398. The lists were
drawn; the English world assembled; the champions presented
themselves; but the King, exasperating the spectators of all
classes who had gathered in high expectation to see the sport,
cast down his wardour, forbade the combat, and exiled
Mowbray for life and Henry for a decade. Both lords obeyed
the royal commands. Mowbray soon died; but Henry, astounded by what he deemed ingratitude and injustice, lived
and schemed in France.

*   *   *   *   *

The year which followed was an unveiled despotism, and
Richard, so patient till his vengeance was accomplished,
showed restlessness and perplexity, profusion and inconse-
quence, in his function. Escorted by his faithful archers from
Cheshire, he sped about the kingdom beguiling the weeks with
feasts and tournaments, while the administration was left to
minor officials at Westminster or Ministers who felt they were
neither trusted nor consulted. Financial stringency followed
royal extravagance, and forced loans and heavier taxes
angered the merchants and country gentry.

During 1398 there were many in the nation who awoke to
the fact that a servile Parliament had in a few weeks suspended
many of the fundamental rights and liberties of the realm.
Hitherto for some time they had had no quarrel with the King.
They now saw him revealed as a despot. Not only the old nobility, who in the former crisis had been defeated, but all the
gentry and merchant classes, were aghast at the triumph of
absolute rule. Nor did their wrath arise from love of constitutional practices alone. They feared, perhaps with many reasons
not known to us, that the King, now master, would rule over

their heads, resting himself upon the submissive shoulders of the mass of the people. They felt again the terror of the social revolution which they had tasted so recently in the Peasants' Revolt. A solid amalgamation of interest, temper, and action united all the classes which had raised or found themselves above the common level. Here was a King, now absolute, who would, as they muttered, let loose the mob upon them.

In February of 1399 died old John of Gaunt, "time-honoured Lancaster." Henry, in exile, succeeded to vast domains, not only in Lancashire and the north but scattered all over England. Richard, pressed for money, could not refrain from a technical legal seizure of the Lancaster estates in spite of his promises; he declared his cousin disinherited. This challenged the position of every property-holder. And forthwith, by a fatal misjudgment of his strength and of what was stirring in the land, the King set forth in May upon a punitive expedition, which was long overdue, to assert the royal authority in Ireland. He left behind him a disordered administration, deprived of troops, and a land violently incensed against him. News of the King's departure was carried to Henry. The moment had come; the coast was clear, and the man did not tarry. In July Henry of Lancaster, as he had now become, landed in Yorkshire, declaring that he had only come to claim his lawful rights as heir to his venerated father. He was immediately surrounded by adherents, particularly from the Lancaster estates, and the all powerful Northern Lords led by the Earl of Northumberland. The course of his revolt followed exactly that of Isabella and Mortimer against Edward II seventy-two years before. From York Henry marched across England, amid general acclamation, to Bristol, and just as Isabella had hanged Hugh Despenser upon its battlements, so now did Henry of Lancaster exact the capital forfeit from William Scrope, Earl of Wiltshire, Bushy, and Greene, King Richard's Ministers and representatives.

It took some time for the news of Henry's apparition and all that followed so swiftly from it to reach King Richard in the depths of Ireland. He hastened back, though baffled by stormy seas. Having landed in England on July 27, he made a rapid three weeks' march through North Wales in an attempt to gather forces. What he saw convinced him that all was over. The whole structure of his power, so patiently and subtly built up, had vanished as if by enchantment. The Welsh, who would have stood by him, could not face the advancing power of what was now all England. At Flint Castle he submitted to Henry, into whose hands the whole administration had now passed. He rode through London as a captive in his train. He was lodged in the Tower. His abdication was extorted; his death had become inevitable. The last of all English kings whose hereditary right was indisputable disappeared for ever beneath the portcullis of Pontefract Castle. Henry, by and with the consent of the Estates of the Realm and the Lords Spiritual and Temporal, ascended the throne as Henry IV, and thereby opened a chapter of history destined to be fatal to the medieval baronage. Although Henry's lineage afforded good grounds for his election to the Crown, and his own qualities, and still more those of his son, confirmed this decision, a higher right in blood was to descend through the house of Mortimer to the house of York, and from this after a long interval the Wars of the Roses broke out upon England.

*   *   *   *   *

The character of Richard II and his place in the regard of history remain an enigma. That he possessed qualities of a high order, both for design and action, is evident. That he was almost from childhood confronted with measureless difficulties and wrongful oppressions against which he repeatedly made head is also plain. The injuries and cruelties which he suffered at the hands of his uncle Gloucester and the high nobility may perhaps be the key to understanding him. Some historians have felt that he was prepared not only to exploit Parliamentary and legal manœuvres against the governing classes, but perhaps even that he would use social forces then and for many generations utterly submerged. At any rate, the people for their part long cherished some such notion of him. These unhappy folk, already to be numbered by the million, looked to Richard with hopes destined to be frustrated for centuries. All through the reign of Henry IV the conception they had formed of Richard was idealised. He was deemed, whether rightly or wrongly, a martyr to the causes of the weak and poor. Statutes were passed declaring it high treason even to spread the rumour that he was still alive.

We have no right in this modern age to rob him of this shaft of sunlight which rests upon his harassed, hunted life. There is however no dispute that in his nature fantastic error and true instinct succeeded each other with baffling rapidity. He was capable of more than human cunning and patience, and also of foolishness which a simpleton would have shunned. He fought four deadly duels with feudal aristocratic society. In 1386 he was overcome; in 1389 he was victorious; in 1397–98 he was supreme; in 1399 he was destroyed.

The Usurpation of Henry Bolingbroke

A LL power and authority fell to King Henry IV, and all who had run risks to place him on the throne combined to secure his right, and their own lives. But the opposite theme endured with strange persistency. The Court of France deemed Henry a usurper. His right in blood was not valid while Richard lived, nor even afterwards when the lineage was scrutinised. But other rights existed. The right of conquest, on which he was inclined to base himself, was discarded by him upon good advice. But the fact that he was acclaimed by the Estates summoned in Richard's name, added to a near right by birth, afforded a broad though challenged foundation for his reign. Many agreeable qualities stand to his credit. All historians concur that he was manly, capable, and naturally merciful. The beginning of his reign was disturbed by the tolerance and lenity which he showed to the defeated party. He who had benefited most from the violent spasm and twist of fortune which had overthrown Richard was the least vindictive against Richard's adherents. He had been near the centre of all the stresses of the late reign; he had been wronged and ill-used; yet he showed a strong repugnance to harsh reprisals. In the hour of his accession he was still the bold knight, surprisingly moderate in success, averse from bloodshed, affianced to growing constitutional ideas, and always dreaming of ending his life as a Crusader. But the sullen, turbulent march of events frustrated his tolerant inclinations and eventually soured his generous nature.

From the outset Henry depended upon Parliament to make good by its weight the defects in his title, and rested on the theory of the elective, limited kingship rather than on that of absolute monarchy. He was therefore alike by mood and need a constitutional King. Great words were used at his accession. "This honourable realm of England, the most abundant angle of riches in the whole world," said Archbishop Arundel, "has been reduced to destruction by the counsels of children and widows. Now God has sent a man, knowing and discreet, for governance, who by the aid of God will be governed and counselled by the wise and ancient of his realm."

"The affairs of the kingdom lie upon us," said the Archbishop. Henry would not act by his own will nor of his own "voluntary purpose or singular opinion, but by common advice, counsel, and consent." Here we see a memorable advance in practice. Parliament itself must not however be deemed a fountain of wisdom and virtue. The instrument had no sure base. It could be packed or swayed. Many of the Parliaments of this period were dubbed with epithets: "the Good Parliament," "the Mad Parliament," "the Merciless Parliament," were fresh in memory. Moreover, the stakes in the game of power played by the great nobles were far beyond what ordinary men or magnates would risk. Who could tell that some sudden baronial exploit might not overset the whole structure upon which they stood? As each change of power had been attended by capital vengeance upon the vanquished there arose in the Commons a very solid and enduring desire to let the great lords cut each other's throats if they were so minded. Therefore the Commons, while acting with vigour, preferred to base themselves upon petition rather than resolution, thus throwing the responsibility definitely upon the most exalted ruling class.

Seeking further protection, they appealed to the King not to judge of any matter from their debates or from the part taken in them by various Members, but rather to await the collective decision of the House. They strongly pressed the doctrine of "grievances before supply," and although Henry refused to accept this claim he was kept so short of money that in practice it was largely conceded. During this time therefore Parliamentary power over finance was greatly strengthened. Not only did the Estates supply the money by voting the taxes, but they began to follow its expenditure, and to require and to receive accounts from the high officers of the State. Nothing like this had been tolerated by any of the Kings before. They had always condemned it as a presumptuous inroad upon their prerogative. These great advances in the polity of England were the characteristics of Lancastrian rule, and followed naturally from the need the house of Lancaster had to buttress its title by public opinion and constitutional authority. Thus Parliament in this early epoch appears to have gained ground never held again till the seventeenth century.

But although the spiritual and lay Estates had seemed not only to choose the sovereign but even to prescribe the succession to the Crown, and the history of these years furnished precedents which Stuart lawyers carefully studied, the actual power of Parliament at this time must not be overstated. The usurpation of Henry IV, the establishment of the rival house in the person of Edward IV, the ousting of Edward V by his uncle, were all acts of feudal violence and rebellion, covered up by declaratory statutes. Parliament was not the author, or even the powerful agent, in these changes, but only the apprehensive registrar of these results of martial and baronial struggles. Elections were not free: the pocket borough was as common in the fifteenth as in the eighteenth century, and Parliament was but the tool and seal of any successful party in the State. It had none the less been declared upon Parliamentary authority, although at Henry's instance, that the crown should pass to the King's eldest son, and to his male issue after him. Thus what had been the English usage was overridden by excluding an elder line dependent on a female link. This did not formally ban succession in the female line, but such was for a long time the practical effect.

On one issue indeed, half social, half religious, King and Parliament were heartily agreed. The Lollards' advocacy of a Church purified by being relieved of all worldly goods did not command the assent of the clergy. They resisted with wrath and vigour. Lollardy had bitten deep into the minds not only of the poorer citizens but of the minor gentry throughout the country. It was in essence a challenge first to the Church and then to the wealthy. The Lollards now sought to win the lay nobility by pointing out how readily the vast treasure of the Church might provide the money for Continental war. But this appeal fell upon deaf ears. The lords saw that their own estates stood on no better title than those of the Church. They therefore joined with the clergy in defence of their property. Very severe laws were now enacted against the Lollards. The King declared, in full agreement with the Estates, that he would destroy heresies with all his strength. In 1401 a terrible statute, *De Heretico Comburendo*, condemned relapsed heretics to be burnt alive, and left the judgment solely to the Church, requiring sheriffs to execute it without allowing an appeal to the Crown. Thus did orthodoxy and property make common cause and march together.

*   *   *   *   *

But the Estates of the Realm considered that their chief immediate safeguard lay in the blotting out of the eclipsed faction. They were the hottest against Richard and those who had been faithful to him. Henry might have been able to stem this tide of cowardly retribution but for a sinister series of events. He and most of his Court fell violently ill through something they had eaten, and poison was suspected. The Welsh, already discontented, under the leadership of Owen Glendower, presently espoused Richard's cause. The slowness of communication had enabled one set of forces to sweep the country while the opposite had hardly realized what was happening. Now they in their turn began to move. Five of the six former Lords Appellant, finding themselves in the shade, formed with friends of Richard II a plot to seize the usurping prince at Windsor. Recovered from his mysterious sickness, riding alone by dangerous roads, Henry evaded their trap. But armed risings appeared in several parts of the country. The severity with which these were quelled mounted to the summit of government. The populace in places joined with the Government forces. The townsfolk at Cirencester beheaded Lord Lumley and the Earls of Kent and Salisbury, the last a Lollard. The conspiracy received no genuine support. All the mercy of Henry's temper could not moderate the prosecutions enforced by those who shared his risks. Indeed in a year his popularity was almost destroyed by what was held to be his weakness in dealing with rebellion and attempted murder. Yet we must understand that he was a braver, stronger man than these cruel personages below him.

The unsuccessful revolt, the civil war which had begun for Richard after his fall, was fatal to the former King. A sanctity dwelt about his person, and all the ceremonial and constitutional procedure which enthroned his successor could not rob him of it. As he lay in Pontefract Castle he was the object of many sympathies both from his adherents and from the suppressed masses. And this chafed and gnawed the party in power. Richard's death was announced in February 1400. Whether he was starved, or, as the Government suggested, went on hunger strike, or whether more direct methods were used, is unknowable. The walls of Pontefract have kept their secret. But far and wide throughout England spread the tale that he had escaped, and that in concealment he awaited his hour to bring the common people of the time to the enjoyment of their own.

All this welled up against Henry of Bolingbroke. He faced continual murder plots. The trouble with the Welsh deepened into a national insurrection. Owen Glendower, who was a remarkable man, of considerable education, carried on a war which was the constant background of English affairs till 1409. The King was also forced to fight continually against the Scots. After six years of this harassment we are told that his natural magnanimity was worn out, and that he yielded himself to the temper of his supporters and of his Parliament in cruel deeds. It may well be so.

His most serious conflict was with the Percys. These lords of the Northern Marches, the old Earl of Northumberland and his fiery son Hotspur, had for nearly three years carried on the defence of England against the Scots unaided and almost entirely at their own expense. They also held important areas for the King in North Wales. They could no longer bear the burden. They demanded a settlement of the account. The Earl presented a bill for £60,000. The King, in bitter poverty, could offer but £40,000. Behind this was a longer tale. The Percys had played a great part in placing Henry on the throne. But Edmund Mortimer, Hotspur's brother-in-law, had joined Glendower in rebellion, and the family were now under suspicion. They held a great independent power, and an antagonism was perhaps inevitable. Hotspur raised the standard of revolt. But at Shrewsbury on July 21, 1403, Henry overcame and slew him in a small, fierce battle. The old Earl, who was marching to his aid, was forced to submit, and pardon was freely extended to him. Parliament was at pains to absolve him from all charges of treason and rebellion and declared him guilty of trespass alone. This clemency was no doubt due to the necessities of the Border and to lack of any other means of defending it against the Scots. The Earl therefore addressed himself to this task, which secured his position at the head of strong forces.

But two years later, with his son's death at heart, he rebelled again, and this time the conspiracy was far-reaching. Archbishop Scrope of York and Thomas Mowbray, Earl of Nottingham, were his principal confederates. The programme of the rebellion was reform, and all personal issues were avoided. Once again Henry marched north, and once again he was successful. Northumberland was driven across the Border, where for some years he remained a menace. Scrope and Mowbray fell into the hands of the King's officers, and Henry, in spite of the appeals of the Archbishop of Canterbury, allowed them to be beheaded after a summary trial. Scrope's execution caused a profound shock throughout the land, and many compared it with the murder of Thomas Becket. At the same time the King's health failed. He was said to be smitten with leprosy, and this was attributed to the wrath of God. The diagnosis at least was incorrect. He had a disfiguring affection of the skin, and a disease of the heart, marked by fainting fits and trances. He was physically a broken man. Henceforward his reign was a struggle against death as well as life.

He still managed to triumph in the Welsh war, and Owen Glendower was forced back into his mountains. But Parliament took all advantages from the King's necessities. Henry saw safety only in surrender. He yielded himself and his burdens to the Estates with the constitutional deference of a modern sovereign. They pressed him hard, and in all the ways most intimately galling. Foreigners, not even excepting the Queen's two daughters, were to be expelled. A Council must be nominated by the King which included the Parliamentary leaders. The accounts of Government expenses were subjected to a Parliamentary audit. The King's own Household was combed and remodelled by unfriendly hands. The new Council demanded even fuller powers. The King pledged himself to govern only by their advice. By these submissions Henry became the least of kings. But he had transferred an intolerable task to others. They had the odium and the toil. They were increasingly unworthy of the trust.

*　　*　　*　　*　　*

A new figure now came upon the scene. Henry's eldest son, the Prince of Wales, showed already an extraordinary force and quality. He had led the charge against Hotspur at Shrewsbury. He had gained successes in Wales. It was only after the virtual defeat of Glendower that Prince Henry was free to turn to large political intrigue. As his father's health declined he was everywhere drawn into State business. He accepted all duties, and sought only for more. Pressed by his adherents, principally his half-uncles, the three Beaufort brothers, to take over the Government from the failing hands of an invalid, he headed a demand that the King should abdicate in his favour. But Henry of Bolingbroke, though tottering, repulsed the proposal with violent indignation. There was a stern confrontation of father and son at Westminster in 1411. The King's partisans appeared to be the more numerous or more resolute. The Prince withdrew abashed. He was removed from the presidency of the Council and his adherents were dismissed from office. He hid his head in retirement. His opponents even charged him with embezzling the pay of the Calais garrison. From this he cleared himself decisively. But there can be no doubt that the dying sovereign still gripped convulsively the reins of power. Misgovernment and decrepitude remained for a while successfully enthroned. In 1412, when the King could no longer walk and scarcely ride, he was with difficulty dissuaded by his Council from attempting to command the troops in Aquitaine. He lingered through the winter, talked of a Crusade, summoned Parliament in February, but could do no business with it. In March, when praying in Westminster Abbey, he had a prolonged fit, from which he rallied only to die in the Jerusalem Chamber on March 20, 1413.

Thus the life and reign of King Henry IV exhibit to us another instance of the vanities of ambition and the harsh guerdon which rewards its success. He had had wrongs to avenge and a cause to champion. He had hardly dared at first to aim at the crown, but he had played the final stake to gain it. He had found it less pleasing when possessed. Not only physically but morally he sank under its weight. His years of triumph were his years of care and sorrow. But none can say he had not reason and justice behind his actions, or that he was not accepted by the country at large. Upon his death a new personality, built upon a grand historic scale, long hungry for power, ascended without dispute the throne not only of England, but very soon of almost all Western Christendom.

The Empire of Henry V

A GLEAM of splendour falls across the dark, troubled story medieval England. Henry V was King at twenty-six. He felt, as his father had never done, sure of his title. He had spent his youth in camp and Council; he had for five or six years intermittently conducted the government of the kingdom during his father's decline. The romantic stories of his riotous youth and sudden conversion to gravity and virtue when charged with the supreme responsibility must not be pressed too far. It may well be true that "he was in his youth a diligent follower of idle practices, much given to instruments of music, and fired with the torches of Venus herself." But if he had thus yielded to the vehement ebullitions of his nature this was no more than a pastime, for always since boyhood he had been held in the grasp of grave business.

In the surging realm, with its ailing King, bitter factions, and deep social and moral unrest, all men had for some time looked to him; and succeeding generations have seldom doubted that according to the standards of his day he was all that a king should be. His face, we are told, was oval, with a long, straight nose, ruddy complexion, dark, smooth hair, and bright eyes, mild as a dove's when unprovoked, but lion-like in wrath; his frame was slender, yet well-knit, strong and active. His disposition was orthodox, chivalrous and just. He came to the throne at a moment when England was wearied of feuds and brawl and yearned for unity and fame. He led the nation away from internal discord to foreign conquest; and he had the dream, and perhaps the prospect, of leading all Western Europe into the high championship of a Crusade. Council and Parliament alike showed themselves suddenly bent on war with France. As was even then usual in England, they wrapped this up in phrases of opposite import. The lords knew well, they said, "that the King will attempt nothing that is not to the glory of God, and will eschew the shedding of Christian blood; if he goes to war the cause will be the renewal of his rights, not his own wilfulness." Bishop Beaufort opened the session of 1414 with a sermon upon "Strive for the truth unto death" and the exhortation "While we have time, let us do good to all men." This was understood to mean the speedy invasion of France.

The Commons were thereupon liberal with supply. The King on his part declared that no law should be passed without their assent. A wave of reconciliation swept the land. The King declared a general pardon. He sought to assuage the past. He negotiated with the Scots for the release of Hotspur's son, and reinstated him in the Earldom of Northumberland. He brought the body, or reputed body, of Richard II to London, and re-interred it in Westminster Abbey, with pageantry and solemn ceremonial. A plot formed against him on the eve of his setting out for the wars was suppressed, by all appearance with ease and national approval, and with only a handful of executions. In particular he spared his cousin, the young Edmund Mortimer, Earl of March, who had been named as the rival King, through whose family much that was merciless was to follow later.

During the whole of 1414 Henry V was absorbed in warlike preparations by land and sea. He reorganised the Fleet. Instead of mainly taking over and arming private ships, as was

the custom, he, like Alfred, built many vessels for the Royal
Navy. He had at least six "great ships," with about fifteen hundred smaller consorts. The expeditionary army was picked and
trained with special care. In spite of the more general resort to
fighting on foot, which had been compelled by the long-bow,
six thousand archers, of whom half were mounted infantry,
were the bulk and staple of the army, together with two
thousand five hundred noble, knightly, or otherwise substantial
warriors in armour, each with his two or three attendants and
aides.

In 1407 Louis, Duke of Orleans, the decisive power at the
Court of the witless French King, Charles VI, had been murdered at the instigation of the Duke of Burgundy, and the strife
of the two parties which divided France became violent and
mortal. To this the late King of England had owed the comparative relief from foreign menace which eased the closing
years of his reign. At Henry V's accession the Orleanists had
gained the preponderance in France, and unfurled the Ori-
flamme against the Duke of Burgundy. Henry naturally allied
himself with the weaker party, the Burgundians, who, in their
distress, were prepared to acknowledge him as King of France.
When he led the power of England across the Channel in con-
tinuation of the long revenge of history for Duke William's
expedition he could count upon the support of a large part of
what is now the French people. The English army of about ten
thousand fighting men sailed to France on August 11, 1415,
in a fleet of small ships, and landed without opposition at the
mouth of the Seine. Harfleur was besieged and taken by the
middle of September. The King was foremost in prowess:

Once more unto the breach, dear friends, once more;
Or close the wall up with our English dead.

In this mood he now invited the Dauphin to end the war by single combat. The challenge was declined. The attrition of the siege, and disease, which levied its unceasing toll on these medieval camps, had already wrought havoc in the English expedition. The main power of France was now in the field. The Council of War, on October 5, advised returning home by sea.

But the King, leaving a garrison in Harfleur, and sending home several thousand sick and wounded, resolved, with about a thousand knights and men-at-arms and four thousand archers, to traverse the French coast in a hundred-mile march to his fortress at Calais, where his ships were to await him. All the circumstances of this decision show that his design was to tempt the enemy to battle. This was not denied him. Marching by Fécamp and Dieppe, he had intended to cross the Somme at the tidal ford, Blanchetaque, which his great-grandfather had passed before Crécy. Falsely informed that the passage would be opposed, he moved by Abbeville; but here the bridge was broken down. He had to ascend the Somme to above Amiens by Boves and Corbie, and could only cross at the ford of Béthencourt. All these names are well known to our generation. On October 20 he camped near Péronne. He was now deeply plunged into France. It was the turn of the Dauphin to offer the grim courtesies of chivalric war. The French heralds came to the English camp and inquired, for mutual convenience, by which route His Majesty would desire to proceed. "Our path lies straight to Calais," was Henry's answer. This was not telling them much, for he had no other choice. The French army, which was already interposing itself, by a right-handed movement across his front fell back before his advance-guard behind the Canche river. Henry, moving by Albert, Frévent, and Blangy, learned that they were before him in

apparently overwhelming numbers. He must now cut his way
through, perish, or surrender. When one of his officers, Sir
Walter Hungerford, deplored the fact "that they had not but
one ten thousand of those men in England that do no work to-
day," the King rebuked him and revived his spirits in a speech
to which Shakespeare has given an immortal form:

> If we are marked to die, we are enough
> To do our country loss; and if to live,
> The fewer men, the greater share of honour.

"Wot you not," he actually said, "that the Lord with these
few can overthrow the pride of the French?" [1] He and the "few"
lay for the night at the village of Maisoncelles, maintaining
utter silence and the strictest discipline. The French headquarters were at Agincourt, and it is said that they kept high revel
and diced for the captives they should take.

The English victory of Crécy was gained against great odds
upon the defensive. Poitiers was a counter-stroke. Agincourt
ranks as the most heroic of all the land battles England has
ever fought. It was a vehement assault. The French, whose
numbers have been estimated at about twenty thousand, were
drawn up in three lines of battle, of which a proportion remained mounted. With justifiable confidence they awaited the
attack of less than a third their number, who, far from home
and many marches from the sea, must win or die. Mounted
upon a small grey horse, with a richly jewelled crown upon his
helmet, and wearing his royal surcoat of leopards and lilies,
the King drew up his array. The archers were disposed in six
wedge-shaped formations, each supported by a body of men-
at-arms. At the last moment Henry sought to avoid so desperate a battle. Heralds passed to and fro. He offered to yield

[1] *Gesta Henrici V*, English Historical Society, ed. B. Williams.

Harfleur and all his prisoners in return for an open road to Calais. The French prince replied that he must renounce the crown of France. On this he resolved to dare the last extremity. The whole English army, even the King himself, dismounted and sent their horses to the rear; and shortly after eleven o'clock on St Crispin's Day, October 25, he gave the order, "In the name of Almighty God and of Saint George, Avaunt Banner in the best time of the year, and Saint George this day be thine help." The archers kissed the soil in reconciliation to God, and, crying loudly, "Hurrah! Hurrah! Saint George and Merrie England!" advanced to within three hundred yards of the heavy masses in their front. They planted their stakes and loosed their arrows.

The French were once again unduly crowded upon the field. They stood in three dense lines, and neither their cross-bowmen nor their battery of cannon could fire effectively. Under the arrow storm they in their turn moved forward down the slope, plodding heavily through a ploughed field already trampled into a quagmire. Still at thirty deep they felt sure of breaking the line. But once again the long-bow destroyed all before it. Horse and foot alike went down; a long heap of armoured dead and wounded lay upon the ground, over which the reinforcements struggled bravely, but in vain. In this grand moment the archers slung their bows, and, sword in hand, fell upon the reeling squadrons and disordered masses. Then the Duke of Alençon rolled forward with the whole second line, and a stubborn hand-to-hand struggle ensued, in which the French prince struck down with his own sword Humphrey of Gloucester. The King rushed to his brother's rescue, and was smitten to the ground by a tremendous stroke; but in spite of the odds Alençon was killed, and the French second line was beaten hand to hand by the English chivalry and yeomen. It recoiled like the first, leaving large numbers of unwounded and still larger numbers of wounded prisoners in the assailants' hands.

Now occurred a terrible episode. The French third line, still intact, covered the entire front, and the English were no longer in regular array. At this moment the French camp-followers and peasantry, who had wandered round the English rear, broke pillaging into the camp and stole the King's crown, wardrobe, and Great Seal. The King, believing himself attacked from behind, while a superior force still remained unbroken on his front, issued the dread order to slaughter the prisoners. Then perished the flower of the French nobility, many of whom had yielded themselves to easy hopes of ransom. Only the most illustrious were spared. The desperate character of this act, and of the moment, supplies what defence can be found for its ferocity. It was not in fact a necessary recourse. The alarm in the rear was soon relieved; but not before the massacre was almost finished. The French third line quitted the field without attempting to renew the battle in any serious manner. Henry, who had declared at daybreak, "For me this day shall never England ransom pay," [1] now saw his path to Calais clear before him. But far more than that: he had decisively broken in open battle at odds of more than three to one the armed chivalry of France. In two or at most three hours he had trodden underfoot at once the corpses of the slain and the will-power of the French monarchy.

After asking the name of the neighbouring castle and ordering that the battle should be called Agincourt after it, Henry made his way to Calais, short of food, but unmolested by the still superior forces which the French had set on foot. Within five months of leaving England he returned to London, having, before all Europe, shattered the French power by a feat of arms which, however it may be tested, must be held unsur-

[1] *Chronicles of London,* ed. C. L. Kingsford, p. 119.

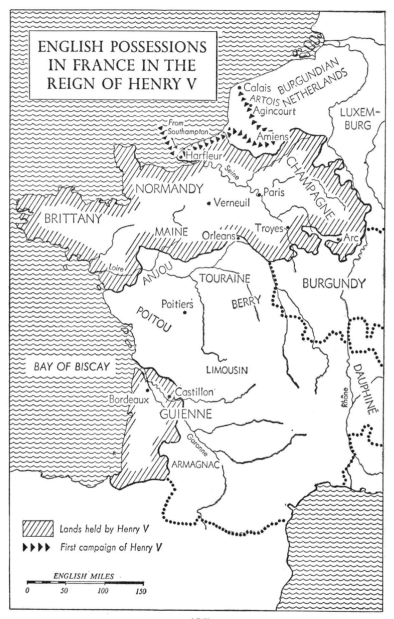

ENGLISH POSSESSIONS
IN THE
REIGN OF HENRY V

Calais BURGUNDIAN
ARTOIS NETHERLANDS
Agincourt
LUXEM-
BURG
From
Southampton
Amiens
Harfleur
Seine
NORMANDY
CHAMPAGNE
Paris
BRITTANY
Verneuil
MAINE
Orleans
Troyes
Arc
ANJOU
TOURAINE
BURGUNDY
Poitiers
BERRY
POITOU
Loire
BAY OF BISCAY
LIMOUSIN
Castillon
Bordeaux
Rhône
DAUPHINÉ
GUIENNE
Garonne
ARMAGNAC

///// Lands held by Henry V

▶ ▶ ▶ ▶ First campaign of Henry V

ENGLISH MILES
0   50   100   150

passed. He rode in triumph through the streets of London with spoils and captives displayed to the delighted people. He himself wore a plain dress, and he refused to allow his "bruised helmet and bended sword" to be shown to the admiring crowd, "lest they should forget that the glory was due to God alone." The victory of Agincourt made him the supreme figure in Europe.

When in 1416 the Holy Roman Emperor Sigismund visited London in an effort to effect a peace he recognised Henry as King of France. But there followed long, costly campaigns and sieges which outran the financial resources of the Island and gradually cooled its martial ardour. A much larger expedition crossed the Channel in 1417. After a hard, long siege Caen was taken; and one by one every French stronghold in Normandy was reduced in successive years. After hideous massacres in Paris, led by the Burgundians, hot-headed supporters of the Dauphin murdered the Duke of Burgundy at Montereau in 1419, and by this deed sealed the alliance of Burgundy with England. Orleanist France was utterly defeated, not only in battle, but in the war. In May 1420, by the Treaty of Troyes, Charles VI recognised Henry as heir to the French kingdom upon his death and as Regent during his life. The English King undertook to govern with the aid of a Council of Frenchmen, and to preserve all ancient customs. Normandy was to be his in full sovereignty, but on his accession to the French throne would be reunited to France. He was accorded the title "King of England and Heir of France." To implement and consolidate these triumphs he married Charles's daughter Catherine, a comely princess, who bore him a son long to reign over impending English miseries.

"It was," says Ranke, "a very extraordinary position which Henry V now occupied. The two great kingdoms, each of which by itself has earlier or later claimed to sway the world, were (without being fused into one) to remain united for ever under him and his successors. . . . Burgundy was bound to him by ties of blood and by hostility to a common foe." [1] He induced Queen Johanna of Naples to adopt his eldest brother as her son and heir. The King of Castile and the heir of Portugal were descended from his father's sisters. Soon after his death the youngest of his brothers, Humphrey of Gloucester, married Jacqueline of Holland and Hainault, who possessed other lands as well. "The pedigrees of Southern and Western Europe alike met in the house of Lancaster, the head of which thus seemed to be the common head of all." It seemed to need only a Crusade, a high, sacred common cause against the advancing Ottoman power, to anneal the bonds which might have united, for a space at least, all Europe under an Englishman. The renewal of strife between England and France consumed powerful contingents which could have been used in defending Christendom against the Turkish menace.

This was the boldest bid the Island ever made in Europe. Henry V was no feudal sovereign of the old type with a class interest which overrode social and territorial barriers. He was entirely national in his outlook: he was the first King to use the English language in his letters and his messages home from the front; his triumphs were gained by English troops; his policy was sustained by a Parliament that could claim to speak for the English people. For it was the union of the country gentry and the rising middle class of the towns, working with the common lawyers, that gave the English Parliament thus early a character and a destiny that the States-General of France and the Cortes of Castile were not to know. Henry stood, and with him his country, at the summit of the world. He was himself endowed with the highest attributes of manhood. "No sovereign," says Stubbs, "who ever reigned has won from con-

[1] *History of England,* vol. i, p. 84.

temporary writers such a singular unison of praise. He was religious, pure in life, temperate, liberal, careful, and yet splendid, merciful, truthful, and honourable; 'discreet in word, provident in counsel, prudent in judgment, modest in look, magnanimous in act'; a brilliant soldier, a sound diplomatist, an able organiser and consolidator of all forces at his command; the restorer of the English Navy, the founder of our military, international, and maritime law. A true Englishman, with all the greatnesses and none of the glaring faults of his Plantagenet ancestors."

Ruthless he could also be on occasion, but the Chroniclers prefer to speak of his generosity and of how he made it a rule of his life to treat all men with consideration. He disdained in State business evasive or cryptic answers. "It is impossible" or "It shall be done" were the characteristic decisions which he gave. He was more deeply loved by his subjects of all classes than any King has been in England. Under him the English armies gained an ascendancy which for centuries was never seen again.

*　　*　　*　　*　　*

But glory was, as always, dearly bought. The imposing Empire of Henry V was hollow and false. Where Henry II had failed his successor could not win. When Henry V revived the English claims to France he opened the greatest tragedy in our medieval history. Agincourt was a glittering victory, but the wasteful and useless campaigns that followed more than outweighed its military and moral value, and the miserable, destroying century that ensued casts its black shadow upon Henry's heroic triumph.

And there is also a sad underside to the brilliant life of England in these years. If Henry V united the nation against France he set it also upon the Lollards. We can see that the Lollards were regarded not only as heretics, but as what we should now call Christian Communists. They had secured as their leader Sir John Oldcastle, a warrior of renown. They threatened nothing less than a revolution in faith and property. Upon them all domestic hatreds were turned by a devout and credulous age. It seemed frightful beyond words that they should declare that the Host lifted in the Mass was a dead thing, "less than a toad or a spider." Hostility was whetted by their policy of plundering the Church. Nor did the constancy of these martyrs to their convictions allay the public rage. As early as 1410 we have a strange, horrible scene, in which Henry, then Prince of Wales, was present at the execution of John Badby, a tailor of Worcestershire. He offered him a free pardon if he would recant. Badby refused and the faggots were lighted, but his piteous groans gave the Prince hope that he might still be converted. He ordered the fire to be extinguished, and again tempted the tortured victim with life, liberty, and a pension if he would but retract. But the tailor, with unconquerable constancy, called upon them to do their worst, and was burned to ashes, while the spectators marvelled alike at the Prince's merciful nature and the tailor's firm religious principles. Oldcastle, who, after a feeble insurrection in 1414, fled to the hills of Herefordshire, was captured at length, and suffered in his turn. These fearful obsessions weighed upon the age, and Henry, while King of the world, was but one of its slaves. This degradation lies about him and his times, and our contacts with his personal nobleness and prowess, though imperishable, are marred.

Fortune, which had bestowed upon the King all that could be dreamed of, could not afford to risk her handiwork in a long life. In the full tide of power and success he died at the end of August 1422 of a malady contracted in the field, probably dysentery, against which the medicine of those times could not make head. When he received the Sacrament and heard the penitential psalms, at the words "Build thou the walls of Jerusalem" he spoke, saying, "Good Lord, thou knowest that my intent has been and yet is, if I might live, to re-edify the walls of Jerusalem." This was his dying thought. He died with his work unfinished. He had once more committed his country to the murderous dynastic war with France. He had been the instrument of the religious and social persecution of the Lollards. Perhaps if he had lived the normal span his power might have become the servant of his virtues and produced the harmonies and tolerances which mankind so often seeks in vain. But Death drew his scythe across these prospects. The gleaming King, cut off untimely, went to his tomb amid the lamentations of his people, and the crown passed to his son, an infant nine months old.

Joan of Arc

A BABY was King of England, and two months later, on the death of Charles VI, was proclaimed without dispute the King of France. Bedford and Gloucester, his uncles, became Protectors, and with a Council comprising the heads of the most powerful families attempted to sustain the work of Henry V. A peculiar sanctity enshrined the hero's son, and the glory of Agincourt played radiantly around his cradle. Nurses, teachers, and presently noble guardians, carefully chosen for the boy's education and welfare, were authorised to use "reasonable chastisement" when required. But this was little needed, for the child had a mild, virtuous, honest, and merciful nature. His piety knew no bounds, and was, with hunting and a taste for literature, the stay and comfort of his long, ignominious, and terrifying pilgrimage. Through his father he inherited the physical weakness of the house of Lancaster, and through his mother the mental infirmities of Charles VI. He was feeble alike in body and mind, unwise and unstable in his judgments, profuse beyond his means to his friends, uncalculating against his enemies, so tender-hearted that it was even said he would let common thieves and murderers live, yet forced to bear the load of innumerable political executions. Flung about like a shuttlecock between the rival factions; presiding as a helpless puppet over the progressive decay of English society and power; hovering bewildered on the skirts of great battles; three times taken prisoner on the field; now paraded with all kingly pomp before Parliaments, armies, and crowds, now led in mockery through the streets, now a captive, now a homeless fugitive, hiding, hunted, hungry; afflicted from time to time by phases of total or partial idiocy, he endured in the fullest measure for nearly fifty years the extreme miseries of human existence, until the hand of murder dispatched him to a world which he was sure would be better, and could hardly have been worse than that he had known. Yet with all his shame of failure and incompetence, and the disasters these helped to bring upon his country, the English people recognised his goodness of heart and rightly ascribed to him the quality of holiness. They never lost their love for him; and in many parts of the country wherever the house of Lancaster was stubbornly defended he was venerated both as saint and martyr.

*   *   *   *   *

At the time of the great King's death the ascendancy of the English arms in France was established. In his brother, John, Duke of Bedford, who went to France as Regent and Commander-in-Chief, a successor of the highest military quality was found. The alliance with Burgundy, carrying with it the allegiance and the sympathies of Paris, persisted. The death, in October 1422, of the French king, who had signed the Treaty of Troyes, while it admitted the English infant to the kingship of France, nevertheless exposed his title to a more serious challenge. South of the Loire, except of course in Gascony, the Dauphin ruled and was now to reign. The war continued bitterly. Nothing could stand against the English archers. Many sieges and much ravaging distressed the countryside. In 1423 the Scots and French under the Earl of Buchan defeated the English at Beaugé, but three other considerable actions ended in English victories. At Cravant, in August 1423, the French found themselves aided by a strong Scottish contingent. These Scotsmen were animated by a hatred of the English which stood out above the ordinary feuds. But the

English archers, with their Burgundian allies, shot most of them down. At Verneuil a year later this decision was repeated. Buchan, who had been made Constable of France after Beaugé, had induced his father-in-law, the Earl of Douglas, to bring over a new Scots army and to become Constable himself. The French, having had some success, were inclined to retire behind the Loire, but the rage of the Scots, of whom there were no fewer than five thousand under Douglas, Constable of Scotland, was uncontrollable. They forced a battle, and were nearly all destroyed by the arrow storm. Douglas, Buchan, and other Scottish chieftains fell upon the field, and so grievous was the slaughter of their followers that it was never again possible to form in these wars a separate Scottish brigade.

The English attempt to conquer all vast France with a few thousand archers led by warrior nobles, with hardly any money from home, and little food to be found in the ruined regions, reached its climax in the triumph of Verneuil. There seemed to the French to be no discoverable way to contend against these rugged, lusty, violent Islanders, with their archery, their flexible tactics, and their audacity, born of victories great and small under varying conditions and at almost any odds. Even five years later at the "Battle of the Herrings," gained in February 1429 by Sir John Falstaff, odds of six to one could not prevail. A convoy of four hundred wagons was bringing to the front the herrings indispensable to the English army during Lent. They were suddenly attacked on the road. But they formed their wagons into what we should now call a laager; the archers stood between and upon them, and at ranges greater than the muskets of Marlborough, Frederick the Great, or Napoleon could ever attain broke the whole assault. Yet the Dauphin, soon to be King Charles VII, stood for France, and everywhere, even in the subjugated provinces, a dull, deep sense of nationality, stirring not only in gentlefolk, but in all who could rise above the submerged classes, centred upon him.

At this time the loves and the acquisitiveness of the Duke of Gloucester, who in Bedford's absence in France became Protector of the English child-King, drove a wedge between England and Burgundy. Jacqueline, Princess of Hainault, Holland, and Zeeland, and heir to these provinces, a woman of remarkable spirit, at the high tide of her nature had been married for reasons of Burgundian policy to the Duke of Brabant, a sickly lout fifteen years of age. She revolted from this infliction, took refuge in England, and appealed to Gloucester for protection. This was accorded in full measure. Gloucester resolved to marry her, enjoy her company, and acquire her inheritance. Some form of divorce was obtained for Jacqueline from the Anti-Pope Benedict XIII, and the marriage took place early in 1423. This questionable romance gave deep offence to the Duke of Burgundy, whose major interests in the Low Countries were injured. Philip of Burgundy saw the world vindictively from his own standpoint. Hitherto his wrath against the treacherous murderers of his father had made him the Dauphin's relentless foe. But this English intrigue gave him a countervailing cause of personal malice, and when Gloucester in State correspondence accused him of falsehood, and in company with Jacqueline descended with a considerable force upon Hainault and Holland, his attachment to English interests became profoundly deranged. Although both Bedford in France and the English Council at home completely disclaimed Gloucester's action, and were prodigal in their efforts to repair the damage, and the Pope was moved by Philip of Burgundy to be tardy in the necessary annulments, the rift between England and Burgundy dates from this event. During these years also the Duke of Brittany detached himself from the English interest and hearkened to the appeals and offers of the French King. By the Treaty of Saumur in October 1425 he obtained the supreme direction of the war against the English. Although no results came to either side from his command the confederacy against France was weakened, and opportunity, faint, fleeting, was offered to the stricken land. The defects of the Dauphin, the exhaustion of the French monarchy, and the disorder and misery of the realm had however reached a pitch where all hung in the balance.

*   *   *   *   *

There now appeared upon the ravaged scene an Angel of Deliverance, the noblest patriot of France, the most splendid of her heroes, the most beloved of her saints, the most inspiring of all her memories, the peasant Maid, the ever-shining, ever-glorious Joan of Arc. In the poor, remote hamlet of Domrémy, on the fringe of the Vosges Forest, she served at the inn. She rode the horses of travellers, bareback, to water. She wandered on Sundays into the woods, where there were shrines, and a legend that some day from these oaks would arise one to save France. In the fields where she tended her sheep the saints of God, who grieved for France, rose before her in visions. St Michael himself appointed her, by right divine, to command the armies of liberation. Joan shrank at first from the awful duty, but when he returned attended by St Margaret and St Catherine, patronesses of the village church, she obeyed their command. There welled in the heart of the Maid a pity for the realm of France, sublime, perhaps miraculous, certainly invincible.

Like Mahomet, she found the most stubborn obstacle in her own family. Her father was scandalised that she should wish to ride in male attire among rough soldiers. How indeed could she procure horses and armour? How could she gain access to the King? But the saints no doubt felt bound to set her fair upon her course. She convinced Baudricourt, governor of the neighbouring town, that she was inspired. He recommended her to a Court ready to clutch at straws. She made a perilous journey across France. She was conducted to the King's presence in the immense stone pile of Chinon. There, among the nobles and courtiers in the great hall, under the flaring torches, she at once picked out the King, who had purposely mingled with the crowd. "Most noble Lord Dauphin," she said, "I am Joan the Maid, sent on the part of God to aid you and the kingdom, and by His order I announce that you will be crowned in the city of Rheims." The aspersion that he was a bastard had always troubled Charles, and when the Maid picked him out among the crowd he was profoundly moved. Alone with him, she spoke of State secrets which she must either have learned from the saints or from other high authority. She asked for an ancient sword which she had never seen, but which she described minutely before it was found. She fascinated the royal circle. When they set her astride on horseback in martial guise it was seen that she could ride. As she couched her lance the spectators were swept with delight.

Policy now, if not earlier, came to play a part. The supernatural character of the Maid's mission was spread abroad. To make sure that she was sent by Heaven and not from elsewhere, she was examined by a committee of theologians, by the Parlement of Poitiers, and by the whole Royal Council. She was declared a virgin of good intent, inspired by God. Indeed, her answers were of such a quality that the theory has been put forward that she had for some time been carefully nurtured, and trained for her mission. This at least would be a reasonable explanation of the known facts.

Orleans in 1429 lay under the extremities of siege. A few thousand English, abandoned by the Burgundians, were slowly reducing the city by an incomplete blockade. Their self-confidence and prestige hardened them to pursue the attack of a fortress deep in hostile territory, whose garrison was four times their number. They had built lines of redoubts, within which they felt themselves secure. The Maid now claimed to lead a convoy to the rescue. In armour plain and without ornament, she rode at the head of the troops. She restored their spirits; she broke the spell of English dominance. She captivated not only the rough soldiery but their hard-bitten leaders. Her plan was simple. She would march straight into Orleans between the strongest forts. But the experienced captain, Dunois, a bastard of the late Duke of Orleans, had not proposed to lead his convoy by this dangerous route. As the Maid did not know the map he embarked his supplies in boats, and brought her by other ways into the besieged town almost alone. She was received with rapture. But the convoy, beaten back by adverse winds, was forced after all to come in by the way she had prescribed; and in fact it marched for a whole day between the redoubts of the English while they gaped at it dumbfounded.

The report of a supernatural visitant sent by God to save France, which inspired the French, clouded the minds and froze the energies of the English. The sense of awe, and even of fear, robbed them of their assurance. Dunois returned to Paris, leaving the Maid in Orleans. Upon her invocation the spirit of victory changed sides, and the French began an offensive which never rested till the English invaders were driven out of France. She called for an immediate onslaught upon the besiegers, and herself led the storming parties against them. Wounded by an arrow, she plucked it out and returned to the charge. She mounted the scaling-ladders and was hurled half stunned into the ditch. Prostrate on the ground, she commanded new efforts. "Forward, fellow-countrymen!" she cried. "God has delivered them into our hands." One by one the English forts fell and their garrisons were slain. The Earl of Suffolk was captured, the siege broken, and Orleans saved. The English retired in good order, and the Maid prudently restrained the citizens from pursuing them into the open country.

Joan now was head indeed of the French army; it was dangerous even to dispute her decisions. The contingents from Orleans would obey none but her. She fought in fresh encounters; she led the assault upon Jargeau, thus opening the Loire above Orleans. In June 1429 she marched with the army that gained the victory of Patay. She told Charles he must march on Rheims to be crowned upon the throne of his ancestors. The idea seemed fantastic: Rheims lay deep in enemy country. But under her spell he obeyed, and everywhere the towns opened their gates before them and the people crowded to his aid. With all the pomp of victory and faith, with the most sacred ceremonies of ancient days, Charles was crowned at Rheims. By his side stood the Maid, resplendent, with her banner proclaiming the Will of God. If this was not a miracle it ought to be.

Joan now became conscious that her mission was exhausted; her "voices" were silent; she asked to be allowed to go home to her sheep and the horses of the inn. But all adjured her to remain. The French captains who conducted the actual operations, though restive under her military interference, were deeply conscious of her value to the cause. The Court was timid and engaged in negotiations with the Duke of Burgundy. A half-hearted attack was made upon Paris. Joan advanced to the forefront and strove to compel victory. She was severely wounded and the leaders ordered the retreat. When she recovered she again sought release. They gave her the rank and revenue of an earl.

But the attitude both of the Court and the Church was changing towards Joan. Up to this point she had championed the Orleanist cause. After her "twenty victories" the full character of her mission appeared. It became clear that she served

God rather than the Church, and France rather than the Orleans party. Indeed, the whole conception of France seems to have sprung and radiated from her. Thus the powerful particularist interests which had hitherto supported her were estranged. Meanwhile she planned to regain Paris for France. When in May 1430 the town of Compiègne revolted against the decision of the King that it should yield to the English, Joan with only six hundred men attempted its succour. She had no doubt that the enterprise was desperate. It took the form of a cavalry sortie across the long causeway over the river. The enemy, at first surprised, rallied, and a panic among the French ensued. Joan, undaunted, was bridled from the field by her friends. She still fought with the rearguard across the causeway. The two sides were intermingled. The fortress itself was imperilled. Its cannon could not fire upon the confused *mêlée*. Flavy, the governor whose duty it was to save the town, felt obliged to pull up the drawbridge in her face and leave her to the Burgundians.

She was sold to the rejoicing English for a moderate sum. To Bedford and his army she was a witch, a sorceress, a harlot, a foul imp of black magic, at all costs to be destroyed. But it was not easy to frame a charge; she was a prisoner of war, and many conventions among the warring aristocrats protected her. The spiritual arm was therefore invoked. The Bishop of Beauvais, the learned doctors of Paris, pursued her for heresy. She underwent prolonged inquisition. The gravamen was that by refusing to disown her "voices" she was defying the judgment and authority of the Church. For a whole year her fate hung in the balance, while careless, ungrateful Charles lifted not a finger to save her. There is no record of any ransom being offered. Joan had recanted under endless pressure, and had been accorded all the mercy of perpetual imprisonment on bread and water. But in her cell the inexorable saints appeared to her again. Entrapping priests set her armour and man's clothes before her; with renewed exaltation she put them on. From that moment she was declared a relapsed heretic and condemned to the fire. Amid an immense concourse she was dragged to the stake in the market-place of Rouen. High upon the pyramid of faggots the flames rose towards her, and the smoke of doom wreathed and curled. She raised a cross made of firewood, and her last word was "Jesus!" History has recorded the comment of an English soldier who witnessed the scene. "We are lost," he said. "We have burnt a saint." All this proved true.

Joan was a being so uplifted from the ordinary run of mankind that she finds no equal in a thousand years. The records of her trial present us with facts alive to-day through all the mists of time. Out of her own mouth can she be judged in each generation. She embodied the natural goodness and valour of the human race in unexampled perfection. Unconquerable courage, infinite compassion, the virtue of the simple, the wisdom of the just, shone forth in her. She glorifies as she freed the soil from which she sprang. All soldiers should read her story and ponder on the words and deeds of the true warrior, who in one single year, though untaught in technical arts, reveals in every situation the key of victory.

Joan of Arc perished on May 29, 1431, and thereafter the tides of war flowed remorselessly against the English. The boy Henry was crowned in Paris in December amid chilly throngs. The whole spirit of the country was against the English claim. Burgundy became definitely hostile in 1435. Bedford died, and was succeeded by lesser captains. The opposing Captain-in-Chief, Dunois, instead of leading French chivalry to frontal attacks upon the English archer array, acted by manœuvre and surprise. The French gained a series of battles. Here they caught the English men-at-arms on one side of the river while their archers were on the other; there by a cannonade they forced a disjointed English attack. The French artillery now became the finest in the world. Seven hundred engineers, under the brothers Bureau, used a heavy battering-train of twenty-two inches calibre, firing gigantic stone balls against the numberless castles which the English still held. Places which in the days of Henry V could be reduced only by famine now fell in a few days to smashing bombardment. All Northern France, except Calais, was reconquered. Even Guienne, dowry of Eleanor of Aquitaine, for three hundred years a loyal, contented fief of the English Crown, was overrun. It is remarkable however that this province almost immediately revolted against France, called upon the English to return, and had to be subdued anew. The Council of competing noble factions in England was incapable of providing effective succour. The valiant Talbot, Earl of Shrewsbury, was killed with most of his English in his foolhardy battle of Castillon in 1453. The surviving English made terms to sail home from La Rochelle. By the end of that year, through force or negotiation, the English had been driven off the Continent. Of all their conquests they held henceforward only the bridgehead of Calais, to garrison which cost nearly a third of the revenue granted by Parliament to the Crown.

York and Lancaster

AS Henry VI grew up his virtues and simpleness became
equally apparent. He was not entirely docile. In 1431
when he was ten years old Warwick, his preceptor, reported
that he was "grown in years, in stature of his person, and also
in conceit and knowledge of his royal estate, the which causes
him to grudge any chastising." He had spoken "of divers matters not behoveful." The Council had in his childhood made a
great show of him, brought him to ceremonies, and crowned
him with solemnity both in London and Paris. As time passed
they became naturally inclined to keep him under stricter control. His consequence was maintained by the rivalry of the
nobles, and by the unbounded hopes of the nation. A body of
knights and squires had for some years been appointed to
dwell with him and be his servants. As the disastrous years in
France unfolded he was pressed continually to assert himself.
At fifteen he was already regularly attending Council meetings.
He was allowed to exercise a measure of prerogative both in
pardons and rewards. When the Council differed it was agreed
he should decide. He often played the part of mediator by
compromise. Before he was eighteen he had absorbed himself
in the foundation of his colleges at Eton and at Cambridge. He
was thought by the high nobles to take a precocious and un-
healthy interest in public affairs which neither his wisdom nor
experience could sustain. He showed a feebleness of mind and
spirit and a gentleness of nature which were little suited to the
fierce rivalries of a martial age. Opinion and also interests were
divided upon him. Flattering accounts of his remarkable in-

telligence were matched by other equally biased tales that he was an idiot almost incapable of distinguishing between right and wrong. Modern historians confirm the less complimentary view. At the hour when a strong king alone could re-create the balance between the nation and the nobility, when all demanded the restraint of faction at home and the waging of victorious war without undue expense abroad, the throne was known to be occupied by a devout simpleton suited alike by his qualities and defects to be a puppet.

These were evil days for England. The Crown was beggarly, the nobles rich. The people were unhappy and unrestful rather than unprosperous. The religious issues of an earlier century were now dominated by more practical politics. The empire so swiftly gained upon the Continent was being cast away by an incompetent and self-enriching oligarchy, and the revenues which might have sent irresistible armies to beat the French were engrossed by the Church.

The princes of the house of Lancaster disputed among themselves. After Bedford's death in 1435 the tension grew between Gloucester and the Beauforts. Cardinal Beaufort, Bishop of Winchester, and one of the legitimised sons of John of Gaunt's third union, was himself the richest man in England, and a prime master of such contributions as the Church thought it prudent to make to the State. From his private fortune, upon pledges which could only be redeemed in gold, he constantly provided the Court, and often the Council, with ready money. Leaning always to the King, meddling little with the ill-starred conduct of affairs, the Beauforts, with whom must be counted William de la Pole, Earl of Suffolk, maintained by peaceful arts and critical detachment an influence to which the martial elements were often forced to defer. The force of this faction was in 1441 turned in malice upon the Duke of Gloucester. He was now wedded, after the invalidation of his marriage with his wife Jacqueline, to the fair Eleanor Cobham, who had long been his mistress. As the weakest point in his array she was singled out for attack, and was accused with much elaboration of lending herself to the black arts. She had made, it was alleged, a wax figure of the King, and had exposed it from time to time to heat, which wasted it away. Her object, according to her accusers, was to cause the King's life to waste away too. She was declared guilty. Barefoot, in penitential garb, she was made to walk for three days through the London streets, and then consigned to perpetual imprisonment with reasonable maintenance. Her alleged accomplices were put to death. This was of course a trial of strength between the parties and a very real pang and injury to Gloucester.

The loss of France, as it sank in year by year, provoked a deep, sullen rage throughout the land. This passion stirred not only the nobility, but the archer class with their admiring friends in every village. A strong sense of wounded national pride spread among the people. Where were the glories of Crécy and Poitiers? Where were the fruits of famous Agincourt? All were squandered, or indeed betrayed, by those who had profited from the overthrow and murder of good King Richard. There were not lacking agitators and preachers, priestly and lay, who prepared a national and social upheaval by reminding folks that the true line of succession had been changed by violence. All this was an undercurrent, but none the less potent. It was a background, shadowy but dominant. Exactly how these forces worked is unknown; but slowly, ceaselessly, there grew in the land, not only among the nobility and gentry, strong parties which presently assumed both shape and organisation.

At twenty-three it was high time that King Henry should marry. Each of the Lancastrian factions was anxious to provide him with a queen; but Cardinal Beaufort and his brothers, with their ally, Suffolk, whose ancestors, the de la Poles of Hull, had founded their fortunes upon trade, prevailed over the Duke of Gloucester, weakened as he was by maladministration and ill-success. Suffolk was sent to France to arrange a further truce, and it was implied in his mission that he should treat for a marriage between the King of England and Margaret of Anjou, niece of the King of France. This remarkable woman added to rare beauty and charm a masterly intellect and a dauntless spirit. Like Joan the Maid, though without her inspiration or her cause, she knew how to make men fight. Even from the seclusion of her family her qualities became well known. Was she not then the mate for this feeble-minded King? Would she not give him the force that he lacked? And would not those who placed her at his side secure a large and sure future for themselves?

Suffolk was well aware of the delicacy and danger of his mission. He produced from the King and the lords an assurance that if he acted to the best of his ability he should not be punished for ill consequences, and that any errors proved against him should be pardoned in advance. Thus fortified he addressed himself to his task with a zeal which proved fatal to him. The father of Margaret, René of Anjou, was not only cousin of the French King, his favourite and his Prime Minister, but in his own right King of Jerusalem and of Sicily. These magnificent titles were not sustained by practical enjoyments. Jerusalem was in the hands of the Turks, he did not own a square yard in Sicily, and half his patrimony of Anjou and Maine was for years held by the English army. Suffolk was enthralled by Margaret. He made the match; and in his eagerness, by a secret article, agreed without formal authority that Maine should be the reward of France. So strong was the basic power of Gloucester's faction, so sharp was the antagonism against France, so loud were the whispers that England had been betrayed in her wars, that the clause was guarded as a deadly secret. The marriage was solemnised in 1445 with such splendour as the age could afford. Suffolk was made a marquis, and several of his relations were ennobled. The King was radiantly happy, the Queen faithfully grateful. Both Houses of Parliament recorded their thanks to Suffolk for his public achievement. But the secret slumbered uneasily, and as the sense of defeat at the hands of France spread through ever-widening circles its inevitable disclosure boded a mortal danger.

During the six years following the condemnation of his wife Eleanor in 1441 Gloucester had been living in retirement, amusing himself with collecting books. His enemies at this grave juncture resolved upon his final overthrow. Suffolk and Edmund Beaufort, nephew of the Cardinal, supported by the Dukes of Somerset and Buckingham, with the Queen in their midst and the King in their charge, arrested Gloucester when he came to a Parliament summoned at St Edmondsbury, where an adequate royal force had been secretly assembled. Seventeen days later Gloucester's corpse was displayed, so that all could see there was no wound upon it. But the manner of Edward II's death was too well known for this proof to be accepted. It was generally believed, though wrongly, that Gloucester had been murdered by the express direction of Suffolk and Edmund Beaufort. It has however been suggested that his death was induced by choler and amazement at the ruin of his fortunes.

It soon appeared that immense forces of retribution were on foot. When in 1448 the secret article for the cession of Maine became public through its occupation by the French anger was expressed on all sides. England had paid a province, it was said, for a princess without a dowry; traitors had cast away much in the field, and given up the rest by intrigue. At the root of the fearful civil war soon to rend the Island there lay this national grief and wrath at the ruin of empire. All other discontents fused themselves with this. The house of Lancaster had usurped the throne, had ruined the finances, had sold the conquests, and now had stained their hands with foul murder. From these charges all men held the King absolved alike by his good heart and silly head. But henceforward the house of York increasingly becomes a rival party within the State.

Edmund Beaufort, now Duke of Somerset, became commander of the army in France. Suffolk remained at home to face a gathering vengeance. The Navy was disaffected. Bishop Moleyns, Keeper of the Privy Seal, sent to Portsmouth to pay what could be paid to the Fleet, was abused by the sailors as a traitor to the country, and murdered in a riot of the troops about to reinforce Somerset in France. The officer commanding the fortresses which were to be ceded to France had refused to deliver them. The French armies advanced and took with a strong hand all that was now denied. Suffolk was impeached. The King and Margaret strove, as in honour bound, to save him. Straining his prerogative, Henry burked the proceedings by sending him in 1450 into a five years' exile. We now see an instance of the fearful state of indiscipline into which England was drifting. When the banished Duke was crossing the Channel with his attendants and treasure in two small vessels, the *Nicholas of the Tower,* the largest warship in the Royal Navy, bore down upon him and carried him on board. He was received by the captain with the ominous words "Welcome, traitor," and two days later he was lowered into a boat and beheaded by six strokes of a rusty sword. It is a revealing sign of the times that a royal ship should seize and execute a royal Minister who was travelling under the King's special protection.

In June and July a rising took place in Kent, which the Lancastrians claimed to bear the marks of Yorkist support. Jack Cade, a soldier of capacity and bad character, home from the wars, gathered several thousand men, all summoned in due form by the constables of the districts, and marched on London. He was admitted to the city, but on his executing Lord Say, the Treasurer, in Cheapside, after a mob trial, the magistrates and citizens turned against him, his followers dispersed under terms of pardon, and he himself was pursued and killed. This success restored for the moment the authority of the Government, and Henry enjoyed a brief interlude in which he devoted himself anew to his colleges at Eton and Cambridge, and to Margaret, who had gained his love and obedience.

As the process of expelling the English from France continued fortresses fell, towns and districts were lost, and their garrisons for the most part came home. The speed of this disaster contributed powerfully to shock English opinion and to shake not only the position of individual Ministers but the very foundations of the Lancastrian dynasty. With incredible folly and bad faith the English broke the truce at Fougères in March 1449. By August 1450 the whole of Normandy was lost. By August 1451 the whole of Gascony, English for three centuries, had been lost as well, and of all the conquests of Henry V which had taken England eleven years of toil and blood to win only Calais remained. Edmund Beaufort, the King's commander, friend, and Lancastrian cousin, bore the blame for unbroken defeat, and this reacted on the King himself. England became full of what we should call "ex-Service men," who did not know why they had been beaten, but were sure they had been mishandled and had fought in vain. The nobles, in the increasing disorder, were glad to gather these hardened fighters to their local defence. All the great houses kept bands of armed retainers, sometimes almost amounting to private armies. They gave them pay or land, or both, and uniforms or liveries bearing the family crest. The Earl of Warwick, perhaps the greatest landowner, who aspired to a leading part in politics, had thousands of dependants who ate what was called "his bread," and of these a large proportion were organised troops proud to display the badge of the Bear and the Ragged Staff. Other magnates emulated this example according to their means. Cash and ambition ruled and the land sank rapidly towards anarchy. The King was a helpless creature, respected, even beloved, but no prop for any man. Parliament, both Lords and Commons, was little more than a clearing-house for the rivalries of nobles.

A statute of 1429 had fixed the county franchise at the forty-shilling freeholder. It is hard to realise that this arbitrarily contracted franchise ruled in England for four hundred years, and that all the wars and quarrels, the decision of the greatest causes, the grandest events at home and abroad, proceeded upon this basis until the Reform Bill of 1832. In the preamble to this Act it was alleged that the participation in elections of too great a number of people "of little substance or worth" had led to homicides, riots, assaults, and feuds. So was a backward but enduring step taken in Parliamentary representation. Yet never for centuries had the privilege of Parliament stood so high. Never for centuries was it more blatantly exploited.

The force of law was appropriated by intrigue. Baronial violence used or defied legal forms with growing impunity. The Constitution was turned against the public. No man was safe in life or lands, or even in his humblest right, except through the protection of his local chief. The celebrated Paston

Letters show that England, enormously advanced as it was in comprehension, character, and civilisation, was relapsing from peace and security into barbaric confusion. The roads were insecure. The King's writ was denied or perverted. The royal judges were flouted or bribed. The rights of sovereignty were stated in the highest terms, but the King was a weak and handled fool. The powers of Parliament could be turned this way and that according as the factions gripped it. Yet the suffering, toiling, unconquerable community had moved far from the days of Stephen and Maud, of Henry II and Thomas à Becket, and of King John and the barons. There was a highly complex society, still growing in spite of evils in many regions. The poverty of the Executive, the difficulties of communication, and the popular strength in bills and bows all helped to hold it in balance. There was a public opinion. There was a collective moral sense. There were venerated customs. Above all there was a national spirit.

*   *   *   *   *

It was upon this community that the agonies of the Wars of the Roses were now to fall. We must not underrate either the great issues which led to the struggle or the conscious, intense, prolonged efforts made to avert it. The need of all men and their active desire was for a strong and capable Government. Some thought this could only be obtained by aiding the lawful, established régime. Others had been for a long time secretly contending that a usurpation had been imposed upon them which had now become incompetent. The claims and hopes of the opposition to the house of Lancaster were embodied in Richard, Duke of York. According to established usage he had a prior right to the crown. York was the son of Richard, Earl of Cambridge, and grandson of Edmund, Duke of York, a younger brother of John of Gaunt. As the great-grandson of Edward III he was the only other person besides Henry VI with an unbroken male descent from Edward III, but in the female line he had also a superior claim through his descent from Gaunt's elder brother, Lionel of Clarence. By the Act of 1407 the Beauforts—Gaunt's legitimised bastards—had been barred from the succession. If Henry VI should succeed in annulling the Act of 1407 then Edmund Beaufort (Somerset) would have a better good male claim with York. It was this that York feared. York had taken Gloucester's place as first Prince of the Blood. After Gloucester's death there survived no male of the legitimate house of Lancaster save Henry VI. Around York and beneath him there gathered an immense party of discontent, which drove him hesitantly to demand a place in the Government, and eventually, through Queen Margaret's increasing hostility, the throne itself.

A Yorkist network grew up in all parts of the country, but mainly in the South and West of England, in Kent, in London, and in Wales. It was significant that Jack Cade, at the head of the Kentish insurgents, had pretended to the name of Mortimer. It was widely believed that the Yorkists, as they began to style themselves, had procured the murder of Bishop Moleyns at Portsmouth, and of Suffolk on the high seas. Blood had thus already flowed between the houses of Lancaster and York.

In these conditions the character of Richard of York deserves close study. He was a virtuous, law-respecting, slow-moving, and highly competent prince. Every office entrusted to him by the Lancastrian régime had been ably and faithfully discharged. He had given good service. He would have been content with the government of Calais and what was left of France, but being deprived of this for the sake of Somerset he accepted the government of Ireland. Not only did he subdue part of that island, but in the very process he won the goodwill of the Irish people. Thus we see on the one side a weak King with a defective title in the hands of personages discredited by national disaster, and now with blood-guilt upon them, and on the other an upright and wise administrator supported by a nation-wide party and with some superior title to the crown.

Anyone who studies the argument which now tore the realm will see how easily honest men could convince themselves of either cause. When King Henry VI realised that his right to the throne was impugned he was mildly astonished. "Since my cradle, for forty years," he said, "I have been King. My father was King; his father was King. You have all sworn fealty to me on many occasions, as your fathers swore it to my father." But the other side declared that oaths not based on truth were void, that wrong must be righted, that successful usurpation gained no sanctity by time, that the foundation of the monarchy could only rest upon law and justice, that to recognise a dynasty of interlopers was to invite rebellion whenever occasion served, and thus dissolve the very frame of English society; and, finally, that if expediency were to rule, who could compare the wretched half-wit King, under whom all was going to ruin, with a prince who had proved himself a soldier and a statesman of the highest temper and quality?

All England was divided between these two conceptions. Although the Yorkists predominated in the rich South, and the Lancastrians were supreme in the warlike North, there were many interlacements and overlaps. While the townsfolk and the mass of the people, upon the whole, abstained from active warfare in this struggle of the upper classes and their armed retainers, and some thought "the fewer nobles the better," their own opinion was also profoundly divided. They venerated the piety and goodness of the King; they also admired the virtues and moderation of the Duke of York. The attitude and feeling of the public, in all parts and at all times, weighed heavily with both contending factions. Thus Europe witnessed the amazing spectacle of nearly thirty years of

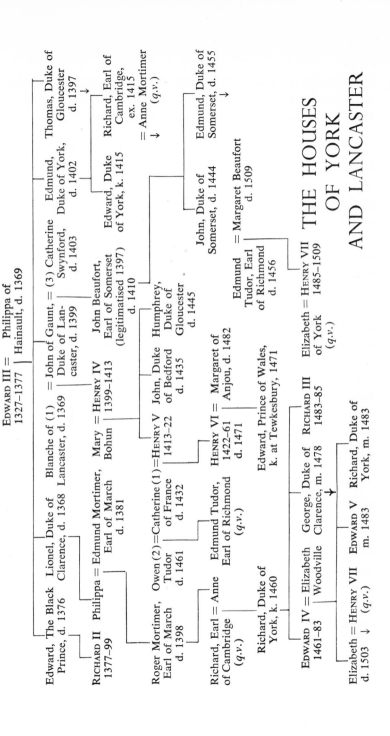

THE HOUSES
OF YORK
AND LANCASTER

EDWARD III = Philippa of
1327–1377   Hainault, d. 1369

Edward, The Black Prince, d. 1376

Lionel, Duke of Clarence, d. 1368

John of Gaunt, Duke of Lancaster, d. 1399 = Blanche of Lancaster, d. 1369 (1)

(3) Catherine Swynford, d. 1403

Edmund, Duke of York, d. 1402

Thomas, Duke of Gloucester, d. 1397 →

RICHARD II 1377–99

Philippa = Edmund Mortimer, Earl of March, d. 1381

Mary = HENRY IV 1399–1413 Bohun

John Beaufort, Earl of Somerset (legitimatised 1397), d. 1410

Edward, Duke of York, k. 1415

Richard, Earl of Cambridge, ex. 1415 = Anne Mortimer (q.v.) →

Roger Mortimer, Earl of March, d. 1398

Owen (2) = Catherine (1) = HENRY V 1413–22 Tudor, of France, d. 1461 d. 1432

John, Duke of Bedford, d. 1435

Humphrey, Duke of Gloucester, d. 1445

John, Duke of Somerset, d. 1444

Edmund, Duke of Somerset, d. 1455 →

Richard, Earl of Cambridge (q.v.) = Anne Edmund Tudor, Earl of Richmond (q.v.)

HENRY VI = Margaret of 1422–61 Anjou, d. 1482 d. 1471

Edmund Tudor, Earl of Richmond, d. 1456 = Margaret Beaufort, d. 1509

Richard, Duke of York, k. 1460

Edward, Prince of Wales, k. at Tewkesbury, 1471

Elizabeth = HENRY VII of York 1485–1509 (q.v.)

EDWARD IV = Elizabeth 1461–83 Woodville

George, Duke of Clarence, m. 1478 →

RICHARD III 1483–85

Elizabeth = HENRY VII d. 1503 → (q.v.)

EDWARD V m. 1483

Richard, Duke of York, m. 1483

ferocious war, conducted with hardly the sack of a single town, and with the mass of the common people little affected and the functions of local government very largely maintained.

* * * * *

In 1450 the ferment of discontent and rivalries drew the Duke of York into his first overt act. He quitted his government in Ireland and landed unbidden in Wales. During the Parliamentary session of the following year a member of the Commons, one Young, boldly proposed that the Duke of York should be declared heir to the throne. This demand was formidable, not only for its backing, but for its good sense. The King had now been married for six years and had no child. The repute in which he stood made it seem unlikely that he would have any. Ought he not, men asked at this time, to designate his successor? If not York, whom then? It could only be Somerset or another representative of the Beaufort line. One can see how shrewdly this thrust was made. But the King, animated certainly by Margaret, repulsed it with unwonted vigour. He refused to abandon his hope of progeny, and, as soon as the Parliament had dispersed, sent the presumptuous Member to the Tower. At this time, also, he broke with the Duke of York, who retired to his castle at Ludlow, on the borders of Wales.

Disgusted by the Government's failure to restore order and justice at home, and to prevent military disasters in France, York became more and more convinced that the Beaufort party, which dominated the weak-willed King, must be driven from power. Prayers and protests had failed; there remained the resort to arms. Accordingly, on February 3, 1452, York sent an address to the citizens of Shrewsbury, accusing Somerset of the disgrace in France and of "labouring continually about the King's Highness for my undoing, and to corrupt my blood and to disinherit me and my heirs and such persons as be about me . . . Seeing that the said Duke ever prevaileth and ruleth about the King's person, and advises him so ill that the land is likely to be destroyed, I may full conclude to proceed in all haste against him with the help of my kinsmen and friends." On this he marched from Shrewsbury towards London, with an army of several thousand men, including artillery. He moved into Kent, plainly expecting that those who had marched with Jack Cade would rally to his cause. The response was disappointing. London closed its gates against his emissaries. The King was carried by Margaret, Somerset, and the Lancastrian interests to Blackheath, with a superior force. Civil war seemed about to begin.

But York felt himself the weaker. He was constitutionally averse from violence. Norfolk was on his side, and other great nobles, but the Earl of Warwick, twenty-four years old, was with the King. Every effort was made to prevent bloodshed. Parleys were unending. In the event York dispersed his forces and presented himself unarmed and bareheaded before King Henry, protesting his loyalty, but demanding redress. His life hung by a thread. Few about the King's person would have scrupled to slay him. But all knew the consequences. York stood for a cause; he was supported by the Commons; half the nation was behind him; his youthful son, the Earl of March, had a second army on foot on the Welsh border. York declared himself "the King's liegeman and servant." Since he was supported by the Commons and evidently at the head of a great party, the King promised that "a sad and substantial Council" should be formed of which he should be a member. The Court had still to choose between Somerset and York. The Queen, always working with Somerset, decided the issue in his favour. He was appointed Constable of Calais, garrisoned by the only regular troops in the pay of the Crown, and was in fact for more than a year at the head of affairs both in France and at home.

Then in quick succession a series of grave events occurred.

The disasters culminated in France. Talbot's attempt to re-conquer Gascony failed; he was defeated at Castillon in July 1453, and Bordeaux fell in October. Somerset, the chief com-mander, bore the burden of defeat. In this situation the King went mad. He had gone down to Wiltshire to spend July and August. Suddenly his memory failed. He recognised no one, not even the Queen. He could eat and drink, but his speech was childish or incoherent. He could not walk. For another fifteen months he remained entirely without comprehension. Afterwards, when he recovered, he declared he remembered nothing. The pious Henry had been withdrawn from the worry of existence to an island of merciful oblivion. His body gaped and drivelled over the bristling realm.

When these terrible facts became known Queen Margaret aspired to be Protector. But the adverse forces were too strong for the Lancastrian party to make the challenge. Moreover, she had another preoccupation. On October 13 she gave birth to a son. How far this event was expected is not clear, but, as long afterwards with James II, it inevitably hardened the hearts of all men. It seemed to shut out for ever the Yorkist claim. Hitherto neither side had been inclined to go to ex-tremes. If Lancaster ruled during the life of Henry, York would succeed at his death, and both sides could accommodate themselves to this natural and lawful process. Now it seemed there would be a Lancastrian ascendancy for ever.

The insanity of the King defeated Somerset: he could no longer withstand York. Norfolk, one of York's supporters, presented a petition against him to the Council, and in Decem-ber 1453 he was committed to the Tower. The strength of York's position bore him to the Protectorate. He moved by Parliamentary means and with great moderation, but he was not to be withstood. He obtained full control of the Executive, and enjoyed the support of both Houses of Parliament. He had not long to show his qualities, but an immediate improvement in the administration was recognised. He set to work with cool vigour to suppress livery and maintenance and to restore order on the roads and throughout the land. He did not hesitate to imprison several of his own most prominent adherents, among them the Earl of Devonshire, for levying a private war. If he refrained from bringing Somerset, who was still imprisoned, to trial, this was only from mercy. His party were astounded at his tolerance. When the Government was in his hands, when his future was marred by the new heir to the Crown, when his power or his life might be destroyed at any moment by the King's recovery, he kept absolute faith with right and justice. Here then is his monument and justification. He stands before history as a patriot ready to risk his life to protect good government, but unwilling to raise his hand against the State in any personal interest.

Surprises continued. When it was generally believed that Henry's line was extinct he had produced an heir. When he seemed to have sunk into permanent imbecility he suddenly recovered. At Christmas 1454 he regained all his faculties. He inquired whether he had been asleep and what had happened meanwhile. Margaret showed him his son, and told him she had named him Edward. Hitherto he had looked with dull eyes upon the infant. Every effort to rouse him had been in vain. Now he was as good as he had ever been. He held up his hands and thanked God, and, according to the Paston Letters, he said he "never knew till that time, nor wist not what was said to him, nor wist where he had been while he had been sick, till now." He sent his almoner to Canterbury with a thank-offering, and declared himself "in charity with all the world," remarking that he "only wished the lords were too."

The Wars of
the Roses

IN the spring of 1455 the Red Rose of Lancaster bloomed
again. York ceased legally to be Protector from the moment that the King's mental recovery was known; he made no
effort to retain the power. Queen Margaret took the helm.
Somerset was not only released but restored to his key position.
York's government of Calais, which had been conferred upon
him for seven years, was handed back to his rival. He was no
longer invited to the King's Council board; and when a Great
Council of peers was convened at Leicester he feared that he
was summoned only to be tried. He retired to Sandal, in Yorkshire, and, being joined by the Earls of Warwick and Salisbury,
together with a large company of nobles, strongly attended, he
denounced Somerset as the man who, having lost Normandy
and Guienne, was now about to ruin the whole kingdom.
York's lords agreed upon a resort to arms. With three thousand men they marched south. At the same time the Duke of
Norfolk appeared at the head of several thousand men, and
Shrewsbury and Sir Thomas Stanley of a few thousands more.
All these forces moved towards London, with St Albans as
their point of concentration. The King, the Queen, Somerset,
and the Court and Lancastrian party, with their power, which
numbered less than three thousand men, moved to Watford
to meet them.

St Albans was an open town. The ancient, powerful monastery there had prevented the citizens from "girding themselves about with a great wall," lest they should become presumptuous. For this reason it was a convenient rendezvous. The King's army got there first, and the royal standard was unfurled in St Peter's Street and Hollowell Street. York, Salisbury, and Warwick did not wait for the heavy reinforcements that were approaching them. They saw that their forces had the advantage and that hours counted. This time there was a fight. It was a collision rather than a battle; but it was none the less decisive. Lord Clifford held for the King the barrier across the street, which York attacked with archery and cannon; but Warwick, circling the town, came in upon him from behind, slew him, and put the royal troops to flight. Somerset was killed "fighting for a cause which was more his own than the King's." The Duke of Buckingham and his son were wounded by arrows; Somerset's son, the Earl of Dorset, was captured sorely wounded and carried home in a cart. The King himself was slightly wounded by an arrow. He did not fly, but took refuge in a tradesman's house in the main street. There presently the Duke of York came to him, and, falling upon his knees, assured him of his fealty and devotion. Not more than three hundred men perished in this clash at St Albans, but these included an extraordinary proportion of the nobles on the King's side. The rank and file were encouraged to spare one another; the leaders fought to the death. The bodies of Somerset and Clifford lay naked in the street for many hours, none daring to bury them. The Yorkist triumph was complete. They had now got the King in their hands. Somerset was dead. Margaret and her child had taken sanctuary. The victors declared their devotion to the royal person and rejoiced that he was rid of evil counsellors. Upon this Parliament was immediately summoned in the King's name.

Historians have shrunk from the Wars of the Roses, and

most of those who have catalogued their events have left us only a melancholy and disjointed picture. We are however in the presence of the most ferocious and implacable quarrel of which there is factual record. The individual actors were bred by generations of privilege and war, into which the feudal theme had brought its peculiar sense of honour, and to which the Papacy contributed such spiritual sanction as emerged from its rivalries and intrigues. It was a conflict in which personal hatreds reached their maximum, and from which mass effects were happily excluded. There must have been many similar convulsions in the human story. None however has been preserved with characters at once so worldly and so expensively chiselled.

Needless causes of confusion may be avoided. Towns must not be confused with titles. The mortal struggle of York and Lancaster did not imply any antagonism between the two well-known English counties. York was in fact the stronghold of the Lancastrians, and the Yorkists founded their strength upon the Midlands and the south of England. The ups and downs of fortune were so numerous and startling, the family feuds so complicated, the impact of national feeling in moments of crisis so difficult to measure, that it has been the fashion to disparage this period. Only Shakespeare, basing himself largely upon Hall's *Chronicle,* has portrayed its savage yet heroic lineaments. He does not attempt to draw conclusions, and for dramatic purposes telescopes events and campaigns. Let us now set forth the facts as they occurred.

*　　*　　*　　*　　*

St Albans was the first shedding of blood in strife. The Yorkists gained possession of the King. But soon we see the inherent power of Lancaster. They had the majority of the nobles on their side, and the majesty of the Crown. In a few months they were as strong as ever. Continual trials of strength were made. There were risings in the country and grim assemblies of Parliament. Legality, constitutionalism, and reverence for the Crown were countered, but not yet overthrown, by turbulent and bloody episodes. The four years from 1456 to 1459 were a period of uneasy truce. All seemed conscious of the peril to themselves and to their order. But Fate lay heavy upon them. There were intense efforts at reconciliation. The spectacle was displayed to the Londoners of the King being escorted to Westminster by a procession in which the Duke of York and Queen Margaret walked side by side, followed by the Yorkist and Lancastrian lords, the most opposed in pairs. Solemn pledges of amity were exchanged; the Sacrament was taken in common by all the leaders; all sought peace where there was no peace. Even when a kind of settlement was reached in London it was upset by violence in the North. In 1459 fighting broke out again. A gathering near Worcester of armed Yorkists in arms dispersed in the presence of the royal army and their chiefs scattered. York returned to Ireland, and Warwick to his captaincy of Calais, in which he had succeeded Somerset.

War began in earnest in July 1460. York was still in Ireland; but the Yorkist lords under Warwick, holding bases in Wales and at Calais, with all their connections and partisans, supported by the Papal Legate and some of the bishops, and, on the whole, by the Commons, confronted the Lancastrians and the Crown at Northampton. Henry VI stood entrenched, and new cannon guarded his line. But when the Yorkists attacked, Lord Grey of Ruthven, who commanded a wing, deserted him and helped the Yorkists over the breastworks. The royal forces fled in panic. King Henry VI remained in his tent, "sitting alone and solitary." The victors presented themselves to him, bowing to the ground. As after St Albans, they carried him again to London, and, having him in their power once more, ruled in his name. The so-called compromise in which all the Estates of the Realm concurred was then attempted. "The Duke of York," says Gregory's *Chronicle* "kept King Harry at Westminster by force and strength, till at last the King, for fear of death, granted him the Crown, for a man that hath but little wit will soon be afeared of death." Henry was to be King for life; York was to conduct the government and succeed him at his death. All who sought a quiet life for the nation hailed this arrangement. But the settlement defied the fact that Queen Margaret, with her son, the Prince of Wales, was at liberty at Harlech Castle, in Wales. The King in bondage had disinherited his own son. The Queen fought on.

With her army of the North and of North Wales Margaret advanced to assert the birthright of her son. The Duke of York, disdaining to remain in the security of Sandal Castle until his whole strength was gathered, marched against her. At Wakefield on December 30, 1460, the first considerable battle of the war was fought. The Lancastrians, with superior forces, caught the Yorkists by surprise, when many were foraging, and a frightful rout and massacre ensued. Here there was no question of sparing the common men; many hundreds were slaughtered; but the brunt fell upon the chiefs. No quarter was given. The Duke of York was killed; his son, the Earl of Rutland, eighteen years old, was flying, but the new Lord Clifford remembering St Albans, slaughtered him with joy, exclaiming, "By God's blood, thy father slew mine; and so will I do thee, and all thy kin." Henceforward this was the rule of the war. The old Earl of Salisbury, caught during the night, was beheaded immediately by Lord Exeter, a natural son of the Duke of Buckingham. Margaret's hand has been discerned in this severity. The heads of the three Yorkist nobles were

ENGLAND AND WALES
DURING THE
WARS OF THE ROSES

SCOTLAND

Berwick
Norham
Hedgley Moor ✗
Bamborough
Dunstanburgh
Alnwick

Newcastle
Hexham ✗
Durham

Battlefields marked ✗

Middleham

York
Clitheroe ✗ Towton
Wakefield ✗
Sandal Castle

Ravenspur

Holt
Nottingham
Harlech
Shrewsbury
Bosworth ✗
✗ Losecoat Field
WALES
Ludlow
Coventry
Mortimers Cross ✗
Northampton
Worcester
Edgecot
Stony Stratford
Milford Haven
Tewkesbury
Dunstable
Watford ✗ St. Albans
London ✗ Barnet

Cerne Abbey

Dartmouth

exposed over the gates and walls of York. The great Duke's head, with a paper crown, grinned upon the landscape, summoning the avengers.

Hitherto the struggle had been between mature, comfortable magnates, deeply involved in State affairs and trying hard to preserve some limits. Now a new generation took charge. There was a new Lord Clifford, a new Duke of Somerset, above all a new Duke of York, all in the twenties, sword in hand, with fathers to avenge and England as the prize. When York's son, hitherto Earl of March, learned that his father's cause had devolved upon him he did not shrink. He fell upon the Earl of Wiltshire and the Welsh Lancastrians, and on February 2, 1461, at the Battle of Mortimer's Cross, near Hereford, he beat and broke them up. He made haste to repay the cruelties of Wakefield. "No quarter" was again the word. Among those executed after the battle was Owen Tudor, a harmless notable, who, with the axe and block before him, hardly believed that he would be beheaded until the collar of his red doublet was ripped off. His son Jasper lived, as will be seen, to carry on the quarrel.

The victorious Yorkists under their young Duke now marched to help the Earl of Warwick, who had returned from Calais and was being hard pressed in London; but Queen Margaret forestalled him, and on February 17, at the second Battle of St Albans, she inflicted upon Warwick a bloody defeat. Warwick, who was at this time the real leader of the Yorkist party, with many troops raised abroad and with the latest firearms and his own feudal forces, had carried the captive King with him and claimed to be acting in his name. But Margaret's onset took him by surprise. "Their prickers [scouts] came not home to bring tidings how nigh the Queen was, save one came and said that she was nine mile off." Warwick and Norfolk escaped; half their army was slaughtered. King Henry had been carted to the scene. There, beneath a large tree, he watched what happened with legitimate and presently un-concealed satisfaction. Two knights of high renown in the French war, one the redoubtable Sir Thomas Kyriel, had been appointed as his warders and guardians. Above all they were to make sure no harm came to him. They therefore remained with him under his tree, and all were surrounded by the victorious army. Among the many captains of consequence whom Margaret put to death in cold blood the next morning these two cases needed special consideration. King Henry said he had asked them to bide with him and that they had done so for his own safety. Queen Margaret produced her son Edward, now seven years old, to whose disinheritance the King had perforce consented, and asked this child, already precociously fierce, to pronounce. "Fair son, with what death shall these two knights die whom you see there?" "Their heads should be cut off" was the ready answer. As Kyriel was being led away to his doom he exclaimed, "May the wrath of God fall on those who have taught a child to speak such words." Thus was pity banished from all hearts, and death or vengeance was the cry.

*　　*　　*　　*　　*

Margaret now had her husband safe back in her hands, and with him the full authority of the Crown. The road to London was open, but she did not choose to advance upon it. The fierce hordes she had brought from the North had already disgraced themselves by their ravages far and wide along their line of march. They had roused against them the fury of the countryside. The King's friends said, "They deemed that the Northern men would have been too cruel in robbing if they had come to London." The city was, upon the whole, steadfast in the Yorkist cause, but it was also said, "If the King and Queen had come with their army to London they would have had all things as they wished." We cannot judge the circumstances fully. Edward of York was marching with the triumphant army of Mortimer's Cross night and day to reach London. Warwick had joined him in Oxfordshire with the survivors of St Albans. Perhaps King Henry pleaded that the capital should not become a battlefield, but at any rate Margaret and her advisers did not dare to make it so. Flushed with victory, laden with spoil, reunited with the King, the Lancastrians retired through Dunstable to the North, and thus disguised the fact that their Scottish mercenaries were already joggling home with all that they could carry. According to Holinshed, "The Queen, having little trust in Essex, less in Kent, and least of all in London, . . . departed from St Albans into the North Country, where the foundation of her strength and refuge only rested."

This was the turning-point in the struggle. Nine days after the second Battle of St Albans Edward of York entered London. The citizens, who might have submitted to Margaret and the King, now hailed the Yorkists with enthusiasm. They thanked God and said, "Let us walk in a new vineyard, and let us make a gay garden in the month of March, with this fair white rose and herb, the Earl of March." [1] It was a vineyard amid thorns. The pretence of acting in the King's name could serve no longer. The Yorkists had become without disguise traitors and rebels against the Crown. But the mood of the youthful warrior who had triumphed and butchered at Mortimer's Cross recked little of this charge. As he saw it, his father had been ruined and killed through respect for the majesty of Henry VI. He and his friends would palter no longer with such conceptions. Forthwith he claimed the crown; and such was the feeling of London and the strength of his army, now upon the spot, that he was able to make good show of public authority for his act. He declared himself King, and on March 4,

[1] Gregory's *Chronicle*.

1461, was proclaimed at Westminster with such formalities as were possible. Henceforward he declared that the other side were guilty of treason, and that he would enforce upon them every penalty.

These assertions must now be made good, and King Edward IV marched north to settle once and for all with King Henry VI. Near York the Queen, with the whole power of Lancaster, confronted him not far from Tadcaster, by the villages of Saxton and Towton. Some accounts declare that a hundred thousand men were on the field, the Yorkists having forty and the Lancastrians sixty thousand; but later authorities greatly reduce these figures.

On March 28 the Yorkist advance-guard was beaten back at Ferry Bridge by the young Lord Clifford, and Warwick himself was wounded; but as heavier forces arrived the bridge was carried, Clifford was slain, and the Yorkist army passed over. The next day one of the most ruthless battles on English soil was fought. The Lancastrians held a good position on rising ground, their right flank being protected by the flooded stream of the Cock, in many places unfordable. Although Edward's army was not complete and the Duke of Norfolk's wing was still approaching, he resolved to attack. The battle began in a blinding snowstorm, which drove in the faces of the Lancastrians. Under this cover clumps of Yorkist spearmen moved up the slope. The wind gave superior range to the archery of the attack and the Lancastrian shafts fell short, while they themselves suffered heavily. Under this pressure the decision was taken to advance downhill upon the foe. For six hours the two sides grappled furiously, with varying success. At the height of the battle Warwick is said to have dismounted and slain his horse to prove to his men he would not quit them alive. But all hung in the balance until late in the afternoon, when the arrival of the Duke of Norfolk's corps upon the ex-

posed flank of the Lancastrians drove the whole mass into retreat, which soon became a rout.

Now the Cock beck, hitherto a friend, became an enemy.
The bridge towards Tadcaster was block with fugitives. Many
thousands of men, heavily armoured, plunged into the swollen
stream, and were drowned in such numbers that hideous
bridges were formed of the corpses and some escaped thereby.
The pursuit was carried on far into the night. Margaret and
her son escaped to York, where King Henry had been observ-
ing the rites of Palm Sunday. Gathering him up, the imperious
Queen set out with her child and a cluster of spears for the
Northern border. The bodies of several thousand Englishmen
lay upon the field. Edward, writing to his mother, conceals his
own losses, but claims that twenty-eight thousand Lancastrian
dead had been counted. It is certain that the flower of the Lancastrian nobility and knighthood fell upon the field. For all
prisoners there was but death. The Earl of Devonshire and
"the bastard of Exeter" alone were spared, and only for a day.
When Edward reached the town of York his first task was to
remove the heads of his father and others of Margaret's victims and to replace them with those of his noblest captives.
Three months later, on June 28, he was crowned King at
Westminster, and the Yorkist triumph seemed complete. It
was followed by wholesale proscriptions and confiscations.
Parliament in November 1461 passed an Act of Attainder
which, surpassing all previous severities, lapped a hundred and
thirty-three notable persons in its withering sweep. Not only
the throne but one-third of the estates in England changed
hands. It was measure for measure.

*　　*　　*　　*　　*

After Towton the Lancastrian cause was sustained by the
unconquerable will of Queen Margaret. Never has her tenacity
and rarely have her vicissitudes been surpassed in any woman.

Apart from the sullen power of Lancaster in the North, she had the friendly regard of two countries, Scotland and France. Both had felt the heavy arm of England in former reigns; both rejoiced at its present division and weakness. The hatred of the Scots for the English still excited by its bitterness the wonder of foreigners. When Louis XI succeeded his father, Charles VII, in 1461, the year of Towton, he found his country almost a desert, horrible to see. The fields were untilled; the villages were clusters of ruined hovels. Amid the ruins, the weeds and brushwood—to use a term which recurs—of what were formerly cultivated and fertile fields there dwelt a race of peasants reduced to the conditions and roused to the ferocity of wolves. All this was the result of the English invasion. Therefore it was a prime aim of Scottish and French policy, always moving hand-in-hand, to foster the internal strife of England and to sustain the weaker party there.

Margaret, as Queen of England and Princess of France, was an outstanding personage in the West of Europe. Her qualities of courage and combativeness, her commanding, persuasive personality, her fury against those who had driven her and her husband from the throne, produced from this one woman's will-power a long series of desperate, forlorn struggles after the main event had been decided, and after the lapse of years for one brief spell reversed it. English national interests did not enter her mind. She had paid her way with Scotland by the surrender of Berwick. She clinched her bargain with Louis XI by mortgaging Calais to him for 20,000 gold livres.

In 1462 Margaret, after much personal appeal to the Courts of France, Burgundy, and Scotland, found herself able to land with a power, and whether by treachery or weakness the three strongest Northern castles, Bamburgh, Alnwick, and Dunstanburgh, opened their gates to her. Louis XI had lent her the services of a fine soldier, Pierre de Brézé, who under her spell spent his large fortune in her cause. In the winter of 1462 therefore King Edward gathered his Yorkist powers, and, carrying his new train of artillery by sea to Newcastle, began the sieges of these lost strongholds. The King himself lay stricken with measles at Durham, and Lord Warwick conducted the operations. The heavy cannon, each with its pet name, played havoc with the masonry of the castles. So vigorously were the sieges conducted that even Christmas leave was forbidden. Margaret, from Berwick, in vain attempted the relief of Alnwick. All three fortresses fell in a month.

The behaviour of Edward at this moment constitutes a solid defence for his character. This voluptuous young King, sure of his position, now showed a clemency unheard of in the Wars of the Roses. Not only did he pardon the Lancastrian nobles who were caught in the fortresses, but he made solemn pacts with them and took them into his full confidence. The Duke of Somerset and Sir Ralph Percy, on swearing allegiance, were not merely allowed to go free, but restored to their estates. Percy was even given the guardianship of two of the castles. Somerset, son of the great Minister slaughtered in the first Battle of St Albans, was admitted to even higher favour. Having made his peace, he was given a high command and a place in the inner councils of the royal army. In this new position at first he gave shrewd military advice, and was granted special pensions by the King.

Edward's magnanimity and forgiveness were ill repaid. When Margaret returned with fresh succours from France and Scotland in 1463 Percy opened the gates of Bamburgh to the Scots, and Alnwick was betrayed about the same time by a soured Yorkist officer, Sir Ralph Grey. Meanwhile Queen Margaret, with King Henry in her hands, herself besieged the castle of Norham, on the Tweed, near Berwick. Once again Edward and the Yorkists took the field, and the redoubtable

new artillery, at that time esteemed as much among the leading nations as atomic weapons are to-day, was carried to the
North. The great guns blew chunks off the castles. Margaret
fled to France, while Henry buried himself amid the valleys
and the pious foundations of Cumberland. This was the final
parting of King Henry VI and his Queen—Queen she was.
Margaret took the Prince with her on her travels. These were
remarkable. With the Duke of Exeter, six knights, and her
faithful Pierre de Brézé she landed at Sluys, and appealed to
the renowned chivalry of the house of Burgundy. She came
"without royal habit or estate"; she and her seven waiting-
women had only the clothes they were wearing. Brézé paid for
their food. Nevertheless she was treated even in this adverse
Court with royal honours. Philip, Duke of Burgundy, was
aged; his son Charles was surnamed "the Bold." The ambas-
sadors of England were active. Margaret got nothing from
Burgundy except the gifts and courtesies which old-time hospitality would afford to "a dame in distress." It is however
from these contacts that our knowledge of Margaret's adventures is derived.

Chastellain, the Burgundian chronicler, recorded her tales.
Thus only has history heard how she, King Henry, and her son
had lived for five days without bread, upon a herring each day
between them. At Mass once the Queen found herself without
even a penny for the offertory. She asked a Scottish archer near
by to lend her something. "Somewhat stiffly and regretfully"
he drew a groat from his purse. At the latest disaster at
Norham, recounted the Queen, she had been captured by
plundering Yorkist soldiers, robbed, and brought before the
captain to be beheaded. Only a quarrel of her captors over the
spoil delayed her execution. But there stood a Yorkist squire,
and to him she turned, "speaking pitifully." "Madam," he said,
"mount behind me, and Monseigneur the Prince in front, and

I will save you or die, seeing that death is more likely to come to me than not." Three-a-back they plunged into the forest, Margaret in terror for her son's life, on which her cause depended. The Yorkist squire now rode off. The forest was a known haunt of bandits, and mother and son crouched in its recesses. Soon there appeared a man of hideous and horrible aspect, with obvious intention to kill and rob. But once more Margaret, by her personal force, prevailed. She said who she was, and confided her son, the heir to the throne, to the brigand's honour. The robber was faithful to his charge. The Queen and the Prince at last both reached the shelter of the fugitive King.

*   *   *   *   *

Edward's clemency had been betrayed by Percy, but he did not withdraw his confidence from Somerset. The King was a man capable of the most bloody deeds when compelled, as he thought, by necessity, and at the same time eager to practise not only magnanimity, but open-hearted confidence. The confidence he showed to Somerset must have led him into deadly perils. This third Duke was during the beginning of 1463 high in the King's favour. "And the King made full much of him, in so much he lodged with the King in his own bed many nights, and sometimes rode a-hunting behind the King, the King having about him not passing six horse at the most, and yet three were of the Duke's men of Somerset."

When in the autumn of 1463 he went to the North Somerset and two hundred of his own men were his bodyguard. At Northampton, where bitter memories of the battle lingered, the townsfolk were first astounded and then infuriated to see this bearer of an accursed name in company with their Yorkist sovereign. Only King Edward's personal exertions saved his new-found follower from being torn to pieces. After this he found it necessary to provide other employment for Somerset and his escort. Somerset was sent to Holt Castle, in Denbighshire. The brawl at Northampton we must suppose convinced him that even the King could not protect him from his Yorkist foes. At Christmas 1463 Somerset deserted Edward and returned to the Lancastrian side. The names of these great nobles were magnets in their own territories. The unstable Duke had hoped to gain possession of Newcastle, and many of his adherents on the report that he was in the neighbourhood came out to him; but he was driven away, and they were caught and beheaded.

Again the banner of Lancaster was raised. Somerset joined King Henry. Alnwick and Bamburgh still held out. Norham and Skipton had been captured, but now Warwick's brother Montagu with a substantial army was in the field. On April 25, 1464, at Hedgeley Moor, near Alnwick, he broke and destroyed the Lancastrian revolt. The leaders perished on the field, or afterwards on the block. Sir Ralph Percy fought to the death, and used the expression, remarkable for one who had accepted pardon and even office from King Edward, "I have saved the bird in my bosom." What was this "bird?" It was the cause of Lancaster, which might be dissembled or even betrayed under duress, but still remained, when occasion served, the lodestar of its adherents. There were many who had this bird in their bosoms, but could never have coined Percy's grand phrase or stooped to his baseness.

Edward's experiment of mercy in this quarrel was now at an end, and the former rigours were renewed in their extreme degree. Somerset, defeated with a small following at Hexham on May 15, 1464, was beheaded the next morning. Before the month was out in every Yorkish camp Lancastrian nobles and knights by dozens and half-dozens were put to death. There was nothing for it but to still these unquiet spirits. John Tiptoft, Earl of Worcester, Constable of England, versed in the civil war, and with Italian experience, presided over drumhead courts-martial, and by adding needless cruelties to his severities justified a vengeance one day to be exacted.

Meanwhile the diplomacy of the English Crown had effected a fifteen years' truce with the King of Scotland, and was potent both at the Courts of France and Burgundy. Margaret remained helpless at Bar-le-Duc. Poor King Henry was at length tracked down near Clitheroe, in Lancashire, and conveyed to London. This time there was no ceremonial entry. With his feet tied by leather thongs to the stirrups, and with a straw hat on his head, the futile but saintly figure around whom such storms had beaten was led three times round the pillory, and finally hustled to the Tower, whose gates closed on him, yet not—this time—for ever.

With the fall of Alnwick only one fortress in the whole kingdom still resisted. The castle of Harlech, on the western sea, alone flaunted the Red Rose. Harlech stood a siege of seven years. When it surrendered in 1468 there were found to be but fifty effective men in the garrison. With two exceptions, they were admitted to mercy. Among them was a child of twelve, who had survived the rigours of the long blockade. He was the nephew of Jasper, the grandson of Owen Tudor, and the future founder of the Tudor dynasty and system of government. His name was Richmond, later to become King Henry VII.

The Adventures
of Edward IV

KING EDWARD IV had made good his right to the Crown upon the field. He was a soldier and a man of action; in the teeth of danger his quality was at its highest. In war nothing daunted or wearied him. Long marches, hazardous decisions, the marshalling of armies, the conduct of battles, seemed his natural sphere. The worse things got the better he became. But the opposite was also true. He was at this time a fighting man and little more, and when the fighting stopped he had no serious zest for sovereignty. The land was fair; the blood of youth coursed in his veins; all his blood debts were paid; with ease and goodwill he sheathed his sharp sword. It had won him his crown; now to enjoy life.

The successes of these difficult years had been gained for King Edward by the Neville family. Warwick or Montagu, now Earl of Northumberland, with George Neville, Archbishop of York, had the whole machinery of government in their hands. The King had been present only at some of the actions. He could even be reproached for his misguided clemency, which had opened up again the distresses of civil war. His magnanimity had been at length sternly repressed by his counsellors and generals. In the first part of his reign England was therefore ruled by the two brothers, Warwick and Northumberland. They believed they had put the King on the throne, and meant him to remain there while they governed.

The King did not quarrel with this. In all his reign he never fought but when he was forced; then he was magnificent. History has scolded this prince of twenty-two for not possessing immediately the statecraft and addiction to business for which his office called. Edward united contrasting characters. He loved peace; he shone in war. But he loved peace for its indulgences rather than its dignity. His pursuit of women, in which he found no obstacles, combined with hunting, feasting, and drinking to fill his life. Were these not the rightful prizes of victory? Let Warwick and Northumberland and other anxious lords carry the burden of State, and let the King be merry. For a while this suited all parties. The victors divided the spoil; the King had his amusements, and his lords their power and policy.

Thus some years slipped by, while the King, although gripping from time to time the reins of authority, led in the main his life of pleasure. His mood towards men and women is described in the well-chosen words by the staid Hume:

"During the present interval of peace, he lived in the most familiar and sociable manner with his subjects, particularly with the Londoners; and the beauty of his person, as well as the gallantry of his address, which, even unassisted by his royal dignity, would have rendered him acceptable to the fair, facilitated all his applications for their favour. This easy and pleasurable course of life augmented every day his popularity among all ranks of men. He was the peculiar favourite of the young and gay of both sexes. The disposition of the English, little addicted to jealousy, kept them from taking umbrage at these liberties. And his indulgence in amusements, while it gratified his inclination, was thus become, without design, a means of supporting and securing his Government." After these comparatively mild censures the historian proceeds to deplore the weakness and imprudence which led the King to stray from the broad, sunlit glades of royal libertinage on to the perilous precipices of romance and marriage.

One day the King a-hunting was carried far by the chase. He rested for the night at a castle. In this castle a lady of quality, niece of the owner, had found shelter. Elizabeth Woodville, or Wydvil, was the widow of a Lancastrian knight, Sir John Grey, "in Margaret's battle at St Albans slain." Her mother, Jacquetta of Luxemburg, had been the youthful wife of the famous John, Duke of Bedford, and after his death she had married his steward, Sir Richard Woodville, later created Earl Rivers. This condescension so far below her station caused offence to the aristocracy. She was fined £1,000 as a deterrent to others. Nevertheless she lived happily ever after, and bore her husband no fewer than thirteen children, of whom Elizabeth was one. There was high as well as ordinary blood in Elizabeth's veins; but she was an austere woman, upright, fearless, chaste and fruitful. She and her two sons were all under the ban of the attainder which disinherited the adherents of Lancaster. The chance of obtaining royal mercy could not be missed. The widow bowed in humble petition before the youthful conqueror, and, like the tanner's daughter of Falaise, made at first glance the sovereign her slave. Shakespeare's account, though somewhat crude, does not err in substance. The Lady Elizabeth observed the strictest self-restraint, which only enhanced the passion of the King. He gave her all his love, and when he found her obdurate he besought her to share his crown. He spurned the counsels of prudence and worldly wisdom. Why conquer in battles, why be a king, if not to gain one's heart's desire? But he was well aware of the dangers of his choice. His marriage in 1464 with Elizabeth Woodville was a secret guarded in deadly earnest. The statesmen at the head of the Government, while they smiled at what seemed an amorous frolic, never dreamed it was a solemn union, which must shake the land to its depths.

* * * * *

Warwick's plans for the King's future had been different. Isabella of the house of Spain, or preferably a French princess, were brides who might greatly forward the interests of England. A royal marriage in those days might be a bond of peace between neighbouring states or the means of successful war. Warwick used grave arguments and pressed the King to decide. Edward seemed strangely hesitant, and dwelt upon his objections until the Minister, who was also his master, became impatient. Then at last the truth was revealed: he had for five months been married to Elizabeth Woodville. Here then was the occasion which sundered him from the valiant King-maker, fourteen years older, but also in the prime of life. Warwick had deep roots in England, and his popularity, whetted by the lavish hospitality which he offered to all classes upon his many great estates, was unbounded. The Londoners looked to him. He held the power. But no one knew better than he that there slept in Edward a tremendous warrior, skilful, ruthless, and capable when roused of attempting and of doing all.

The King too, for his part, began to take more interest in affairs. Queen Elizabeth had five brothers, seven sisters, and two sons. By royal decree he raised them to high rank, or married them into the greatest families. He went so far as to marry his wife's fourth brother, at twenty, to the Dowager Duchess of Norfolk, aged eighty. Eight new peerages came into existence in the Queen's family: her father, five brothers-in-law, her son, and her brother Anthony. This was generally thought excessive. It must be remembered that at this time there were but sixty peers, of whom not more than fifty could ever be got to Parliament on one occasion. All these potentates were held in a tight and nicely calculated system. The arrival of a new nobility who had done nothing notable in the war and now surrounded the indolent King was not merely offensive, but politically dangerous to Warwick and his proud associates.

But the clash came over foreign policy. In this sad generation England, lately the master, had become the sport of neighbouring states. Her titled refugees, from one faction or the other, beset the Courts of Western Europe. The Duke of Burgundy had been shocked to learn one morning that a Duke of Exeter and several other high English nobles were actually begging their bread at the tail of one of his progresses. Ashamed to see such a slight upon his class, he provided them with modest dwellings and allowances. Similar charities were performed by Louis XI to the unhappy descendants of the victors of Agincourt. Margaret with her retinue of shadows was welcomed in her pauper stateliness both in Burgundy and in France. At any moment either Power, now become formidable as England had waned, might support the exiled faction in good earnest and pay back the debts of fifty years before by an invasion of England. It was the policy of Warwick and his connection to make friends with France, by far the stronger Power, and thus obtain effectual security. In this mood they hoped to make a French match for the King's sister. Edward took the opposite line. With the instinct which afterwards ruled our Island for so many centuries, he sought to base English policy upon the second strongest state in Western Europe. He could no doubt argue that to be the ally of France was to be in the power of France, but to be joined with Burgundy was to have the means of correcting if not of controlling French action. Amid his revelries and other hunting he nursed a conqueror's spirit. Never should England become a vassal state; instead of being divided by her neighbours, she would herself, by dividing them, maintain a balance. At this time these politics were new; but the stresses they wrought in the small but vehement world of English government can be readily understood nowadays.

The King therefore, to Warwick's chagrin and alarm, in 1468 married his sister Margaret to Charles the Bold, who had in 1467 succeeded as Duke of Burgundy. Thus not only did these great lords, who at the constant peril of their lives and by all their vast resources had placed him on the throne, suffer slights and material losses by the creation of a new nobility, but they had besides to stomach a foreign policy which they believed would be fatal to England, to the Yorkist party, and to themselves. What help could Burgundy give if France, joined to the house of Lancaster, invaded England? What would happen to them, their great estates, and all who depended upon them, in such a catastrophe? The quarrel between the King and Warwick, as head of the Nevilles, was not therefore petty, or even, as has often been suggested, entirely personal.

The offended chiefs took deep counsel together. Edward continued to enjoy his life with his Queen, and now and again, with others. His attention in public matters was occupied mainly with Lancastrian plots and movements, but underneath and behind him a far graver menace was preparing. The Nevilles were at length ready to try conclusions with him. Warwick's plan was singular in its skill. He had gained the King's brother, Clarence, to his side by whispering that but for this upstart brood of the Woodvilles he might succeed Edward as King. As bond it was secretly agreed that Clarence should marry Warwick's daughter Isabella.

When all was ready Warwick struck. A rising took place in the North. Thousands of men in Yorkshire under the leadership of various young lords complained in arms about taxation. The "thrave," a levy paid since the days of Athelstan, became suddenly obnoxious. But other grievances were urged, par-

ticularly that the King was swayed by "favourites." At the
same time in London the House of Commons petitioned
against lax and profuse administration. The King was now
forced to go to the North. Except his small bodyguard he had
no troops of his own, but he called upon his nobles to bring
out their men. He advanced in July to Nottingham, and there
awaited the Earls of Pembroke and Devon, both new creations
of his own, who had marshalled the levies of Wales and the
West. As soon as the King had been enticed northwards by
the rebellion Warwick and Clarence, who had hitherto
crouched at Calais, came to England with the Calais garrison.
Warwick published a manifesto supporting the Northern
rebels, "the King's true subjects" as he termed them, and urged
them "with piteous lamentations to be the means to our Sovereign Lord the King of remedy and reformation." Warwick was
joined by many thousands of Kentish men and was received
with great respect in London. But before he and Clarence
could bring their forces against the King's rear the event was
decided. The Northern rebels, under "Robin of Redesdale,"
intercepted Pembroke and Devon, and at Edgcott, near Ban-
bury, defeated them with a merciless slaughter, a hundred and
sixty-eight knights, squires, and gentlemen either falling in the
fight or being executed thereafter. Both Pembroke and later
Devon were beheaded.

The King, trying to rally his scattered forces at Olney, in
Buckinghamshire, found himself in the power of his great
nobles. His brother, Richard of Gloucester, known to legend
as "Crookback" because of his alleged deformity, seemed his
only friend. At first he attempted to rally Warwick and
Clarence to their duty, but in the course of conversation he
was made to realise that he was their captive. With bows and
ceremonies they explained that his future reign must be in
accordance with their advice. He was conveyed to Warwick's

castle at Middleham, and there kept in honourable but real restraint under the surveillance of the Archbishop of York. At this moment therefore Warwick the King-maker had actually the two rival Kings, Henry VI and Edward IV, both his prisoners, one in the Tower and the other at Middleham. This was a remarkable achievement for any subject. To make the lesson even plainer, Lord Rivers, the Queen's father, and John Woodville, her brother, were arrested and executed at Kenilworth without any pretence of trial. Thus did the older nobility deal with the new.

But the relations between Warwick and the King did not admit of such simple solutions. Warwick had struck with suddenness, and for a while no one realised what had happened. As the truth became known the Yorkist nobility viewed with astonishment and anger the detention of their brave, victorious sovereign, and the Lancastrians everywhere raised their heads in the hopes of profiting by the Yorkist feud. The King found it convenient in his turn to dissemble. He professed himself convinced that Warwick and Clarence were right. He undertook to amend his ways, and after he had signed free pardons to all who had been in arms against him he was liberated. Thus was a settlement reached between Warwick and the Crown. King Edward was soon again at the head of forces, defeating Lancastrian rebels and executing their leaders, while Warwick and all his powerful connections returned to their posts, proclaimed their allegiance, and apparently enjoyed royal favour. But all this was on the surface.

*   *   *   *   *

In March 1470, under the pretence of suppressing a rebellion in Lincolnshire, the King called his forces to arms. At Losecoat Field he defeated the insurgents, who promptly fled; and in the series of executions which had now become customary after every engagement he obtained a confession from

Sir Robert Welles which accused both Warwick and Clarence of treason. The evidence is fairly convincing; for at this moment they were conspiring against Edward, and shortly afterwards refused to obey his express order to join him. The King, with troops fresh from victory, turned on them all of a sudden. He marched against them, and they fled, astounded that their own methods should be retorted upon themselves. They sought safety in Warwick's base at Calais; but Lord Wenlock, whom he had left as his deputy, refused to admit them. Even after they had bombarded the sea-front he made it a positive favour to send a few flagons of wine to Clarence's bride, who, on board ship, had just given birth to a son. The King-maker found himself by one sharp twist of fortune deprived of almost every resource he had counted upon as sure. He in his turn presented himself at the French Court as a suppliant.

But this was the best luck Louis XI had ever known. He must have rubbed his hands in the same glee as when he visited his former Minister, Cardinal Jean Balue, whom he kept imprisoned in an iron cage at Chinon because he had conspired with Charles the Bold. Two years earlier Edward as the ally of Burgundy had threatened him with war. Now here in France were the leaders of both the parties that had disputed England for so long. Margaret was dwelling in her father's Anjou. Warwick, friend of France, vanquished in his own country, had arrived at Honfleur. With gusto the stern, cynical, hard-pressed Louis set himself to the task of reconciling and combining these opposite forces. At Angers he confronted Margaret and her son, now a fine youth of seventeen, with Warwick and Clarence, and proposed brutally to them that they should join together with his support to overthrow Edward. At first both parties recoiled. Nor can we wonder. A river of blood flowed between them. All that they had fought for during these cruel years was defaced by their union. Warwick and Margaret had slain with deliberation each other's dearest friends and kin. She had beheaded his father Salisbury, slain his uncle York and his cousin Rutland. He for his part had executed the two Somersets, father and son, the Earl of Wiltshire, and many of her devoted adherents. The common people who had fallen in their quarrel, they were uncounted. In 1459 Margaret had declared Warwick attainted, a terrible outlawry. In 1460 he had branded her son as bastard or changeling. They had done each other the gravest human injuries. But they had one bond in common. They hated Edward and they wanted to win. They were the champions of a generation which could not accept defeat. And here, as indeed for a time it proved, appeared the means of speedy triumph.

Warwick had a fleet, commanded by his nephew, the bastard of Fauconberg. He had the sailors in all the seaports of the south coast. He knew he had but to go or send his summons to large parts of England for the people to take arms at his command. Margaret represented the beaten, disinherited, proscribed house of Lancaster, stubborn as ever. They agreed to forgive and unite. They took solemn oaths at Angers upon a fragment of the Holy Cross, which luckily was available. The confederacy was sealed by the betrothal of Margaret's son, the Prince of Wales, to Warwick's younger daughter, Anne. No one can blame Queen Margaret because in the ruin of her cause she reluctantly forgave injuries and welcomed the King-maker's invaluable help. She had never swerved from her faith. But for Warwick the transaction was unnatural, cynical and brutal.

Moreover, he overlooked the effect on Clarence of the new marriage he had arranged for his daughter Anne. A son born of this union would have had a great hope of uniting torn, tormented England. It was reasonable to expect the birth of an heir to these prospects. But Clarence had been swayed in his desertion of his brother by thoughts of the crown, and although he was now named as the next in succession after Margaret's son the value of his chance was no longer high. Edward had been staggered by his brother's conduct. He did not however allow his personal resentment to influence his action. A lady in attendance upon the new Duchess of Clarence proved to be a discreet and accomplished emissary of the King. She conveyed to Clarence soon after he fled from England that he had only to rejoin his brother for all to be pardoned and forgotten. The new agreement between Warwick and Margaret decided Clarence to avail himself of this fraternal offer, but not immediately. He must have been a great dissembler; for Warwick was no more able to forecast his actions in the future than his brother had been in the past.

King Edward was by now alarmed and vigilant, but he could scarcely foresee how many of his supporters would betray him. Warwick repeated the process he had used a year before. Fitzhugh, his cousin, started a new insurrection in Yorkshire. Edward gathered some forces and, making little of the affair, marched against the rebels. Warned by Charles of Burgundy, he even expressed his wish that Warwick would land. He seems to have been entirely confident. But never was there a more swift undeception. Warwick and Clarence landed at Dartmouth in September 1470. Kent and other southern counties rose in his behalf. Warwick marched to London. He brought the miserable Henry VI from his prison in the Tower, placed a crown on his head, paraded him through the capital, and seated him upon the throne.

At Nottingham Edward received alarming news. The major part of his kingdom seemed to have turned against him. Suddenly he learned that while the Northern rebels were moving down upon him and cutting him from his Welsh succours, and while Warwick was moving northward with strong forces, Northumberland, Warwick's brother, hitherto faithful, had made his men throw up their caps for King Henry. When Edward heard of Northumberland's desertion, and also of rapid movements to secure his person, he deemed it his sole hope to fly beyond the seas. He had but one refuge—the Court of Burgundy; and with a handful of followers he cast himself upon his brother-in-law. Charles the Bold was also cautious. He had to consider the imminent danger of an attack by England and France united. Until he was sure that this was inevitable he temporised with his royal refugee relation. But when it became clear that the policy of Warwick was undoubtedly to make war upon him in conjunction with Louis XI he defended himself by an obvious manœuvre. He furnished King Edward with about twelve hundred trustworthy Flemish and German soldiers and the necessary ships and money for a descent. These forces were collected secretly in the island of Walcheren.

*   *   *   *   *

Meanwhile the King-maker ruled England, and it seemed that he might long continue to do so. He had King Henry VI a puppet in his hand. The unhappy man, a breathing ruin sitting like a sack upon the throne, with a crown on his head and a sceptre in his hand, received the fickle caresses of Fortune with the same mild endurance which he had shown to her malignities. Statutes were passed in his name which annihilated all the disinheritances and attainders of the Yorkist Parliament. A third of the land of England returned to its old possessors. The banished nobles or the heirs of the slain returned from poverty and exile to their ancient seats. Meanwhile all preparations were made for a combined attack by England and France on Burgundy, and war became imminent.

But while these violent transformations were comprehensible to the actors, and the drama proceeded with apparent success, the solid bulk of England on both sides was incapable of following such too-quick movements and reconciliations. Almost the whole population stood wherever it had stood before. Their leaders might have made new combinations, but ordinary men could not believe that the antagonism of the Red and the White Rose was ended. It needed but another shock to produce an entirely different scene. It is significant that, although repeatedly urged by Warwick to join him and her husband, King Henry, in London, and although possessed of effective forces, Margaret remained in France, and kept her son with her.

In March 1471 Edward landed with his small expedition at Ravenspur, a port in Yorkshire now washed away by the North Sea, but then still famous for the descent of Henry of Bolingbroke in 1399. The King, fighting for his life, was, as usual, at his best. York shut its gates in his face, but, like Bolingbroke, he declared he had only come to claim his private estates, and bade his troops declare themselves for King Henry VI. Accepted and nourished on these terms, he set forth on his march to London. Northumberland, with four times his numbers, approached to intercept him. Edward, by extraordinary marches, manœuvred past him. All Yorkist lords and adherents in the districts through which he passed joined his army. At Warwick he was strong enough to proclaim himself King again. The King-maker, disconcerted by the turn of events, sent repeated imperative requests to Margaret to come at once, and at Coventry stationed himself in King Edward's path. Meanwhile his brother Northumberland followed Edward southward, only two marches behind. In this dire strait Edward had a resource unsuspected by Warwick. He knew Clarence was his man. Clarence was moving from Gloucestershire with considerable forces, ostensibly to join Warwick; but Edward, slipping round Warwick's flank, as he had out-marched and out-witted Northumberland, placed himself between Warwick and London, and in the exact position where Clarence could make his junction with him.

Both sides now concentrated all their strength, and again large armies were seen in England. Edward entered London, and was cordially received by the bewildered citizens. Henry VI, who had actually been made to ride about the streets at the head of six hundred horsemen, was relieved from these exertions and taken back to his prison in the Tower. The decisive battle impended on the North Road, and at Barnet on April 14, 1471, Edward and the Yorkists faced Warwick and the house of Neville, with the new Duke of Somerset, second son of Edmund Beaufort, and important Lancastrian allies.

Throughout England no one could see clearly what was happening, and the Battle of Barnet, which resolved their doubts, was itself fought in a fog. The lines of battle overlapped; Warwick's right turned Edward's left flank, and *vice versa*. The King-maker, stung perhaps by imputations upon his physical courage, fought on foot. The new Lord Oxford, a prominent Lancastrian, whose father had been beheaded earlier in the reign, commanding the overlapping Lancastrian left, found himself successful in his charge, but lost in the mist. Little knowing that the whole of King Edward's rear was open to his attack, he tried to regain his own lines and arrived in the rear of Somerset's centre. The badge of a star and rays on his banners was mistaken by Warwick's troops for the sun and rays of King Edward. Warwick's archers loosed upon him. The mistake was discovered, but in those days of treason and changing sides it only led to another blunder. It was assumed that he had deserted. The cry of treason ran through Warwick's hosts. Oxford, in his uncertainty, rode off into the gloom. Somerset, on the other flank, had already been routed.

Warwick, with the right wing, was attacked by the King and the main Yorkist power. Here indeed it was not worth while to ask for mercy. Warwick, outnumbered, his ranks broken, sought to reach his horse. He would have been wise in spite of taunts to have followed his usual custom of mounting again on the battle-day after walking along the lines; for had he escaped this zigzag story might have ended at the opposite point. But north of the town near which the main struggle was fought the King-maker, just as he was about to reach the necessary horse, was overtaken by the Yorkists and battered to death. He had been the foremost champion of the Yorkist cause. He had served King Edward well. He had received ill-usage from the youth he had placed and sustained upon the throne. By his depraved abandonment of all the causes for which he had sent so many men to their doom he had deserved death; and for his virtues, which were distinguished, it was fitting that it should come to him in honourable guise.

*   *   *   *   *

On the very day of Barnet Margaret at last landed in England. Somerset, the fourth Duke, with his father and his elder brother to avenge, fresh from the distaster at Barnet, met her and became her military commander. On learning that Warwick was slain and his army beaten and dispersed the hitherto indomitable Queen had her hour of despair. Sheltering in Cerne Abbey, near Weymouth, her thought was to return to France; but now her son, the Prince of Wales, nearly eighteen, in whose veins flowed the blood of Henry V, was for fighting for the crown or death. Margaret rallied her spirits and appeared once again unbroken by her life of disaster. Her only hope was to reach the Welsh border, where strong traditional Lancastrian forces were already in arms. The King-maker aberration had been excised. The struggle was once again between Lancaster and York. Edward, near London, held interior lines. He strove to cut Margaret off from Wales. Both armies marched incessantly. In their final march each covered forty miles in a single day. The Lancastrians succeeded in reaching the goal first, but only with their troops in a state of extreme exhaustion. Edward, close behind, pressed on, and on May 3 brought them to battle at Tewkesbury.

This battle was simple in its character. The two sides faced each other in the usual formation of three sectors, right, centre, and left. Somerset commanded Margaret's left, Lord Wenlock and the Prince of Wales the centre, and Devon her right. King Edward exercised a more general command. The Lancastrian position was strong; "in front of their field were so evil lanes, and deep dykes, so many hedges, trees, and bushes, that it was right hard to approach them here and come to hands." [1] Apparently the Lancastrian plan was to await the attack which the Yorkists were eager to deliver. However, Somerset saw an opportunity for using one of the "evil lanes" to pierce the Yorkist centre, and, either without consulting the other generals or in disagreement with them, he charged forward and gained a momentary success. But King Edward had foreseen his weakness in this quarter. He manfully withstood the irruption upon his main body, and two hundred spears he had thrown out wide as a flank guard fell upon Somerset at a decisive moment and from a deadly angle. The Lancastrians' wing recoiled in disorder. The Yorkists advanced all along the line. In their turn they fell upon their enemies' now unguarded flank, and the last army of the house of Lancaster broke into ruin. Somerset the Fourth evidently felt that he had not been supported at the critical moment. Before flying from the field he dashed out Wenlock's brains with his mace. This protest, while throwing a gleam upon the story of the battle, did not affect the result.

[1] *The Arrival of Edward IV.*

The Lancastrians were scattered or destroyed. Somerset and many other notables who thought themselves safe in sanctuary were dragged forth and decapitated. Margaret was captured. The Prince of Wales, fighting valiantly, was slain on the field, according to one chronicler, crying in vain for succour to his brother-in-law, the treacherous Clarence. Margaret was kept for a show, and also because women, especially when they happened to be queens, were not slaughtered in this fierce age.

Richard of Gloucester hastened to London. He had a task to do at the Tower. As long as the Prince of Wales lived King Henry's life had been safe, but with the death of the last hope of Lancaster his fate was sealed. On the night of May 21 the Duke of Gloucester visited the Tower with full authority from the King, where he probably supervised the murder of the melancholy spectator who had been the centre of fifty years of cruel contention.

When King Edward and his victorious army entered London, always their partisan, especially at such moments, the triumph of the Yorkist cause was complete.

> Once more we sit in England's royal throne,
> Re-purchas'd with the blood of enemies:
> What valiant foemen like to autumn's corn,
> Have we mow'd down, in tops of all their pride!
> Three Dukes of Somerset, threefold renown'd
> For hardy and undoubted champions;
> Two Cliffords, as the father and the son,
> And two Northumberlands: two braver men
> Ne'er spurr'd their coursers at the trumpet's sound;
> With them, the two brave bears, Warwick and Montagu,
> That in their chains fetter'd the kingly lion,
> And made the forest tremble when they roar'd.
> Thus have we swept suspicion from our seat,
> And made our footstool of security.

Come hither, Bess, and let me kiss my boy.
Young Ned, for thee thine uncles and myself
Have in our armours watch'd the winter's night;
Went all a-foot in summer's scalding heat,
That thou might'st repossess the crown in peace;
And of our labours thou shalt reap the gain.

*   *   *   *   *

The rest of the reign of Edward IV may be told briefly. The King was now supreme. His foes and his patrons alike were dead. He was now a matured and disillusioned statesman. He had every means of remaining complete master of the realm while leading a jolly life. Even from the beginning of his reign he had been chary of calling Parliaments. They made trouble; but if money were needed they had to be called. Therefore the cry in those days which sobered all sovereigns was, "The King should live of his own." But this doctrine took no account of the increasing scope of government. How could the King from his paternal estates, together with certain tolls and tithes, fifteenths, and a few odd poundages, and the accidents of people dying intestate or without adult heirs, or treasure-trove and the like, maintain from these snips an administration equal to the requirements of an expanding society? Still less on this basis could full-blooded wars be waged against France as was expected. It was difficult indeed even to defend the Scottish Border. One had to make use of the warlike nobility of the North, whose hereditary profession was to keep the Marches. Money —above all, ready money. There was the hobble which cramped the medieval kings; and even now it counts somewhat.

Edward was resolved to have as little to do with Parliament as possible, and even as a boy of twenty in the stress of war he tried hard and faithfully to "live of his own." Now that he was victorious and unchallenged, he set himself to practise the utmost economy in everything except his personal expenses, and to avoid any policy of adventure abroad which might drive him to beg from Parliament. He had a new source of revenue in the estates of the attainted Lancastrians. The Crown had gained from the Wars of the Roses. Many were the new possessions which yielded their annual fruit. Thus so long as there was peace the King could pay his way. But the nobility and the nation sought more. They wanted to reconquer France. They mourned the loss of the French provinces. They looked back across their own miseries to the glories of Agincourt, Poitiers, and Crécy. The King, the proved warrior, was expected to produce results in this sphere. It was his intention to do the least possible. He had never liked war, and had had enough of it. Nevertheless he obtained from the Parliament considerable grants for a war in alliance with Burgundy against France.

In 1475 he invaded France, but advanced only as far as Picquigny, near Amiens. There he parleyed. Louis XI had the same outlook. He too saw that kings might grow strong and safe in peace, and would be the prey and tool of their subjects in war. The two kings sought peace and found it. Louis XI offered Edward IV a lump sum of 75,000 crowns, and a yearly tribute of 50,000. This was almost enough to balance the royal budget and make him independent of Parliament. Edward closed on the bargain, and signed the treaty of Picquigny. But Charles the Bold, his ally of Burgundy, took it amiss. At Péronne, in full assembly, with all the English captains gathered, he declared that he had been shamefully betrayed by his ally. A most painful impression was created; but the King put up with it. He went back home and drew for seven successive years this substantial payment for not harrying France, and at the same time he pocketed most of the moneys which Parliament had voted for harrying her.

At this date the interest of these transactions centres mainly upon the character of Edward IV, and we can see that though he had to strive through fierce deeds and slaughter to his throne he was at heart a Little-Englander and a lover of ease. It by no means follows that his policy was injurious to the realm. A long peace was needed for recovery from the horrible civil war. The French Government saw in him with terror all the qualities of Henry V. They paid heavily to hold them in abeyance. This suited the King. He made his administration live thriftily, and on his death he was the first King since Henry II to leave not debts but a fortune. He laboured to contain national pride within the smallest limits, but meanwhile he let the nation grow strong again. He who above all others was thought to be the spear-point became a pad; but at that time a good pad. It may well be, as has been written, that "his indolence and gaiety were mere veils beneath which Edward shrouded profound political ability." [1]

There came a day when he had to call Parliament together. This was not however to ask them for money. What with confiscations, the French tribute, and the profits of his private trading ventures, he could still make his way. His quarrel was with his brother Clarence. Although the compact made between these brothers before Barnet and Tewkesbury had been strictly kept, Edward never trusted Clarence again. Nothing could burn out from his mind the sense that Clarence was a traitor who had betrayed his cause and his family at one decisive moment and had been rebought at another. Clarence for his part knew that the wound although skinned over was unhealed; but he was a magnificent prince, and he sprawled buoyantly over the land. He flouted the King, defying the royal courts; he executed capital sentences upon persons who had offended him in private matters, and felt himself secure. He may have discovered the secret of Edward's alleged pre-con-

[1] J. R. Green.

tract of marriage with Eleanor Butler which Richard of Gloucester was later to use in justifying his usurpation. Certainly if Edward's marriage to Elizabeth Woodville were to be proved invalid for this reason Clarence was the next legitimate heir, and a source of danger to the King. When in January 1478 Edward's patience was exhausted he called the Parliament with no other business but to condemn Clarence. He adduced a formidable catalogue of crimes and affronts to the Throne, constituting treason. The Parliament, as might be expected, accepted the King's view. By a Bill of Attainder they adjudged Clarence worthy of death, left the execution in the hands of the King, and went home relieved at not having been asked to pay any more taxes.

Clarence was already in the Tower. How he died is much disputed. Some say the King gave him his choice of deaths. Certainly Edward did not intend to have a grisly public spectacle. According to Shakespeare the Duke was drowned in a butt of Malmsey wine. This was certainly the popular legend believed by the sixteenth century. Why should it not be true? At any rate no one has attempted to prove any different tale. "False, fleeting, perjured Clarence" passed out of the world astonished that his brother should have so long a memory and take things so seriously.

Other fortunes had attended Richard of Gloucester. Shortly after the death of Henry VI he got himself married to Anne, daughter of the dead King-maker and co-heiress to the vast Warwick estates. This union excited no enthusiasm; for Anne had been betrothed, if not indeed actually married, to the young Prince Edward, killed at Tewkesbury. Important interests were however combined.

Queen Elizabeth over the course of years had produced not only five daughters, but two fine boys, who were growing up. In 1483 one was twelve and the other nine. The succession to the Crown seemed plain and secure. The King himself was only forty. In another ten years the Yorkist triumph would have become permanent. But here Fate intervened, and with solemn hand reminded the pleasure-loving Edward that his account was closed. His main thought was set on securing the crown to his son, the unfledged Edward V; but in April 1483 death came so suddenly upon him that he had no time to take the necessary precautions. Although always devoted to Queen Elizabeth, he had lived promiscuously all his life. She was in the Midlands, when, after only ten days' illness, this strong King was cut down in his prime. The historians assure us that this was the penalty of debauchery. It may well have been appendicitis, an explanation as yet unknown. He died unprepared except by the Church, and his faithful brother Richard saw himself suddenly confronted with an entirely new view of his future.

Richard III

THE King died so suddenly that all were caught by surprise. A tense crisis instantly arose. After Barnet and Tewkesbury the old nobility had had to swallow with such grace as they could muster the return of the surviving Woodvilles to the sunlight of power and favour. But throughout England the Queen's relations were viewed with resentment or disdain, while the King made merry with his beautiful, charming mistress, Jane Shore. Now death dissolved the royal authority by which alone so questionable a structure could be sustained. His eldest son, Edward, dwelt at Ludlow, on the Welsh border, under the care of his uncle, the second Lord Rivers. A Protectorate was inevitable. There could be no doubt about the Protector. Richard of Gloucester, the King's faithful brother, renowned in war, grave and competent in administration, enriched by Warwick's inheritance and many other great estates, in possession of all the chief military offices, stood forth without compare, and had been nominated by the late King himself. Around him gathered most of the old nobility. They viewed with general distaste the idea of a King whose grandfather, though a knight, had been a mere steward to one of their own order. They deplored a minority and thereafter the rule of an unproved, inexperienced boy-King. They were however bound by their oaths and by the succession in the Yorkist line that their own swords had established.

One thing at least they would not brook: Queen Elizabeth and her low-born relations should no longer have the ascendancy. On the other hand, Lord Rivers at Ludlow, with numerous adherents and family supporters, had possession of the new King. For three weeks both parties eyed one another and parleyed. It was agreed in April that the King should be crowned at the earliest moment, but that he should come to London attended by not more than two thousand horsemen. Accordingly this cavalcade, headed by Lord Rivers and his nephew, Grey, rode southward through Shrewsbury and Northampton. They had reached Stony Stratford when they learned that Gloucester and his ally, the Duke of Buckingham, coming to London from Yorkshire, were only ten miles behind them. They turned back to Northampton to greet the two Dukes, apparently suspecting no evil. Richard received them amicably; they dined together. But with the morning there was a change.

When he awoke Rivers found the doors of the inn locked. He asked the reason for this precaution. Gloucester and Buckingham met him with scowling gaze and accused him of "trying to set distance" between the King and them. He and Grey were immediately made prisoners. Richard then rode with his power to Stony Stratford, arrested the commanders of the two thousand horse, forced his way to the young King, and told him he had discovered a design on the part of Lord Rivers and others to seize the Government and oppress the old nobility. On this declaration Edward V took the only positive action recorded of his reign. He wept. Well he might.

The next morning Duke Richard presented himself again to Edward. He embraced him as an uncle; he bowed to him as a subject. He announced himself as Protector. He dismissed the two thousand horsemen to their homes; their services would not be needed. To London then! To the coronation! Thus this melancholy procession set out.

The Queen, who was already in London, had no illusions. She took sanctuary at once with her other children at Westminster, making a hole through the wall between the church and the palace to transport such personal belongings as she could gather.

The report that the King was in duress caused a commotion in the capital. "He was to be sent, no man wist whither, to be done with God wot what." [1] But Lord Hastings reassured the Council that all was well and that any disturbance would only delay the coronation, upon which the peace of the realm depended. The Archbishop of York, who was also Chancellor, tried to reassure the Queen. "Be of good cheer, madam," he said, "for if they crown any other than your son whom they now have with them, we shall on the morrow crown his brother whom you have with you here." He even gave her the Great Seal as a kind of guarantee. He was not in any plot, but only an old fool playing for safety first and peace at any price. Presently, frightened at what he had done, he managed to get the Great Seal back.

The King arrived in London only on May 4, and the coronation, which had been fixed for that date, was necessarily postponed. He was lodged at the Bishop of London's palace, where he received the fealty of all the lords, spiritual and temporal. But the Protector and his friends felt that it was hardly becoming that he should be the guest of an ecclesiastic, and when the Queen's friends suggested that he might reside at the Hospital of the Knights of St John in Clerkenwell Richard argued that it would be more fitting to the royal dignity to dwell in one of his own castles and on his own ground. The Tower was a residence not only commodious but at the same time safe from any popular disorder. To this decision the lords of the Council gave united assent, it not being either easy or safe for the minority to disagree. With much ceremony and protestations of devotion the child of twelve was conducted to the Tower, and its gates closed behind him.

[1] More.

London was in a ferment, and the magnates gathered there gazed upon each other in doubt and fear. The next step in the tragedy concerned Lord Hastings. He had played a leading part in the closing years of Edward IV. After the King's death he had been strong against the Woodvilles; but he was the first to detach himself from Richard's proceedings. It did not suit him, nor some of the other magnates, that all power should rapidly be accumulating in Richard's hands. He began to be friendly with the Queen's party, still in the sanctuary of Westminster Abbey. Of what happened next all we really know is that Hastings was abruptly arrested in council at the Tower on June 13 and beheaded without trial on the same day. Sir Thomas More late in the next reign wrote his celebrated history. His book was based of course on information given him under the new and strongly established régime. His object seems to have been less to compose a factual narrative than a moralistic drama. In it Richard is evil incarnate, and Henry Tudor, the deliverer of the kingdom, all sweetness and light. The opposite view would have been treason. Not only is every possible crime attributed by More to Richard, and some impossible ones, but he is presented as a physical monster, crookbacked and withered of arm. No one in his lifetime seems to have remarked these deformities, but they are now very familiar to us through Shakespeare's play. Needless to say, as soon as the Tudor dynasty was laid to rest defenders of Richard fell to work, and they have been increasingly busy ever since.

More's tale however has priority. We have the famous scene at the Council in the Tower. It was Friday, June 13. Richard arrived in the Council chamber about nine, apparently in good humour. "My lord," he said to Bishop Morton, "you have very good strawberries in your garden at Holborn. I pray you let us have a mess of them." The Council began its business. Richard asked to be excused for a while; when he returned between ten and eleven his whole manner was changed. He frowned and glared upon the Council, and at the same time clusters of armed men gathered at the door. "What punishment do they deserve," demanded the Protector, "who conspire against the life of one so nearly related to the King as myself, and entrusted with the government of the realm?" There was general consternation. Hastings said at length that they deserved the punishment of traitors. "That sorceress my brother's wife," cried Richard, "and others with her—see how they have wasted my body with sorcery and witchcraft." So saying, he is supposed to have bared his arm and showed it to the Council, shrunk and withered as legend says it was. In furious terms he next referred to Jane Shore, with whom Hastings had formed an intimacy on the late King's death. Hastings, taken aback, replied, "Certainly if they have done so heinously they are worth a heinous punishment." "What?" cried Crookback. "Dost thou serve me with 'ifs' and 'ands?' I tell thee they have done it, and that I will make good upon thy body, traitor!" He struck the Council table with his fist, and at this signal the armed men ran in, crying "Treason!" and Hastings, Bishop Morton, and the Archbishop of York with some others were seized. Richard bade Hastings prepare for instant death. "I will not dine until I have his head." There was barely time to find a priest. Upon a log of wood which lay by chance in the Tower yard Hastings was decapitated. Terror reigned.

Richard had ordered his retainers in the North to come to London in arms under his trusted lieutenant, Sir Richard Ratcliffe. On the way south Ratcliffe collected Lords Rivers, Vaughan, Grey, and the commanders of the two thousand horse from the castles in which they were confined, and at Pomfret cut off their heads a few days after Hastings had suffered. Their executions are undisputed fact.

Meanwhile the Queen and her remaining son still sheltered

in sanctuary. Richard felt that it would be more natural that the two brothers should be together under his care, and he moved the purged Council to request the Queen to give him up. The Council contemplated the use of force in the event of a refusal. Having no choice, the Queen submitted, and the little prince of nine was handed over in Westminster Hall to the Protector, who embraced him affectionately and conducted him to the Tower, which neither he nor his brother was ever to leave again. Richard's Northern bands were now approaching London in considerable numbers, many thousands being expected, and he felt strong enough to take his next step. The coronation of Edward V had been postponed several times. Now a preacher named Shaw, brother of the Lord Mayor of London, one of Richard's partisans, was engaged to preach a sermon at St Paul's Cross. Taking his text from the Book of Wisdom, "Bastard slips shall not take deep root," he impugned Edward IV's marriage with Elizabeth Woodville upon a number of grounds, including sorcery, violation of the alleged previous betrothal to Eleanor Butler, and the assertion that the ceremony had been performed in an unconsecrated place. He argued from this that Edward's children were illegitimate and that the crown rightly belonged to Richard. The suggestion was even revived that Edward IV himself had not been his father's son. Richard now appeared, accompanied by Buckingham, evidently expecting to be publicly acclaimed; but, says More, "the people were so far from crying 'King Richard!' that they stood as if turned into stones for wonder of this shameful sermon." Two days later the Duke of Buckingham tried his hand, and according to an eye-witness he was so eloquent and well rehearsed that he did not even pause to spit; but once again the people remained mute, and only some of the Duke's servants threw up their caps, crying, "King Richard!"

Nevertheless on June 25 Parliament met, and after receiving

a roll declaring that the late King's marriage with Elizabeth was no marriage at all and that Edward's children were bastard it petitioned Richard to assume the crown. A deputation, headed by the Duke of Buckingham, waited on Richard, who was staying at the house of his mother, whose virtue he had aspersed. With becoming modesty Richard persistently refused; but when Buckingham assured him of their determination that the children of Edward should not rule and that if he would not serve the country they would be forced to choose some other noble he overcame his conscientious scruples at the call of public duty. The next day he was enthroned, with much ceremony. At the same time the forces which Ratcliffe had sent from the North were reviewed in Finsbury Fields. They proved to be about five thousand strong, "evil apparelled . . . in rusty harness neither defensible nor scoured." The City was relieved to find that the reports of their strength and numbers had been exaggerated.

The coronation of King Richard III was fixed for July 6, and pageants and processions diverted the uneasy public. As an act of clemency Richard released the Archbishop of York from arrest, and transferred Bishop Morton of Ely to the easier custody of Buckingham. The coronation was celebrated with all possible pomp and splendour. Particular importance was attached to the religious aspect. Archbishop Bourchier placed the crowns on the heads of the King and Queen; they were anointed with oil; they received the Sacrament in the presence of the assembly, and finally repaired to a banquet in Westminster Hall. The King now had a title acknowledged and confirmed by Parliament, and upon the theory of the bastardy of Edward's children he was also the lineal successor in blood. Thus the whole design seemed to have been accomplished. Yet from this very moment there began that marked distrust and hostility of all classes towards King Richard III which all his arts and competence could not allay. "It followed," said the chronicler Fabyan, whose book was published in 1516, "anon as this man had taken upon him, he fell in great hatred of the more part of the nobles of his realm, insomuch that such as before loved and praised him . . . now murmured and grudged against him in such wise that few or none favoured his party except it were for dread or for the great gifts they had received of him."

It is contended by the defenders of King Richard that the Tudor version of these events has prevailed. But the English people who lived at the time and learned of the events day by day formed their convictions two years before the Tudors gained power or were indeed a prominent factor. Richard III held the authority of government. He told his own story with what facilities were available, and he was spontaneously and almost universally disbelieved. Indeed, no fact stands forth more unchallengeable than that the overwhelming majority of the nation was convinced that Richard had used his power as Protector to usurp the crown and that the princes had disappeared in the Tower. It will take many ingenious books to raise this issue to the dignity of a historical controversy.

No man had done more to place Richard upon the throne than the Duke of Buckingham, and upon no one had the King bestowed greater gifts and favours. Yet during these first three months of Richard's reign Buckingham from being his chief supporter became his mortal foe. His motives are not clear. Perhaps he shrank from becoming the accomplice in what he foresaw would be the closing act of the usurpation. Perhaps he feared for his own safety, for was he not himself of royal blood? He was descended both through the Beauforts and Thomas of Woodstock from Edward III. It was believed that when the Beaufort family was legitimated by letters patent under King Richard II, confirmed by Henry IV, there had been a reservation rendering them incapable of inheriting the crown; but this reservation had not been a part of the original document, but had only been written in during the reign of Henry IV. The Duke of Buckingham, as a Beaufort on his mother's side, possessed the original letters patent under the Great Seal, confirmed in Parliament, in which no such bar was mentioned. Although he guarded this secret with all needful prudence he must now look upon himself as a potential claimant to the crown, and he must feel none the safer if Richard should so regard him. Buckingham's mind was troubled by the knowledge that all the ceremony and vigour with which Richard's ascent to the throne had been conducted did not affect the general feeling that he was a usurper. In his castle at Brecknock he began to talk moodily to his prisoner, Bishop Morton; and the Bishop, who was a master of the persuasive arts and a consummate politician, undoubtedly gained a great hold upon him.

*   *   *   *   *

Meanwhile King Richard began a progress from Oxford through the Midlands. At every city he laboured to make the best impression, righting wrongs, settling disputes, granting favours, and courting popularity. Yet he could not escape the sense that behind the displays of gratitude and loyalty which naturally surrounded him there lay an unspoken challenge to his Kingship. There was little concealment of this in the South. In London, Kent, Essex, and throughout the Home Counties feeling already ran high against him, and on all men's lips was the demand that the princes should be liberated. Richard did not as yet suspect Buckingham, who had parted from him at Gloucester, of any serious disaffection. But he was anxious for the safety of his crown. How could he maintain it while his nephews lived to provide a rallying point for any combination of hostile forces against him? So we come to the principal crime ever afterwards associated with Richard's name. His interest is plain. His character was ruthless. It is certain that the helpless children in the Tower were not seen again after the month of July 1483. Yet we are invited by some to believe that they languished in captivity, unnoticed and unrecorded, for another two years, only to be done to death by Henry Tudor.

According to Thomas More's story, Richard resolved in July to extirpate the menace to his peace and sovereignty presented by the princes. He sent a special messenger, by name John Green, to Brackenbury, the Constable of the Tower, with orders to make an end of them. Brackenbury refused to obey. "Whom should a man trust," exclaimed the King when Green returned with this report "when those who I thought would most surely serve at my command will do nothing for me?" A page who heard this outburst reminded his master that Sir James Tyrell, one of Richard's former companions in arms, was capable of anything. Tyrell was sent to London with a warrant authorising Brackenbury to deliver to him for one night all the keys of the Tower. Tyrell discharged his fell commission with all dispatch. One of the four gaolers in charge of the princes, Forest by name, was found willing, and with Dighton, Tyrell's own groom, did the deed. When the princes were asleep these two assassins pressed the pillows hard down upon their faces till they were suffocated, and their bodies were immured in some secret corner of the Tower. There is some proof that all three murderers were suitably rewarded by the King. But it was not until Henry VII's reign, when Tyrell was lying in the Tower under sentence of death for quite a separate crime, that he is alleged to have made a confession upon which, with much other circumstantial evidence, the story as we know it rests.

In the reign of Charles II, when in 1674 the staircase leading to the chapel in the White Tower was altered, the skeletons of two young lads, whose apparent ages fitted the two princes, were found buried under a mass of rubble. They were examined by the royal surgeon, and the antiquaries reported that they were undoubtedly the remains of Edward V and the Duke of York. Charles accepted this view, and the skeletons were reburied in Henry VII's Chapel at Westminster with a Latin inscription laying all blame upon their perfidious uncle "the usurper of the realm." This has not prevented various writers, among whom Horace Walpole is notable, from endeavouring to clear Richard of the crime, or from attempting to cast it, without any evidence beyond conjecture, upon Henry VII. However, in our own time an exhumation has confirmed the view of the disinterested authorities of King Charles's reign.

Buckingham had now become the centre of a conspiracy throughout the West and South of England against the King. He had reached a definite decision about his own claims to the crown. He seems to have assumed from his knowledge of Richard that the princes in the Tower were either dead or doomed. He met at this time Margaret, Countess of Richmond, survivor of the Beaufort line, and recognised that even if the house of York were altogether set aside both she and her son Henry Tudor, Earl of Richmond, stood between him and the crown. The Countess of Richmond, presuming him to be still Richard's right-hand man, asked him to win the King's consent to a marriage between her son Henry of Richmond and one of King Edward's daughters, Elizabeth, still in sanctuary with their mother at Westminster. Richard would never have entertained such a project, which was indeed the extreme opposite to his interests. But Buckingham saw that such a marriage would unite the claims of York and Lancaster, bridge the gulf that had parted England for so long, and enable a tremendous front to be immediately formed against the usurper.

The popular demand for the release of the princes was followed by a report of their death. When, how, and by whose hand the deed had been done was not known. But as the news spread like wildfire a kind of fury seized upon many people. Although accustomed to the brutalities of the long civil wars, the English people of those days still retained the faculty of horror; and once it was excited they did not soon forget. A modern dictator with the resources of science at his disposal can easily lead the public on from day to day, destroying all persistency of thought and aim, so that memory is blurred by the multiplicity of daily news and judgment baffled by its perversion. But in the fifteenth century the murder of the two young princes by the very man who had undertaken to protect them was regarded as an atrocious crime, never to be forgotten or forgiven. In September Richard in his progress reached York, and here he created his son Prince of Wales, thus in the eyes of his enemies giving confirmation to the darkest rumours.

All Buckingham's preparations were for a general rising on October 18. He would gather his Welsh forces at Brecknock; all the Southern and Western counties would take up arms; and Henry, Earl of Richmond, with the aid of the Duke of Brittany, would land with a force of five thousand men in Wales. But the anger of the people at the rumoured murder of the princes deranged this elaborate plan. In Kent, Wiltshire, Sussex, and Devonshire there were risings ten days before the appointed date; Henry of Richmond was forced to set sail from Brittany in foul weather on October 12, so that his fleet was dispersed; and when Buckingham unfurled his flag at Brecknock the elements took sides against him too. A terrific storm flooded the Severn valley, and he found himself penned on the Welsh border in a district which could not supply the needs of his army, and unable, as he had planned, to join the rebels in Devonshire.

King Richard acted with the utmost vigour. He had an army and he marched against rebellion. The sporadic risings in the South were suppressed. Buckingham's forces melted away, and he himself hid from vengeance. Richmond reached the English coast at last with only two ships, and sailed westwards towards Plymouth, waiting for a sign which never came. Such was the uncertainty at Plymouth that he warily made further inquiries, as a result of which he sailed back to Brittany. Buckingham, with a high price on his head, was betrayed to Richard, who lost not an hour in having him slaughtered. The usual crop of executions followed. Order was restored throughout the land, and the King seemed to have established himself securely upon his throne.

He proceeded in the new year to inaugurate a series of enlightened reforms in every sphere of Government. He revived the power of Parliament, which it had been the policy of Edward IV to reduce to nullity. He declared the practice of raising revenue by "benevolences" illegal. Parliament again legislated copiously after a long interval. Commerce was protected by a series of well-meant if ill-judged Acts, and a land law was passed to regulate "uses," or, as we should now say, trusts. Attempts were made to please the clergy by confirming their privileges, endowing new religious foundations, and extending the patronage of learning. Much care was taken over the shows of heraldry and pageantry; magnanimity was shown to fallen opponents, and petitioners in distress were treated with kindness. But all counted for nothing. The hatred which Richard's crime had roused against him throughout the land remained sullen and quenchless, and no benefits bestowed, no sagacious measures adopted, no administrative successes achieved, could avail the guilty monarch.

An impulsive gentleman, one Collingbourne, formerly

Sheriff of Worcester, was so much incensed against the King that he had a doggerel rhyme he had composed nailed on the door of St Paul's:

> The Catte, the Ratte, and Lovell our dogge
> Rulyth all Englande under a Hogge.

Catesby, Ratcliffe, Viscount Lovell, and Richard, whose badge was a boar, saw themselves affronted. But it was not only for this that Collingbourne suffered an agonising death at the end of a year. He was undoubtedly a rebel, actively engaged in conspiracy.

Even Richard's own soul rebelled against him. He was haunted by fears and dreams. He saw retribution awaiting him round every corner. "I have heard by creditable report," says Sir Thomas More, "of such as were secret with his chamberers, that after this abominable deed done he never had quiet in his mind, he never thought himself sure. Where he went abroad, his eyes whirled about, his body privily fenced, his hand ever on his dagger, his countenance and manner like one always ready to strike again. He took ill rest at nights, lay long waking and musing; sore wearied with care and watch, he rather slumbered than slept. Troubled with fearful dreams, suddenly sometimes started he up, leapt out of his bed and ran about the chamber. So was his restless heart continually tossed and tumbled with the tedious impression and stormy remembrance of his most abominable deed."

*   *   *   *   *

A terrible blow now fell upon the King. In April 1484 his only son, the Prince of Wales, died at Middleham, and his wife, Anne, the daughter of the King-maker, whose health was broken, could bear no more children. Henry Tudor, Earl of Richmond, now became obviously the rival claimant and successor to the throne. Richmond, "the nearest thing to royalty the Lancastrian party possessed," was a Welshman, whose grandfather, Owen Tudor, executed by the Yorkists in 1461, had married, if indeed he married, Henry V's widow, Catherine of France, and whose father Edmund had married the Lady Margaret Beaufort. Thus Richmond could trace his descent through his mother from Edward III, and on his father's side had French royal blood in his veins as well as a shadowy claim to descent from Cadwallader and the legendary ancient kings of Britain, including King Arthur. His life had been cast amid ceaseless trouble. For seven years of childhood he had been besieged in Harlech Castle. At the age of fourteen, on the defeat of the Lancastrians at Tewkesbury, he was forced to flee to Brittany. Thereafter exile and privation had been his lot. These trials had stamped themselves upon his character, rendering him crafty and suspicious. This, however, did not daunt a proud spirit, nor cloud a wise and commanding mind, nor cast a shadow over his countenance, which was, we are told, "smiling and amiable, especially in his communications."

All hopes in England were now turned towards Richmond, and it was apparent that the marriage which had been projected between him and Edward IV's eldest daughter Elizabeth offered a prospect of ending for ever the cruel dynastic strife of which the land was unutterably weary. After the failure of Buckingham's rebellion Richmond and his expedition had returned to Brittany. The Duke of Brittany, long friendly again accorded shelter and subsistence to the exile and his band of perhaps five hundred Englishmen of quality. But King Richard's diplomacy was active. He offered a large sum of money for the surrender of his rival. During the illness of the Duke of Brittany the Breton Minister, Landois, was disposed to sell the valuable refugee. Richmond however, suspecting the danger, escaped in the nick of time by galloping hell for leather into France, where, in accordance with the general policy of keeping English feuds alive, he was well received by the French regent, Anne. Meanwhile the Duke of Brittany, recovering, reproved his Minister and continued to harbour the English exiles. In France Richmond was joined by the Earl of Oxford, the leading survivor of the Lancastrian party, who had escaped from ten years' incarceration and plunged once again into the old struggle. As the months passed many prominent Englishmen, both Yorkist and Lancastrian, withdrew themselves from Richard's baleful presence, and made their way to Richmond, who from this time forth stood at the head of a combination which might well unite all England.

His great hope lay in the marriage with the Princess Elizabeth. But in this quarter Richard had not been idle. Before the rebellion he had taken steps to prevent Elizabeth slipping out of sanctuary and England. In March 1484 he made proposals to the Dowager Queen, Dame Elizabeth Grey as he called her, of reconciliation. The unhappy Queen did not reject his overtures. Richard promised in a solemn deed "on his honour as a King" to provide maintenance for the ex-Queen and to marry her daughters suitably to gentlemen. This remarkable document was witnessed not only by the Lords Spiritual and Temporal, but in addition by the Lord Mayor of London and the Aldermen. In spite of the past the Queen had to trust herself to this. She quitted sanctuary. She abandoned the match for her daughter with Richmond. She and the elder princesses were received at Richard's Court and treated with exceptional distinction. At the Christmas Court at Westminster in 1484 high revels were held. It was noticed that the changes of dress provided for Dame Elizabeth Grey and her daughters were almost royal in their style and richness. The stigma of bastardy so lately inflicted upon Edward's children, and the awful secret of the Tower, were banished. Although the threat of invasion was constant, gaiety and dancing ruled the hour. "Dame Elizabeth" even wrote to her son by her first marriage, the Marquis of Dorset, in Paris, to abandon Richmond and come home to share in the new-found favour. More surprising still, Princess Elizabeth seems to have been by no means hostile to the attentions of the usurper. In March 1485 Queen Anne died, probably from natural causes. Rumours were circulating that Richard intended to marry his niece himself, in order to keep her out of Richmond's way. This incestuous union could have been achieved by Papal dispensation, but Richard disavowed all intention of it, both in Council and in public. And it is indeed hard to see how his position could have been strengthened by marrying a princess whom he had declared illegitimate. However that may be, Richmond was thereby relieved of a great anxiety.

All through the summer Richmond's expedition was preparing at the mouth of the Seine, and the exodus from England of substantial people to join him was unceasing. The suspense was wearing to Richard. He felt he was surrounded by hatred and distrust, and that none served him but from fear, or hope of favour. His dogged, indomitable nature had determined him to make for his crown the greatest of all his fights. He fixed his headquarters in a good central position at Nottingham. Commissions of muster and array were ordered to call men to arms in almost every county. Departing perforce from the precepts he had set himself in the previous year, he asked for a "benevolence," or "malevolence" as it was described, of thirty thousand pounds. He set on foot a disciplined regular force. He stationed relays of horsemen every twenty miles permanently along the great roads to bring news and carry orders with an organised swiftness hitherto unknown in England. This important development in the postal system had been

inaugurated by Edward IV. At the head of his troops he ceaselessly patrolled the Midland area, endeavouring by strength
to overawe and by good government to placate his sullen subjects. He set forth his cause in a vehement proclamation, de-
nouncing ". . . one, Henry Tydder, son of Edmund Tydder,
son of Owen Tydder," of bastard blood both on his father's
and mother's side, who of his ambition and covetousness pretended to the crown, "to the disinheriting and destruction of
all the noble and worshipful blood of his realm for ever." But
this fell cold.

On August 1 Richmond embarked at Harfleur with his
Englishmen, Yorkist as well as Lancastrian, and a body of
French troops. A fair wind bore him down the Channel. He
evaded the squadrons of "Lovell our Dogge," doubled Land's
End, and landed at Milford Haven on the 7th. Kneeling, he
recited the psalm *Judica me, Deus, et decerne causam meam.*
He kissed the ground, signed himself with the Cross, and gave
the order to advance in the name of God and St George. He
had only two thousand men; but such were his assurances of
support that he proclaimed Richard forthwith usurper and
rebel against himself. The Welsh were gratified by the prospect
of one of their race succeeding to the crown of mighty England. It had been for ages a national dream. The ancient Britons would come back into their own. Richard's principal chief-
tain and officer, Rhys ap Thomas, considered himself at first
debarred by his oath of allegiance from aiding the invader. He
had declared that no rebels should enter Wales, "except they
should pass over his belly." He had however excused himself
from sending his only son to Nottingham as a hostage, assuring
Richard that nothing could bind him more strongly than his
conscience. This now became an obstacle. However, the
Bishop of St David's offered to absolve him from his oath, and
suggested that he might, if still disquieted, lay himself upon

the ground before Richmond and let him actually step over his belly. A more dignified but equally satisfactory procedure was adopted. Rhys ap Thomas stood under the Molloch Bridge near Dale while Henry of Richmond walked over the top. Anything like a scandalous breach of faith was thus avoided. The Welsh gentry rallied in moderate numbers to Richmond, who displayed not only the standard of St George, but the Red Dragon of Cadwallader. With five thousand men he now moved eastwards through Shrewsbury and Stafford.

*   *   *   *   *

For all his post-horses it was five days before the King heard of the landing. He gathered his army and marched to meet his foe. At this moment the attitude of the Stanleys became of decisive importance. They had been entrusted by the King with the duty of intercepting the rebels should they land in the West. Sir William Stanley, with some thousands of men, made no attempt to do so. Richard thereupon summoned Lord Stanley, the head of the house, to his Court, and when that potentate declared himself "ill of the sweating sickness" he seized Lord Strange, his eldest son, to hold him answerable with his life for his father's loyalty. This did not prevent Sir William Stanley with the Cheshire levies from making friendly contact with Richmond. But Lord Stanley, hoping to save his son, maintained till the last moment an uncertain demeanour.

The city of York on this occasion stood by the Yorkist cause. The Duke of Norfolk and Percy, Earl of Northumberland, were Richard's principal adherents. "The Catte and the Ratte" had no hope of life but in their master's victory. On August 17, thus attended, the King set forth towards Leicester at the head of his army. Their ordered ranks, four abreast, with the cavalry on both flanks and the King mounted on his great white charger in the centre, made a formidable impression upon beholders. And when on Sunday, the 21st, this

· 497 ·

whole array came out of Leicester to meet Richmond near the village of Market Bosworth it was certain that a decisive battle impended on the morrow.

Appearances favoured the King. He had ten thousand disciplined men under the royal authority against Richmond's hastily gathered five thousand rebels. But at some distance from the flanks of the main army, on opposite hill-tops, stood the respective forces, mainly from Lancashire and Cheshire, of Sir William Stanley and Lord Stanley, the whole situation resembling, as has been said, four players in a game of cards. Richard, according to the Tudor historians, although confessing to a night of frightful dreams and demon-hauntings, harangued his captains in magnificent style. "Dismiss all fear. . . . Every one give but one sure stroke and the day is ours. What prevaileth a handful of men to a whole realm? As for me, I assure you this day I will triumph by glorious victory or suffer death for immortal fame." He then gave the signal for battle, and sent a message to Lord Stanley that if he did not fall on forthwith he would instantly decapitate his son. Stanley, forced to this bitter choice, answered proudly that he had other sons. The King gave orders for Strange's execution. But the officers so charged thought it prudent to hold the stroke in suspense till matters were clearer. "My lord, the enemy is past the marsh. After the battle let young Stanley die."

But even now Richmond was not sure what part Lord Stanley and his forces would play. When, after archery and cannonade, the lines were locked in battle all doubts were removed. The Earl of Northumberland, commanding Richard's left, stood idle at a distance. Lord Stanley's force joined Richmond. The King saw that all was lost, and, shouting "Treason! Treason!" hurled himself into the thickest of the fray in the desperate purpose of striking down Richmond with his own hand. He actually slew Sir William Brandon, Richmond's standard-bearer, and laid low Sir John Cheney, a warrior renowned for his bodily strength. He is said even to have reached Richmond and crossed swords with him. But at this moment Sir William Stanley's three thousand, "in coats as red as blood," fell upon the struggling Yorkists. The tides of conflict swept the principals asunder. Richmond was preserved, and the King, refusing to fly, was borne down and slaughtered as he deserved.

One foot I will never flee, while the breath is my breast within.
As he said, so did it he—if he lost his life he died a king.

Richard's crown, which he wore to the last, was picked out of a bush and placed upon the victor's head. The Duke of Norfolk was slain fighting bravely; his son, Lord Surrey, was taken prisoner; Ratcliffe was killed; Catesby, after being allowed to make his will, was executed on the field; and Henry Tudor became King of England. Richard's corpse, naked, and torn by wounds, was bound across a horse, with his head and long hair hanging down, bloody and hideous, and in this condition borne into Leicester for all men to see.

*　　*　　*　　*　　*

Bosworth Field may be taken as closing a long chapter in English history. Though risings and conspiracies continued throughout the next reign the strife of the Red and the White Rose had in the main come to an end. Neither won. A solution was reached in which the survivors of both causes could be reconciled. The marriage of Richmond with the adaptable Princess Elizabeth produced the Tudor line, in which both Yorkists and Lancastrians had a share. The revengeful ghosts of two mangled generations were laid for ever. Richard's death also ended the Plantagenet line. For over three hundred years this strong race of warrior and statesmen kings, whose gifts and vices were upon the highest scale, whose sense of authority and Empire had been persistently maintained, now vanished from the fortunes of the Island. The Plantagenets and the proud, exclusive nobility which their system evolved had torn themselves to pieces. The heads of most of the noble houses had been cut off, and their branches extirpated to the second and third generation. An oligarchy whose passions, loyalties, and crimes had for long written English history was subdued. Sprigs of female or bastard lines made disputable contacts with a departed age. As Cœur de Lion said of his house, "From the Devil we sprang and to the Devil we shall go."

At Bosworth the Wars of the Roses reached their final milestone. In the next century the subjects of the Tudors liked to consider that the Middle Ages too had come to a close in 1485, and that a new age had dawned with the accession of Henry Tudor. Modern historians prefer to point out that there are no sharp dividing lines in this period of our history, and that Henry VII carried on and consolidated much of the work of the Yorkist Kings. Certainly the prolongation of strife, waste, and insecurity in the fifteenth century had aroused in all classes an overpowering desire for strong, ordered government. The Parliamentary conception which had prevailed under the house of Lancaster had gained many frontiers of constitutional rights. These were now to pass into long abeyance. Not until the seventeenth century were the old maxims, "Grievances before supply," "Responsibility of Ministers in accordance with the public will," "The Crown the servant and not the master of the State," brought again into the light, and, as it happened, the glare of a new day. The stir of the Renaissance, the storm of the Reformation, hurled their new problems on the bewildered but also reinspired mortals of the new age upon which England entered under the guidance of the wise, sad, careful monarch who inaugurated the Tudor dictatorship as King Henry VII.

INDEX

Abbeville, 343, 403
Acre, siege of, 227, 232
Adrian IV, Pope, 327
Ætius, 58, 61
Agincourt, Battle of, 404–8, 410
Agricola, 29–30, 32, 40
Aidan, St, 80
Alaric the Visigoth, 54
Albany, house of, 322
Albigenses, 266
Albion, 13
Alcuin, 85, 95
Aldershot, rout of Danes near, 125
Aldhelm of Malmesbury, 87
Aldred, Archbishop of York, 167
Alençon, 153
Alençon, Charles, Count of, at Crécy, 345–7
Alençon, John, first Duke of, at Agincourt, 405
Alexander II, King of Scotland, 258
Alexander III, King of Scotland, 301
Alfred the Great, King of the English, 104–28; prepared to help Mercia, 101; builds up country's strength, 102, 116–18, 123–4; at Battle of Ashdown, 105–6; King of Wessex, 108; makes peace with Danes, 108, 112, 116–17, 119–20; a fugitive, 113–114; defeats Danes at Ethandun, 116; his treatment of defeated enemy, 116, 125–6; navy of, 118–19; Book of Laws of, 120; achievements of, 122, 127; and third Viking invasion, 123–6; son of, 124; death of, 127; genealogical tree of, 133; Scots king descended from, 325; mentioned, 56, 67
Alfred, Prince, son of Ethelred, 144
Alnwick Castle, 452, 455–6
Alphege, St, Archbishop of Canterbury, 137, 140
America, Viking discovery of, 91, 93, 97
Andelys, 239
Angers, 465–6
Angevin Empire, 197, 204; loss of, 247
Angles, the tribe, 65
Anglesey (Mona), Roman attack on, 23; subjugation of, 29; Edwin reduces, 77; shire of, 299

Anglican Church, 82; effect of Conquest on, 176–7; fourteenth-century unpopularity of, 359–60
Anglo-Saxon: England, 82–7; art and culture, 87; administration, 132, 174. *See also* Saxons
Anglo-Saxon Chronicle, 56; on William the Conqueror, 171–2; on Stephen's reign, 192–4; mentioned, 121, 125
Anjou, Duchy of, Maine taken from, 157, 171, 188; Henry II, Count of, 196–7, 203; King John's claim to, 242; Arthur does homage for, 244
Anne, Queen of Richard III, 466, 477, 492, 495
Anne of Bohemia, Queen of Richard II, 383–4
Anselm, Archbishop of Canterbury, 177, 208
Antioch, 181, 227, 231
Antonine Wall, 41
Antoninus Pius, Emperor, 41
Appledore, Vikings at, 124
Aquitaine, Duchy of, in Henry II's Empire, 196, 203; given to Richard, 213; John's claim to, 242, 244; Black Prince in, 354; England acquires in full sovereignty, 356
Archers: of William I, 162–4; longbow, 300, 307, 332; cover invading troops, 340; at Crécy, 345–7, 355; defeated by gunpowder, 353–4; at Poitiers, 356; invincibility of English, 415; French strategy defeats, 423
Army, Roman, in Britain, 35, 49–50; Saxon method of raising, 115, 118, 124, 174; feudal method of raising, 155, 172, 295–7, 299; mercenary, of King John, 258, 264; rise of paid regular, 297, 299; of William Wallace, 305; the long-bow and, 332–3, 345–7; expeditionary, of Edward III, 338–41; hired, 368; expeditionary, of Henry V, 402; private, of great nobles, 431
Arsuf, Battle of, 233
Arteveldt, Jacques van, 338–40
Arthur, King, 58–61
Arthur, Prince, of Brittany, 243–6
Artillery, French, 422–3; of Edward IV, 452–3

INDEX

Arundel, Richard, Earl of, Lord Appellant, 383–6
Arundel, Thomas, Archbishop of Canterbury, 382, 392, 397
Ascalon, Battle of, 181
Ashdown, Battle of, 105–6
Asser, Bishop of Sherborne, on Alfred, 104–6, 114, 122; on Danes in Mercia, 109; on Battle of Ethandun, 116
Assizes, 200
Athelney, Isle of, 113
Athelstan, King of the English, 130–2
Attainder, Act of, after Towton, 450
Augustine, St, 74–6, 80–1
Augustus, Emperor, 30, 33–4
Avignon, Popes in, 359
Avranches, Compromise of, 212
Axholme, 282

Badby, John, 411
Bakewell, 129
Ball, John, 371–2
Balliol, house of, 302, 321
Balliol, John, King of Scotland, 302–4
Balue, Cardinal Jean, 465
Bamburgh Castle, 451–2, 455
Bannockburn, Battle of, 313–15
Barnet, Battle of, 470–1
Barons, feudal, 168–9, 172–4; revolts of, 179, 183; charter guaranteeing rights of, 182; manorial courts of, 185, 216, 221, 288; Henry I antagonises, 186–7, 190–1; regain power under Stephen, 192–3, 198; Henry II curbs power of, 215–6; John antagonises, 248, 252, 258; and Magna Carta, 252–7, 279; invite French king into England, 258–9; wars of, under Henry III, 259–64; angered at foreign favourites, 267–70; Simon de Montfort leads, 271; form commission to reform Government, 272–3; split in, 276; turn against de Montfort, 277–80; Edward I seeks to curb, 286–7, 288; oppose Edward I, 295–6; speak as leaders of national opposition, 296–7; gain control of Curia, 212, 316; seek control of Household, 315–16; oppose Edward II, 315–19; of Scotland, James I disciplines, 322–3; Mortimer's quarrel with, 334–5
Bath, Edgar's coronation at, 134
Battle, Abbot of, 369
Battle, trial by, 218
Bayeux Tapestry, 156

Bayonne, 333
Beaker people, 7
Beaufort, Cardinal, Bishop of Winchester, 401, 425, 427
Beaufort, Lady Margaret, 493
Beauforts, house of, barred from succession, 433, 486–7. See also Somerset, Duke of, Buckingham, 2nd Duke of
Beaugé, Battle of, 414
Beauvais, Bishop of, 421
Bec, Abbey of, 177
Becket, Thomas, Archbishop of Canterbury, 205–6; quarrel of, with Henry II, 207–11; martyrdom of, 211–12
Bede, the Venerable, 82–3, 87; history of, 56–7, 65
Bedford, 119; siege of castle at, 264
Bedford, John, Duke of, Queen of Naples and, 409; Protector, 413; Regent and Commander-in-Chief in France, 414–15; Joan of Arc in hands of, 421; death of, 422; wife of, 459; mentioned, 416
Belgæ, 12–13, 18
Benedict IX, Pope, 177
Benedict XIII, Anti-Pope, 416
Benfleet, Danes defeated at, 125
Berengaria of Navarre, Queen of Richard I, 231
Berkeley Castle, murder of Edward III in, 251
Berkhamsted, 167
Berkshire, subjugated by Offa, 85; manifesto of rectors of, 269
Bertha, Queen, of Kent, 74
Bertrand du Guesclin, 357
Berwick, sacked by Edward I, 304; ceded to Edward III, 336; surrendered to Scotland, 451
Berwick, Treaty of, 350
Bible, Wyclif's translation of, 361
Bigod—see Norfolk, Earl of
Black Death, 352–3; aftermath of, 367–72; enduring legacies of, 374
Blackheath, Lancastrians at, 437
Blacklow Hill, 313
Blackstone Edge, 42
Boadicea, Queen, 23–7
Bohemia, influence of Wyclif on, 276
Bohun, Henry de, 314
Boniface, St, 83, 87
Bordeaux, siege of, 294; English possession of, 333; fall of, 438

INDEX

Cade, Jack, 430, 433
Cadwallon, King of North Wales, 78–9; Tudor descent from, 493
Cadyand, landing at, 340
Caen, burial of the Conqueror in, 171; Edward III captures, 342; Henry V captures, 408
Caerleon-on-Usk, 35, 50
Calais, besieged by Edward III, 348–51; burghers of, 351; ceded to England, 356; murder of Gloucester at, 385; Henry V marches to, 402–6; sole French possession of England, 423, 430; mortgaged to Louis XI, 451; Warwick and Clarence land from, 463; refused admittance to, 465; mentioned, 398
Caledonia, people of, 29, 32–3; Roman campaign in, 30, 32; Roman wall across, 41
Cambridge, Henry VI founds King's College at, 424, 430
Cambridgeshire, Peasants' Revolt in, 373
Campbell, house of, 325
Canterbury, Augustine founds church at, 74; coins from mint of, 85; sack of, 137; death of Becket at, 210–12; selection of Archbishop of, 249–50; mentioned, 79–80, 81, 140
Cantiaci, 64
Canute, King of the English, 138–42, 144
Caractacus, 20–2
Carausius, 51–2
Carlisle, 40, 258
Carucage, 230
Cassivellaunus, 16–17
Castillon, Battle of, 423, 438
Castles, Norman, 169, 172; in Stephen's reign, 193–4; siege engines against, 301
Catesby, Sir William, 492, 499
Cathares, 265
Catherine, Queen of Henry V, 408; marries Owen Tudor, 493
Cavalry, Arthurian, 61; Norman, 162; eclipse of mailed, 300; long-bows against, 332–3, 346–7
Celtic, inroads on Britain, 9–14; survivals in Saxon Britain, 63–4; missionaries, 80; art, 87
Celtic Churches, 71–7, 80–2
Cerdic, 65
Cerne Abbey, 471

Chaluz, 240
Chancery, the, 291
Chariot-fighting, 16
Charles I, Holy Roman Emperor (Charlemagne), 84–6, 97, 123
Charles III, Holy Roman Emperor (the Fat), 123
Charles IV, Holy Roman Emperor, 346
Charles III, King of France (the Simple), 131, 143
Charles IV, King of France, 319, 337
Charles VI, King of France, 402; daughter of, 384; recognises Henry V as his heir, 408; death of, 413–14
Charles VII, King of France (Dauphin) and Henry V, 402–5; reigns in Southern France, 414; weakness of, 417; Joan of Arc recognises, 418; coronation of, 420; abandons Joan, 421
Charles Martel, 90
Château Gaillard, 239, 247
Chaucer, Geoffrey, 379
Cheney, Sir John, 499
Cheshire, Peasants' Revolt in, 374
Chester, Ranulf de Blundevill, Earl of, 258–60
Chester, Ranulf de Gernon, Earl of, 196
Chester, Roman base at, 23, 35, 42, 50; Vikings raid, 135; submits to William, 167
Chester-le-Street, 112
Chichester, see transferred to, 177
Chinon, death of Henry II at, 214
Chippenham, Battle of, 113, 116
Christianity, in Roman Empire, 44–5, 71; British, 71–7, 79–82; Ireland converted to, 71–3; English conversion to, 73–8, 80–1; first international organisation, 88–9; conversion of Danes to, 111, 116, 125
Church, the, British *versus* Papal, 73–7, 79–82; sanctuary of learning and knowledge, 88–9; power and riches of, 89, 98, 205, 425; Viking raids and, 95–6, 98; Norman relations with, 143; effect of Conquest on English, 176–7; Stephen antagonises, 192; challenge of, to State, 205–7; raises money for Richard's ransom, 236; John seizes lands of, 249; opposes Papal sovereignty of England, 251; supports Henry III, 259–60; foreigners appointed to benefices of, 269;

299, 311; arbitrates in Scottish succession, 302; at war with Scotland, 304–7; and Ireland, 329; mentioned, 275

Edward II, plan to marry Margaret of Scotland, 301; marriage of, 306; weakness of, 311, 315; favourites of, 312, 316, 318; defeated at Bannockburn, 313–15; builds up royalist party, 318; murder of, 319

Edward III, used as pawn in deposition of father, 319; Balliol's concessions to, 336; minority of, 333–5; marriage of, 334; French wars of, 238–51, 354–7; Navy of, 339–40; money-raising methods of, 341; at Crécy, 343–8; Parliamentary development in reign of, 357–9; old age and death of, 362–3; descendants of, and Wars of Roses, 432–3; mentioned, 332

Edward IV, accession of, 393; Earl of March, 437; Duke of York, 446; enters London, 448, 470, 473; declared King, 448–50; ill-requited clemency of, 452–5, 457; character of, 457–8, 474–6; marriage of, 459–60, 476–7, 484; makes alliance with Burgundy, 461–2; Warwick plots against, 462–3, 464–5; in hands of Warwick, 463; Warwick and Margaret combine against, 465–6; makes overtures to Clarence, 466–7; followers desert, 467–8; Burgundy supports, 468; defeats Warwick, 469–71; defeats Margaret at Tewkesbury, 471–2; "lives of his own," 473–6; and death of Clarence, 477; death of, 478, 479; question of legitimacy of, 484

Edward V, ousting of, 393, 484; under protection of Earl Rivers, 479; Richard obtains possession of, 480; in Tower, 481; question of legitimacy of, 484–5; murder of, 488–9

Edward, Prince of Wales (the Black Prince), at Crécy, 343–4, 347–8; at Poitiers, 354–6; death of, 363

Edward, Prince of Wales, son of Henry VI, birth of, 438–9; disinherited by father, 444; fierceness of, 447; with his mother in escape and exile, 453–4, 465; betrothal of, 466, 477; lands in England, 471; death of, 473

Edward Balliol, King of Scotland, 336

Edward Bruce, King of Ireland, 329

Edwin, Earl, 159, 162, 167

Edwin, King of Northumbria, 77–8

Egbert, King of Northumbria, 102

Egbert, King of Wessex, 104

Eginhard, on Viking raids, 96

Egypt, Jerusalem in hands of, 181

Eleanor of Aquitaine, Queen of Henry II, divorce and marriage of, 196–7, 203; estranged from Henry, 202, 213; Richard leaves England in charge of, 230, 235–6; at death of Richard, 240; and accession of John, 243; Arthur attacks, 245–6; death of, 248

Eleanor of Castile, Queen of Edward I, 294

Eleanor of Provence, Queen of Henry III, 268, 280, 294

Elfric, Abbot of Eynsham, Catholic Homilies of, 134

Elizabeth, Princess, marriage of, with Henry Tudor, 489, 493–4, 499; Richard III and, 495

Elizabeth Woodville, Queen of Edward IV, 459; ennoblement of family of, 460, 479; question of validity of marriage of, 477, 484; children of, 477; takes sanctuary, 481–2, 484, 489; accused of witchcraft, 483; taken into favour, 494

Ella, 65

Ella, King of Northumbria, 99

Ellandun, Battle of, 104

Ely, 144, 282; Castle of, 168

Emma of Normandy, Queen, 140, 143–4

England, barbaric and heathen, 70; Christianity reaches, 72–8; conflict between Roman and British Churches in, 75–6, 80–2; Northumbrian overlordship of, 76–8; Anglo-Saxon, 82–7; Viking attacks on, 90–1, 94–102, 123–6, 135–8; poor defences of, 98, 148–9; Danes settle in, 102–3, 109, 110–12; reconquest of, 128, 130–2; administrative reconstruction of, under Edgar, 132–4; Saxon monarchy of, 145, 147; political weakness in, under Edward the Confessor, 147–9; justification for Norman invasion of, 155; Norman invasion of, 159–65, 166–8; subjugation of, 168–9, 172; Norman castles arise in, 168–9, 172; French culture in, 169; effect of Norman conquest on, 172–8; Saxon local government retained in, 174–5;

INDEX

land, 326–7; effect of Black Death on, 368–72
Fitzgerald family, 328, 330
Flagellants, 353
Flanders, William I allied to, 157; assists in Norman invasion, 160; County of, 203; campaign of Edward I in, 296; embargo on wool trade with, 337–8; French vengeance on, 340
Flint Castle, 389
Florentine bankers, 291, 341
Forest, Charter of the, 296
Fortescue, Sir John, 377
Forth, river, Romans reach, 30
France, Arab threat to, 90; Viking raids on, 91, 97, 122–3; assists in Norman invasion, 160; seeks to weaken Norman dukes, 169, 187, 203–4; war between England and, 188, 204–5, 237–40, 293–5, 303–6, 336–51, 354–7, 368, 400–08, 409–10, 414–23, 475; Henry II's possessions in, 195–7, 203–4; crusading zeal in, 227; feeling of unity in, 243; regains Normandy, 246–7; Henry III sails for, suppression of Albigenses in, 265–7; Constitution of, 275; Scotland's alliance with, 294, 304, 321, 336, 350; Scottish ruling houses and, 321; army of, 333; concessions to (1327), 333; English claim to throne of, 337; defeat of 355–7; alliance of Richard II with, 384; mortal strife of parties in, 402; Henry VI crowned king of, 413–4; Scots army in, 414; conception of nationality in, 415, 421; English driven from, 419, 422–3, 425, 430, 438; truce with, 427, 430; Maine ceded to, 427; helps Margaret of Anjou, 450–3; havoc caused by wars in, 451; English refugees in, 461; Warwick seeks alliance with, 460; combines with England against Burgundy, 468; Edward IV's treaty with, 475; Henry Tudor takes refuge in, 493–4
Franchise, statute of 1429 fixing, 431
Franks, kings of, 123; in Palestine, 181; jury originating among, 217
Frederick I, Holy Roman Emperor (Barbarossa), 213; Crusade of, 227, 231
Frederick II, Holy Roman Emperor, 269, 270

French: of fourteenth century compared with English, 376–7; artillery, defeats English, 423
Fréteval, 209–10
Froissart, quotations from, 319, 339, 342–3; on Crécy, 342–8, 348
Fulk, King of Jerusalem, 195
Fyrd, Saxon militia, 115, 118, 124, 299; at Hastings, 161–3; supports the Conqueror, 168; supports Rufus, 179

Galloway, 324
Garter, Order of the, 362
Gascony, English possessions in, 197, 333; Simon de Montfort governor of, 271; declared forfeit, 293; campaigns in, 294, 354; barons refuse to serve in, 295–6; mercenaries from, 299; seized by Charles IV, 319; warfare on frontiers of, 336–7, 340; English confirmed in possession of, 356; loss of, 430, 438
Gaul, 3, 53
Gauls, British affinities to, 29
Gaveston, Piers, 312, 318
Genoese cross-bowmen, 340, 343; at Crécy, 345–6
Geoffrey, Count of Anjou, 190, 195
Geoffrey, Duke of Brittany, 213, 243
Geoffrey of Monmouth, 59–60
Gerald of Windsor, 328
Gerberoi, 170
Germanus, St, 55–6, 72
Germany, Roman wars in, 3, 4; invaders from, 56, 61, 65–9; Crusading zeal in, 227, 231; Cœur de Lion imprisoned in, 233
Ghent, 338–40
Gildas the Wise, 56–63, 82
Gisors, 240
Glendower, Owen, 396–8
Gloucester, 24, 260
Gloucester, Humphrey, Duke of, at Agincourt, 405; marriages of, 409, 416, 425; Protector, 413, 416; Beaufort's plot against, 425–8; death of, 428
Gloucester, Thomas of Woodstock, Duke of, 379–80, 390
Gloucester, Gilbert de Clare, Earl of, 280–3
Gloucester, Richard de Clare, Earl of, 276–7
Gloucester, Robert, Earl of, 191, 195
Gloucester, Statute of, 288

by Cœur de Lion, 233; struggle for crown of, 232; titular kingdom of, 427

Jews, acquire land, 289–90; expulsion of, 290–1

Joan of Arc, visions of, 417; convinces King and Court, 417–18; victories of, 418–20; seeks to go home, 420; trial and execution of, 421–2

John, King of Bohemia, 346

John, King of England, rebels against his father, 213–4; plots against Richard, 234, 235–6, 239; estates of, 234; forgiven by Richard, 237; ascends throne, 240, 243; character of, 242; refuses to attend French Court, 244–5; captures and kills Arthur, 245–6; loses French provinces, 247; antagonises barons, 248, 252, 258; quarrels with Papacy, 249–50; in partnership with Papacy, 251–2; signs Magna Carta, 254; death of, 254, 258–9; in Ireland, 329

John II, King of France, 355–6

John of Gaunt—see Lancaster, Duke of

Julius Cæsar, determines on conquest of Britain, 3–6; campaigns of, 15–17

Julius Classicianus, 28

Jury system, 217–220, 222

Justices: of labour, 370; royal, 186, 219; travelling, 220

Jutes, 65

Kenilworth, 282

Kent, Celtic conquest of, 12–14; Roman conquest of, 20; Jutish conquest of, 57, 64–5; converted to Christianity, 74; Offa's subjugation of, 85; unites with Wessex, 84; Viking attacks on, 124, 137; rallies to Harold, 162; Peasants' Revolt in, 372; Cade's rebellion in, 430, 433; Yorkists sympathies of, 433, 437, 448; supports Warwick, 467; feeling against Richard III in, 487, 490

Kent, Edmund, Plantagenet, Earl of, 334

Kent, Thomas Holland, third Earl of, 395

Kildare, Viking raids on, 96

Kilkenny, Statutes of, 330

King's Bench, Court of, 220

King's Council—see Curia Regis

King's courts, 186, 216–22

King's Peace, 216

Knights Templars, 226

Kyriel, Sir Thomas, 447

Labourers, Statute of (1351), 370

Labrador, 97

Lambeth, provincial Council of, 292; sacked in Peasants' Revolt, 373

Lancaster, house of, accession to throne of, 389; disputes among lords of, 425; faction against, 426–7, 430; loss of France blamed on, 430; predominant in North, 434, 448, 450; recovers power after St Albans, 442; attempts to reconcile with Yorkists, 443; defeat of, at Towton, 449–50; execution of leaders of, 455; marriage uniting Yorkists with, 489, 499

Lancaster, John of Gaunt, Duke of, 367; in Brittany, 354; joins Wyclif in campaign against Church, 360–1; burning of Savoy Palace of, 373; Wyclif loses support of, 376; in Spain, 378, 382; joins Richard II, 384–5; death of, 388; legitimatised bastards of, 433

Lancaster, Henry, Earl of, 334

Lancaster, Thomas, Earl of, 317–18

Lancaster, Thomas, of, in Ireland, 330

Land tenure, Anglo-Saxon, 148, 174; Norman, based on military service, 155, 173–4; Magna Carta and, 256; and Statutes of Westminster and, 288–9

Lanfranc, Archbishop of Canterbury, 177, 205–7

Langland, William, 369, 371

Langton, Stephen, Archbishop of Canterbury, 249; opposes Papal sovereignty of England, 251; influences barons, 252; at Runnymede, 254; character of, 261–2; mentioned, 263

Langton, Walter, Bishop of Lichfield, 292

Law, sovereignty of, 256–7

Laws, Alfred's Book of, 120; of Edward the Confessor, 120, 182. See also Common Law

Le Mans, 244; Battle of, 214, 228

Lea, river, boundary of Danelaw, 119; Danish ships in, 126

Leicester, Danes in, 103; captured from Danes, 128; Great Council of peers at, 440

Leinster, King of, 327

St Vaast, 341
St Valery, 160
Saint-Clair-sur-Epte, Treaty of, 143
Saint-Matthieu, Battle of, 293
Saintonge, 197, 333
Saladin, 226, 231–2
"Saladin tithe," 227
Salisbury, 173, 334, 373
Salisbury, John, third Earl of, 395
Salisbury, Richard Neville, fifth Earl of, 440, 444
Salisbury, William de Longespée, Earl of, 252
Sandal Castle, 440, 444
Sandwich, Ethelred's fleet at, 137
Saracens, 226, 232
Saumur, Treaty of, 417
Saxon Chronicle—see *Anglo-Saxon*
Saxons, raid British coast, 48, 51; combine with Picts and Scots, 52–5; settle in Britain, 57, 62–5; Arthur and, 61; cruelty of, 65; society under, 65–7; Christianity brought to, 73–6; last battle between Britons and, 79; defeated by Danes, 98–103; local militia of, 115, 118; resistance of, to Normans, 166–8; support William, 167–8; Henry II appeases, 183. *See also* Anglo-Saxon; West Saxons
Saxton, 449
Say, Lord, 430
Scandinavia, invasion of England from, 158–60; threatened invasion from, 173; Crusading fleet from, 227. *See also* Vikings
Scarborough Castle, 312
Scotland, Viking raids on, 96–7; Canute King of, 140; submits to William I, 171; Llewellyn's plans in, 271; in alliance with France, 294–5, 304, 321, 336, 350; war with, 295, 304–8, 312–15, 320–3, 335–6; plans to unite English throne with, 301, 320, 322; Edward arbitrates in succession to the throne, 302–3; Edward conquers, 304; nationalism in, 304; wins independence, 320; disunity in, 321, 324–5, 336; cession of land to Edward III, 333, 336; sanctity of royal house in, 325; feudal justice and clan law in, 325; Church in, 326; abandonment of English claims to, 334; Balliol conquers with help of Edward, 336; helps Margaret against Edward, 450–3

Scots, raid Roman Britain, 41, 48; combine with Picts and Saxons, 52–5; submit to Athelstan, 130–2; Norman frontier against, 182; assist barons against John, 258; hatred for English among, 322; Percy's part in wars against, 396; send army to fight in France, 414; in army of Margaret of Anjou, 448
Scottish Christian Church, 73
Scottish islands, Vikings in, 96–7; Hardrado recruits in, 158; mercenaries to Ireland from, 328
Scrope, Richard, Archbishop of York, 397
Scrope, William, Earl of Wiltshire, 388–9
Scutage, Henry II imposes, 206; Richard imposes, 230, 236; and Magna Carta, 255
Seljuk Turks, 180
Serfdom, ending of, 368–9, 373, 374–5, 383
Severn valley, 75, 85, 281
Severus, Emperor, 41
Sheen Lodge, Richmond, 363
Sheriffs, Saxon, 132, 148; retained by Normans, 174–5; collect King's revenue, 185
Shetlands, 97, 324
Shire courts, 134, 175, 220
Shore, Jane, 479, 483
Shrewsbury, 268, 436–7, 497; Battle of, 396
Shrewsbury, John Talbot, first Earl of, 423, 438
Shrewsbury, John Talbot, second Earl of, 440
Sicily, Norman kings of, 212; Richard and Philip Augustus in, 231; Henry III accepts, for son, 270; feudal kingdom in, 327, 427
Siena, 291
Sigismund, Holy Roman Emperor, 408
Silchester, 12
Silures, 29
Simeon of Durham, 101
Simon de Montfort—*see* Montfort, Simon de
Skipton Castle, 455
Sluys, battle off, 339
Smithfield, Wat Tyler at, 373
Socage, 256
Somerset, Alfred takes refuge in, 113; Peasants' Revolt in, 374

Danes, 108, 112, 116–17; Danish victories in, 113; Alfred's measures to strengthen, 118; genealogical tree of house of, 133; rallies to Harold, 162; manorial system in, 174
West Saxons, defeated by Offa, 85; defeat Danes, 105–6
Westminster, Parliament meets in, 358; Richard II compelled to submit in, 381
Westminster, Provisions of, 273; repudiation of, 276–7; re-enactment of, 283
Westminster, Statutes of, 288–9
Westminster Abbey, Harold crowned in, 157; William I crowned in, 167; rebuilt by Henry III, 283; Elizabeth Woodville takes sanctuary in, 480–2, 484, 489
Westmoreland, Rufus conquers, 179
Wheathampstead, 12
Whitby, Synod of, 80
White Ship, loss of, 188
Wihtgar, West Saxon, 65
William I, King of England (William of Normandy, the Conqueror), gets promise of crown from Edward, 146, 153; parentage of, 153; minority of, 154; gets promise of crown from Harold, 156; invasion of England by, 160–5, 166–8; ruthlessness of, 166–9; crowned at Westminster, 167; fights in France, 169–70; death of, 170–1; character of, 171–2; his achievements in England, 172–6, 215; uses juries, 217; "colloquy" of, 274
William II, King of England, 170, 179, 182
William the Clito, 188
William the Marshal, and Richard I, 228; and accession of John, 243; supports John, 258; Regent for Henry, 259, 262; death of, 264
William of Wykeham, 382
Wilton, Battle of, 108; massacre in, 136
Wiltshire, Celtic conquest of, 12; British place-names of, 64; Danes ravage, 127; Peasants' Revolt in, 374; rising against Richard III in, 490
Wiltshire, William Scrope, Earl of, 388–9
Winchelsea, Robert, Archbishop of Canterbury, 295
Winchester, founding of, 12; sacked by Danes, 138; death of Waltheof at,

168; treasury in, 185; hostile to John, 258; riots in, 373
Winchester, Statute of, 289
Winchester, Treaty of, 198
Windmill Hill, near Avebury, 7
Witan, 119
Witan, the Saxon, 119, 148, 157
Woodville, Elizabeth—*see* Elizabeth Woodville, Queen
Woodville, John, 464
Wool trade, embargo on, 337–8; raising money from, 341
Worcester, 258, 443
Worcester, John Tiptoft, Earl of, 455
Wroxeter, 23
Wyclif, John, 360–1; persecution of followers of, 375; failure of, in his own day, 376

York, Roman, 35, 39, 41, 50; Saxon, 77–8; Christianity in, 79; Vikings take, 100–2; submits to Ethelfleda, 128; vassal prince in, 132; Harold in, 159; William I in, 167; Duke of York's head exposed at, 444, 450; Queen Margaret in, 449–50; Edward IV in, 450, 469; supports Richard III, 497
York, Edward, Duke of—*see* Edward IV, King
York, Richard, Duke of, in Ireland, 433–6, 443; right of, to crown, 432–6; character of, 433, 439; and Calais, 433, 440; lands in Wales, 436; King breaks with, 436–7; seeks to displace Somerset, 436; declares his loyalty to Henry, 437, 441; Protector during King's insanity, 438–9, 440; takes up arms, 440; Henry grants succession to, 444; death of, 444
York, house of, and Cade's rebellion, 430, 433; and succession to throne, 432–3; predominant in South, 433–4; resorts to arms, 440, 442–3; attempts to reconcile, with Lancastrians, 443; claims the crown, 448; victory of, 448–50; marriage uniting Lancastrians with, 489–90, 499–500
Yorkshire, Danes defeated in, 130; Sweyn subdues, 138; William's "waste" of, 167; Peasants' Revolt in, 374; Henry of Lancaster lands in, 388; rebellions in, against Edward IV, 462–3, 467–8

TYPOGRAPHY AND
BINDING DESIGN
BY
AVERY FISHER

MAPS BY
JAMES MACDONALD

COMPOSITION, PRESSWORK
AND BINDING
BY
KINGSPORT PRESS, INC.
KINGSPORT, TENNESSEE